THE BRIDGE

Enza Gandolfo is a Melbourne writer and honorary professor in creative writing at Victoria University. She is interested in the power of stories to create understanding and empathy, with a focus on feminist and political fiction. *The Bridge* was shortlisted for the Stella Prize, while Enza's first novel, *Swimming* (2009), was shortlisted for the Barbara Jefferis Award. She also writes short stories and essays, and has co-authored three books, including *Inventory: on op shops* (2007) and *It Keeps Me Sane: women craft wellbeing* (2009).

THE BRIDGE

ENZA GANDOLFO

SCRIBE
Melbourne • London

Scribe Publications
18–20 Edward St, Brunswick, Victoria 3056, Australia
3754 Pleasant Ave, Suite 100, Minneapolis, Minnesota 55409, USA
2 John Street, Clerkenwell, London, WC1N 2ES, United Kingdom

First published by Scribe in Australia and New Zealand 2018
Reprinted 2019 (twice)
Published by Scribe in North America 2019

Front cover images, top: © Vera Lair. Middle: ©Thad/Getty Images.
Bottom: © Leanne Surfleet.
Back cover image, top: © Aliaksei Kaponia.

Typeset in Adobe Garamond Pro by the publishers

Printed and bound in the UK by CPI Group (UK) Ltd, Croydon CR0 4YY

Scribe Publications is committed to the sustainable use of natural resources
and the use of paper products made responsibly from those resources.

9781947534469 (US edition)
9781925713015 (Australian edition)
9781925548938 (e-book edition)

A catalogue record for this book is available from the National Library
of Australia.

scribepublications.com
scribepublications.com.au

For the men who built the West Gate Bridge:
the victims and the survivors

For Teresa Corcoran (1959–2005)

1970

The factories rang their end-of-shift sirens, and herds of workers dashed through cyclone-wire gates towards their cars and bikes, or the narrow footpaths that lead to railway stations and bus stops. Sweat dripped from foreheads and armpits, down the backs of their necks. Trailed by the stench of rubber and glue, of animal fat, of burnt metal and sawdust, the women turned their thoughts to home, to dinner, to gathering scattered children, while the men headed straight for the pub.

Antonello changed into jeans and a t-shirt, grabbed his satchel, and clocked off. His mates, Sam and Slav, called after him, keen to entice him to the Vic, to a game of pool and a few drinks before dinner.

'You're not going home? Henpecked already,' Sam yelled. Antonello laughed and shook his head. Since he'd confessed he preferred to spend his evenings at home with Paolina, Sam teased him at every opportunity.

'Newlyweds. It'll wear off,' he heard an older bloke telling Sam. 'Give it six months.'

But he wasn't going straight home. Today, as had become his habit of late, Antonello walked north along the Yarra, almost to the point where it met the Maribyrnong.

At the riverbank he sat on a boulder and watched the descending sun rain silver and gold on the river. From Coode Island and the dockyards, he could hear the distant rattle of chains, the thump of hammers, and the groan of motors as cranes hoisted containers on and off ships, on and off trucks. In the distance, the city centre, flat and one-dimensional, faded behind a soft mist. Nearby, the leaves of the ghost gums fluttered, and two adolescent fishermen laughed as they chased squawking gulls away from their bait bucket.

In his notebooks, amid sketches of the river and birdlife, his family, and Paolina, he'd rendered the West Gate Bridge under construction in all its various stages and moods, with and without the tons of building equipment and the piles of raw materials sprawled around its base on both sides of the river. The bridge, with and without the builders, all men — riggers, carpenters, boilermakers, ironworkers, crane drivers — in their overalls or shorts and blue singlets, steel-capped work boots and hard hats; an army at its beckoning. There were detailed pencil and charcoal sketches of the bridge in the daytime, caught under a blazing Melbourne sun, the two spans towering over the river like prehistoric reptiles with mouths agape. There were quick, watercolour drawings capturing the bridge at either end of the day — at dawn and at dusk — when in the soft light it rose from the earth, grey and ethereal and indistinguishable from the clouds.

From a distance the bridge, so diminished, reminded Antonello of a high-wire on which a tightrope artist might balance; a thin line across a blue sky. That bridge bore no resemblance to the one he was working on, with its eight vehicle lanes ready to bear the weight of the city's progress. Up close, when he was standing under the base of one of the twenty-eight piers, each a massive tower of concrete — that bridge was sometimes monstrous.

The two arms rising from opposite sides were advancing towards each other; soon the West Gate would span the Yarra River. Soon.

Antonello began sketching the bridge long before Premier Bolte signed off on the contracts. Studying the artist's representations and architects' blueprints in the newspapers — the solid piers, the long roadway, the spires, the snaking expanse across the water — he drew his own bridge: lines, curves, shadows.

He imagined driving over the West Gate. He imagined flying.

To bridge a river, especially one as wide as the Yarra, was a grand ambition.

Once, when Antonello was a boy, his grandfather had taken him to the wharf in Messina to see the ferry leave Sicily for mainland Italy.

'They say they're going to build a bridge so that we can walk across the sea,' said Nonno Giovanni.

'Who is going to build it, Nonno?' he asked, awestruck. 'What kind of man can build a bridge across the sea?'

'It's nonsense,' Nonno Giovanni said. 'Impossible. The sea can't be conquered, and only Jesus can walk on water.'

Just after five o'clock, Paolina snuck up behind Antonello, slipping her hands over his eyes.

'*Cara mia*,' he said, folding his hands over hers.

She sat next to him. 'The bridge looks gloomy.'

'It's the clouds,' he replied, turning his attention to her. Paolina wore her blonde hair in one long plait, but strands had escaped, and floated in the breeze. He paused for a moment and smiled. She moved closer and kissed him. He didn't want her to stop. Before he met Paolina, public displays of affection between couples embarrassed him. With past girlfriends, he'd controlled his desires, waited until they were able to find a quiet, private place, but not with Paolina. Not even now that they were married and could go home and make love whenever they wanted to. He searched for her hand as they walked; if they were sitting, he pushed his leg against hers; if they were standing, he wrapped his arm around her waist. His body gravitated towards her. He loved to touch her hair, her skin, the soft hollow of her neck. He hadn't known it was possible to spend so many hours kissing.

One of the boys fishing downriver wolf-whistled; they stopped kissing and laughed. Paolina rested her head on Antonello's shoulder. 'I think you are in love with that bridge.'

'Maybe,' he admitted. 'You know it's going to be the biggest —'

'Yes, yes,' she interrupted, 'I know.' She stretched her arms wide and grinned, and Antonello watched, captivated, as the dimples transformed her face. 'The longest, most amazing bridge, higher, taller, more spectacular than the one across Sydney Harbour ... You're lucky I'm not one of those jealous Sicilian women.'

There was a maternal indulgence in Paolina's voice, making her seem older than her twenty years. Antonello assumed it was an attitude primary-school teachers cultivated. He assumed it was her training, that she acquired it along with the ability to organise whole days into a series of learning activities she mapped onto a weekly grid.

A container ship slid silently under the half-made bridge. Grey foam splashed onto the bank. The tugboat guiding the ship down the river blew its horn, and the punt travelling across from the east side stopped and waited. Antonello reached for his pencil again: his hand danced across the page, and the lines transformed into a ship stacked with containers floating on the rippled water.

'You're so talented. You'd make a great art teacher,' Paolina said, running her hands through his thick black hair.

'I'm happy being a rigger,' he said without looking up from the sketch, absorbed in capturing the smaller details now — the masts and towers, the flags.

When he first told his brothers that Paolina was a teacher, Vince asked, 'So she's clever?'

'Yes,' he'd confirmed, with pride.

'They say a man should never marry a woman who is smarter than him.'

'Are you saying I'm dumb?'

All three brothers laughed.

'Well, maybe not as smart as Mamma thinks you are,' Vince said, grabbing Antonello in a playful stranglehold, as if they were boys playing on the street in the village.

He proposed to Paolina six months after their first date, and when she said yes, he asked her again and again, 'Are you sure?'

'Of course I'm sure,' she said with a laugh as he slipped the gold ring on her finger. 'You're the most handsome man I know.'

'More handsome that Marcello Mastroianni in *La Dolce Vita*?' he teased. They had seen the movie at La Scala in Footscray, with Sam and his fiancée Alice, and the two women had declared Mastroianni a heartthrob.

That Paolina chose him was a miracle. He still said thank-you prayers at night before he slid into their bed. *Bellissima e molto buona.* Would Paolina one day regret marrying him — a labourer with no education?

'Come on, let's go,' Paolina said. 'It smells like dead fish and burnt oil here.'

Antonello raised his head and sniffed the air. 'You have a better sense of smell than me. Working down here, I've stopped noticing it.' Before he closed his notebook, he gazed at the completed sketch: the bridge, half-made, reaching across the river from both sides. A promise not yet fulfilled.

But they were close to finishing. In a few more months, the bridge would be whole, and when they relinquished it to the city, they'd make history. A bunch of working blokes would forever be part of Melbourne.

Chapter 1

It was late Thursday morning during Paolina's third week with her Grade 3 class. This was her fourth appointment as a replacement teacher, her second at the same school. Agnes Hunt, the permanent teacher who was now on maternity leave, had warned her that there were several mischief-makers who needed constant surveillance, and they'd already made themselves known: Marisa Percelli had twisted her ankle doing back flips between the desks, the Papageorgiou triplets had brought matches to school and set the bins on fire, and Gary Dyson spat hand-rolled paper missiles across the room whenever she wasn't looking. But more concerning to Paolina were the students who were struggling and found every activity a challenge.

Terri, whose turn it was to read, was short and shy, with pale skin and green eyes that she hid behind a long fringe. She stood up as one of the Papageorgiou boys — Paolina hadn't got as far as telling them apart — passed her the book. She was trembling and already her face was turning red.

'Oh no, not her, we'll be here all day,' yelled out Willie, the class talker, from the back of the room, where he was supposed to be facing the wall with his hands on his head in an enforced five-minute silence. Giggles rippled along the desks.

Paolina ignored him and focused on Terri. The girl's tongue flapped about, her lips opened and closed, she alternately sucked and bloated her cheeks, but nothing came out. It was as if the words were glue in her mouth. When she finally found her voice, some words came out in a rush of spit, while others were stretched beyond recognition as she painstakingly sounded out each letter. Around the room students were twitching and fiddling, and some were sniggering. Paolina was thinking about how to help the girl, how to spare her any further embarrassment, when she noticed Jimmy, a smallish boy she'd caught fighting the day before, scribbling in his book. She tiptoed across the room and stood by his desk. In the margins of the novel, there were pencil sketches of birds — not the stick-birds other children his age drew, but fully formed sparrows, and seagulls, and a half-drawn heron, its long, sharp beak protruding from a small head with, as yet, no body. She hesitated for a moment, then snatched the pencil out of Jimmy's hand. Startled, he knocked his book and it tumbled to the floor. Around him, the students laughed. Terri continued stuttering and stammering through her allotted page. Paolina gave the class the stern look she'd been practising since her lecturer at Melbourne Teachers' College told her she needed to be more serious when disciplining her students. Firm but fair.

A few streets away, Emilia washed the coffee cups and put away the single remaining piece of lemon cake. Both her son Antonello and his father, Franco, had been too nervous to eat their breakfast before their meeting at the bank. But of course they were famished afterwards.

'Asking for a loan feels like begging,' Franco had said days earlier, trying to convince Emilia to come with him to the bank.

'Wait until we save the money,' she insisted.

But Franco refused to postpone buying a new car. 'I earn the money, and I'll buy a car if I want to.'

Franco was a firecracker, too easy to ignite. When they disagreed, they could argue for days. Emilia knew that Antonello hated his father's inability to control his temper, and the ease with which she goaded him, so to put an end to the ongoing battle he'd volunteered to take the morning off and go to the bank with Franco.

The bank manager, a benign middle-aged man in a grey suit who apparently thought getting his message across to a migrant required long pauses between every word, happily agreed to the loan, and now Franco was working in the garden and, Emilia assumed, dreaming about his new car as if it weren't going to cost them a small fortune, with the interest and bank fees.

Emilia stirred the pasta sauce simmering on the back burner. Garlic and onions, basil and chilli, homemade pork sausage and tomato passata, a pinch of sugar and a splash of their own wine — well, more than a splash, but she wouldn't tell her daughter, Carmela, who, since the maternal and child health nurse at the council told her even one drop of alcohol could damage a child's brain, had been on a constant campaign to stop Emilia using wine in her cooking. Carmela was trying to be more *Australiana*, and as a result, she had eliminated wine, and garlic (bad breath) and chilli (too spicy), from her diet. Carmela's food was bland and boring (though Emilia couldn't blame Australia; her oldest daughter was a terrible cook), so most days Carmela came for lunch, with her children and her husband, before Marco's afternoon shift at the foundry. Emilia didn't mind: all her married life in Italy, she'd shared the cooking with her mother-in-law and youngest sister-in-law, and even though they had their own kitchens in their own separate sections of the three-storey house, all three households ate together.

When Emilia had suggested to Antonello that he and Paolina might move in with them, at least until they had saved enough for their own house, he'd laughed.

'I don't think that would be a good idea,' he said finally when she asked him what was so funny. 'You're too bossy.'

She'd thrown her tea towel at him, but she knew he was right. It was nostalgia. She was grateful to no longer share her kitchen.

As she set the table, the sun streamed in through the louvre windows, creating soft, warm stripes across the room. It was 15 October, her mother's eighty-fourth birthday. She'd sent her money and later, after dinner, she'd call. Her mother's hearing had deteriorated and Emilia would have to shout. The thin phone line was an inadequate channel for the weight of their emotions.

Emilia checked the sauce once more. It was spicier than, and not as sweet as, her mother's. The memory rolled in: she a short ten-year-old, standing on a stool so she could look into the pot. *'Attenzione a non troppo peperoncino, basta, basta!'* Her mother pinching her arm to stop her adding the extra chilli.

Just after 11.40 am, Antonello arrived on site and made his way to the lift, where he'd arranged to meet Slav and Sam. Even though drinking before a shift was against company policy, almost everyone had a liquid lunch on payday. To avoid problems, the workers went to the Vic and the Commercial, leaving the Railway to the engineers. Most of the workers from the local factories and refineries were paid on Thursdays, so all three bars would be crowded until the clock hit one, when the men downed their pints and rushed back to work.

Des, a boilermaker, tapped Antonello on the arm. 'Wouldn't go up there if I was you — it's a fucking circus. They reckon they can't get rid of the buckles caused by those heavy blocks you guys heaved up there, so they're going to take the bolts out. Bob's real fucking pissed, but they're the bloody bosses.'

Des belonged to a group of *Australiani* who kept their distance from the *dagos* and *wogs*. He'd never spoken to Antonello before.

'Bob said they did it on the other side,' Antonello said.

'Yeah. So they say, mate,' Des replied. 'I reckon it's time to look for another job. Those engineers are losing it.'

Antonello watched Des until he disappeared into the portable where they clocked on and off. He scanned the site. It was busy. As well as the normal clutter of materials — steel rods, sacks of concrete, boxes of bolts, spools of wire rope and metal chain, enormous pipes and poles — there were several workers manoeuvring cranes and forklifts around the site and its many obstacles.

Antonello thought back to the first time he strolled along the river with his brothers. They'd only been in Australia a few days. No running motors, no horns, and no shouting. No stench of burning diesel. No bridge. He remembered watching the fishermen — young men and boys, mainly, but a couple of older blokes too — casting their lines into the water and then wedging the rod into a pipe hammered into the ground so their hands were free for a cigarette and a beer. The water was a murky brown — so unlike the rivers in Sicily — but the fish swam in it and none of the fishermen's buckets were empty. They'd felt hopeful for their lives in Australia.

Over the years, Antonello and his brothers had spent many hours fishing along the river. The Yarra, one old fisherman had told Antonello, was called the Birrarung, once, long ago, when his ancestors had the run of the place. He'd taught them how to catch eels. 'You Italians are the only white people I've met that understand they're good eatin',' he said. The brothers took the eels home to their mother, who cooked them in a soupy stew the family loved.

Most of the fishermen resented the bridge and the way their river, their favourite fishing spot, the one their grandfathers and great-grandfathers had fished during the tough times when there was little else to eat, the one they had discovered as kids with their mates, the one where they had taught their sons to fish — the sons who'd come back from Vietnam without an arm, without a best friend, who were themselves only when they were fishing — was being destroyed. 'Who needs a fucking bridge anyway? We don't want those rich bastards coming over to the west,' was the general sentiment.

'You can't stand in the way of progress,' Bob had said when Antonello asked what he thought, even though Bob too enjoyed fishing.

When Antonello checked his watch, it was 11.45. Sam and Slav should've been heading down. He looked up at the men on the span. Bob was surrounded by his crew, including Ted, a new rigger who was saving for a surfing trip to Bali and had volunteered to replace Antonello on the morning shift. Bob was pacing. He seemed agitated.

Des had been worried about the bolts, but surely, Antonello thought, they wouldn't take the bolts out unless it was safe. Not unless all the engineers and foremen agreed. He knew that Bob would not agree. 'Shortcuts are never a good idea': Bob's golden rule. It was annoying sometimes — Antonello and the other riggers in Bob's crews, especially the younger ones, often tried to sway Bob, but he wouldn't be swayed. Once, after a long disagreement, Bob lined up the crew and, like an army sergeant, marched along, pointing at them and yelling, 'My responsibility isn't just to get the job done. It's to your families, to make sure you fucking morons get home in one piece at the end of every day.' They grumbled. One of the blokes called Bob 'an old nanna', but they followed his instructions to the letter.

It had been a tough couple of months on the job. Cantilevering the box-girders, a half-span at a time, manoeuvring them into position on the piers, supporting it with trusses and cables, was a slow and delicate process. The spans had given the crews trouble on the east side, and after the last box was lifted into place, buckles had appeared in the steel, leaving the whole east side unstable. 'They shoulda fucking lowered the span back down, but no, no, they put in some braces and had a go at strengthening it while it was still up in the fucking air,' Bob reported when he came back from the east side.

It had been mid-morning, and Antonello and the others were sitting in the crowded lunchroom, waiting for the rain to ease.

'But of course, later the spans didn't join up as they should've.' Bob used his hands to show a gap between the two sides of the roadway. 'Never seen buckles like that, like fucking tumours suddenly popping out … So what did they do? What ya reckon? They took out some bolts. They took the fucking bolts out. Can you believe it?' Bob glared at the men. No one responded, and he continued. 'First I thought, what fucking idiot came up with that idea? I was worried the whole thing was going to come down. I was ready to fucking run for my life. But it worked, it fucking worked,' he said, grinding his cigarette butt into the ashtray. 'They took thirty bolts out, like pulling teeth — like Frankenstein pulling out the monster's teeth with tweezers — but it fucking worked, and no more buckles.'

'My son, Freddy, when he was a nipper, tied a string around his tooth and tied the string around the door handle. That worked. Might suggest it to the engineers,' said Johnno, one of the older riggers. The men laughed, and Bob shook his head. 'It was me old man's idea — he had dementia, kept telling the kids stories about the old days,' Johnno added.

'Bet the tooth came out alright,' said Sam with a grin. 'Sounds like your old man, even with dementia, got more know-how than most of those engineers.'

'Wouldn't surprise me. And the tooth fairy gave Freddy his penny, no question asked.'

'A penny! Strewth, no way a kid would settle for a penny these days,' one of the other blokes said.

'Yep,' Johnno responded, 'even the Tooth Fairy has put her prices up.'

The laughter swept through the lunchroom like a cool breeze at the end of a hot spell, and the conversation moved on. Johnno began his usual rant against the Vietnam Moratorium Campaign, which was being supported by the unions, including his *fucking union*. And no one was thinking about the soldiers who were conscripted and were taking the brunt of the blame. Bob, like many of the other blokes, was actively involved. Antonello watched him move away to avoid an argument with Johnno.

When it came time to lift the last spans onto piers 10 and 11 on the west side, they'd been extra careful, pulling each box as close to the concrete pier as possible, inch by inch, like children might pull a go-kart up a steep hill. Once it reached the top, it was lowered onto rolling beams and slotted into position. But the two half-boxes weren't the same height. It was a repeat of the problems on the east side. The engineers ordered huge concrete blocks. The riggers hoisted ten of them, each one weighing 8 tons, up to the top and spread them across the higher span to force it down. It hadn't worked: the spans buckled.

Bob wouldn't want them to take the bolts out, not unless it was safe. But up there the engineers were the bosses.

On the span, several men were working frantically; he couldn't see what they were doing, but he could sense the urgency of it. And the despair — whatever they were trying wasn't working. Something was wrong, very wrong. As Antonello whispered a short prayer, *Please God, keep them safe*, and made the sign of the cross over his chest, there were a series of loud, eerie pinging and popping sounds, like shots from a rifle, and the men on the span scattered.

'What the bloody hell was —' yelled a man standing next to Antonello, but before he could finish, the massive span shifted. Men struggled to keep upright. The span groaned and screeched as metal scraped on metal.

There was a thunderous crack, followed by more screeching and rasping. And a hailing of dust and concrete and sharp flakes of rust.

'Fuck, it's going to fall, the fucking bridge is going to fall …' The voice came from behind Antonello. 'We need to get out of here!'

On the ground some men were stopping and looking up, some were yelling, others were running. Antonello was too stunned to move. He couldn't make sense of what was happening. What *was* happening? Was the whole bridge going to collapse? How could they get the men down?

'We have to do something,' he said to the men close by. 'We have to help.'

'It's too fucking late,' someone said. 'They're goners.'

There was an agonising groan as the span the rigging team had spent the last few days hoisting up moved again. It was caving in the centre now, and the men were trapped midair. They stumbled, slid, and slipped. They were bashed by the flying debris; their arms reached for the sides of the girder, for something, but there was nothing. Gas bottles, drums, pieces of timber, chains, and bolts spun and rolled and fell over the edges, turning into airborne missiles.

Another jolt; the span was almost vertical now. A stiff-legged derrick loosed from its mooring catapulted towards the river, its long metal arms flaying violently, a giant possessed. And now the men: the men were falling, falling off, falling through the air and into the river below. They were screaming, but their cries were muffled by the bridge's own deathly groans.

As soon as the span left dangling seemed to slow down, to stop, Antonello moved towards it. And towards the river, praying, *Mary, mother of God, please let them be safe*. Chanting it over and over again. Thinking of Sam and Slav and Bob, hoping they were in the water and that they'd surface and swim back. They were strong swimmers — he'd dived with them at the local pool — and they'd be safe … they had to be safe.

As he moved closer to the bridge, he noticed cracks forming two-thirds down pier 11. It had been a solid column of concrete, built to hold up tons of roadway, tons of traffic, but the small cracks were quickly widening and expanding. The pier was crumbling. There was a jolt and the span slipped further, slowly at first and then faster, and faster again.

The pier could no longer support the weight of the collapsing span. Soon it would plummet to the ground. He was in its path.

'Run, fucking run! It's coming down.' The scream came from behind him.

'Bloody hell!' More shouts and screams. Everywhere, men running. 'Move! Run!'

A hand grabbed his arm. He turned and ran with the others away from the bridge, towards the road. It was difficult to see; the air was thick with dust. A sudden gush of wind smacked him hard — he stumbled, fell, his left knee bashing hard against the sharp edge of an overturned bench. His leg ached but he stood up and ran, and ran until he reached a crane and crawled behind it. Concrete and steel hurtled downwards, heavy and hard. As it struck the ground, there was a thunderous crash, the ground shook, and the crane rocked back and forth and almost toppled on top of him.

There were several explosions, followed by the roar of flames. The stink of burning diesel, of burning steel, of burning flesh. His throat stung. His eyes were gritty and sore. There was a loud, piercing buzz. For several seconds he held his breath; he shut his eyes tight and didn't make a sound. Crouched against the crane, he waited for death to claim him. This was surely the end of everything. The tons of concrete and steel he'd spent months hoisting up were crashing down towards him. He would be crushed. This was the end. He would never see Paolina again. A policeman would arrive at their small bungalow, and she would open the door, smiling, but she would know even before they told her that he was dead, and her smile would disappear. When she was sad, her face lost its animation, her lips shrank until they were a thin, pale line. He'd vowed to give her a happy life. When he proposed to her, on a picnic by the river, the half-made bridge behind them, he promised to make her smile every day, many times a day. He promised they'd be together forever. *Please God,* he prayed. *Please God.*

A crash. A loud and thunderous boom resounded across the neighbourhood.

In Emilia's kitchen, the floor vibrated; a ceramic Sicilian horse and cart that had made the long journey with them on the ship slid off the edge of the dresser and hit the floor, shattering. In the cupboard, glasses clinked and rattled as they fell against one another. Emilia reached for the crucifix on the wall above the door and steadied it, made the sign of the cross, and said a quick prayer: '*Ti prego Sant'Antonio mantenere la mia famiglia sicura.*' She turned off the gas and ran out the door.

Standing at her front gate, watching the billows of smoke and dust over the bridge, Emilia knew something awful had happened. Franco ran towards her from the back garden, a shovel in his hand.

'Was it an earthquake?' she asked.

'It sounded like a bomb,' Franco said as he threw down the shovel, and they both started to make their way towards the river — neither of them mentioned the bridge or Antonello, but that's where they were heading.

In Paolina's classroom, the windows rattled. Children screamed, pushed their chairs back, and raced to the window, to the door, spilling out into the yard like locusts. She was powerless to stop them.

In the yard, Paolina ran over to the principal. 'Please look after my class. That came from the direction of the West Gate — something's happened to the bridge, I have to go.' She didn't wait for a response. Once outside the school gates, she ran as fast as she could, trying not to think. She could taste the bitter panic in her mouth; the foreboding, the dark future snapping at her heels. She ran past workers pouring out of local factories, past mothers with babies and toddlers on their hips, and shift workers in pyjamas standing at their front gates, all of them staring in the distance at the furious black smoke threatening to devour the city.

'Fuck, the bridge fell!'

'No, it couldn't be the bridge ...'

'Was it a bomb?'

She knew the way without thinking, without looking, so many afternoons she'd walked it, alone and with Antonello. Twenty minutes, longer if they strolled, stopping to kiss, to catch each other's eye, to admire a house or a garden, to build a fantasy life in which they might own a house of their own. Now she was running, running down through the main street of the shopping centre, running towards the bridge, towards the smoke, running around people who now clogged the footpaths and the road, who were standing still, who weren't moving fast enough.

'Was it an explosion?'

'Was it the West Gate?'

'Not that bloody bridge.'

'It hasn't even been finished yet —'

'Please God, not the bridge.'

One woman, catching Paolina's eye, called out, 'Can't imagine anyone surviving, can you?' Paolina resisted the urge to stop and slap the woman. How could people say these things, how could they voice them? Her parents' friends and relatives did it all the time when they talked about Vietnam. *So many of our young men getting killed. All the ones coming back are so damaged.* Did they forget her brother was one of those soldiers? Those words pricked at the fear and the anxiety, they prodded at the pain. Some days those words pierced all her resolve until she was immobilised by it.

Didn't they know that to speak of death was to call it forth, to bring it into being?

Paolina ignored the voices and the questions, and the smoke, now a long towering mushroom in the sky, and focused on getting to the bridge.

'Mrs ... Mrs.' There was a child tugging at her dress. He grabbed her arm and she almost tripped. It was her student, Jimmy.

'What are you doing here? You were supposed to stay at school.'

'But Mrs, you said it was the bridge. My dad works on the bridge. I want to make sure he's alright.'

'I don't know what's happened,' she said. 'I don't know if it's the bridge.'

She should take him back, but they were already closer to the bridge than to the school. He barely reached her waist, a skinny boy. *Skinny as a rake*: silly phrase, but it described him perfectly. They kept moving forward. And now they were part of a thick swarm of people heading for the West Gate. As soon as they turned onto Hyde Street, the crowd gasped. A huge span had fallen and crashed, a concrete column had collapsed. The air was dust and smoke and grit. And thick with the stench of diesel and petroleum.

She could see flames and flying sparks; the riverbank was a mountain of mangled steel and concrete; there were crushed buildings and overturned cranes. Mud from the river flats was splattered on the road, on the cars parked along the street, and on the weatherboards of the small row of houses across the road; the thick black sludge hung from awnings, windowsills, and fence posts like sleeping bats from trees. Windows and windscreens were shattered. The ground was littered with debris, and they had to watch where they walked. In the distance, sirens and alarms, as police cars, ambulances, and fire trucks sped towards them. A TV news helicopter circled above. The emergency workers were already rushing onto the site.

One young policeman was left to manage the crowd. 'Get back, stay back,' he said, waving them across the road.

Jimmy and Paolina stopped. Even over all the noise she heard the voices of men, shouting, screaming, wailing.

'My son works on the bridge,' an elderly man said as he moved towards the policeman. 'I have to find him. Please, they're calling for help.'

'Please stay back.' The young officer put his arm on the man's shoulder and softened his voice. 'We need to let the rescuers do their job. You'll get in the way, and it's dangerous. They know what they're doing. They'll help your son.' The man inched back.

A small group of men carrying sledgehammers and shovels pushed to the front.

'Members of the public, please stay back.'

But the men didn't stop. 'We're from the foundry and we're here to help.'

The officer let them through.

'What happened?' a woman called out.

'I don't know,' he said. 'Please move back.'

'We'll have to wait here,' Paolina told Jimmy. They struggled to see the site through the smoke, but they could hear the cries for help, the calling out of names, the calling out of instructions and directions.

As the first of the men, covered in dust, in mud and oil, came stumbling through the rubble and smoke — ghostly figures, disorientated and dazed — the crowd gravitated towards them. Some of these men were limping; they had broken arms and legs, dislocated shoulders; they were bruised and bleeding. But they were finding their way out, helping one another to find a way out.

Slowly the more seriously injured appeared, carried on stretchers, groaning and howling. Paolina drew Jimmy closer. They both examined each man. These were living, the survivors. No sign of Jimmy's father. No sign of Antonello. Where was her husband?

Antonello, my husband. She'd become accustomed to having a husband. To introducing him: *my husband. This is my husband, Antonello. Il mio marito, Nello.* He promised they'd be together forever. That they'd make a beautiful life together, buy a house, and have children. He was dependable. He kept his promises. He had to be safe. He had to be. *Jesus, please keep him safe.*

She didn't know what to do. Anchored to the spot by Jimmy's small hand gripping her wrist, she chanted a prayer in a low whisper. *Hail Mary, full of grace, Our Lord is with thee, blessed art thou among women, and blessed is the fruit of thy womb, Jesus.*

'Have you heard anything?' Emilia asked when she caught sight of Paolina.

'I've seen some men stumbling out, but I don't know who to ask.'

'Do you know what happened?' Franco asked.

'No, lots of speculation, but nothing … I'm hoping …'

'Sant'Antonio will look after my son.' Emilia made the sign of the cross over her chest. She coughed. 'I can hardly breathe.' Floating around them were flakes of rust and ash, as well as the thick smoke from the fires. Paolina's throat was scratchy and irritated too. Emilia coughed again — she seemed to be choking — and Franco rubbed her back with his hand.

'You go home,' Paolina said. 'I'll wait.'

'Not until I see my son.' Emilia held her handkerchief over her mouth.

As the first dead appeared, bodies on stretchers covered roughly with white sheets, an eerie silence fell over the crowd. They stopped asking questions and shouting speculations, and even the most boisterous lowered their voices to whispers, which were drowned out by the noise of the helicopters and sirens, by the shouts of rescue workers and police.

Like everyone else, Emilia, Franco, and Paolina, with Jimmy holding on to her hand, stared at the bodies lined up on the road. Paolina was close enough to make out the shape of each man, to see the hand or foot the ambulance officers failed to cover. She didn't turn away each time until she was sure the body wasn't Antonello's. She scrutinised the injured; she scanned the wreckage over and over again. Fear thrashed against Paolina's chest, it pushed against her clenched teeth. She refused to give it voice, to abandon herself to it.

Around her she heard the cries and screams of family members — wives and parents, children — as they recognised a familiar scratched wristwatch, a pair of steel-capped boots, a red sock, the shape of a body under the white sheet now stained with blood. She imagined those men would've been up on the top of the bridge and didn't stand a chance. Where was Antonello when the bridge collapsed?

A group of older women, most of them with their aprons on, took their rosary beads from their pockets and formed a circle. Emilia joined them. She brought her own beads to her lips, kissed the small silver cross, and began to pray. Each woman chanted low prayers in her native tongue — in Italian, in Greek, in Maltese, in Spanish.

Paolina noticed Franco standing alone and glaring at the broken bridge, his face sagged, deep furrows marking the corners of his mouth. He chain-smoked his thin, tight, hand-rolled cigarettes; the small grey butts littered the ground around him.

When Jimmy's hand slipped away, Paolina grabbed him by the shoulder, but he shook himself free and was instantly out of reach, lunging towards a man so covered in mud and blood he seemed, at least to Paolina, unrecognisable.

'Dad, Dad! It's me.' Jimmy wrapped his arms around the man's legs so they both almost toppled over. The man took several seconds to react, to recognise his son. Then he patted the boy on the head and embraced him; they inched towards a gutter and sank together to the ground. Paolina reached for her gold crucifix.

'Paolina,' Carmela, Antonello's sister, called out as she pushed her pram towards Paolina. 'Nello will be okay,' Carmela sobbed when she reached her. 'Mamma says he's the lucky one.'

She rocked the pram that held her youngest child. Paolina squeezed her sister-in-law's arm. Luck was fickle; she didn't want to depend on it.

'He wasn't supposed to be on site. He took the morning off to go to the bank with your father. He went in early to meet Sam and Slav for lunch.'

Was that bad luck?

The baby began to cry and Carmela picked him up. He had brown eyes and olive skin. His head was covered in spiky black hair, as dark as Antonello's. Paolina wanted children, but they'd decided to wait until they saved a house deposit. Now Paolina wished she was already pregnant and Antonello's child was in her belly. What if something happened to him? What if he were dead? She might've lost him and their future, the family they were going to have together.

She'd foreseen the bridge falling. It fell in her nightmares, collapsing over and over again. It fell on those days when he was late home, when the wind turned into a gust. He told her she worried too much, that the bridge was safe, *he* was safe. She closed her eyes. *Nello, please be alive.*

One hour and then a second hour passed, and with them Paolina's anxiety rose. One old woman howled as her son limped towards her. A younger woman knelt by the body of her brother. 'I can't go home and tell Mum you're dead,' she cried. 'I can't.' A woman dressed in a Salvation Army uniform gathered the sister in her arms. 'My mother loved him best,' the girl wailed.

They waited. Some paced. Others leant against fences and cars, talked in soft whispers to the strangers they found themselves next to. The road transformed into a large waiting room, each person praying that their son, husband, father, brother would be the lucky one, the one who defied the odds and survived.

Paolina closed her eyes to stop herself crying and recalled sitting with Antonello on the banks of the Yarra, watching him draw the bridge. Witnessing the pleasure drawing gave him. He found pleasure so easily. She knew what trauma could do to a man: her father suffered from depression, a result of his experiences as a prisoner of war in Russia. He sulked for weeks, even months, at a time. Her mother coped by keeping the house quiet and dark and still. Blinds rolled down. Doors closed.

Television and radios off or barely audible. It was as if the sunlight were scalding, all sound deafening. She and Giacomo spent their childhoods orchestrating outings to escape, to find places out of their parents' reach where they could play with abandon. Now Giacomo had returned from Vietnam, withdrawn and depressed, all joy leached from his life. Antonello was content and uncomplicated. Not boisterous, just quiet and warm and full of a naïve delight. She loved how he surrendered to life, whether it was dancing at the San Remo Ballroom, going to the movies at La Scala, or taking the train and the tram all the way to St Kilda for a picnic lunch under the large palms.

'Paolina.' Bob's wife, Sandy, tapped her on the shoulder and she opened her eyes. They embraced. Paolina sank into Sandy's shoulder and they both wept.

The last time the two women had seen each other was at Paolina and Antonello's wedding. Sandy had danced all night. She was vivacious and funny. While all the other women her age were dressed as Queen Elizabeth lookalikes in their pastel two-piece suits with matching box hats, Sandy wore a flowing purple kaftan, and Paolina recalled the swirl of her dress as Bob spun her around the dance floor.

Sandy's face was red and blotchy, and even in her flowing skirt, even with her silver bangles and large shell earrings, she looked old. 'Any news on Nello?' she asked, hooking her arm under Paolina's.

'No. Any news about Bob?'

'No, no news, but I know … I can already feel he's gone.'

'We can't give up hope, Sandy.'

'He's been good at staying out of trouble, but not this time,' Sandy whispered. 'He'll have done everything he could for the crew, especially Antonello …'

There was nothing more to say, and they both fell silent. Nothing to do but wait.

Chapter 2

The air was dense, black, and brittle, and Antonello coughed and coughed, but he couldn't clear his throat. His lips were dry and swollen, his hands and face coated in a coarse grit and sticky brown mud. His leg throbbed; his eyes were scratchy and difficult to open. He was stunned. There was a persistent ringing in his ears. It muffled but didn't block other sounds: gas exploding and fuel igniting into flames, the spit and spark of the fires, the rivets popping and the cries and screams of men calling for help, calling out names, groaning in pain. He stretched his arms out in front of him, but the air swallowed them whole. Trembling, he pulled them back. The world was a thick fog, more dense than the winter fogs that descended on his childhood village, cloaking each house in its own mist. As a child, he stood on the balcony during those fogs, imagining he was the last living person in the world, alone, king of the new world. But the fantasies were short-lived. Anxiety crept over him, beginning in his belly, rising like bile, until he was choking. He raced back inside, searching for his brothers, for his sisters, for his mother, calling out their names, relief coming slowly when he heard their voices, soothing him, and felt their touch, his mother ruffling his hair or his brother Vince swinging him around until he was dizzy.

As his eyes adjusted, he could make out the shape of the devastation. It reminded him of those images of wartime European cities in history textbooks. The aftermath of battles lost. The ground was mud and slush, shards of glass, crushed concrete, twisted steel, and men half buried and motionless, men crawling out of the mud and from under the debris.

They stumbled out, dazed and disorientated, trembling and unsteady, from behind cranes and forklifts. These ghost walkers were being drawn towards the fallen span, towards the voices of their trapped mates. He could see that his bridge, smashed and mangled, everything in its way ground to ash and powder, had finally stopped falling. It was a wreck; a ruined battleship, sinking into the sludge.

He thought about Paolina, about his parents. They'd be in a panic, and he knew he should let them know he was alive. But he could not leave the site — first he had to find the others. 'A crew is like an army platoon,' he heard Bob's voice echoing in his head. 'You never leave one of your men behind.' He moved closer to the wreckage. There was work to be done. Men to be rescued. He heard his name, *Nello, Nello* ... but between him and the trapped man there were several fires, their angry flames, the heat, and the bellowing towers of dense black smoke blocking his path.

Please, please let them be alive. The prayer was a chant, a wish, a hope. Not Bob, not Sam, not Slav.

Like the other men who escaped injury, Antonello didn't go home. He joined firemen and police, and men from neighbouring factories who raced down to the bridge to help. Armed with shovels and crowbars, and sledgehammers, they were digging through rocks and concrete, cutting through steel beams with oxyacetylene torches, trying to untangle the mess. They were in dinghies searching the river. They dived under the fallen concrete and steel. The mud clung to them, coating their skin, weighing them down, making it difficult for them to breathe, to keep their eyes open, to find the bodies of their mates and pull them out of the river.

It might've been hours since the collapse, his legs were so heavy and tired, his arms aching. But if someone told him it was only minutes ago, he would've believed them too. He avoided talking, communicating with others in gestures, as they struggled to dislodge concrete and steel. Some of the trapped men caught sight of their mates through the dusty fog, recognising them, calling their names, but it was hard, frustrating work and not all the trapped men could be reached — not until the fires were put out, until steel was hauled away, until the emergency workers stabilised the bridge. Bodies accumulated on the roadside in a long line, silent and still. Ten, twelve, then twenty, then twenty-five …

When Antonello saw Sam, he was sitting on a concrete block, his arm in a sling; a Salvo was handing him a drink. Antonello tried to leap towards him, but his knee buckled and he stumbled.

'Nello!' Sam yelled as he caught sight of him.

Sam is alive. The relief choked the breath out of him. Muddy water dripped from Sam's hair, from his clothes, from his eyes. Even so, Antonello could see he was crying. He had never seen Sam cry. They were best mates. They played together. They fished together. They drank together. They went out dancing together. Once they picked up two girls and the four went to a hotel, booked a room, and spent the night. They were so drunk and shameless. It was before Alice. Before Paolina. They sometimes remembered that night and their brashness. Slav was pissed off with them for leaving him behind. He said they were supposed to be the Rat Pack together — trouble was, Slav said, they were Dean and Frank, inseparable, and he wasn't sure who he was … Peter or Sammy Jr or Joey.

Where was Slav now? They had promised him that next time, they wouldn't leave him behind.

Sam struggled to his feet, put his good arm around his friend's shoulder, and pulled him close. 'I thought I was a goner.' His voice wavered. His body seemed light and vulnerable, as if all the strength had been leached out of him, as if he were melting. He leant into Antonello to keep upright.

'Me too,' Antonello replied, helping Sam sit back down.

'Any sign of Slav? Bob?'

Antonello shook his head. Behind Sam the mutilated bridge remained imperious, glaring down at the devastation on the bank, at the fires burning, at the men dead and dying, as if it were the one who had been betrayed.

'I'm going back to look for them,' Antonello said, as he turned to limp towards the bridge, leaving Sam alone. 'You stay here, mate.'

Sam was safe; now he'd search for Slav and for Bob. He was prepared to shift and carry concrete and steel until he found them. He didn't want to think about what he'd seen: the piers collapsing and the span cracked in half as the men fell to their deaths. He didn't want to think about Bob, standing on the top with the crew. He didn't want to think about Slav either, about him falling and the full weight of the span coming down on top of him. After all, Sam had been up there too. Sam was alive. There was hope.

When a policeman asked him his name and if he'd contacted his family, he noticed for the first time the people gathered on the road behind the barriers. Paolina and his parents would be there waiting, worrying. Reluctantly, he moved towards the crowd. He heard his mother call out his name before he saw her, and then he saw Paolina, and his sister, Carmela, and his father and other people, and they were running towards him. Paolina reached him first. She held him and sobbed. His mother touched his face again and again, as if she didn't believe he were real. He should've been glad to see them, especially Paolina, but he felt only shame. The sensation of it was overwhelming and persistent, its tentacles around his neck, pressing down on his heart.

'I need to go back and help,' he said, pulling away from his mother and Paolina. 'I can't leave them.'

But before he could go, Sandy called out to him.

'I saw Sam,' she told him. 'He said Bob was up the top. Arguing with the bosses about the bolts.' She held his hand. 'I know he's gone. They tell me not to give up hope. But I know.'

'I won't stop looking until we find him,' Antonello promised.

'I'm glad you're okay,' she said, raising her other hand and patting Antonello on the cheek. Her skin was ice against his hot and gritty face. 'Bob told me ... He said he was worried about the bridge, a couple of days ago. He never talked bad about that bloody bridge. Not to me. He said he wouldn't forgive himself if something happened to you — to the other guys as well, but especially to you, his favourite. You're like a son to him.' She whispered the last six words.

'I know. I know. I've got to go back, Sandy.' He pulled away and she let go of his hand.

'Please.' Paolina stood in front of him. 'Please don't go back. There are plenty of rescuers, your brothers are helping — they'll find the others.'

'I can't leave them,' he said, moving away. As he made his way back towards the wreckage, slowly, picking through the rubble, he noticed a crushed helmet, several odd boots, a pair of thick prescription glasses, the lenses intact, and a mangled red lunchbox. He kicked the lunchbox out of his way, but it only moved a couple of inches. He imagined a woman, a mother or a wife, packing the lunchbox earlier that day: 'Cheese sandwiches, love.' Would that man come home again? The ground was sludge — mud and oil and blood. The emergency workers were carrying in sacks of sand to cover the ground, but there'd never be enough sand.

There were men everywhere now — the survivors, the rescuers, ambos, cops — but the initial frenzy had passed. And as the sun set, and the darkness, a black shroud, descended, hope dissipated. There was no chance of finding anyone else alive. Exhausted, Antonello joined a group gathered around a makeshift campfire. His knee was swollen and throbbing; his mouth was dry and powdery. One of the Salvos, an older man, pointed to a small stool and handed him a cup of tea. 'You should get that knee seen to,' he said.

'Thanks, it'll be fine,' Antonello said. The tea was bitter, but it was hot and soothing.

'It went like a pack of cards,' he heard someone say.

No, he thought, *not like a pack of cards. No, that wasn't how it went.*

Another man, his arm in a sling, his face covered in mud, said, '"Pull the bolts out," they told us, and some of us said it was a fucking bad idea, but no, they did it anyway. The steel turned blue, fucking blue.'

'They realised too bloody late it was a mistake, the biggest mistake ever,' another guy added, 'and that dickhead engineer calls out, "Put them back!" But there was no puttin' them back — the holes had disappeared and the whole fucking bridge was slipping away under our feet. I knew we were rooted.' He shook his head, and a bloke sitting next to him put his arm around his shoulder.

'I don't know how I'm here. Or why. Why am I alive? Bernie's dead, you know.' Antonello hadn't noticed Johnno until he started speaking. He was sitting on a piece of concrete, bent over, his eyes staring at the liquid in his cup. He was in Bob's crew and Antonello thought about asking him if he'd seen Bob, but he couldn't speak. Words seemed impossible to him. He did not know where words came from or how they might make it from his throat out into the world.

'He was doing the timesheets and scheduling for next week's shifts. I called in to tell him I was going to take a week off to go fishing with my son. I was telling Bernie about how my son isn't the same since Vietnam. Bernie said if I wanted, I could borrow his boat, take Fred out on the bay. We talked about trout and salmon, and the best bait — we argued about bait, friendly-like; he said he'd bet me anything if I used prawn I'd catch … I promised to bring him back a fish. I left the hut just in time. I heard a screeching sound. And then popping, like gunshots. I felt it … dust and gravel, it felt like rain at first … I looked up and I saw the fucking thing falling, the whole fucking thing. I ran out of the way, but it crushed the hut. I should've done something, called Bernie, but there was no time. It went down so fast.'

'Nothing you could do, Johnno. Too bloody quick.'

'Bernie was a good bloke.'

'May he rest in peace,' another man said, making the sign of the cross.

Bernie had two daughters: Catherine and Margaret. Their photographs were pinned to the board behind Bernie's small, cluttered desk, with its stacks of messy files. Those girls were orphaned now.

Good men. Family men. Bernie and Slav and Bob.

After the tea they went back to helping with the rescue. Hope of finding the missing men was running out. Everything lying in the way of the bridge was pulverised. But Antonello didn't want to leave. He didn't want to go home.

The remains of the bridge formed a rugged landscape, barren, bleak. Beneath the fallen concrete and steel, there were the relics of another world, another time, buried, already, in the past. They dug, they uncovered, they removed the rubble, but they could not resurrect that lost world.

It was well after midnight before they found Slav's body. The weight of the discovery bore down on Antonello, and he collapsed.

'You fainted,' the ambo told him when he came to. 'You'll be okay but you're exhausted, and that knee needs to rest.'

'I'll be fine,' he said. 'Just need a minute.'

'Is there someone who can drive you home? Otherwise we'll have to take you to the hospital, and they've already got more on their hands than they can handle.'

'I'll take him home.' His father had been waiting for him. 'Joe took your mother and Paolina home, he'll be back with the car any minute.'

At the bungalow, Paolina ran a bath for him and heated some soup.

'Please,' he said to Paolina, 'please, don't say anything.'

'Okay,' she said, her hand on his shoulder as he sat at the table. 'But eat something.'

He wasn't hungry. He swallowed a couple of spoonfuls and pushed the bowl away, stood up, and walked into the bedroom, where he collapsed onto the bed. Sleep drew him but as soon as he closed his eyes, he saw the span falling, the men falling; heard their screams.

Chapter 3

Things that were solid crumbled. Fell. Things that should've been said hadn't been said. Problems had been ignored, wished away. The collapsing bridge, the falling men, played like a film on a big screen, over and over again in his mind, and each time, no matter how hard he tried, he couldn't change the ending. He tossed restlessly for several hours. As soon as dawn broke, he climbed out of bed, careful not to wake Paolina, left her a short note, and went back to the bridge.

The dust had settled. The roadway was clear now. The bodies were gone. There was one police car and two news vans, but there were no reporters or cops in sight. On the road, not far from where Antonello was standing, an old couple held hands and watched the rescuers. A woman and her teenage son also stood close by. The boy held his mother's hand and was trying to drag her away.

On the site, there were several crews at work removing large concrete rocks and carrying them with wheelbarrows and small trailers to the riverbank. A couple of men armed with oxyacetylene torches were cutting through the steel. There were two cranes lifting larger boulders off the site. A group of men in suits and hard hats — inspectors, Antonello assumed — were walking around the site and making notes. Two Salvation Army workers stood at a small table set up with tea and thermoses, listening to the news on the radio, where a journalist was talking about seeing the collapse from a helicopter: 'It was as if a child had a tantrum with his construction set and bashed it to the ground.' Antonello shuddered and moved away until the radio was only a dull murmur.

The two snaking arms of the bridge reached across the river, longing to be one. On the bank the fallen span was a twisted wreck, and the crumbled column was a mountain of rubble. The bridge was broken, mournful. If left for long enough, it would be devoured by the river.

Bob was one of three men presumed dead but not yet recovered. He was buried under tons of steel and concrete. Antonello lowered himself to the ground, bent his head, and closed his eyes. He'd known Bob for six years. Bob was his first boss; he was a mate, like family.

'Always jobs for riggers,' Bob had said at their first meeting. 'You need a brain and lots of muscle. Your uncle Charlie says you're a smart kid, a hard worker. And it's hard work, no question about it. Not for a wuss.'

'Yes, sir.' Antonello's father had instructed him to call Bob *sir*. But Bob was a big bloke who wore blue overalls and a green army beanie over his shoulder-length grey hair. He had a beard and a permanent tan. He didn't look to Antonello like someone who would want to be called 'sir'.

'Call me Bob,' he said. 'Sir is for them white-collar blokes in suits, them blokes with diplomas.' He stretched the last word out to its limit, *dee-plo-mahs*. 'Those blokes are so far up their arses they can't find themselves.' He laughed and patted Antonello on the back. 'I ain't as scary as I look. You look a little scrawny, but we can build you up.'

They were standing on the footpath of a building site on a busy road in the city. There were several men working on the site, and Antonello could feel their eyes on him.

'You'll have to go to tech at night to get your certificates,' Bob told him.

'Okay.' Antonello was nervous; most *Australiani* he had ever spoken to for any length of time — the doctor, his teachers, the teller at his parents' bank — had made him feel as if he were the only one in the room that didn't get the joke.

'Are you sure? Can you read and write in English? You don't seem to speak much.' Bob winked, and Antonello noticed his eyes. They were as blue as the sea of the Stretto di Messina on the summer afternoons when he and his grandfather gazed at it from the seats in front of Fontana del Nettuno.

'My English isn't too bad. I think I'll be right.' Antonello remembered relaxing, even though he had no idea what it'd take to get his certificates and if his English would be up to it.

'Well, you seem like a good kid.'

Antonello waited for Bob to add 'for a wog or a dago', but he didn't.

'Are you okay with heights?'

'Heights?' Antonello repeated.

'Yes, heights. If you're going to be a fucking rigger you need to be able to work up high.' Bob pointed to the sky. 'We spend half our bloody lives on the top of buildings, on steel beams, up high. Are you going to be okay with that?'

Antonello climbed his first ladder as a three-year-old, passing tools to his father, who was on a constant mission to fix and repair their house. First there was the stone house in Vizzini, which was old and damp and had an unending list of things to be done — loose tiles on the roof, cracked windows, broken shutters, leaves clogging up gutters ... And when they bought their Australian house, he seemed to be in the process of painting and repainting either the inside or the outside every summer holidays. Antonello's older brothers were better at staying out of sight.

'I think I'm okay,' he said. 'I'm okay on the roof of our house and on ladders.'

'The roof of your bloody house.' Bob laughed and clapped his hands hard, and his whole body shook. 'The roof of your house isn't high. To a rigger, the roof of a house is like a fucking kid's stool. I'm talking about fucking bridges, about multi-storey buildings, ship masts — though I'm not planning to do any ship work. A closed shop, that.'

'I think I'll be fine,' Antonello said. He wasn't sure — *would* he be fine?

'Bonza. I'll give you a go because Charlie's a mate, a good bloke — best bricklayer this side of the planet — and you seem like an okay kid. But if you can't do height work, you've got Buckley's chance of bein' a fucking rigger, remember that.'

It wasn't until a month or so later that Antonello did his first real height job. They were working on a half-built office block. On the ground the crane driver was waiting to lift the next set of steel frames to the twelfth floor. Bob instructed the crew to make their way along the narrow steel beams to the edge of the building, where the crane driver was waiting for their signal. Antonello was on the right side of the building, following Bob. He was fine until he looked down at the ground and froze. He couldn't move, or speak. He was hot and flushed, and his forehead was covered in sweat; drops ran down his face and into his eyes, but he dared not raise his arms to wipe it off. His body swayed and rocked, and he couldn't make it stop.

'Are you okay, Nello?' Bob asked.

When Antonello didn't respond, Bob went over to him. 'Don't fucking look down,' he said.

Slowly and with care, he placed Antonello's right hand on his shoulder. 'Hold on to me. Breathe. Don't hold your breath.'

'I can't move.'

'You can move. I won't let you fall. One step at a time, don't go freaking out on me.'

Light-headed and nauseous, Antonello made it back onto the ground. His knees were trembling; his heart was thumping. He threw up his breakfast into a bin they used for wood scraps.

'Bloody hell. Can't be taking that home to Sandy for the fire.'

'What's up with you two?' the crane driver called out. 'Are we doing this or what?'

'Let's do it after lunch,' Bob said.

'Whatever. Thought you were in a fucking hurry.'

But Bob didn't say anything to anybody, and thirty minutes later, he insisted Antonello go up again. 'You got two fucking choices, mate: either you get over it or bloody give it away and find another job. Rigging is height work. It is fucking dangerous, that's true, but there are plenty of old riggers around. We're careful — one hand for the boss, one hand for yourself — and we keep an eye out for ourselves and our mates.'

'Not sure if I can go back up there.'

'You need to get back on the fucking bike. You're a good kid. I've got used to you and I don't want to break in some new guy.'

Antonello went back up.

By the time they were working on the bridge, Bob told everyone that Antonello was 'not a bad rigger, not bad at all, built up some muscles, not too shabby'. Bob would wink at Antonello and they'd both remember the day on the steel scaffolding when he nearly quit.

'Nello, Nello, are you okay?' It was Sam, standing above him, his arm in a cast. Sam lowered himself to the ground. 'Back's a bit stiff.' His voice was hoarse.

Before Antonello could respond, Sam continued, 'I thought I might find you here. Paolina's worried.'

'She rang you?'

'No, I dropped in to see you.'

'They haven't found Bob yet,' Antonello said.

'I know, mate, but you can't sit here all day waiting. It's almost lunchtime.'

'Why not? If it was us, Bob'd be in there, digging.'

'Some of us are going to mass this afternoon, a special mass at St Augustine's. Come with us.'

'No,' Antonello said, shaking his head.

'It might help,' Sam said, reaching out to put his good arm around Antonello's shoulder.

'I don't want to go to church. I don't want to have anything to do with God.' Antonello was surprised by his own words, but he knew as soon as he said them that they were true.

'You don't mean that, Antonello,' Sam said.

'I mean it.'

'When the bridge started to shake and they couldn't put the bolts back in, I knew the span was going to fall, and I started praying. I closed my eyes and I prayed. I could feel myself falling, but I kept my eyes closed and kept praying —'

'Stop it, Sam. Stop it. I don't want to hear it. So you're grateful God saved you … but I bet every single man was praying in those last moments and it didn't fucking do most of them any good. Think about Bernie; you couldn't get more devout than Bernie. He would've been praying. And Slav too, bet even Bob … Do you think you or me — do you think God heard us and not them, not Slav or Bob, are we so special?'

Like most Sicilians, Antonello had invested a great deal of time and energy in God. Not just going to mass every week, not just the hours of his childhood spent as an altar boy, at Sunday school, lining up during Easter parades, and helping out at the local holy festivals for one of the three patron saints of his village, but the hours of prayer, and the whispered confessions, the pouring out of secret hopes and dreams. Blind faith, stupid blind faith, given over in a pious submission to a God who was supposed to be better than man, more loving and kind. But all this had been wasted. God was cruel.

'It wasn't God's fault, Nello, you know that.'

Antonello imagined God as a monstrous man in full tantrum, bashing the bridge to the ground. Like a toddler with a construction set, the radio journalist had said. 'No, I don't know that. I don't know.' He shook Sam's hand off his shoulder. 'If he exists and he's almighty and all-seeing, and fucking everywhere, why didn't he stop it, and stop all the other awful things happening in the world? If he watches and does nothing, that makes him cruel and sadistic. I prefer to think he doesn't exist at all. I've wasted enough time praying and going to church and giving him pennies I can't afford to give.'

In the days that followed, the newspapers printed the first lists of the dead. The men's names, their ages, the names of their streets and suburbs. They also listed the injured and their physical conditions, categorised as either satisfactory or serious, and in some cases explicated with *will be operated on today, might go home tomorrow, improving* — as if they were hospital staff giving updates to worried relatives. Not named were the missing, the unidentified, their wives and girlfriends, their fathers and mothers, their brothers and sisters, waiting in the hope their loved one would be the exception, the one found alive.

The front pages of the paper featured the survivors. The men who rode the bridge down holding on to a girder or bouncing in the internal cavity of the span, the ones who were able to outrun it — with the help of a gust of wind created by the collapse itself — the ones who caught the last or second-last lift down and made it to the ground, the ones who moved out of the lunch or first-aid hut just before the weight of the bridge crushed it to the ground, the ones who fell into the river and weren't pounded by falling metal or concrete, the ones who were able to find shelter behind a crane or truck, and the ones who woke up in hospital with broken bones and deep scars, their eyes glued together with thick black oil and no memory beyond the initial collapse. Antonello was described as a twenty-two-year-old rigger, from Footscray. A Sicilian migrant with a pretty young wife. They printed a photograph of him and Paolina on their wedding day, which he found out later his mother had given the reporter. The caption read, *Lucky escape for newlyweds.*

Emilia wanted to give thanks to God: it was a miracle that Antonello was alive. On the day of the bridge collapse, waiting for the news, she had pledged offerings to San Giuseppe, to Sant'Antonio, and to the Madonna della Lettera, the patron saint of Messina. Afterwards, she insisted Franco drive her across the city to St Anthony's Shrine Catholic Church in Hawthorn to light candles and make the promised donations. She went to her local church, St Augustine's, and lit row after row of candles; she sent her mother money to give to the Madonna's church in Messina. She understood that if God and the saints listened to your prayers, you had to pay your debts. Antonello was the *lucky one*, but luck couldn't be taken for granted. And on the day the bridge fell, there were several hours when she thought his luck had run out.

She was a forty-three-year-old mother of four when she discovered she was pregnant with Antonello. She was furious. Each of her children's births had been more difficult than the last, and in between there were six miscarriages. Her periods were less regular and lighter and she considered herself no longer fertile, able to enjoy sex with Franco without anxiety. But Antonello was a healthy, happy baby, born at the end of the war, into a world at peace. *You had to be grateful for that.*

In Vizzini, the war had been a distant ogre. Occasionally there were bombings in the nearby hills, sending people scattering into church basements, but the village was never targeted. However, they had their losses too. Vizzini sent its sons to fight, and Emilia's favourite uncle was one of thirty-three local boys killed. She remembered her mother's youngest brother as jovial and kind, always willing to carry his young niece on his shoulders, to spin her in circles, to tickle her until she laughed so much the tears rolled down her cheeks. Starving in a prisoner-of-war camp near the Italian and German border, he and a friend had escaped. They were caught and beaten so badly that several of his ribs were broken and his lungs collapsed. Two days later, the war was over and he lay in a hospital bed, dying. Emilia's grandparents travelled non-stop for two days, but by the time they reached the hospital he was dead, and all they could do for their youngest child was buy a cheap suit and weep over his grave.

Her grandmother came back wracked by grief, but she remade her life. Emilia didn't think she had that strength. Antonello was her baby. Named after her favourite fifteenth-century artist, Antonello da Messina, whose painting of the Madonna hung on the wall of her childhood kitchen. She believed he was destined to be an artist, to leave a legacy, to live a long life.

Emilia remembered her uncle as she lit candles to thank God and all the saints for her son's life. And she prayed for the other women, including her friends Sandy and Marisa, Slav's aunt, who weren't so lucky, whose men hadn't survived the bridge collapse. And she prayed for the men, who died without the last rites, that God would forgive their sins, and welcome their souls into heaven.

The collapsing bridge buried the hut that contained all the work cards and the time clock, as well as Bernie, the only one who knew how many workers clocked on that morning, and so it took a couple of days to confirm that there were sixty men on the site. Sixteen men at the top and more men in the hollow tunnel of the span, most working to strengthen the bridge. They fell 150 feet to the ground. There were men in the huts, in the cranes, in the elevator, and on the ground below. In *The Age* on 16 October it was reported that thirty-two men were confirmed dead, not all had been identified, and the names of several men could not be released until relatives — some living overseas — could be notified. There were eighteen men in hospital, six of them in a serious condition, and three workers, including Bob, were unaccounted for. Rescue workers continued digging through the rubble.

The rescuers found Bob's body on the third day after the collapse, crushed, and almost unrecognisable. He'd been wedged under tons of debris.

Sandy asked Antonello to speak at Bob's funeral.

'Do it for Sandy,' Paolina said, trying to give him courage. They were sitting drinking coffee at the small square table in the front room of their two-room bungalow.

'You have no fucking idea how hard this is for me,' Antonello yelled at Paolina. It was the first time he'd raised his voice at her. It shocked both of them, and neither spoke for several minutes. Antonello ran his hands over the surface of the table, speckled red and white. The table was secondhand. As soon as they had put out the word they needed one, plus a few chairs and a wardrobe, their aunts and uncles opened up their garages and furniture poured out. These older relatives who, after years of hard work in textile factories, in motor-vehicle manufacturing plants, on building sites, and on the railways, had renovated their kitchens, updated bedrooms, and bought new furniture — some of it ornate and imported — were unable to discard what was useful and functional. Paolina made green curtains they could pull across the window for privacy. In a small glass cabinet, given to them by Zia Teresa, Paolina displayed their wedding presents: crystal glasses and gold coffee cups, a water jug engraved with swirling flowers. They hung pictures on the wall, including a reproduction of Antonello da Messina's *Virgin Annunciata*. On Paolina's request one of her aunts had sent the print from Sicily. She had framed it and given it to Antonello on their first night as a married couple. Next to it was one of his watercolour sketches of the half-made bridge. The bridge at sunset, its snaking curves reflected as ripples of light on the river. When Paolina had suggested framing and hanging his sketch on the wall, he said, 'Only real art belongs on the wall.' She wrapped her arms around him. 'This is as real as art gets, and I want it on our wall.' He was embarrassed but also secretly pleased. *La nostra prima casa*. The bungalow everyone else called tiny and cramped was an oasis, bright and warm and magical.

Now the room closed in on Antonello. It was airless and stuffy. *Like a coffin*, he thought, *like a coffin*. He avoided looking at the sketch. He avoided looking at Paolina. Unable to sit any longer, he got up and pulled the sketch off the wall. Paolina flinched.

'Get this fucking thing out of here,' he said, dropping it hard on the table. The glass shook in the frame. 'I never want to see it again.'

'Okay,' Paolina whispered, reaching her arm out to touch him. 'I will. Please, Nello, sit down, talk to me.'

He resisted the urge to push her hand off his shoulder. Every muscle was tense and taut, ready to snap. The heat rising, rage burning hot, a fever, inevitable, uncontrollable, explosive. And destructive. He recognised his father in himself. Anger was his father's master: it pulled the strings, cracked the whip, and his father was weak and helpless in its wake. He blasphemed. He abused. He cursed. He smashed plates, punched holes in walls, threatened. And the family scattered, terrified. Now that rage was aroused in Antonello, like a wild animal waking to find himself trapped. He feared it was untameable — furious and feral. The desire to surrender was irresistible. If he stayed in the bungalow, he would yield to it. And so he left, slamming the door shut behind him and running fast, with no idea where he was going.

Not to the bridge. Away from the bridge.

The anger pounded through the soles of his feet. His knee screamed with pain, but he kept running. Fools. He and all the other men were fools. They had believed the lies. The bridge was so important. Bringing a city together. They worked so bloody hard on that bridge, as if they were called to it. Tough and dangerous work. But they felt lucky to be doing it. Fools. They were fools, so excited to erect the trusses, to slide the spine units into place. Long days, double shifts, so eager to see it come together, piece by piece, taking shape. Each arm, east and west, reaching out to the other with an irresistible longing.

He and Slav and Sam, so happy to be working on the bridge. It was a big job. Essential and important work, so everyone said. His cousins, his soccer mates, even some of his *Australiani* neighbours who hated the dagos who'd taken over their street, patted him on the back when they saw him. *Hey, heard you're working on the West Gate Bridge.*

Why didn't he and the other workers pay more attention? Why didn't they listen to the unions? The English companies didn't care — it was all about the schedule, not the men, he knew that. There had been enough fuck-ups, so many demarcation disputes, a never-ending inventory of problems. They should never have trusted them. How many times had the engineers asked them to do work they were not qualified for? Laughing it off as if anyone could do any job, as if they were all unskilled idiots, replaceable.

Initially he'd gone to all the stop-work meetings, voted to down tools, and marched off the site. So many strikes, sometimes it seemed they were at a stop-work meeting or on strike and picketing the site every week. A day or a half-day lost in a fortnight. But nothing had changed, and over time they'd gotten sick of it, they'd given up. He wanted to save up for a house, Sam for a wedding. They caved. They joined more than one union, so they could do what the engineers asked, even when they didn't have the right training. They started voting against the strikes. The companies continued to blame the men for the delays and the mounting costs, the timelines stretched further and further. The bridge had become the butt of jokes in the newspapers and on the TV news, on talkback radio, at barbecues, at the bar in pubs across both sides of the river. *That bridge ain't ever going to be finished.* The government blamed the companies, the companies blamed the unions, the unions blamed the companies, but in the end the workers were always the scapegoats. They were the ones who paid the price for other people's bad decisions.

Sweat dripped down his neck. His knee throbbed. The pain intensified. When he stopped running, he found himself at the Altona end of Francis Street, outside the Footscray Cemetery. His knee was the size of a football. He gazed across the cemetery. It was a bleak, arid landscape, a wasteland of concrete tombstones. There were few trees. And some splashes of colour from the bouquets of decaying flowers, of faded plastic flowers.

He could see that there were mounds of dirt and empty plots waiting for the dead. It was here that on the next day, and the day after, and the day after that, he'd stand watching his workmates being lowered into the ground. It was next to those plots he would stand, watching other men's wives and children, mothers and fathers, brothers and sisters, weeping. Bob would end up here. And Slav too. Slav, who grew up with a view of the Adriatic Sea, here between two major roads, surrounded by truck fumes and car exhaust.

Nauseous, Antonello leant against the cyclone fence, which rattled under his weight. He vomited. The acrid stench made him gag, and he threw up again. The back of his throat ached. His eyes watered over, and for moments the world was a blur. When he recovered himself, he looked up. On the other side of the fence an old woman dressed in black — including a black scarf and thick tights — was staring at him.

'Are you okay?' she asked in a Greek accent, and he noticed that around her neck hung a thick gold chain and a cross. Without waiting for a response, she asked, 'You Greek?'

'Sorry.' Antonello shook his head. She backed away from the fence. 'Sorry, I'm okay. Just a bit sick. Sorry, not Greek. Italian.'

The woman shrugged. '*Una faccia una razza,*' she said.

'You speak Italian?'

'No,' she said. 'Only this. My Italian neighbour likes to say this.'

Antonello nodded. It was a common enough saying among Italian and Greeks in Melbourne. It translated to *one face, one race* or *we are all wogs here.* It wasn't only the Australians who couldn't tell the Greeks and Italians apart; even the Greeks and Italians could get it wrong. And there was a connection between the two ethnic groups, even though most Italians hadn't met any Greeks, and most Greeks hadn't met an Italian before they arrived in Australia.

'Here, you have one of these,' she said, handing him barley sugar through the gap in the fence. 'Sometimes I cry too much, I feel sick. Sugar helps.'

Antonello took the lolly. *Please don't ask me,* he thought, *please don't ask me why I'm here.*

'Before my son died, I laughed all day. Now it is hard to laugh. My daughters say I must stop crying. I try. I smile at home. I am a good mother to them. I am a good grandmother. But in the daytime, they go to work and I come here to cry.'

'I'm sorry,' he said. He wanted to ask her how she managed smiling at home, not crying. How she managed these two lives. How she managed to keep living.

'Will you come to see my boy?' She pointed to a row of graves to their left. His first impulse was to say no, but the woman caught him in her gaze, her green eyes beckoning. Initially he had assumed she was his mother's age, but strands of grey hair were visible under the scarf, and the skin around her eyes was much more heavily wrinkled than Emilia's. Perhaps she was older, or perhaps grief had aged her.

'Okay,' he said.

'The gate is there,' she responded, pointing to a spot further along the fence.

Antonello unwrapped the barley sugar as he limped along the path. She waited for him on the other side of the gate.

'You're hurt?'

'Just my knee, it'll be okay,' he said, taking the bucket of flowers she was carrying. It was full of arum lilies, but they weren't white like the ones in his parents' garden — these were a mournful purple, and their odour was musty and damp. She led him along the cracked concrete path, between one of several long rows of graves, until they reached a black marble tombstone.

'My Dimitri and his father,' she said. Antonello set the bucket on the ground.

The headstone was divided into three sections. On the left there was a photograph of a man in his early fifties, bald, with a large bulbous nose and black eyes. He was dressed in a suit and tie, his expression serious. Beneath it, *Eleftherios Pantelidis, 1909–1969*, was engraved in gold letters. The rest of the script was in Greek, and Antonello didn't understand it. In the centre of the headstone there were two photographs, both of the same young man. In one he was wearing a leather jacket, unzipped, over a white t-shirt. He leant against a motorbike in a James Dean pose, thumbs of both hands in his jean pockets, slick coiffed black hair, eyes gazing into the distance, and only the slightest hint of a grin. In the second photograph, a close-up, Antonello could see his green eyes, same green as his mother's. *Dimitri Pantelidis, 1952–1968*.

'My husband can't live after my son died,' she said as she reached out to touch the photograph of her son. 'One day he fell to the ground and did not get up again. I wanted to die too. But I breathe. I walk. I stand. I don't fall.' She pointed to the blank section of the headstone. 'One day. One day I will be here too. Everybody comes here one day.'

Antonello felt it again, the craving to be dead. If only he could fall to the ground and not get up again, like Eleftherios. To fall into a long and deep sleep.

'People say my husband loved my son too much. But *I* love my son too much. I gave birth to him. I fed him. I looked after him. My husband was weak. He left me to suffer alone.' She pulled the dead flowers from the vase and cleaned the grave, wiping it with a damp cloth. Antonello threw the dead flowers in the bin. When he came back, she had filled the vases with clean water and was arranging the lilies. She worked in silence, and he was grateful she didn't ask him questions.

'I need to go now,' he said.

'God bless you,' she said. As he walked away, she took her rosary beads from her pocket and turned back to the grave.

He drifted back towards the bungalow slowly. His knee was still aching. He avoided the streets from which the broken bridge might be visible. His rage, temporarily subdued, had retreated but it hadn't disappeared — he could feel it there, gnawing at edges of his consciousness. In its place, a pulsating anxiety. If he hadn't swapped shifts with Ted, he would most likely be dead. He should've been there with his mates. He should've fallen with the bridge, with Bob. He should've been crushed in the lift with Slav. If he shared these thoughts with the other men, with Paolina, or with his parents, they'd probably think him crazy. He was alive. He should be grateful for his life, he knew that, but he wasn't grateful, and he had no idea how he was supposed to manage living, breathing, being with Paolina.

Back in the bungalow, Paolina wrapped the sketch in newspaper and put it away in the top shelf of the wardrobe, underneath her rarely used dowry linen. From the bungalow window, she gazed out into the backyard. Her father was clearing a garden bed ready for the next planting; Giacomo was sitting on the small brick fence that surrounded the fig tree, smoking. His hand was trembling. The bridge collapse was an accident, it was not a war. With time she hoped that Antonello would return to the man he was before the accident, the man she fell in love with.

'I was worried,' Paolina said when he finally came home.

'I'm sorry I yelled at you,' he responded, collapsing exhausted onto the bed.

'I understand you're angry.'

'I've never been this angry. I want to punch something, someone. I want to find the person responsible and hit them as hard as I can.'

'Nello, that isn't going to make anything any better,' Paolina said. She lay alongside him on the bed so they were looking at each other. She caressed his face with one hand.

'I know ... But how could they let this happen? They killed so many men. They could've killed all of us, they didn't give a damn. I'm angry at them. I'm angry at myself. Bob and Slav and Ted and so many others are dead and I'm not ...' He was sobbing now, the tears streaming down his face.

'Nello, please don't say that. If you ... When I think that you might've ... you might've died too ...' Paolina inched closer and wrapped her arms around him.

Antonello buried his head in her shoulder. Death, wilful death, at his own hand, was impossible. He'd made a commitment to Paolina; whatever happened now happened to the two of them. He wasn't Eleftherios, he would not drop dead from grief. He would not leave Paolina.

'We let the bridge collapse. We knew there were problems ... and we didn't do enough,' he whispered.

'It wasn't your fault,' she whispered back. 'Not yours or Bob's or Slav's or Sam's.'

Paolina held Antonello until he fell asleep. In the early morning when he woke, the bungalow was unfamiliar and he was as disorientated as an orphaned child waking up on his first morning in a dormitory. In Vizzini, his childhood bedroom was on the top floor, up three flights of stairs. The room was wall-to-wall beds, a double bed and a single bed, pushed together. There were no windows, and the wall was a partition that didn't reach the ceiling. On the other side, his sisters' room was identical. He was surrounded by the sounds of his brothers and sisters breathing, snoring, farting. He heard their dreams and nightmares. He belonged in that room. They should've stayed in Sicily. What madness had possessed his parents, what madness had made them take the family away from their home?

Ten days after the collapse, Antonello gave the eulogy at Bob's funeral. Bob as a boss. Bob as a mate, like family, like an uncle. Bob as a joker, as a dyed-in-the-wool Bulldogs fan. He talked about Bob's love of the bridge, because Sandy asked him to. *Bob was proud of being a rigger and a bridge builder,* Sandy said to him before the funeral. *Don't forget.* So he held back his anger; he didn't mention betrayal, he didn't criticise the companies or the engineers. It was there on the tip of his tongue, but he held back.

After the funeral, the mourners gathered in the front bar of the Vic. Paolina and Emilia helped the other women to pass around trays of sandwiches, while the men drank and smoked too much as they told their favourite jokes and stories about Bob.

The men also talked about Bolte's long speeches on grief and tragedy. He had guaranteed that a Royal Commission would investigate, and that workers would not return to the site until it was safe. And he had declared that finishing the bridge would be a way of honouring the dead.

'Well, the job does have to be finished,' he heard Johnno say. Antonello watched the men down their beers and make pledges to return. He was shocked and disappointed that so many of them seemed to have bought the Premier's empty promises.

As soon as he could, Antonello slipped out of the pub and headed for the riverbank, keeping his back to the ruined bridge. Behind him, the punt was crossing from east to west. Once the bridge was built, there wouldn't be any need for the punt. He would miss it. On weekends, there was a carnival atmosphere. From a small food stall on the side of the road, a father and son sold fish and chips, party pies and pasties. Drivers lined their cars up, waiting for the ferry, and went to buy hot fried food. It was here Antonello ate his first Chiko Roll, hot and peppery. And his first ice-cream from the local Mr Whippy van — not as good as the gelato back home, but sweet and soft and creamy.

On the ferry, he loved to hang over the rail, watching the river and feeling the spray on his face. As the punt forged a channel through the water, children ran in between cars and bicycles, and adults lit cigarettes and caught up with neighbours and workmates, as if they might be on a yacht sailing the Pacific instead of an old punt chugging across the Yarra.

He tried to picture the river and the bank long ago, when it was called Birrarung and the only way across was in canoes. Was it possible to turn time back? He imagined destroying what remained of the bridge — blowing it up, or pulling it down, every last piece. He imagined gathering all the survivors together so they could tear the bridge down. They were the bridge builders: they had built it, and they could take it apart. Return the river to itself. If only he could make a ghost of the bridge. He would go back for that. He would go back to obliterate it.

He kept going until he was almost in Williamstown. From a phone booth, he rang his brother Vince. Vince didn't ask any questions. He arrived in his old Holden, picked Antonello up, and without a word drove him home the long way, through Newport and Altona, avoiding the bridge.

At Slav's funeral, Antonello gave another eulogy, and as he spoke, the words floated over the congregation, shrouding the church. He couldn't hear his own voice above the sound of Slav's Aunt Marisa sobbing.

In the fortnight after the collapse, Antonello attended eleven funerals: Catholic, Orthodox, Anglican, Presbyterian, and even Jehovah's Witness. There was no difference — each family was heartbroken. There was nothing to say, nothing that could be said. The survivors — some in bandages and casts, or leaning on walking sticks — turned up dressed in suits and ties and sat behind the families of the dead, wounded sentinels unsure of their obligations. Outside, after each service, some were as silent and withdrawn as Antonello; others were loud and angry; some were militant, their voices punching fists of rage into the crisp spring air. Their bridge was in ruins, their mates dead. They were all lost.

2009

Chapter 4

As if orchestrated by a callous conductor, the morning came crashing into the room. First the warning bells of the railway gates, followed by the blaring horns of the first trains — one city-bound, one headed for Werribee. Then the screech of the exhaust brakes as the semi-trailers, weighed down by replenished tanks from the refineries and the CSR sugar plant, were caught by the lights at the intersection of Francis and Hyde on their way to the freeway. Mrs Nguyễn's ageing Alsatian, Wes, his deep bark setting off other dogs in a call-and-response. The rasping cries of the wattle birds. The neighbourhood was waking from its slumber as grumpy as an old man after a big night: joints aching, belly churning, and head screaming. It was 6.05 am. Mandy Neilson sighed and wrapped the pillow around her head to block her ears, and imagined the quiet stillness in the neighbourhood when her grandmother first moved into the house as a young bride in the 1940s, almost seventy years ago.

All her life Mandy had lived in this house, but all her life she had dreamt of moving to the country. A cottage on a riverbank: nothing too grand, something small and isolated, surrounded by bush or forest.

The idea of the cottage, she'd inherited from her mother. 'A pie-in-the-sky dream,' her father, Tom, had called it. He wasn't being cruel, just realistic. 'Wishing don't make it so, Sal,' he said whenever her mother brought it up. In her last year, Sal was too sick to get out of bed. By that time, even if they'd won the lotto, or her father had picked every trifecta for the whole racing season, there was no likelihood of a cottage for Sal.

Before the illness, Sal was a formidable woman, tall and strong. She ruled the house and was social, and *socially minded*. Women from the street gathered in her kitchen in the mornings drinking tea, sharing stories and gossip. She volunteered at the school tuck shop once a week and cooked extra food for an elderly neighbour whose children were ruthless and neglectful. Yet in that last year of her life, she became gaunt. Her voice was barely audible; to catch her words, Mandy lowered her ear to her mother's lips. Sal lost interest in people. Refused to let the neighbours in. She reserved her strength for her children, John and Mandy, but especially for Mandy, her youngest. In the afternoons, after school, Mandy sat on her mother's bed. They ignored the traffic and Sal's shallow breathing, and conjured up their dream home: a short stroll to the river where Tom and John could fish, a large and rambling garden — a section for vegetables and a section for flowers — surrounded by native bush where they could meander without ever seeing another person. They flicked through the magazines Sal's sisters brought when they came to visit, and tore out pictures of gardens, of furniture. Of cottages like theirs.

Mandy kept her mother's clippings in an old suitcase under her bed. They were dried and yellowed. They were waiting.

The neighbourhood was going through a real-estate boom, and all sorts of people were moving in. *Posh people*, her father would've called them. *Posh and up themselves*. Last week, after years of thinking about it, Mandy had organised a property valuation. A woman in a black suit, high heels, and a silk scarf in the company's yellow and red arrived with a clipboard and a tick-the-box list. She marched through the house, inspecting and making notes. Mandy, embarrassed, sat in the kitchen waiting for the verdict. The house was a dump, a rickety double-fronted weatherboard. Her parents had inherited the mortgage from their parents, and with it the accumulated wear and tear. With the help of a mate who knew a bit about plumbing, her father had moved the toilet inside and put a shower head over the bathtub. It leaned a little to the left, and they hadn't been able to get rid of the hammering in the pipes.

Mandy had repainted a room or two, but otherwise there had been little upkeep since it was built in the 1920s. It was old and tired. The stumps at the back of the house were rotting, and the hallway sloped downwards. The house couldn't stand on its own two feet. The roof leaked — over the bath (not such a big issue) and in a couple of places along the hallway. On days when the rain was a downpour, Mandy placed buckets in prime locations before she left for work, just in case. They never overflowed, but once when her daughter, Jo, and Jo's best friend, Ashleigh, were in the house alone during a storm, they filled the buckets with tap water, right up to the rim. When Mandy came home she panicked, and even rang a couple of local plumbers to get quotes to have the roof fixed, until Jo and Ashleigh broke into a fit of giggles and confessed.

There were cracks in the plaster in every room. Outside, there were missing weatherboards. Mould in the bathroom grew around the base of the bathtub and ran up and down the walls. It couldn't be stopped, even with bleach and hot water and hours of Mandy's scrubbing. The first time they moved the furniture in Jo's bedroom, when she had insisted on redecorating, they were surprised to find that under Jo's bed the pale carpet was a rich royal blue, and the roses, everywhere else a washed-out pink, were a deep red. At the inspection, Mandy half expected the agent to laugh and say, 'You think someone will want to buy this dump? Seriously?' But it seemed even with the traffic and the pollution, even with the Mobil terminal across the road, her run-down house would sell and she would be able to afford a couple of acres somewhere in central Victoria.

She'd sell at the end of the year, once Jo finished school. She hadn't told Jo; it made sense to wait until after her exams. No point causing her extra stress. Mandy imagined herself sitting in the passenger seat of the removal van, all her possessions stacked in the back. She imagined staring into the rearview mirror as the house, the tanks, and the West Gate Bridge disappeared.

Down the hallway, Jo slept as if the traffic were a soft lullaby sung to her by her mother — though that would've been a different mother because Mandy couldn't hold a tune, and her lullabies, when she'd attempted them, hadn't soothed Jo to sleep.

'... romantic thing you've ever done? Something to make your partner take notice. Ring us now.'

Without opening her eyes, Jo raised an arm and slammed the snooze button on the alarm. The radio stopped and she slipped further down under the warm doona. The station played top-100 hits, and in between three comedians, the morning radio hosts, delivered endless jokes, mostly at the expense of celebrities and politicians, but also at the expense of a string of people who rang in to tell their stories. The hosts invented silly pranks, and from across the city eager listeners volunteered to participate. There were numerous wedding proposals and even a couple of on-air weddings; people confessed sins and secrets as if the radio weren't a public broadcasting service, as if there were no possibility of their loved ones discovering they had been betrayed, lied to, deceived. The hosts revelled in devising competitions that required people who were willing to look ridiculous and foolish — to turn up on the steps of Parliament House in their underwear or to sit all morning in their bathers on deckchairs on the steps of Flinders Street Station. The stunts were childish and not even funny; Jo never considered taking part, no matter the prize. There were times, though, even as she rolled her eyes at these people, when she envied them and their propensity for joy and abandonment — their willingness to be ridiculed and laughed at, to allow their secrets and flaws to be exposed.

'They're bogans. Not a brain between them,' Ash had said one day in response to Jo's bewilderment that a young woman had given her name and suburb.

'Bad enough she's a nymphomaniac with a weird fetish, but telling the whole world, so embarrassing,' Jo said.

With the hope they might catch the afternoon sun, they were sitting in a row on a wooden bench, the skirts of their school uniforms hitched up and their legs stretched long. A group of boys were playing handball against the brick wall of the canteen, and the regular thump of the ball and the boys' yelps and shouts broke the silence of the deserted school yard. The junior students were back in class. Jo and Ash, with Mani and Laura, had a free period. They and the boys should've been in the library studying.

'In VCE you don't have time to waste,' their History teacher said as she rushed past pushing a trolley of books. The girls waited until she disappeared into the staff room and burst out laughing.

'Wonder if Ms Sacks heard you talking about nymphs with a fetish for men with big bellies. She's running to the staff room to tell them about Kinky Jo,' Mani said.

'Jo? Kinky, as if,' Ash laughed.

When the bell rang, they stood up, pulled down their skirts, and rushed off to collect books from their lockers. Jo thought about Ash's *as if*. As if anyone would believe boring, anxious Jo could be kinky, is that what Ash thought?

The radio started up again but as the first bars of Lady Gaga's 'Just Dance' came on, Jo hit the snooze button. Moments later, she heard her mother's bedroom door open.

'Jo,' Mandy called out. 'Are you awake?'

Jo pulled the doona over her head. She felt her mother's irritation, the silent, seething scent of it wafting down the hallway.

'There are some things,' Mandy had taken to saying, 'that aren't worth fighting about.' It had become an automatic response at the end of their frequent arguments. In Jo it spawned an uncontrollable loathing, like nausea brought on by an unexpected swallow of rancid milk. This loathing and the accompanying urge to yell abuse at her mother had become compulsive. Mandy's inane questions — *How was school? Did you hang out with Ashleigh today? Do you want chicken for dinner?* — her lame clothes, her boring unhealthy dinners, so irritated Jo that it seemed impossible to imagine a future in which they might get along.

'I'm always walking on eggshells and biting my tongue,' Jo overheard Mandy telling Mrs Nguyễn over the fence. 'Everyone tells me to grit my teeth because surviving the teenage years is tough, but it's a temporary stage and we'll get along better when Jo's older.'

'Of course. She's young, a teenager. It's all those hormones,' Mrs Nguyễn said.

'I've no idea how mothers and daughters get along, or even if it's possible. I'm winging it,' Mandy said. 'Sometimes I miss my little girl.' Mandy repeated this too often.

'The little girl you miss,' Jo always told Mandy when she brought this up, 'is in your head, all sugar and spice, it isn't me. It was never me.'

'You were such a good child, so —'

'Mum, for fuck's sake.'

Little provocation was needed to trigger these fights. The child her mother conjured up in these conversations reminded Jo of the girls in the junk-mail catalogues, in their pink dresses or polka-dot jumpsuits, grinning as they skipped off the page. Jo had been a chubby child, not like the other girls her age, who were either waif-like ballerinas or lanky football-playing, tree-climbing, somersaulting tomboys. She hated being reminded of her 'fat' days. She hated that her mother remembered with affection the child she wanted to forget.

From bed, Jo could sense her mother stopping to take a deep breath, and then expelling it. Or maybe she was counting: *one, two, three.*

'Jo? Jo!'

'I heard you,' Jo yelled back, and in a whisper, 'Fucking leave me alone.' She rolled over so her back faced the door.

'Don't go back to sleep or you'll be late. I'm going to jump into the shower — then it's all yours.'

When Mandy turned on the shower, there was the usual hammering followed by Mandy's loud cursing. Jo sighed. The house was a dump, no arguing with that, but it was their home and Jo loved it. Her first ever memory was at this house. She was three years old. She didn't remember any of the back story, but she'd been told the details often: after weeks of fighting, her mother had decided to leave her father, packed up all their clothes into two suitcases, and called a taxi. In her memory, it was like a scene from a movie — when they arrived, the taxi door opened, and Grandpa Tom, a tall, lanky man with weathered skin and thick brown hair, was leaning against the verandah post, smoking. When he saw her, he twisted the cigarette butt between his fingers, threw it into the garden, and opened his arms wide. She ran straight to him. He picked her up and swung her around until the world turned into a whirl of shapes and colours. When they stopped spinning, she wrapped her arms around his neck; he smelt of tobacco and sweat. Her small hands ran over the prickles of his unshaven chin.

'Welcome home, Joey girl,' he said, and he took her to the front bedroom. 'This is your room.'

It was light blue, the colour of her grandmother Mary's hydrangeas, which they sometimes made into bouquets to take to church.

'Blue is my favourite colour,' Jo said.

'Is it?' Mandy said with a laugh.

In the room there was one big bed. At the flat, Jo's cot was small and narrow, and squeezed into the corner next to her parents' bed.

'Where is your bed?' Jo asked her mother, and together the three of them toured the house. Every time Mandy told this story, she added, 'Jo didn't ask for her father, not once.'

Holding Grandpa Tom's hand, feeling the rough, calloused skin, she was safe. That memory was a memory of coming home. The house was her home. She loved that everywhere the marks of the past, of her grandparents' and great-grandparents' lives, were there waiting for her to discover. Not cut away under a cosmetic surgeon's knife, gone forever, like Ash's house, renovated several times until the Californian bungalow was a ghostly façade. The inside of the old property had been gutted and a new one architecturally designed. A whole new upstairs floor had been added, which housed the bedrooms, and downstairs there was a big open-plan living area with a long table and a wall of glass windows and doors that looked out into the garden. There were new silver appliances, glistening and glowing, and feature walls in colours with foreign names, like aubergine and turmeric.

Jo couldn't imagine ever selling the house. It would be a betrayal of her grandparents who'd spent a lifetime trying to pay it off, who'd died in debt. Mandy owned it now. Uncle John *made a few good deals* — paid off the last ten thousand and signed the house over to Mandy. 'An act of charity,' Aunt Joy called it.

Jo would inherit it and she would leave it to her children.

'... And what did you skywrite?'

'Well, I wanted them to write, *Jade, you have the sexiest pussy ever.*'

The female host, obviously miffed, said, 'Watch your language.'

'Sure, sure no offence meant. I thought she'd think it was funny. Anyway, the guy wouldn't write that in the sky. He said he would get fined or arrested or something. So in the end we agreed it would say, *Jade, I love you. Marry me?* A bit lame but I thought it'd still be romantic. I thought Jade'd get a real hoot out of it being in the sky, you know. Anyway, I paid him the dough and waited. Well, the arsehole — can I say that on radio?'

'You just did, mate.' The hosts laughed.

'Jo, shower's free,' Mandy yelled.

Jo hit the off button on the radio. 'Okay, I'm there.'

On Saturdays, Jo's shift at the café started at 7.30. If she was out of bed by 7.00, she could manage a shower and breakfast. If she left it any longer, she'd have to skip breakfast, and there was no hope of getting anything at the café until after ten. She threw the covers off, got out of bed, and walked straight down the hallway and into the shower. By the time Mandy called out 'Coffee?', Jo was dressed and heading for the kitchen.

They sat down opposite each other at the square formica table, each in their usual positions, Jo facing the back door and Mandy the hallway. Flicking through that morning's newspaper, Mandy took bites of her toast while Jo poured milk into a bowl of no-name breakfast cereal. They both drank their instant coffee the same way, with milk and no sugar, out of identical heavy Bulldogs mugs. 'Anyone can tell you're mother and daughter,' people had told Jo numerous times. Of course, there were the obvious things: light brown hair that hung straight and flat, and that you could do nothing with, the sort of hair that hairdressers wanted to *highlight*, and the identical scattering of freckles over the bridges of their small noses. But Mandy had hazel eyes, more brown than green, while Jo had her father's smoky-blue eyes, underscored by dark shadows, which intensified after a late night or not enough sleep. She had his olive skin too — it went dark brown at the slightest hint of summer sun — and because her mother and Ash, who were both susceptible to sunburn, were envious, she thought of this as her best feature.

Jo wore two earrings in each ear — an elongated silver loop and a stud in the shape of a tree. On her left shoulder, a tattoo of a flock of black birds. Mandy was one of a handful of women of her generation who hadn't pierced her ears. Mandy said Jo did these things to annoy her, and to be *different*, and to *fit in*. 'Give me a break. Which is it?' Jo retorted whenever the topic came up.

Jo had her ears pierced for the first time when she was eleven; the earrings and the cost of the piercing were a birthday present from her paternal grandmother, Mary. She'd worn earrings ever since. The second piercings were a whim. She was thirteen, and the process involved a sewing needle, boiling water, and a great deal of blood and pain. When Ash turned eighteen and they were both *legal*, they had gone to get tattoos together; Ash's was an eagle feather, on her thigh. Ash's mother listed infections and diseases. Mandy talked about rebellion and regret. Together Jo and Ash were impervious. But it was the last time they had conspired. That was almost six months ago now.

'How did your meeting with the careers teacher go?' Mandy asked.

'Fine.'

'What does that mean?'

Jo shrugged her shoulders in a dismissive gesture she hoped would shut her mother up. The meeting with Mrs Chang hadn't gone anywhere. In her list of preferences for courses she might want to do at university, she had listed Architecture and Urban Design and Planning at the University of Melbourne and RMIT, but Mrs Chang, whose cluttered office was surrounded by brochures on every career imaginable, said, 'Great to aim high. But you need to be practical too. What are you going to do if you don't get in?' She went on to tell Jo that her teachers predicted she would get a 'respectable' VCE score if she 'put her mind to it', probably something in the high 60s, but it was unlikely to get her into any of the courses she'd listed, all requiring scores of 75 or above.

'You could apply for Architecture at Deakin in Geelong, you might get in there.'

'I want to stay in the city,' Jo said.

'What about other careers, teaching? You could teach History or Geography. They seem to be your best subjects,' Mrs Chang suggested.

Jo shook her head. 'I don't want to be a teacher.'

'You're a sensible girl with a level head. You'd make a good paramedic or nurse, or one of the other health professions would suit you. Nutrition. Not physiotherapy, though — everyone wants to be a physio, it's hard to get in.' Mrs Chang was squinting at a list on the computer monitor.

'No, I don't want to look after sick people.'

Mrs Chang showed no sign of disapproval or frustration. 'There are so many jobs to choose from that it can be confusing,' she said. 'Problem is, everyone thinks you have to find the one thing you love — that's a lot of pressure. Most people work to make a living. You just have to find something that you don't mind doing.'

Jo didn't mind waitressing, but could she spend the rest of her life as a waitress? *Follow your passions*, teachers in earlier years advised, but maybe that advice was for the clever people. Like Ash. Ash and Jo read the same books, discussed their essays, and came up with a shared set of ideas, but in the process of writing and handing them in, Ash's essay evolved into an A+ and Jo's dwindled into C−.

Ash was going to be a lawyer. No one suggested a fallback position to her. Their friend Mani planned to study music. She might scrape through VCE if she were lucky, but she didn't care. She had a long list of fallback positions: music teaching or music production or sound technology … Not that she needed them — her band was going to get millions of hits on YouTube and record companies would be killing one another to sign them up, and if that didn't happen they'd go on *Australia's Got Talent*. Laura was doing VCE to placate her parents, but she wanted to be a beautician. She brokered (her father was in finance) a deal with her parents that if she passed VCE, they would pay for a beauty therapy course. Laura's mother was determined to get Laura to university, to make sure she had a degree and a profession. Laura said her mother lit candles at the local church once a week and prayed to St Joseph to change her daughter's mind. But Laura wasn't worried; her parents were sticklers for keeping promises.

Jo sat on the other side of Mrs Chang's desk and stared at the large photograph of Halong Bay, the limestone rocks rising out of the green water and disappearing into the mist. 'Is that where you grew up?'

'My mother came from one of the floating villages in the bay.' Mrs Chang paused and turned to look at the photograph. 'I went last year for a holiday. So many punts and tourists.'

'It's a great photo. Looks peaceful.'

'I took it for my mother. I had it blown up and framed, but she gave it back to me.' Mrs Chang let out a long sigh. She was a tall, slender woman in her late fifties. She wore two- and three-piece suits in pastel colours — baby blue, salmon pink, lavender — with silk blouses and high heels. Her manicured nails were painted in hues that matched her outfits. She was out of place at the school, where most of the teachers dressed in various shades of denim. Jo had trouble imagining her on a boat in Halong Bay.

'Why?'

'She says it is hard enough to forget. Vietnam has a sad history. Sometimes things happen to people that they want to forget.' She glanced at her watch and frowned. 'So, enough chat, Jo. Were you listening to my suggestions? Or is your heart set on studying urban design?'

Mr Williams, Jo's Year 10 Geography teacher, had introduced her to urban design. His passion was 'environmental justice', making industrial areas safer, more liveable. He had a long list of activist 'wins' that included saving forests, saving rivers, and helping secure the vote for Indigenous Australians. Ian, the students called him — at least when the principal wasn't in earshot — and rolled their eyes when he became overly zealous, picking on their plastic drink bottles, on paper wastage, on the clothes they wore, going on about where they were made and how much the manufacturers paid poor workers in Asia. He spent several classes trying to get them to stop eating meat by showing them gruesome videos of abattoirs and chickens in battery farms.

Jo volunteered for one of his 'urban regeneration' projects and helped plant three hundred trees along Stony Creek, the polluted waterway that snaked its way through several industrial suburbs from St Albans to Yarraville. It was hard work. They cleared weeds, broke up the hard topsoil to reach the rich brown loam underneath, and planted drooping sheoak, river red gums, and various acacias — just saplings, most less than 10 centimetres high. For weeks after, Jo researched local trees.

She discovered the western suburbs had fewer trees, and certainly fewer mature trees, than other areas of the city. She discovered the council's list of significant trees and went exploring along the Maribyrnong River, where there were the native kurrajongs and sugar gums, as well as date palms and pepper trees. The majestic old elms, in Stephen Street, in Fairlie Street, and at Footscray Primary School, were her favourites: from their sturdy grey trunks they rose 20 metres, but while their canopies were wide and dense, their roots were shallow and visible, like the veins of her grandmother's hands.

She didn't mention the elms to Ian. They were an introduced species, and he would not approve.

When she was researching the trees, she wasn't worrying. It was as if she'd taken a happy pill. She stopped watching what she was eating, fearful that she was going to put on weight with every mouthful; there were no voices in her head goading her about becoming the fat girl again. Anxiety about the future — about having *no direction*, no talents, no passions — no longer consumed every minute of her day. She stopped spending nights lying in bed creating endless disaster scenarios — her mother dying, the refineries blowing up, a terrorist attack in Melbourne. The conversations with her friends, especially Ash, went unanalysed and she didn't go over them word by word, until even a simple exchange seemed fraught with double meanings, with intimations and innuendo.

But she fell in love with Ian and all her insecurities resurfaced.

'It's a crush, you'll get over it. And he's old and not even that good-looking,' Ash said.

For more than a year Ian was the target of her affections, the main protagonist of her fantasies. She switched subjects to be in his classes. She went to demonstrations to watch him from the sidelines and *accidentally* bumped into him when he was on yard duty at lunch time. She imagined herself knocking on Ian's door. She imagined following him down the hallway of his house, past the *Save the Whale, Climate Change Is Here Now,* and *Plant a Tree and Breathe* posters on the walls, to his bedroom, where they fell onto his bed, where they kissed and fucked and where over and over he declared his love.

What was the difference between fantasy and reality? Was it possible to make fantasies come true?

Since he left the school, Jo hadn't seen Ian. She was grateful that he introduced her to environmental design, to the possibility of regenerating the industrial landscape. But she wasn't going to be an activist. She wasn't going to make the industrial suburbs more liveable. She would be lucky to get a job she didn't hate.

'Maybe if you made a list of possibilities,' Mandy suggested.

'Sure, I'll do that.'

'Jo.'

'What?'

'I am trying to help.'

'Mrs Chang said I could find something I don't mind doing. Like you. You don't mind the deli, do you?'

'Jo, there is no need to be like that.'

Jo didn't respond, and they sat there for a while in silence.

'What do you have planned for today?' Mandy asked in a conciliatory, change-the-subject tone that Jo found even more irritating.

'It's Saturday — my plan's to go to work, like I do every Saturday.' She didn't look up. She wanted to say, *Why do you ask such stupid questions?*

'And after?'

'Studying. Then going out with Ash to Rosie's party,' Jo said.

'I haven't seen Ashleigh for ages.'

'That's because we've got so much fucking — sorry, so much homework.'

'I know it's a hard year, but it's almost over.'

It wasn't just that it was a hard year. Ash had changed; she was more distant, less available. The friendship was waning. Like the first drop in temperature after a long warm summer, the change was subtle at first. No storms. No heavy rains. But Ash was slipping out of Jo's grasp. That was real. It wasn't her imagination. Hanging on to it, pulling it back, was like being on the losing side of one of those tug-of-war games they played when she was in primary school — the more effort she made, the less available Ash became. Whenever they saw each other on a weekend, Jo planned to say something. *Say something.* Only she didn't, and the periods of anxiety had grown longer and more frequent.

For months, Jo had avoided her mother's questions about Ash. What could she say anyway? Even if she did talk to Mandy, what help would Mandy be? The act of confiding was foreign to Jo, even with her mother, even when she was young. When the anxiety attacks first started, she tried explaining to Mandy. The rising panic that came with sweat, and nausea, and dizziness. Mandy didn't understand. She was sympathetic and concerned, but dismissive: 'You don't have anything to worry about.' Jo understood there were problems her mother couldn't fix.

And it wasn't as if she and Ash had stopped being friends. They weren't fighting. Not like they did when they were younger, those *I never want to see you ever again* fights. Those *I wish you'd disappear down a big hole forever* fights. They weren't hanging out after school and on weekends, but they were together every day at school. Just yesterday, at lunchtime, they had been together with Laura and Mani at their usual bench, on the edge of the oval, and everything had seemed normal. They'd talked about going to Rosie's party together, about what they would wear, who was going to take responsibility for organising a card to go with their gift, a voucher for a facial at the local day spa.

'What if I come to your place to get ready? We can drive around and pick up Laura and Mani on the way?' Ash had asked.

'No Kevin?'

'I thought you'd prefer it to be just us.'

'It's not that I don't like Kevin —' Jo began.

'No boys! We can all go single,' Laura interrupted.

'Sure,' Mani said, grinning. 'You just want to flirt all night.'

They all laughed, and Jo watched Ash laugh. Was Ash just pretending they were friends?

'Will you be home for dinner?' Mandy asked.

'No idea — don't worry about dinner. I'll find something to eat.'

'Fine.'

'Fine.'

'It's 7.20,' Mandy said. 'You're gonna be late.'

'Not if I run.' Jo dropped the spoon into the half-eaten cereal, stood up and grabbed her phone, and ran towards the door.

'Have a good day,' Mandy called out, but Jo was gone, the front door slamming shut.

It was almost noon, and the Two Hands Café in Yarraville was overflowing. Late risers were sitting down to massive plates of eggs and bacon, smashed avocado, and sautéed mushrooms, and filmgoers were eating quick lunches before the early-afternoon screenings. There were long queues for takeaway and tables. Jo was clearing plates, her back to the door, when Ash's sister, Jane, tapped her on the shoulder. Ash's mother, Rae, dressed in her designer activewear — striped leggings and a black top that Ash had told Jo cost a fortune — was standing at the end of the queue waiting for a table.

'Hey,' Jane said, 'do we get to jump the queue because we're, like, family? I'm practically your sister. And I'm starving.' Jane was wearing the baggy 'Thrasher' t-shirt that Jo had given her for her thirteenth birthday. Jo noticed the glare from a woman standing ahead of them in the queue.

'She's joking,' Rae said, loudly enough for the woman to hear. 'How are you, Jo? I haven't seen you for a few weeks.'

'I'm good, just so much homework. No time to breathe.'

'I'm going to give VCE a miss,' Jane said.

'We'll see about that.' Rae smiled at her daughter, and Jane frowned.

'I'm going to be a pro skater. I don't need school for that.'

Rae winked at Jo. Jane elbowed her mother. 'Just wait and see.' And all three of them laughed.

'They might have degrees for skateboarders by the time you finish school,' Jo teased.

'But she thinks she's already an expert,' Rae said.

The bell in the kitchen rang. 'Argh, sorry, I have to go,' Jo said. 'I'm sure you'll get a table soon. See ya.'

'Bye, Jo,' Rae said. 'Say hello to your mum, I haven't seen her in ages.'

Jo headed for the kitchen, where the meals for one of her tables were ready to serve. Then a table asked for the bill and another table for water and a third, a large group of what looked like an extended family, wanted to order. By the time she had a chance for a breather, Jane and Rae had been seated at the other end of the restaurant. She was run off her feet for the next half hour and didn't get a chance to talk to them again.

Jane had said 'like family', but they weren't family, even though until recently she had spent at least one, sometimes two, nights a week eating and sleeping at their house. If she and Ash stopped being friends, she wouldn't any longer have anything to do with Ash's family. What would they be to her if she and Ash stopped being friends? Would they slip away, become acquaintances, and then finally strangers?

Normally Jo worked an eight-hour shift, 7.30 to 3.30 or 8.00 to 4.00, but her boss, Ted, had reluctantly agreed to a five-hour shift, because she needed to finish her English essay.

It was a mild spring day, except for the wind — almost a gust that, even when the sun pushed through the clouds, kept the temperature down. Normally by this time of the year, Melburnians could be heard yearning for warmer weather, but the city was still reeling from the Black Saturday bushfires in February. One hundred and seventy-three people dead, thousands of homes and hectares of land destroyed. As Jo left the café, she heard a couple talking about the fires and their hope that this year the holiday season would come with cooler temperatures and more rain.

Jo walked home through the shopping centre to the beat of The Black Eyed Peas' 'Boom Boom Pow'. The lyrics were complete nonsense, but still she loved the song. She thought about all those people enjoying their Saturday off and resented having to do homework. But it was just a few more months. 'Once you have *the certificate*, you'll be ready to go on with your real lives,' Jo's school principal had declared at one of her regular pep talks with the senior students. Jo thought this was an odd thing to say to students, considering some would fail and some would not do as well as they hoped. What would it mean if she failed — would she become stuck like some rabbit in headlights, fixed to the spot, never able to move, or would she be doomed to repeat VCE again and again, *Groundhog Day*–style, until she got it right?

As she approached her front gate, Jo slowed and looked up at the West Gate. The high-wind warning lights were flashing and the traffic was slowed to a crawl. She took her earphones out, and immediately the music was replaced with the rumble of the traffic, the sputter of exhaust pipes, and the squeal of brakes. Across the road the oil tanks cast a sombre shadow. She sighed and headed inside.

Mandy was at work, so Jo spread her books on the kitchen table. Then she opened her laptop and stared at the screen. She was contemplating whether to work on her History assignment — on the goals and consequences of Lenin's New Economic Policy — or her English essay on the nature of reality. The essay was due first, but she'd been avoiding it. The question, 'Is every reality open to interpretation?' was to be answered with reference to Ian McEwan's *Enduring Love*, a strange and difficult novel she hadn't finished reading, and with reference to current events. Keeping up with the daily news was imperative. Her mother had signed up for a subscription to *The Age*, even though Mandy's preference was for the *Herald Sun* and they couldn't afford two newspapers. Most days Jo didn't open the paper, and it remained in the tight cylinder the delivery guy threw from his car into their front yard every morning. Over the months, these dusty corpses accumulated in the corner of the laundry. Still procrastinating, she sent Ash a text message: *Do you want to come over early? Work on the essay?* Jo found it easier to get homework done if they worked together.

'The next-door neighbors are having a family reunion. There's like hundreds of them. And loud Greek music. It's a nightmare, can't get anything done,' Ash said when she arrived. Her hair was up in an untidy bun and she was wearing her gym pants and a tight pink t-shirt.

'Oh God, no, sounds painful. Did you bring your clothes for tonight?'

'I need to go to the library before it closes, to get a couple of books for my Legal Studies essay. I'll go home and get my clothes on the way back. And I haven't decided what I'm going to wear yet.'

'Have you started the essay?' Jo asked as Ash emptied the contents of her backpack onto the table: books, notebooks, her laptop.

'Just rough notes. You?'

'Just starting. Haven't finished reading the novel yet. I mean, a novel about a stalker? Anyway, I watched the film.'

'Jo …' Ash frowned, pointed her finger at Jo, and mimicked Mrs Hunt's British accent. 'The movie isn't the book, and you can get into all sorts of problems in the exam.'

Jo scowled. According to Mrs Hunt, their English teacher, the degradation of the English language could be traced to Hollywood, and it was criminal the way movies dominated the culture, and now even the government had decreed that students study films as part of the curriculum: films don't, can't, replace literature.

'A few more months. Read the novel,' Ash said.

'I will.'

Ash's phone rang.

'Hey, glad you called,' she said. Her smile, the dimples, signs of her obvious pleasure. 'No, this is a good time. Just at Jo's, working on the English essay … No, all good …

'Kevin says hi, I'll go outside,' Ash said, and mouthed, 'Sorry,' as she headed towards the back door. She sat on the edge of the deck, pulling her knees to her chin and leaning her back against a post. As she settled in, she lowered her voice and only an odd word or a laugh made it as far as the kitchen.

On top of the stack of Ash's books there was a red Moleskine notebook: Ash's journal. Over the years, Ash's journals had changed in shape and size — with lines and without lines, with arty covers, with plain covers. Kevin had introduced her to the Moleskines. 'Kevin says that real writers use Moleskine notebooks, like Hemingway and Oscar Wilde,' Ash told Jo. They were standing in a stationery store and Ash was spinning the Moleskine stand.

'Really? Any women writers? I thought writers were poor — these are so expensive. At Bill's Bargains they have notebooks for two dollars.'

'Not this good, Jo. It's my journal, I write in it every day.' Ash caressed the cover and gave Jo a pleading smile. 'Can I borrow ten dollars?'

Jo picked up the notebook and ran her fingers over the cover. When they were younger, Jo often asked: 'What do you write about?' And Ash read out humorous pieces about her parents or their teachers. She read Jo her lists: *stupid things I said this week that I can't take back, things I'll do when this fucking year is over, by the time I'm 40 I'll ...* She documented their lives: the notes they passed in class, the boys they had the hots for, and the Sunday afternoons Mandy coaxed them into watching daggy old films like *Singing in the Rain*. Once she said, 'I've got a Jo list' and read out a sample: *Jo lets me tell her all my bad jokes and she laughs. Jo's there when I need her. Jo makes the best meatballs and spaghetti (and I should know because my nonna is Italian). Jo doesn't care that she doesn't get As. Jo can keep a secret.* Jo loved that list. Ash loved her unconditionally.

But that was the past. Now she couldn't ask. In those days she didn't suspect Ash of having other lists: *All the things I hate about Jo: fat, needy, boring ...*

In the three months since they returned to school for their final semester, this was only the second time Ash had visited on a weekend, and she was on the phone with Kevin. They'd only been out three times: for Jo's birthday, to go to a new Latin American bar Laura's father had a share in, and to Pink's 'Funhouse Tour' concert, which they'd bought tickets for months in advance. Ash said she was busy studying, that if she didn't do well enough she wouldn't get into law, and then what would she do? But most Friday and Saturday nights she went out with Kevin. At school on Mondays, Ash avoided talking about her weekends.

Were they still friends? Still best friends? They only seemed to talk about school and homework. Their conversations were superficial, as if they were just classmates who happened to be caught behind each other in the canteen queue.

'Let sleeping dogs lie,' Grandpa Tom said when Jo or Mandy asked *too many questions*. She'd only been four years old when he got sick. He had lost so much weight his bones were visible; when she hugged him he was all sharp edges. It took him longer to get out of bed, and no matter what her mother cooked, he couldn't finish a full meal. Finally, Mandy had insisted on taking him to the doctor. The diagnosis was cancer. He'd ignored several moles on his back for years, so by the time they did the tests, the cancer was at stage 4 and terminal. Tom said it pissed him off, them knowing. 'Let sleeping dogs lie, why can't women do that?' But they were right, weren't they, to want to know?

Jo's friendship with Ash was a sore she picked and scratched. A journal was personal, full of private thoughts. You had to be invited in; reading another person's journal was like breaking into their house while they were away, like rifling through their drawers, like peeking in through their windows while they were having dinner with their family. During all those years, Ash's journals often within reach, she'd never considered reading them. It was invasive. It was voyeuristic. It was a kind of theft, and once done there'd be no going back.

Jo ran her hand across the smooth red cover. Ash was settling in for a long conversation with Kevin. She was talking and laughing, twisting strands of her long hair around her finger. As Jo slipped the band off and the notebook opened, sunlight and shade danced across the back deck, making patterns over Ash. Stealing glances at Ash, she flipped the pages of the journal.

May 11. Ash wrote in a print-like script, the lines surprisingly straight and even, like rungs on a ladder. It wasn't her usual scribble, the one she used for taking notes in class, for leaving notes in Jo's locker, for leaving messages for her mother on the kitchen table. There was a lengthy description of Kevin's face: wide, open, cute; of his voice: sexy and deep; of the way he held her hand, fingers intertwined; of their long discussions; of how she could be herself with him. *I can be myself with Kevin.* Who was Ash when she was with Jo?

Jo flipped the page over. May 12. A rant about Ash's mother took up several pages — her voice and her rules and the way she told Ash off for spending money on clothes but went out shopping most weekends and bought clothes for herself, and how she forced Ash to do housework even though Ash was overwhelmed with study, and how she monopolised Kevin when he came over … *My mother flirts with Kevin, it's disgusting.*

There were several paragraphs about Ash's grandmother and how pale and sick she was looking, and how it made Ash sad to think she might die. Here the pen was heavier on the page, as if Ash had pressed down with all her weight, with rage. Jo flipped back towards May and April. *Places I want to live. The ultimate playlist.* Jo recognised all the songs on this list as Ash's favourites. No surprises. *The secret playlist.* There were no surprises on that list either. Everyone had songs that they were embarrassed to admit they liked; Ash's included a couple of ABBA and Milli Vanilli classics and even Aqua's 'Barbie Girl', which they had played in their early teens during sleepovers at Ash's place to annoy Ash's mother. A condensed biography of human-rights lawyer Geoffrey Robertson. The words to Eminem's 'Crack a Bottle'. A song so far away from Ash's life, from anything she'd experienced, that Ash's attraction to it seemed voyeuristic, like those people who gather around accidents or are drawn to reading about disasters.

At the sound of footsteps on the deck, Jo shut the notebook and put it back on top of the stack of other books.

For the rest of that afternoon, Jo and Ash worked on their essays. *What is the nature of reality?* They discussed Jed's obsession with Joe, whether Clarissa believed him, whether the 'hero' John Logan, who died trying to rescue the boy, could be admired as a hero if he were betraying his wife by having an affair. All the time Jo was thinking, *what about you, Ash? What about us? Are we still best friends?*

There'd been no mention of Jo in the journal, not once. Not once in all the entries she read. Jo didn't keep a journal, but if she did, Ash would've been there, on every page. When she planned moving out of home, it was with Ash. When she imagined travelling, going to Europe, to Paris and London, to Barcelona, it was with Ash. When she thought about what university to go to, she thought about where Ash would go. In Jo's dreams of a big wedding and a white dress, in which she was floating down the aisle towards the love of her life — a man she hadn't met and couldn't evoke — Ash was there. Ash was the maid of honour, in a long lilac dress, flowers threaded through her hair. Was it possible to go from being central to Ash's world to so much on the periphery that she was invisible? Were they in the process of breaking up?

The first person Jo broke up with was Max, her boyfriend in Year 9. At the beginning of their four-month relationship he was cute and funny, but by the end she hated everything about him, and the sight of him waving at her across the school ground sent her into a frenzy, causing her to escape into the girls' toilets. One afternoon, in her desperation to hide from him, she tripped over a discarded cricket bat and broke her arm. When she told Mandy that she didn't like him anymore, her mother insisted she break up with him. Mandy dialled the phone number for her and sat next to Jo on the bed as Jo said, *I'm breaking up with you. I don't want to be your girlfriend.* They never spoke again. The second person was Craig, whom she'd met at the café one lunchtime. They dated for a few months, and had sex three times. She was determined to lose her virginity. She was the last of her group — Laura, Mani, and Ash had all *done it.* It was almost as disappointing as she'd expected it to be. But not as bad. When she saw Craig around Yarraville, they waved and smiled but didn't stop to talk.

If she and Ash stopped being friends, would they become strangers? Distant acquaintances? Would they give a nod as they passed in the street? Or would Ash be so repulsed that she'd want to run away and hide?

Should I write about that? Imagine that, Ash: Mrs Hunt reading my essay in class, my essay about you and me. Throughout the afternoon, she deliberated about how to bring it up. But what could she say: 'Why haven't you written about me in your journal?' Even in her head she sounded like a wimpy ten-year-old. Like the fat and lonely child she had been before she met Ash.

Chapter 5

Paolina shifted her chair to catch the soft afternoon sun as it came in through the sliding glass doors. In the garden, Antonello was staking the tomato plants. He was wearing old khaki shorts and a singlet, and she could see his strong calf muscles, his strong arms. Her body was broken and weak; all her muscles were limp, and her skin so flabby that it reminded her of being a child forced to wear her older cousin's too-big hand-me-down dresses. Even on good days, walking the fifty steps to the front gate to check the letterbox was a struggle that required too much fortitude; gardening was reduced to short bursts, confined to the raised bed that Antonello had installed so that she could sit on a small wooden stool to tend the plants.

Her granddaughters had helped her plant herbs, basil and parsley, and bulbs — tulips, irises, and jonquils. The bulbs were a gift. 'Secret plants,' her youngest granddaughter called them. 'We can plant them and not tell Nonno. They'll be a surprise.' Antonello's reputation as the sort of gardener who didn't have time for flowers was the butt of many family jokes. The girls called the garden 'Nonno's farm'.

Antonello pounded the wooden stakes with a hammer until they sank into the ground, and he tested each one by rocking it back and forth. The first time she'd seen him garden, he was planting two red rose bushes in the small bed under the bungalow windows. The roses were her choice. 'We'll lie in bed with coffee, look out the window, and see them,' she told him. It was before the bridge collapse, in those romantic first months of their marriage. A Sunday, she guessed; the memory carried with it a sense of the day stretching into tranquility. A grey morning, the sky cloaked in dark and ponderous clouds. Drifting from the open kitchen window of her parents' house was the wistful tones of a Calabrian folk singer, her mother's favourite, the song a lament to a lost lover and a lost country. She remembered making a joke about her parents' poor musical tastes as she inched towards him, as she ran her fingers along his arm. Antonello dropped the spade, wrapped his arms around her waist, and talked about the rain, urging her back into the bungalow. Even though they were married and living in their first home, the prefabricated bungalow in her parents' backyard, they felt like teenagers playing house. That day they giggled as they pulled the blinds down and hung Zia Lina's sign, *Non Disturbare*, on the door.

The sign, cross-stitched in bright reds and blues, the text surrounded by a garland of daisies, had been a kitchen tea gift. 'You're young. If you want to be alone, put this on the door. That way your mother' — Lina elbowed her sister — 'eh, *sorella*? She won't come in with her plate of cotolette or biscotti when you want to be alone.' Both Paolina and her mother blushed, but across the room, which was overflowing with female cousins and aunts, with future sisters-in-law, a future mother-in-law, girlfriends, there were giggles and laughter.

'We can't use that,' Antonello said when he first saw the sign. 'It's like we are putting a notice on the door, letting your parents know we are having sex now.' But they did hang the sign on the door, because in those early days they were impatient, their longing for each other was urgent. Paolina's body, even in its battered current state, remembered, and the memory, along with the sight of Antonello in the garden, resulted in an unexpected feverish desire. She wouldn't act on it — her body didn't have the strength — but its presence was delicious and sweet.

Recently, while sorting and clearing, Paolina had discovered the cross-stitched sign among the handmade linen she had inherited from her mother, which she'd never used but couldn't bear to discard. Her zia's work was fine, the letters constructed from a series of perfect, tiny stitches. She was surprised, though, when she turned the piece over, to find that on the back of the sign there was another embroidered message, in English: *Don't forget to laugh, marriage is funny*. Paolina would've sworn the second message hadn't been there when Zia Lina first gave her the gift. That it hadn't been there all those times she hung the sign on the bungalow door. Lina's English was better than Paolina's mother's, but not so good; she must've recruited a translator.

On that same day, Paolina rang Lina's oldest daughter, Rosa, and they reminisced. They remembered their mothers, and the way the two sisters — the oldest and the youngest, bookending the family of eight — were inseparable.

'They fought so much,' Rosa said. 'Remember?'

'Yes.'

'About everything. About recipes. About childhood memories. About how to make the sauce, the sausages. God, remember once, your mother grabbed the salt shaker that my mother had in her hands and threw it across the room to stop her putting more salt on the sausages?'

'My mother used to say your mother was born with no tastebuds,' Paolina said with a laugh.

'Once, I said to my mother, "Why do we have to do everything with Zia Pina? All you do is fight." She slapped me. "*Tu sei una cretina*", she yelled at me. "*È mia sorrella*".'

After they hung up, Paolina sewed a small tag, 'This is for Rosa', on the *Non Disturbare* sign before she put it back in the drawer.

Outside, Antonello lined up his three rows of ten stakes. As the tomato plants grew, he would train them up the stakes and they'd bear fruit — enough to share with his children, Alex and Nicki, and their families; with the neighbours; with friends. This year Paolina might not be the one to pick them. She might not be the one to put them in paper bags and distribute them. Although the cancer had slowed, it hadn't stopped. Death was as sly and as agile as the black cat skulking in the bushes, its eye on the birds blinded by the lure of Antonello's garden. Her children and her grandchildren would mourn her and move on with their lives, but Antonello would be alone. Alone in the garden. Alone in the house. She couldn't shake the feeling of guilt and sorrow, the sense that she was abandoning him.

Paolina made a cup of tea and sat at the kitchen table. In front of her was that morning's *Herald Sun*. She unfolded it and turned the pages, reading the headlines. The image of the temporary suicide fence on the West Gate Bridge caught her attention; she knew it would've caught Antonello's. The photograph was taken at peak hour, early morning. The traffic heading towards the city was heavy: several lanes of cars and trucks bumper to bumper.

'Four times the number the bridge was made to hold,' Antonello repeated often. The bridge collapsing again was an ongoing possibility. And the falling dreams persisted, though neither mentioned them — what was there left to say? It had been almost forty years now, and she was used to being woken by his cries, by his legs hitting hard against the mattress.

In the months after the collapse, she'd been adamant they should move away, but Antonello refused. In hindsight, she understood he was suffering from post-traumatic stress, but none of the survivors went to counselling. The doctors treated their physical injuries and gave them sleeping tablets.

Antonello and Paolina saw the bridge daily; there was no avoiding it. Whenever they went to the shops or walked to Alex's house or picked up their granddaughters from school, the bridge towered over them. Whenever they took the train into the city or headed for a drive to Williamstown or Altona, it was there, a deep scar on the horizon. Antonello never drove across it, not even to visit Nicki in Port Melbourne, on the other side of the bridge.

Paolina watched him hammer in the last stake. She loved him. She belonged to him, and he to her, but he wasn't the man she married. That Antonello, young and carefree, existed only in her memories and imaginings, constructed from *what ifs* and *if onlys*. He was a phantom lingering at edges of their marriage. For years she prayed he'd return, but he never did.

The bridge was having a bad year. In the summer, a father stopped at the top, picked up his young daughter, and threw her over the side, into the river below, while her helpless brothers, aged two and six, sat in the car watching and crying. A few days later, a teenage boy, bullied at school, strolled onto the bridge — where walkers are banned — and jumped off.

'The West Gate is a well-known suicide spot,' Alex had told her recently.

'I've never heard any reported.'

'There are media protocols to stop the reporting,' Alex had explained. 'After each suicide reported in the newspaper, there is a spate of other suicides, copycatting.' Copycat: an insult her students had often flung at one another. *Copycat from Ballarat* ... It was a child's word, for harmless teasing and mocking, for childish games, for wanting to be included and liked, for wanting to do what your friends were doing.

Paolina turned her attention back to the newspaper article. According to the journalist, it was predicted that the temporary barriers would prevent at least two suicides a month. She whispered a short prayer for all those people in such despair that they saw death as their only option. Even with the cancer and the treatment, which was awful, she could not imagine voluntarily giving up her life.

Antonello left the hammer on the low brick fence that surrounded the garden, discarded his gloves, and limped towards the bench under the lemon tree. His back was stiff. His knee ached. The doctor said he needed a knee reconstruction, but the knee was a legacy, and he didn't think he could have it repaired. His body was sluggish and unreliable. As a young man he had taken his strength for granted. Six days a week of physical labour, extra shifts whenever he could get them, soccer after work, and dancing on Friday and Saturday nights. The first time he danced with Paolina, they waltzed and rocked and twisted around the dance floor, resting only when the band took breaks. She was so light in his arms; he was so strong. He remembered the sweet smell of her jasmine perfume and the pleasure of his hand on the hollow of her back.

Antonello could hear the shouts and laughter of children and their parents making their way to the oval for Saturday afternoon football. He could hear the constant hum of traffic on the bridge. Every day, at least once a day, he gave the bridge his undivided attention. At least once a week this included a pilgrimage to the site to stand in front of the monument to the dead, but today he stayed in the garden and whispered their names: Slav Stronvenji and Bob Westland and young Ted Richards, whose surname he hadn't learnt until after the collapse. It was a prayer of sorts, though not to any God, but to the ghosts, ever present, and to the unfinished business between them.

His past was a web of black tunnels. Some days he was trapped in them for hours. Some days the chanting of the names was the only way to stop the memories, and the pain, but the morning's newspaper articles about the bridge had triggered his anxiety. His hands were shaking. And when he closed his eyes, to calm himself, he was sucked back in time as if through a portal. He could see himself, a young man, standing on the viewing platform, gazing up at the half-made bridge. It was a cold morning, and ominous black clouds threatened rain. He was waiting for Paolina's class. The children, when they arrived after 10.00 am, were wearing scarves and jackets. Twenty-four excited ten-year-olds, lined up in twos on the viewing platform.

In the days beforehand, Paolina had researched bridges as symbols — of crossings and transitions, of journeys between places. Antonello helped her draw pictures of bridges in her workbook and on project paper, pictures she planned to reproduce with coloured chalk on the blackboard. He helped her find copies of the bridge designs and photographs of different kinds of bridges: logs tossed over streams, with people walking across like trapeze artists on balance beams; small wooden bridges for pedestrians; bigger wooden bridges made to be used by horses and carts. Then the modern bridges — the Sydney Harbour, the Golden Gate, and the George Washington.

Slav helped Paolina look for poems and songs about bridges. But they found that many of the poems were about bridges falling, like 'London Bridge Is Falling Down'. She left those off her list, and settled instead on Will Allen Dromgoole's 'The Bridge Builder'.

She and Slav insisted on reading the poem to Antonello. 'This poem is about you and your workmates,' she said, 'building a bridge for the future.'

She asked Antonello if he would talk to her students about the bridge. He told her there were people whose job it was to talk to schoolchildren, but she insisted she wanted him to talk to them too, and he agreed because he knew she was making an effort, working against her own apprehensions.

After the education officer, Robert, had spoken to the children about the bridge and its construction, Antonello told them about his job as a rigger.

'Is it scary up there?' one of the boys asked.

'Sometimes,' Antonello said, 'but you get used to it.'

'How do they stick those giant towers into the water? Seems like they'd fall over,' another kid called out.

'They're called piers or pylons, and they're solid concrete,' Antonello said. 'I can tell you they dug deep holes to put them in.'

'Your husband is cute, Miss,' Antonello heard a girl call out cheekily.

'I am going to be a rigger,' another girl said.

'Girls can't be riggers,' a boy yelled back.

'Yes, they can.'

Soon all the children were arguing, and it took some effort for Paolina to settle them.

'Come on, children, Mr Milovich and Mr Bassillo have work to do. Say thank you and good-bye.'

'Thank you, Mr Milovich, and thank you, Mr Bassillo,' the children called out in a sing-song tone.

Antonello chuckled as he watched them disappearing around the corner. He turned and caught sight of a tanker gliding under the bridge towards Williamstown. On the eastern side, the punt waited for the ship to pass. The piers stood tall and grey, formidable, twenty-eight of them in a row, like gravestones. *Gravestones.* He made the sign of the cross over his chest and said a prayer. *Dear God, please keep the bridge safe.*

'By the time those kids are in high school, the punt will be history. The cars and the trucks will come and go on the bridge, and they won't notice the ships.' Bob came up behind him. They collected their sandwiches from the lunchroom and headed for the riverbank. Crows, gulls, and miners flew around them, undisturbed by the bridge building. The birds flew out towards the tankers and the punt, and circled to land by the men in the hope that they'd be thrown scraps.

'Sometimes I don't think we are ever going to finish this bridge,' Antonello said.

'Me too. But imagine that, a fucking half-made bridge. I'm sure the politicians would love that. I can hear Bolte,' Bob said, and then, mimicking the Premier's measured voice, '"Oh, I'm so pleased to announce the launch of the half-made bridge, a legacy I will be remembered for — alongside the hanging of that mongrel Ryan and ..."' Bob was laughing so much that he couldn't finish the sentence.

Antonello chuckled. 'You could've been a politician, Bob.'

'Sure, and the bridge could be a public art sculpture, but it's meant to be a bridge.'

'Some of the blokes think it's doomed. Sam's mother has been saying it's cursed and that we should get a *strega* to come and take the evil eye off and remove the curse.'

'A strega?'

'A witch.'

'Well, maybe a witch would help. Can't make it much worse. Just when I think things are going smoothly, something else happens. Too many problems, we all know that. What worries me is that everyone is tired of all the problems, all of us — the bosses, the bloody engineers, and the workers too. When everyone is exhausted, that's when problems happen.'

Why hadn't he listened to those premonitions, to those warnings? Antonello gripped the side of the bench. He could feel tears falling.

When he opened his eyes, he caught sight of the prickly pear. The fruit was beginning to turn orange and yellow. His next-door neighbour was on a mission to get Antonello to cut it down. 'You know it's a noxious weed,' she insisted. She said they had a moral obligation to only grow plants native to the area. Their disagreements were usually friendly — they both supported the Greens, they agreed that more should be done to address climate change and to ensure land rights for Indigenous Australians — but he refused to give in on the prickly pears, and no amount of coaxing from Paolina, who said their relationship with Kathy was more important than any plant, would change his mind.

It had taken him a whole afternoon to cut all of the fronds that were growing towards Kathy's side of the fence. But he couldn't bear to cut it down. In the valleys between Vizzini and the neighbouring towns, farmers grew fields of prickly pears and sold the fruit at the market. Prickly pears reminded him of home.

Since he'd stopped work to be with Paolina, he spent most of his spare time in the garden. The broccoli and the broad beans were ready to pick, and soon there would be eggplants and capsicums too. The Italian parsley in Paolina's raised garden had gone wild, and the first shoots of the bulbs the girls helped their grandmother plant were beginning to appear. On their next visit, he'd act out his disapproval, so they could roll their eyes behind his back and laugh. It was so much easier with his grandchildren than it had ever been with his children.

Once, his daughter, Nicki, had asked him about the bridge. She was doing a project for school. He refused to talk about it, but she persisted and persisted. They fought. Their relationship had never been great, but it was worse after that. He should've told her about the bridge, but he was afraid he couldn't tell it as a story or a piece of history. He was afraid to tell her that he'd seen things, known that there were problems, and remained silent. So often he'd told his children to be responsible, to look out for each other and for their friends. How could he tell her that he was at work the day they'd jacked up the box girders on the west side, and that when the two half boxes were not the same height, he didn't insist they take them back down? How could he tell her he was one of the riggers who'd hoisted ten big blocks, each one weighing 8 tons, up to the top and spread them across the higher span to force it down? How could he tell her that he was there early the following morning, only weeks before the collapse, and that he'd known the blocks hadn't worked?

The phone alarm woke Paolina. It was 2.00 pm and she needed to take her medication. She rose slowly from the recliner and went to the bench.

There the pills were lined up in small plastic jars, and on the pinboard was a list: which pills, how many, with or without food, and time of day. She poured a glass of water from the filtered jug and took six pills, one at a time.

She picked up the phone to reset the alarm and noticed a message from her old friend Alice. They had kept in touch even though Alice now lived interstate. Usually they talked on the phone once or twice a year, but since Paolina had told her about the cancer, Alice had been ringing or texting every week.

They'd met at teachers' college in the late 1960s, and it was through Alice that Paolina met Antonello. Alice had invited her to the San Remo Ballroom, and Alice's boyfriend, Sam, came to pick them up. There were two other young men in the front seat. Sam introduced Slav and Antonello.

'I thought Alice said you were Italian,' Antonello said to Paolina once they found a table.

'I am,' she said. 'I was born here, but my parents come from Sicily. It's my hair, isn't it? Everyone thinks I'm Australian because I don't have dark hair. You know, there are Italians with blonde hair.'

'Not many,' he said, 'at least not from the south. I don't remember anyone in the village having blonde hair. Well, there was one woman with white hair, but she was an albino.'

They both laughed. His laugh was hearty and free of any restraint. He was a handsome man, his hair black and wavy, his eyes almost as black as her brother's. She hadn't laughed for weeks. She remembered feeling guilty: she was enjoying herself while her brother was in Vietnam and in danger. She'd considered leaving — catching a cab and going home.

'Where in Sicily is your family from?'

His voice brought her back to the room, where the orchestra were playing 'I'll Be Seeing You' and several couples were already on the dance floor.

'Grammichele. And yours?' she asked.

'Vizzini — not that far from Grammichele,' Antonello said. 'I've been to Grammichele twice — a long time ago now, when I was a child. My father's youngest sister married a man from Grammichele and they lived there. It is much bigger than Vizzini. It has a piazza in the centre with six roads leading to it, I remember. My cousin Andrea took me there, and we spent the afternoon running around the square and up and down the streets until it rained and we sheltered in one of the churches.'

The waiters brought them a bottle of wine, and Antonello poured them a glass each. The band started playing Elvis hits and more couples moved onto the dance floor.

'St Michael's?'

'You know it?'

'No, I've never been,' Paolina said. 'My parents talk about the town so much that I'm sure I could draw you a map with all the main sights. We planned to go back for my cousin's wedding last year, but my brother was conscripted and sent to Vietnam.'

'Sorry, that must be difficult. I was lucky, didn't get called up. Have you heard from your brother?'

'He writes and he seems to be okay. He has nine months to go before his tour of duty is done. God willing, he'll be home soon.'

When the band started playing 'Blue Suede Shoes', Alice was suddenly standing behind them. 'Come on, you two. No one should sit through Elvis. Nello, are you going to ask Paolina to dance?'

'Sorry,' Paolina responded. 'Alice can be bossy.'

'Dance?' Antonello said, turning to Paolina.

Alice laughed as she raced back towards Sam, who was rocking and rolling with an imaginary partner.

'Yes, I'd love to,' Paolina said, pushing back her chair.

Paolina danced with Antonello all night. And when the music allowed it, they talked.

'You remind me of one of my teachers, Signora Bellini. She encouraged me to draw.'

'You draw?' Paolina asked.

'I've always loved drawing. My mother takes the credit. She wanted to name all her children after artists, but my father wouldn't let her. I was the lucky last — all the grandparents' names were used up.'

'So you're an artist?'

Antonello shook his head. 'I'm a rigger who can draw a bit. My mother wanted me to be an artist. "Artists live forever," she says. But my father says artists need to put food on the table like everyone else, and art doesn't pay much.'

'And you — would you prefer to be an artist?'

'No, I like rigging. My father's right, you can't make a living as an artist. Drawing isn't work, it's pleasure, and men need to work to look after their families. What about you? What did you want to do?'

'I wanted to do nursing, but my parents hated the idea — the night shifts, living in the hospital, inappropriate for a good Italian girl. So I chose teaching instead, and I love it — so that was lucky.'

On the way home, Alice and Paolina sat in the back seat again, all three men in front.

'Are you two talking about us?' Sam asked.

'Oh, Sam, you think that's all we have to talk about,' Alice teased. 'Of course. I'm telling Paolina how handsome you are because she can't see that for herself.'

It was Antonello they talked about, in hushed tones.

'Do you like him?' Alice asked.

'He's gorgeous,' Paolina said.

'I think he likes you too,' Alice whispered.

'How do you know?'

'Give me a break. He can't keep his eyes off you. Double dates soon.'

'As if my parents are going to let me go on dates. Good Italian girls stay home with their mammas until they are married.'

'There are ways, even for good girls like you.' Alice put her arm around her friend and, lowering her voice even further, said, 'Leave it to me.'

They giggled, and Paolina was a little girl again, like the little girls in her class who huddled together with their friends and ran in carefree circles around the school ground, able to forget even their worst troubles, as only children can. *He loves me, he loves me not, he loves me …*

'Paolina. Paolina, are you okay?'

Antonello was standing at the door.

'*Si, si come una ragazza*,' she said, and winked. They rarely spoke Italian now that their parents' generation was dead, but she liked to tease him in Italian. There was an extra playfulness that emerged with the language; it pulled them back into their childhoods.

'*Bella Paolina.*' He smiled back. 'We'll be late if we don't hurry.'

'What time is it?' She hadn't expected to fall asleep again, and she was disorientated.

'Almost 3.15. We should leave in the next ten minutes.'

'You're the one that needs to get cleaned up and dressed,' Paolina said.

'Let's be late, we'll be waiting for hours anyway. Can't believe he sees patients on a Saturday.'

But he took off his gumboots, came in, and headed for the bedroom to get changed. Paolina sighed: another trip to the oncologist's crowded and sombre waiting room lay ahead of them. The oncologist was in his forties, and on the wall of his office were pictures of his four children, and what Paolina suspected was his second wife. He was tanned, well-dressed, and always running late, caught up by an emergency or by his tendency to slip into long conversations with his patients about golf or holidays or the weather, as if getting to the point were more painful for him than for them.

But tomorrow was Sunday and, if she wasn't too tired, if the news wasn't too bad, they'd drop in on Alex and his family, and their granddaughters would tell them the stories of their week at school and complain about their parents and their teachers, and they'd all forget for a few hours.

Chapter 6

Carrying a tote bag, a hanger with a couple of skirts, and a bottle of champagne, Ash arrived back at Jo's in a flurry at 7.30. From behind the closed front door, she yelled, 'Hey Jo, let me in,' because she didn't have a free hand to ring the bell.

'Hi, Ashleigh. So good to see you. Can I help?' Mandy said as she let Ash in. 'Looks like you've brought your whole wardrobe.'

Ash handed her a bag and the champagne. 'Thanks, Mandy. You know me — I can't decide what to wear,' Ash said, kissing Mandy on the cheek and heading straight into Jo's bedroom. 'What are you wearing, Jo?'

'My red dress — maybe.' Jo's bed was covered in clothes.

'Great. Can I borrow the blue top? My turn. It'll go with my pencil skirt.'

'Sure.' Jo dug the blue top out from the pile and handed it to Ash.

Since their early teens, when they started buying their own clothes, they often went halves. This required negotiation, but mainly it worked. Ash understood fashion — understood which clothes were in and which weren't, which clothes would mark you as an outsider, which marked you as an insider, so she directed and managed the shopping trips and the decisions on what to purchase, but that suited Jo too. Without Ash, she would've lived in jeans and t-shirts, the wrong kind, and dressing for parties would've been a nightmare. Even with Ash, she found clothes shopping difficult. The mirrors in the tiny dressing-room cubicles highlighted all her faults. Clothes clung to her belly, accentuated her hips and her thighs. In those mirrors, with their harsh spotlights, she became the fat girl again. Ash didn't know about her fat history, or the trip to visit her father and his wife, about them forcing her to go on a diet. There were experiences too shameful to tell even a best friend.

Sometimes, when they were in changing rooms, in dress shops, she let slip, 'I feel fat in this.' Ash laughed at her. 'Are you for real? I can see your ribs.' Or 'If you're fat, I'm fat, because we're the same size. Are you saying I'm fat?' They might have been the same size, but the clothes didn't look the same on them. Jo was taller and had a fuller figure. However, the real difference was to do with styles and combinations. When Jo wore the red dress, she wore ballet flats and tied her hair back in a ponytail. If she wore jewellery at all, it was a fine silver chain with her birthstone, a small ruby, that she had bought with money her father sent for a recent birthday. Ash wore the red dress with six-inch heels; she wore a tight black choker, and against her long slender neck it turned into a swirl of tattooed waves. Ash's mother said it made her look like she belonged on a vampire movie set. The dress had a tie on the right side that could be adjusted. Ash tied it low to create a cleavage.

'Cruiser? Lemon or lime?'

'Lime. Can you put the champagne in the freezer — it's warm.'

Ash moved Jo's clothes to one side and unpacked her bag, spreading her clothes out on Jo's bed, on the chair and desk. They took the drinks into the bathroom. Jo rarely wore make-up, but she enjoyed hanging over the basin, squashed up against Ash, so they could talk to each other's reflections in the mirror as they painted their lips and eyes, as they transformed their faces from ordinary school girls to grown women.

'Hey, try this mascara, it's awesome.' Ash handed Jo the mascara tube. The mascara dyed Jo's brown lashes black.

'I hope Kevin was okay about not coming to the party ... You've got a smudge, there,' Jo said, pointing to Ash's left eyelid.

'Yup — no problem. It's great to hang out, just us girls.' Ash stopped doing her make-up and blew Jo a kiss in the mirror. 'God, who said that once there's a guy around, he has to come to everything? As if we're attached. Anyway, he doesn't like Rosie.'

But Kevin's name was all over the pages of Ash's journal. *Smokin' hot, sexy eyes, warm hands on my breasts …* Remembering those passages, Jo blushed. In the mirror her cheeks turned a blotchy red. Kevin wasn't the problem. Kevin and Ash having sex wasn't the problem, either. Of course they were having sex. Of course she knew that. She shouldn't have read the journal. It was private. It was Ash's private space. No one should have access to your thoughts. She would've hated Ash or anyone else having access to her thoughts … but she wouldn't have risked writing them down, filling up a whole journal with them, tempting fate at having them discovered. Yet Ash was in her thoughts, constantly. All those entries in which Ash fantasised about her future, and often with Kevin — Ash the successful lawyer, the judge, working for the United Nations, working for Amnesty International and married to Kevin, the famous photographer. World renowned. Living in New York. Living in Paris. Jo was nowhere in those scenarios.

Ash raised one leg up on the side of the bathtub and ran the razor over her skin. 'I reckon I'm going to quit my job,' she said. Ash's legs were smooth and hairless; there was nothing to shave.

'You'll cut yourself. There's shaving cream in the cupboard.'

'It'll be fine.'

'Whatever, they're your legs,' Jo said. 'What'll you do about a job?'

Ash went through a long list of possibilities, including the cafés in Yarraville and half the shops at Highpoint Shopping Centre.

Their friendship wasn't equally balanced. Were any friendships equally balanced?

Laura and Mani's friendship wasn't equally balanced, either — though it was closer. Promiscuous Laura had no boundaries, no awareness of the dangers or the consequences, while Mani was the protective and maternal one. Did she get sick of looking out for Laura? Of being the one with all the common sense?

The first few days of high school, Jo had felt lonely and vulnerable. The older students, especially the boys, seemed too big to be at school; everywhere the Year 7 students went, they were in the way. *Get out of the way. Move, you little moron.* There was so much noise. The thump of balls against walls, the yelling and screaming from the football oval and the basketball court. Corridors, crowded and smelly, with half-eaten lunches spilling out of bins, sweaty bodies being pushed and shoved against lockers.

It was their second science lesson and they were put into lab groups — Laura and Mani and Ash and Jo.

'I've just moved to Yarraville,' Ash told them.

'My friends all went to a different school,' Jo said. It was mostly true: the only girls she'd been friendly with, twins Sarah and Allie, went to Mount St Joseph's, and the other girls from her Grade 6 class, even though they had noticed her weight loss and made comments about how 'amazing' she looked, didn't invite her to sit with them in class or at lunchtime.

'Do you guys want to have lunch together?' Ash asked them when the bell rang. Easily, effortlessly, they became friends. Laura and Mani were already a pair. 'We've been joined at the hips since birth,' Mani told them.

Ash and Jo became best friends. BFFs. Besties. They hung out at school and on the weekends. They read the same books and watched the same TV shows. Ash was crazy about horses — Jo didn't get it, but she went and cheered for Ash at the pony-club competitions. When they fought they made up quickly and easily. They stayed over at each other's houses, went to parties together, got their first periods in the same month. Jo loved being part of a pair. When Jo was alone, everyone asked after Ash. But Ash's absence had expanded until there seemed to be a big gaping hole in Jo's evenings and weekends.

She thought about the night at the Latin American bar: that was only three weeks ago. They had learned to tango. They had danced and laughed. It was an awesome night, they all agreed. Jo and Ash had skipped all the way back to Ash's place, where they'd slept in Ash's bed and talked until dawn. Jo had felt *oh so lucky*.

They were together tonight, that was the important thing, and when they were together they had a good time.

Once they were satisfied with their make-up, they modelled different outfits for each other, coming full circle: Jo wore the red dress and Ash the blue top over a pencil skirt. They'd purchased the top, lacy and sleeveless, from an expensive boutique in Yarraville. Squeezed into the fitting room, they both tried it on. They both liked it, but Ash was broke. Ash worked part-time at Happy Paws, walking people's dogs around the neighbourhood. The pay was legal — just — but not great, and she spent the money faster than she earned it.

Jo and Ash had one rule about clothing: the person who contributed the most money wore the dress or top first. Jo had worn the blue top to Ash's eighteenth birthday party.

'It's not fair,' Ash said when Jo arrived, 'you weren't supposed to wear it to my party. Now everyone I know has seen it on you.'

'It'll look different on you,' Jo said, not sure whether Ash was serious.

'It'll look better,' Ash said, deliberately loud. Jo longed to tell Ash to stop acting like a cow, but instead she let the comment pass. It was Ash's birthday. Ash's grandmother was so ill the party had been postponed twice. Now she sat in an armchair in the corner of the crowded lounge room, pale and thin. She managed only a gentle smile as people bent down to give her a kiss on each cheek.

Jo didn't make a fuss; everybody knew they were *bestest best* friends. 'They're like sisters,' was the way Ash's mother described their friendship to other people — at least when Jo was around.

Ash twirled a couple of times in front of the mirror and stood facing Jo.

'Looks great,' Jo said. Ash was pretty and confident and that made all the difference. She had striking auburn hair that (when she didn't spend hours straightening it or having it braided) fell in long waves down her back. Boys stopped to stare at her as she walked past. The wolf-whistles were always for Ash. Adult women called Jo pretty, but boys didn't seem to notice her; she was shyer, less confident, more easily missed.

Mandy said Ash's confidence was a result of her parents and all their *positive reinforcement*. In Ash's household everyone was *special*. All achievements, no matter how small, were celebrated — the first pirouette, the first kick (and the fuss about the first goal ...), the first race, the first story.

'You're so creative,' Ash's father would say when Ash or Jane drew him a picture.

'You're so clever,' Ash's mother would say when Ash or Jane showed her a school project.

When Jo first met Ash's family, she believed Ash's parents were acknowledging what was so: Ash was clever and creative and talented. And so was Jane. But Ash's parents were soon heaping these compliments onto Jo as well. She found them confusing — no one had ever told Jo she was especially talented or clever.

'Ash's parents have done a lot of parenting courses,' Mandy said later to her friend Pam when she thought Jo was out of hearing. 'They think it's important you tell your kids how good they are at everything, even if it's not true. They lie to them.'

'Yep. The positive reinforcement mob. We have a plague of them at school.' Pam's youngest was still at primary school. 'They've moved in from the eastern suburbs.'

'What's the point of having a false sense of yourself? They're setting those kids up for a fall.'

Honesty was Mandy's big thing. The truth: *tell it like it is*. People who knew Mandy said she didn't *suffer fools*, that she *called a spade a spade*. Jo's father, David, said Mandy had no diplomacy and didn't give a shit about other people's feelings.

The only television show that Mandy and Jo sometimes watched together — except the football when the Dogs were playing — was *Australian Idol*. During the early auditions at the beginning of each series, there were numerous overly confident young people who couldn't sing. Mandy squirmed during that part of the show. 'See what happens when people lie to their children about their talents? Those parents should've told their children that they can't sing. Save us all the embarrassment,' Mandy said.

'Maybe his mother likes his singing.'

'Only if she's tone deaf too. It's so cruel.'

'Are you for real, Mum? People will kill for five minutes of fame — no matter what. Don't take it so seriously.'

But she did. She often found it so excruciating she had to leave the room.

———

It was after 8.30 by the time Ash and Jo were ready to go out.

'You need to eat if you're going to keep drinking,' Mandy said.

'There'll be food at the party,' Jo said. 'We need to go. We're already late.'

'I've made eggs, bacon, and toast. It's ready.'

'Thanks, Mandy,' Ash sang out, and then whispered to Jo, 'Let's have a quick bite.'

'Okay,' Jo relented.

'And let's have some champagne with dinner,' Ash said, going over to the freezer.

'What are you girls celebrating?' Mandy asked.

'Almost done with school,' Ash said as she popped the champagne and poured three glasses. 'To us,' she cheered.

While Ash had gone to pick up her clothes, Jo had rehearsed several possible conversations she could have with Ash about their friendship, about what was going on: *Why are you pulling away from me? What have I done? What did I do wrong? Why are you behaving like such an arsehole?* But now they were laughing and giggling and making faces at each other when Mandy wasn't looking. It felt like they were back to being best friends. Was she being stupid? Maybe there was nothing going on. Maybe she didn't appear in the journal because she was so much a part of Ash's life there was nothing to question, there was nothing for Ash to write about, to mull over. Maybe she was imagining problems where there weren't any. Listening too much to the annoying voices in her head, spinning doubts and anxieties, like the monsters in children's stories who stir up trouble while everyone is asleep.

'You girls look so beautiful and so grown up,' Mandy said.

They rolled their eyes and winked at each other.

'Oh God, Mum,' Jo said. 'We are grown up.'

Mandy smiled. 'It's lovely to see you together and having fun.'

'Thanks, Mandy,' Ash said. 'Great eggs.'

'You're welcome.'

When they'd finished eating, Jo said, 'We better go.'

'How are you getting there?' Mandy asked.

'I'm going to drive,' Jo said. Jo was the only one in her group with a car, an ancient secondhand Toyota that Pop Jack, David's father, had left to her in his will, along with money for driving lessons and a sad letter apologising for not sticking around to teach her to drive, as if getting sick and dying were his fault. When she was only little, Pop Jack let her sit in the front seat while Mary, her grandmother, sat in the back. He fancied himself a good defensive driver. As they drove, he annotated his every move. *Look in the rearview mirror before slowing down. See how I'm gentle on the clutch. This car will last forever if you are careful.*

Mary kept the car in the garage for the two years between Pop's death and Jo's sixteenth birthday. Neither Mary nor Mandy drove, so occasionally Mary's next-door neighbour Elena drove the car around the block *to keep the battery alive.*

'Okay ... but ...'

'What? It's just down the road in Willy.'

'Okay. Have a good time, girls. Be careful, and keep an eye out for each other.'

'Chill, Mum. Really, you'd think we were ten.'

They skipped and giggled down the path to the car. Jo drove around the corner while Ash sent Laura a text message. By the time they pulled up outside the row of townhouses where Mani lived, Laura, long blonde hair straightened, in a short, strapless, and very tight lemon dress, was waving at them from the front gate. Mani, cropped dark hair, in a vintage navy dress and cowboy boots, came out the front door. Ash jumped out of the car. 'Let me take a photo of you two,' she said. 'You look like you come from two different planets.'

Mani and Laura wrapped their arms around each other's waists as Ash snapped several photographs. Once they were in the car, Mani told them about Laura's boyfriend putting pressure on Laura to hang out with him all the time and how he'd sent her twenty text messages in the last hour.

'He hasn't sent twenty messages,' Laura said. 'God, you exaggerate.'

'Okay, give me over the phone and I'll count them,' Mani said, snatching the phone out of Laura's hand and sending it soaring across the back seat.

'Stop squabbling, you two,' Ash exclaimed. 'I feel like a parent with naughty toddlers in the back.'

'Okay,' Laura said, giggling, 'maybe he did send twenty messages. But he's crazy in love with me, and who wouldn't be? But now he's saying things like, "When we're married …"'

'As if,' Mani said. 'Why exactly haven't you dropped him yet?'

'I'm not wearing one of those tacky bridesmaid dresses,' Ash said.

'Who said I'm gonna have you guys in my wedding,' Laura replied, laughing.

'Marriage — you're a baby,' Jo said. Laura was *the baby*, the youngest of the group, only seventeen.

Laura responded in a soft, sexy voice. 'But he's so, so cute, I can't keep my hands off him.'

'Give me a break,' Mani shouted. 'If I was your mother, I'd lock you up.'

'Hell. You'd be a dictator mother. When you have kids, I'll have to be there to make sure they have a life.'

When the banter stopped, Ash asked if they had finished their English essay and the conversation moved to homework and study, to the relief of having a night off, to parents and their lectures on VCE and how it was *one year* and if they were *just nuns* for the next few weeks, everything would work out.

'Did your mother actually say "nuns"?' Laura asked.

'No.' Ash shook her head. 'It's one of my grandmother's sayings: *When we were young girls we had to behave like nuns.*'

Jo joined in the laughter, but she was thinking about the nuns that she'd seen at St Augustine's when she was a child, in their long black habits, their hair hidden behind their veils, and only their faces showing. What would it be like to be a nun? To know your whole life was mapped, your future was someone else's responsibility to manage and organise?

Rosie's party was at Sirens, on the Esplanade in Williamstown.

Rosie's parents had booked out the waterfront restaurant, and by the time Jo and her friends arrived the party was spilling off the deck and onto the sand. The guests included Rosie's extended family (Greek on her father's side — enough cousins to fill a soccer stadium — and Irish on her mother's) and most of their class from school, as well as Rosie's friends from tennis and choir.

There was a band playing seventies pop and disco covers. Rosie was a big retro music fan: her bedroom walls were covered with images of David Bowie, Queen, and ABBA. On the dance floor, a couple of Rosie's older relatives and family friends, men and women in their forties, were showing off their disco moves. Generous, half-decimated platters of finger food sat on each of the tables. Waiters offered up trays with champagne and wine and mixed drinks. On the beach, a group of their classmates were sitting on deckchairs around a camp fire. Most of the girls had matching blankets wrapped around their shoulders.

'Fuck,' Ash said. 'Trust Rosie to go all out.'

'I didn't think you could build a fire on Willy beach,' Jo said.

'Rosie's father has *connections*, remember?' Laura whispered.

'And plenty of money,' Jo said.

'There are millions of people in the world worse off than you,' Mandy told Jo when she wanted the things that Ash or Rosie had — the iPhones, the Apple laptops, the concert tickets.

Over the last year, there had been several eighteenth birthdays. Some parties were backyards bashes catered by parents and grandparents; some were held in small church halls or at the local bowling club with take-away pizzas and bring-your-own alcohol. Jo had opted for a small family dinner and a night out with friends. Rosie's party was the first to be held in a fancy restaurant and fully catered.

On the deck, the waiters tentatively balanced trays of drinks as they moved between the guests, some already drunk and unsteady. Jo and Ash grabbed a drink each, while Laura and Mani disappeared onto the dance floor. Jo and Ash talked to friends and gravitated to the fire, where they took a couple of puffs of a joint that Ben, a classmate, was passing around as if there were no adults at the party, and no chance that anyone would object. Assuming they were stoned, Ben inched closer to Ash and Jo, blew smoke in their faces, and tried to grab Jo around the waist.

'Get off me,' she said, and pushed him away.

'You're a dickhead,' Ash said, and they made their way back up to the deck.

As the band started to sing 'SOS', Rosie's mother called out, 'ABBA was my first ever concert.'

Rosie, who was dancing in the middle of their circle, waved her arms in the air and screamed in response, 'I wish I'd been there.'

After the disco set, Rosie's grandfather called out, 'Greek music!' and when the music changed, he threw off his jacket, grabbed Rosie's hand, started to dance. Soon a large circle formed and arms linked. The dancers sprang and leaped and kicked. Jo and Ash and Mani joined the circle, laughing as a couple of older Greek women taught them the steps.

After the third song, Jo, head spinning, broke away from the circle and made her way back down to the fire on the beach. She watched Ash and Mani dancing. She wanted to believe in her friendship with Ash. She wanted to believe she mattered to Ash as much as Ash mattered to her, as much as they had mattered to each other when they were younger. During their first months of friendship, she'd been cautious, but not Ash — Ash had organised sleepovers and outings, had insisted they spend their weekends together. Ash had declared the intimacy of the friendship immediately, introducing Jo to her parents as 'my best friend' when they'd only known each other for a week. Ash had inched herself into all aspects of Jo's life in a way Jo hadn't known was possible, had never experienced.

Jo gazed up at the stars and tried to think about something else. Anything. She wished she had someone who loved her, loved her best of all — someone like Ian. She imagined him arriving at the party, catching sight of her across the room; she imagined them walking off together for a moonlight stroll along the beach … but then she remembered the night, several months after he'd left the school, when she took the tram to Fitzroy and made her way to his house. Once she arrived, she didn't know what to do: all the bravado that had driven her there had come crashing down. Ash would've knocked on the door. Jo aspired to that level of confidence. Instead she hid behind a tree, dreading that he might see her, might report her. Her head whirled with scenarios that involved the school, the police, and her mother. The anxiety had lodged itself in her throat until breathing became difficult. It lodged itself in her legs, so that standing and moving seemed impossible feats. It was a fog over her eyes, a clatter of voices in her head. Her hands trembled. Shivering and cold, and then hot and flushed. It was a cast spell; she knew it would dissipate, but there was no predicting how long it might take.

At seven that night when her mother called her for dinner, she was back in her room, but she had no memory of the trip home. Later, when she opened the photo app on her phone, she found the photographs. Four of the Victorian terrace: one of three pushbikes on the front verandah and the stained and ripped couch on the balcony upstairs; a close-up of the green door; another of the front window with the blinds halfway down; and a more distant shot of three birds in a row on the telephone wires, the house in the background. Sometimes when she flicked through those photos, she became nostalgic for that other life, the life with Ian, as if she'd lived it.

She only stirred when Rosie's father called the guests back onto the deck. They gathered around the two-tier cake to sing happy birthday to Rosie and listen to her parents make speeches about pride and beauty and a bright future and to Rosie's slurred response; everyone, even Rosie's parents, laughed good-naturedly.

After the toast, Jo and Ash headed back across the deck to the fire with the cake and their drinks. They found a couple of chairs, grabbed a blanket each, and settled in.

'Do you ever wonder,' Jo said before she'd even thought about what she was going to say, 'if we'll all be friends once school is over?'

'I guess some of us'll lose touch,' Ash said, champagne in one hand and a forkful of cake in the other. 'We'll be at different universities and we'll meet new people.'

'That's sad, don't you think?' Jo's cake was on a plate on her lap. She'd taken one bite, but now it was stuck in her throat and she couldn't swallow. She took another swig of her champagne. It helped a little; she drank the rest. In the glow from the fire and the moonlight, Ash's long hair, with its red hue, shone against her pale skin.

'Does it have to be sad?' Ash said, letting out a long sigh. 'It could be exciting meeting new people. Don't you think?'

There was a cool breeze, and small frothy waves rolled onto the beach. The white caps formed bubbles that burst before they hit the sand. Along the debris line, cracked shells caught the light and twinkled like stars. A group of girls took off their shoes, hitched up their dresses, and screamed as they raced in and out of the water. The fire was dying down; a young waiter came over to stoke it and add logs from a crate he'd carried across the sand.

'Will we lose touch, you and I?' Jo asked.

'Not if we don't want to,' Ash said.

She wished Ash would laugh and say she was teasing and that of course they'd be friends forever. In the silence that followed, Jo watched Ash eat her cake. Next to her, a couple were kissing — under the blanket, the boy was reaching for the girl's breasts, the girl pushing his hand away, until finally she tossed the blanket aside. 'You're an arsehole.'

The boy whimpered after her, 'Come on, babe.'

'I'm getting another drink. Want one?' Jo said as she scanned the area for one of the waiters who'd been circling all night with trays. The band was on a break, and on the dance floor the few remaining children chased coloured balloons and tied one another up in loose streamers. At the tables, the women wrapped shawls around their shoulders and leaned into their partners.

'No. I thought we might go soon. It's almost midnight, and if you're going to drive …'

'I'm fine,' Jo said.

'Okay, but can we go soon?'

'What's the rush?'

'I promised to walk a couple of stressed-out hounds in the morning, and there's the English essay,' Ash said.

'So what? You're a night owl. You'll be fine in the morning.'

'And I told Kevin I'd give him a ring, and if he was up he might come over.'

'So you have a date with Kevin tonight, that's really the reason.'

'It's not a date, it's a maybe kind of thing.'

'I thought you were going to stay at my place tonight.' Jo knew she sounded pathetic.

'We didn't organise anything, and I'm working tomorrow and we've been hanging out this afternoon and all night.' Ash was forcing a smile. 'And it's been great, but ... well, I'd like to see Kevin. You get it, don't you?'

'Yeah, sure. Great. Let's go.' Jo tried to keep the anger out of her voice.

'Jo, are you okay?' Ash asked.

'I'm fine. Let's go,' she said.

'I'll go and find Laura and Mani. Meet you on the deck,' Ash said.

While Ash went to look for their friends, Jo shook the sand out of her sandals and climbed up the steps to the deck. She leant against the banister. She would not cry, not here, not now. So what if she and Ash stopped being friends? So what if Ash preferred Kevin? What did it matter anyway? She had other friends, Laura and Mani — not best friends, but friends, and she was good at being alone. She could spend hours reading or watching films or lying in bed daydreaming; she didn't need Ash. *I don't need you.* Trouble was, she remembered not having friends, and the way other kids had excluded her. All those lunchtimes sitting alone in the schoolyard, taking tiny, tiny bites of her peanut-butter sandwiches, of her apple — 'eating at a snail's pace', Grandpa Tom called it when she ate like that at home. Purposely slow, making her lunch last the whole hour, so that when busybody Mr Marsh asked, 'Why don't you play with the other girls?' she could shake her head: 'I'm still eating my lunch.' Hours watching other girls. Lucy Girello, with her high pigtail plaits, her skinny legs pumping as she won all the races. Lucy, who had once said to her, 'You're too fat to skip, you might burst a vein. My fat neighbour burst a vein. He blew up and up, his cheeks turned red and he *died.*' Lucy had collapsed to the ground, shaking her legs in the air like a dying beetle. Embarrassed, Jo's cheeks had burnt under the oppressive summer sun, the other girls sniggering, calling out, 'Lucy, you're awful,' and 'Look, she's gone bright red.' No one standing by her side. Alone. She didn't want to go back to being alone, to being the one not sitting around in gossipy groups, not sharing secrets, not laughing. The last one picked for netball. For rounders. For volleyball. She remembered. How pathetic to be so grateful to the twins for letting her sit with them, for letting her walk home with them. Grateful and ashamed.

Most of the remaining guests were sitting at tables or had wandered out to the edges of the deck. Alone, she felt exposed. She wanted to leave. What if she left without them? They could make their own way home. Just as she was considering going, a waiter dipped in her direction and offered her more champagne. He was her age, a tall boy, tired-looking now, his white shirt stained around the cuffs. She grabbed a glass from the tray, drank it in a couple of gulps, and put it down on a nearby table.

'Gee, you must've needed that,' he said. Offering up the tray for another drink, she shook her head.

Finally the others appeared. 'Great party!' Mani said. 'I could stay all night.'

'We can stay longer,' Jo said. 'Ash's in a rush. But if she wanted to stay, we'd be staying.'

'What?' Ash said. 'What are you talking about, Jo?'

'What's up?' Laura asked. She had her shoes in her hands and was covered in sand.

'Nothing. You look like you've been rolling in it,' Jo said, helping Laura brush the sand off her hair.

'Sure have.' Laura grinned. 'The drummer was on a break.'

'Fuck.' Mani hit her on the arm. 'That's where you got to. He's Rosie's brother. What about Rob and marriage and *he's so so cute*?'

'What he doesn't know …' Laura said with a smile. Boys swarmed around Laura. It wasn't just that she was pretty; lots of girls were pretty. Jo guessed it was her easy and joyful nature. Maybe boys were no different to girls, and everyone was drawn to happy people like Laura and Ash.

'Jo, don't you want to go?' Ash said. 'I'd call a taxi, but I'm broke.'

'All set to go, at your command,' Jo responded.

'What is with you?' Ash asked as they moved around other guests.

'Nothing,' Jo said. 'Let's find Rosie.'

Rosie was at the bar talking to an older couple. They waited until she noticed them, and then said their goodbyes. A waiter opened the door for them. Jo didn't notice the step and tripped. The boy caught her arm and helped steady her.

'Are you okay to drive? We could wait awhile. You could have a coffee,' Mani said.

'I'm fine. Really. See, I can find my nose,' Jo said as they stepped out onto the footpath, touching the tip of her nose with her finger. But in truth, she felt drunk: not wasted, just a little tipsy. And angry. *Only if we want to stay friends. Do you want to, Ash?*

Once they were in the car and Jo pulled the seatbelt across her shoulder, she thought, *I shouldn't be driving.*

'Are you okay, Jo?' Laura asked when she didn't turn the key in the ignition.

'I'm fine.' *Ten minutes*, she thought. *And we'll all be in bed.* Jo turned the key in the ignition. As she drove out of the parking space, she asked, 'Mani, do you think you and Laura will be friends after you leave school?'

'Of course,' Mani said from the back seat, grabbing Laura and giving her a hug. 'Tied at the hip. Friends forever. Even if she's a slut.'

'Better a slut than a virgin,' Laura sang out. 'Friends for life. Every slut has to have a Mani.'

'I didn't say we wouldn't be friends,' Ash whispered. 'It's just we don't know, do we, where we'll be or what we'll be doing.'

'But you hope we won't be. You hope you can drop me, hang out with Kevin, and meet new, more interesting people.'

'What's with you two tonight?' Mani asked.

'Nothing,' Jo said. 'Not a fucking thing. Not us. Haven't you heard? We're like sisters.'

Beyonce's 'Single Ladies' came on and Jo turned the volume up. Mani and Laura started singing.

'This is our song, Jo. Ash and Laura are taken,' Mani called out.

Jo snatched a look at them in the rearview mirror and tears slipped down her face — slow steady drops, falling silently. As they turned the corner, the West Gate Bridge came into view. *Almost home, almost there.*

103

She wished the car was empty. She wished she had magic powers that could make them all vanish.

'Please slow down,' Ash said.

Jo's heart throbbed; her hands shook. She was hot and agitated. She was sweating. As she rolled down the windows, the wind rushed in cool and loud, and Mani raised her voice, singing her own lyrics along with Beyoncé: 'Cause if Rob likes it then he'll have to put a ring on it. If Rob likes it he should put cuffs on it!'

Mani and Laura were singing and waving and swinging their arms in the air. The whole car was shaking. Jo was drunk, she knew it now. She couldn't steady herself, she was shivering, her hands were shaking. She should stop the car, but the car was accelerating and she was singing too, and swaying from side to side. She had to keep pace with the beat; she had to go faster, faster, faster.

'Jo, slow down!' Ash yelled over the music and reached for the volume.

'Fuck off,' Jo yelled back, smacking Ash's hand away. 'Leave it on.'

Ash withdrew. Mani and Laura stopped singing.

'What the fuck is going on?'

Don't say anything. Get home. Just drop them off and go home.

You don't fucking give a shit about me. You wrote about all those other people and nothing about me. You can't wait until you don't have to see me again. You're a user. You've used me and now you don't want to …

'Slow down. Jo, please.' Ash was pleading now. 'What's with you? Slow down and talk to me.'

This time Ash managed to switch the radio off. The silence in the car hit Jo like a slap. Jo switched it back on, but instead of music, it was a couple of radio jocks talking. Their voices were irritating, their laughter garish. Jo gripped the steering wheel tighter to stop the trembling. Her body was all pulse and beat, her mouth parched and bitter. The dark night was a stream of speeding lights: lights coming towards her, lights chasing her, lights on the bridge, white and yellow lights shooting back and forwards, lights turning the river into sheets of coloured glass.

They were under the bridge now, and its long concrete tail towered over them.

Focus on the road. Focus on the road.

When the steering wheel slid out of her hand, she tried to grip it again, but it was too late to stop the car slipping across the roadway. 'Don't put your foot on the brake' — Jo remembered someone saying that, but not who had said it. The car spun as if they were on a ride at the show, at Luna Park, lights and screams and the car soaring and not stopping. Jo begging it to stop. *Stop, please stop.* And lifting her foot and smashing it down hard on the brake, and the car skidding, and skating and swerving, and finally her hands finding the steering wheel, the resistance of it, and screeching and groaning and more screaming. And the car airborne, and the barricade, a giant eagle, wings open, flying towards them. Arms up, eyes closed, the bellowing crash of metal against metal, thunderous and explosive.

Chapter 7

'Wake up, wake up. Wake up … Can you open your eyes?'

A hissing and ringing, constant and low-pitched, muffled every-thing else.

'Open your eyes?' The woman's voice was cracked and fragmented; a series of echoes. There was banging, and sirens and alarms and shouting. Jo wanted to cup her ears, but her arms wouldn't move.

'You've been in an accident … an accident. You blacked out. Open your eyes. Open your eyes … We need to get you out of here.'

Clamped tight, her eyes refused to open.

'Let go of the steering wheel.' The woman's hands were cold as she gripped Jo's hands one at a time and pulled them off the steering wheel and onto her lap.

'Can you tell me your name?' There was a pause. 'I'm going to open the door now and take your seatbelt off.' Her voice was harsh and impatient. It reminded Jo of Mr Marsh's voice, of being told off for homework not done properly, of being the source of frustration, of irritation, of having done something wrong and sitting still and quiet and waiting to be punished. The woman yanked at the door until it gave way with a creak and a groan. There was a gush of cold air and the woman's arm reached across Jo's chest to unbuckle the seatbelt. With its release, her body slumped. There was a sharp ache across her belly. She winced and doubled over with the pain.

'Your name's Jo, is that right? My name is Teresa. I'm a paramedic.

I'm here to help you. Jo, you have to open your eyes.' She put the emphasis on 'have to'.

Paramedic. Mrs Chang said, 'You have a level head, you'd make a good paramedic.' But Jo didn't have a level head. She didn't want to drive around the city to collect the dead and dying. The dead and dying ... she remembered Ash and Mani and Laura.

'I don't want to see,' she muttered. The buzzing in her ears was a roar now, as if she were on the tarmac at the airport, as if she'd fallen into an enormous jet engine. And beyond the buzzing, far off in the distance, there were many voices. People shouting. Someone sobbing.

'Where are my friends?'

'We need to get you out of the car.' Teresa again. 'Are you hurt? Can you move your arms?' Teresa's fingers on her pulse, her hands on Jo's forehead.

'Get up — come on, Jo.' Hooking her arm around Jo's shoulder, Teresa eased her out of the car. The pain across her abdomen intensified. Her hands throbbed; she struggled to open and close them.

'Open your eyes.'

Jo finally opened her eyes. Laura and Mani were sitting on the ground. A male paramedic was putting a bandage on Laura's hand. Huddled together wrapped under the same blue blanket, they were both crying. Mani's head was resting on Laura's shoulder. *Friends forever.* Jo turned back to look at the car. The front seat was empty.

'Where is Ash?' Jo asked. Teresa wore a yellow safety jacket over her blue uniform. Her lips were pursed tight and she avoided Jo's eyes. She pointed to Laura and Mani. When Jo looked over at them, they turned away.

'No.' Jo shook her head. 'Ash was in the front seat.'

'Come on, keep walking.'

Walking hurt. She resisted. 'Where are we going?' She was blinded by bright lights in the darkness, and disorientated by voices, so many voices.

'To the hospital.'

'Is Ash there?'

'Come on.'

Jo tried to pull away from Teresa and stumbled. A man came and took her other arm, and together he and Teresa steered her towards the ambulance. Around them there was so much movement. Flashing lights. Sirens. Horns. Cars and trucks zooming past.

'What happened? I don't know what happened.'

Teresa shook her head. 'You had an accident.'

'Where is Ash?' Jo asked again.

'We're going to take you to the hospital. The police will call your parents. They'll have to do a blood alcohol test. Do you understand?'

'No,' Jo repeated. 'Please no.'

'It's the law,' the paramedic said.

Jo pried herself free again. She needed to see Ash. Teresa let out a long sigh. She grabbed Jo's arm, leading her into the back of the ambulance and onto the stretcher.

Once she was lying down, Jo shut her eyes again. As they began moving, she felt nauseous. When she was young she had suffered from motion sickness, especially if she was in the back seat. If Pop Jack was driving, he'd stop so she could walk around. Usually the nausea subsided quickly; she rarely vomited. Lying on the stretcher in the ambulance, she concentrated on not vomiting, on not thinking, on not thinking about Ash, but it didn't work. Bitter and putrid bile spewed out of her mouth and into the bucket that Teresa held under her chin. By the time they arrived at the hospital, she was shaking and cold.

'When can I see Ash?'

No one answered. She knew the worst was to come. She refused to let herself speculate, but already she knew she would be better off dead.

Chapter 8

Mandy had watched Jo and Ash walk to the car. They were grown women, and it wasn't any longer her job to worry about them, but she hadn't moved until the car disappeared around the corner and out of sight. She poured herself the remaining champagne and watched an old movie — *You've Got Mail* — and went to bed. She fell asleep and into a dream in which she was alone on the beach at sunset.

The white foam of the breaking waves was luminous, the horizon a flaming orange and pink. Strolling along the water's edge, carrying her shoes in her hands, the lukewarm water lapping up against her legs, Mandy gazed at the long stretch of beach ahead. There was a light breeze, but she was warm and content.

Without warning, the wind changed direction and the temperature dropped. She heard footsteps: the shuffle of thongs across the sand. But behind her the beach was deserted. Was someone lurking in the shadows? As she quickened her pace, an alarm, shrilling and insistent, rang once and then again and again, bellowing across the dunes. Was it an emergency warning? Should she be running? Where was everyone? She ran towards the road, her feet sinking into the soft sand. The moon slipped behind clouds, into the darkness. The alarm grew louder. She was exhausted, breathless, her heart beating faster, panic rising … She was awake. Hot, disorientated. She kicked the doona off. The alarm was still ringing. It was the doorbell. 3.04 am. Who rang the doorbell in the middle of the night?

'I thought it was you,' she said later to Jo. 'I thought you'd locked yourself out, left your keys behind, or come back too drunk to open the door. I was angry. I wanted to stay in bed. I didn't want to get up.'

The doorbell rang again. And again. There was a pause — only a few seconds, but long enough for Mandy to drop her head back on the pillow.

It rang again and she stumbled out of bed and down the hallway to the door, calling out, 'Is that you, Jo?'

'Mrs Neilson, it's the police.'

Mandy closed her eyes. *This is a dream, just a dream. You can wake up now. It's just a dream; turn around and go back to bed.*

Years earlier, during a spate of particularly disturbing nightmares, Mandy had read an article by a dream therapist who believed the dreamer could alter the shape and direction of their dreams — he suggested it was possible for a person to will themselves out of bad dreams and nightmares. Adopting the therapist's techniques helped her to sleep and to control the dreams she'd begun having after she and David separated. In those dreams, she constantly lost Jo. She lost Jo while they were doing their shopping in the crowded Little Saigon shopping centre, surrounded by the cackle of voices, of vendors calling out their specials, of men and women talking in foreign languages, of long rows of fruit and vegetables, of counters piled high with meat and fish, of wet and slippery floors. She lost Jo in the middle of a crammed street as they waited for the Moomba parade, amid families and picnic baskets and toddlers chasing balloons. She lost Jo in the stands at the football; she lost Jo in a crowded school ground; in the playground at the park. She lost Jo in places she and Jo had never been, were unlikely to ever go — midtown New York, with its flashing neon lights; in a rush of tourists on the Great Wall of China; in giant mazes; at overcrowded heavy-rock concerts. But the most frightening of all the dreams began with an explosion at the Mobil Oil terminal, and huge, monstrous flames flying across the road and threatening the house. In that dream, the police came to the door, knocking and yelling at them to evacuate, *evacuate now*, but Jo was missing and Mandy ran in circles around the house trying to find her …
In those dreams, the terror of losing Jo was so real that Mandy woke up

shaking and shivering, unable to go back to sleep. On those nights, she pulled a chair up close to Jo's bed and watched her daughter sleep. When Mandy read the article about dream therapy in a magazine in the doctor's surgery, she tore out the pages — she hadn't done that before. She hated it when people tore things out of other people's magazines. She took the article home and read and re-read it. Over a couple of months, she taught herself the art of altering her dreams. The moment in the dream when Jo's hand slipped out of hers, she wished the crowd away, or she called Jo's name and Jo materialised.

While the police stood on the other side of the door, Mandy willed the dream to change. *Go back to bed and everything will be fine. Stop the bell. Make them go away. Go back to bed, it's a dream.*

But the doorbell rang again and she knew she was awake.

'Mrs Neilson, please open the door.'

Mandy resisted. She didn't want to open the door, she didn't want to hear what they had to say. She didn't know if Jo was in bed. The bedroom door was closed. She couldn't remember if it was closed when Jo and Ash left. She hadn't heard Jo come in, but it was late. Surely she was in bed.

'Mrs Neilson? Please open the door.' They rang the bell again and knocked on the wooden frame.

'I'm coming,' she said, slowly unlocking and opening the door. On the step there were two police officers, a woman and a man. Behind them, the ghoulish oil tanks glowed under the security lights.

'Are you Mrs Neilson?' the woman asked.

'Yes. Is it Jo?' she said, holding her breath.

'Jo's fine, Mrs Neilson. Jo's been in an accident. She's in hospital, but she's not hurt.'

Mandy's hands were shaking. She began to breathe again.

'I'm Constable Lumina and this is Constable Peters.'

'What about Jo's friends, Ashleigh and Mani and Laura? Jo left with her friend Ashleigh and she was going to drive them home later.'

Constable Lumina was a girl, not much older than Jo. The uniform — the heavy boots, the thick black belt, and the gun — were meant to bestow her with authority, but standing at the door, she looked like a teenager in fancy dress. Too young to be on Mandy's doorstep at 3.00 am. Hesitating, avoiding Mandy's eyes, she let Mandy's question hang in the air between them. Mandy heard the distant rumble of the traffic on the bridge. She breathed in the smell of the petroleum and the sea and Constable Lumina's floral perfume that reminded her of her mother, of being a little girl, of the years of watching her mother deteriorate, of the constant presence of fear.

'Can we come in?' Constable Peters asked. He was older than Constable Lumina, but not by much — in his mid-twenties, perhaps. A solid man. His blue shirt too tight, showing the shape of his muscular arms and chest. Mandy moved aside and the police officers stepped into the hallway.

'Can we sit down?' Constable Lumina said. But none of them moved.

'What about the other girls? What about Ashleigh?'

'Mani and Laura are fine, but I'm afraid Ashleigh died on impact.'

'No.' Mandy shook her head. She felt as if she were standing on a thin, unstable ledge and any moment she might fall into a void. 'But they were here … just hours … they were all dressed up, going to a party, they — couldn't Ashleigh … couldn't they help her?'

'It was too late,' Constable Lumina said, reaching out for Mandy's arm, but Mandy slid back. Her body felt light and thin in the cold. Her nightie was flimsy, an old cotton garment she should've thrown out years ago; it had paint stains and a couple of small holes and it was no shield against the night air. Jo had given Mandy the nightie on her third Mother's Day, the year she and David separated. The year she and Jo moved in with her father. Jo and her grandfather had gone on their first shopping trip together, down to Forges in Footscray. Forges was the only place Tom ever shopped, and then only rarely — that's where he went when he wanted socks and underwear, a new pair of jeans (once every five years), a shirt or a t-shirt. The parcel wrapping was ripped by the time Jo gave it to her, but it was special. The nightie was too big. The nightie was too thin. Mandy wrapped her arms across her body and pulled the nightie tight until it was a twisted knot. She wanted to tell them to go away, to go away and to let her go back to bed. To let this be a dream, a nightmare.

'What happened?' she asked.

'Your daughter was driving. She'd been drinking. We're not sure what caused the accident, but the car spun out of control, and they hit an embankment.'

Mandy wanted to scream. Anger and rage caught in her throat: *that girl, that girl*. She pushed against the wall behind her to stop herself from falling. She couldn't look at the police officers. She stared at her bare feet, her small and pale and cold feet. Both officers were wearing heavy walking boots, like the ones her father used to wear when he worked in the foundry.

'You need to go to the hospital.'

She didn't want to see Jo. She thought she might never want to see Jo again.

'I can't … I don't have a car.'

'We can drive you to the hospital.'

It was cramped with the three of them standing in the narrow hallway, and Mandy longed for them to go. 'I'm not dressed.'

'We can wait.'

But she didn't move.

'I know it's difficult, Mrs Neilson, but Jo needs you.'

She longed to tell them to go away, to fuck off, to leave her alone. What if she didn't want to see Jo? How could she go and see Jo when Ashleigh was dead? 'Ashleigh, poor Ashleigh. And her parents — and Jane. Jane is so young.'

'Yes,' Constable Lumina said, 'it's hard for everyone. Your daughter too. Please, Mrs Nielson, get dressed, and we'll take you to the hospital.'

As she was dressing, Mandy thought about what she hadn't said to Jo and Ashleigh. *You've been drinking, don't drive, take a taxi*. She should've stopped Jo driving. She should've tried. She was a coward, avoiding conflict, instead of being a proper mother; a proper mother would've stopped them.

When she emerged dressed, Constable Lumina led her out of the house, ready to take her by the arm. Mandy shifted away again. She avoided looking up at the street, at the neighbourhood, at the tanks and the bridge.

In the back seat of the police car, as they drove down Hyde Street, Mandy thought about Ashleigh's parents, and Jane, and the police knocking on their door, and the fact that they were grieving for their daughter, their sister, who was gone … forever.

The officers drove to the hospital. Mandy wanted to tell them how beautiful Ashleigh had looked in her blue top, how she was all smiles and laughter. About Jo and Ashleigh with their arms around each other, posing for photographs, and of her jealousy — jealous of their youth, of their lives. And now Ashleigh was dead, and it was all Jo's fault. And if it was Jo's fault, then it was Mandy's fault too. She'd let it happen.

'She was so alive, a few hours ago,' she said, in an attempt to convince the two police officers, and herself, that it was a mistake. It was impossible, she wanted to yell at them, shake them. This wasn't how death happened. She'd watched both her parents die — months of decline, of hospitals, of waiting, of suffering and pain, until they stopped praying for life, for recovery, until all hope abandoned them, until they were praying for death.

The police officers didn't respond.

Bad mother. She was a bad mother. Good mothers knew what to do. They knew how to behave. A good mother wouldn't have let her drunk daughter take the car. A good mother would've stopped them, and Ashleigh, beautiful Ashleigh, would be alive. Mandy's anger flared. In the past, whenever Jo had done something wrong, she'd defended, excused, compensated. But there was no excuse for driving drunk. No defence. No compensating for Ashleigh's death. Mandy didn't want to see Jo. That moment in the back seat of the police car, she experienced a sensation of falling, of falling out of love with her daughter. Like falling in love with Jo, it would, in her memory, seem instantaneous. When Jo was born, Mandy bonded with her immediately. Jo was an easy baby. The nurses said she was lucky. It was only years later, when other women friends had their babies, and she witnessed first-baby blues and anxieties, postnatal depression, and colicky infants that refused to sleep, that she realised how lucky she'd been. Her love for Jo was unconditional — it rose out of her in waves, and even during the recent difficult teenage years, even as Jo rejected her, even as she no longer knew what her daughter thought about, dreamed about, even as she asked questions and Jo was rude and distant, she hadn't doubted her love. It was the one love that would endure anything, survive anything. She had promised Jo that. When David left, Mandy said, 'Your father and I can't live together, we don't love each other anymore, but we'll always love you.' She promised the three- and four- and five-year-old Jo over and over again.

Her love for Jo had been her driving force. On days when the world seemed impossible to negotiate, it kept her going. In its absence, she was left feeling hollow, weighed down by weariness. Leaning against the window in the back of the police car, she had no idea how they'd live through this, past it. Did people manage to live? To move on? Did Jo deserve to? Did either of them?

'Will she go to prison?' Mandy asked the police officers.

Constable Lumina turned to face Mandy. 'She'll be charged, and when she's released from the hospital she'll have to make a statement. And go to court. It'll be up to the courts.'

'But it's likely?'

'Yes, it's likely.'

Chapter 9

Antonello woke in a sweat, his hands gripping the bed post. In his dream the bridge, cut loose from the piers, was a swinging pendulum. He was balancing on a tightrope between the two halves. But the span on the west side cracked, the concrete crumbled, he was falling … He reached out for the tissues on the bedside table and wiped his face. Took a deep breath to calm himself and checked the clock. It was 4.00 am.

'Occupational hazard,' Bob said the first time Antonello told him about his falling dreams, not long after they'd started to work on the bridge. 'Whenever you do height work, the falling comes back. Sandy says that some nights the whole bed shakes, and that isn't because I'm such a stud.' He winked at Antonello.

Many times standing on the half-finished bridge, Antonello had imagined diving off: the flight, the lift, the floating, the soaring, and the final descent into the water. Like all the men, he'd felt the bridge sway, especially on windy days, when the end span shook. The movement, a tremor, travelled along the bridge and through his body in tiny rolling waves; he'd imagine his own falling.

After the collapse, the occasional falling dream turned into a reoccurring nightmare, and each time it catapulted him into the past and left him adrift, as if the present were an alien world he'd landed in by mistake.

To anchor himself, he shifted his body closer to Paolina, until he felt her breath on his face. She'd thrown the covers off her shoulders; both arms were raised above her head. He resisted the urge to reach out, to run his hand over the soft folds of her skin.

'It's not a remission,' the doctor warned them. 'We can't call it that, not yet, but for now the tumour has stopped growing.'

Life without Paolina was unimaginable. This was a cliché and a lie, he knew that. It was what people said when their loved ones were dying. Then, of course, most people went on living. But there were all kinds of living, and some were closer to death than life.

Antonello was certain that without Paolina, he'd shrivel and shrink, until he was like those pickled men in a jar they sold at the craft markets Paolina loved going to on Sunday mornings. The men were made from recycled pantyhose, the surprisingly young craftswoman had told him, standing behind rows and rows of men in jars. She wore a green lace dress and a small box hat with feathers.

'Everything's recycled,' Antonello remembered saying to Paolina. 'Why don't they say *old*?'

Paolina hung her pantyhose in the bathroom to dry. They were so delicate that if his hand accidentally brushed across them, the threads snagged easily on his fingernails, on the rough patches of his skin.

The young craftswoman, with her button nose and sweet smile, reminded him of his mother's Madonna. Emilia had kept the statuette, strung with rosary beads, on her bedroom dresser. Every night, she'd knelt in front of it before bed. His sister, Carmela, the only remaining church-goer in his family, had inherited the statuette. His mother would've described the young woman as angelic. It was disconcerting to think of her sitting at a work table, cutting up old stockings, shaping and stuffing them until they turned into old men, and then shoving them into a jar, the lid screwed on nice and tight.

Paolina's cancer felt like a betrayal. Of course, he knew he was being silly and selfish and ridiculous. Childish, even. But Paolina was going to leave him, and without her his days would be long and empty; life would have no meaning.

He wasn't good at friendship. When Paolina's friends visited, he was polite — he could even be friendly — but he didn't have any friends of his own. His brother Joe dropped in some afternoons, and they paced the garden or strolled down to the creek so that Joe's German shepherd, now old and crippled with arthritis, could take a slow walk. Once a year, they made wine. Sometimes Antonello went rummaging in wrecker's yards or trash-and-treasure markets, excursions instigated by his brother Vince, to buy materials for his many projects — a new shed for one of his children or a cubby house for a grandchild or something for his latest attempt at renovating a section of the house.

Recently, Antonello had overheard his daughter, Nicki, say to Paolina, 'Don't you dare die first and leave us with Dad.' Alex and Nicki — Alexandro and Domenica, but their Italian names printed on their birth certificates were rarely used, mostly forgotten — considered him difficult. Soon he'd be a burden.

'Mamma is the most loving woman I know. I'm sure you love us, but you're not good at showing it. You're moody and hard to be around. What I learnt from you, Dad, is that love isn't enough,' Alex had said once, on the rare occasion when father and son talked, though the conversation had arisen after Antonello criticised Alex for spoiling the girls.

Alex and Nicki rarely talked to Antonello directly. They talked to their mother and she refashioned their requests, their announcements, for him. He overheard their comments and criticisms, not because they said things when they knew he'd overhear them, not because he purposely eavesdropped on them — he would've preferred not to hear — but because they didn't notice him. He was a spectre lurking in the background, invisible and hardly relevant.

Nicki said Paolina should've divorced him. Had she ever considered it? Paolina loved him, he was certain of that, even though their marriage was more difficult than she'd anticipated — but no one ever imagines a difficult marriage.

Over the last decade, a number of Paolina's friends had been widowed or divorced, and they had started new and different lives without their husbands. Did Paolina hope for a life in which she could plan her own destiny, perhaps discover another self? He wanted to die first.

When the depression hit, as it did on a regular basis, it left him depleted. It manifested first as rage — with it, a desire to scream, to tear things apart, to punch walls, to throw furniture. A dark mantle that swamped everything. But he was a volcano that never erupted. He didn't vent his anger as his father had done. That was his only source of pride, as if by not expressing it he was protecting his family from it. The pity was it took so much energy to dam it up, to contain it, that he had nothing left for his children, and so he withdrew, was often absent, silent and alone, sometimes disappearing for hours, for whole days, walking miles across the city until his heart returned to its regular beat, until he stopped shaking, until he could unclench his fists. But even if he was in the house during those episodes, he wasn't present. 'Dad's gone zombie again,' Nicki would complain to Paolina.

Several times he'd considered leaving Paolina and the children, for their own good, but he couldn't bring himself to do it. Leaving was impossible. Where would he have gone? What would that have done to his family? Anyway, without Paolina he didn't exist at all. He'd contemplated suicide, but the thought of Paolina's grief and the legacy he'd leave behind — a coward husband and father — stopped him.

Knowing his children resented him was painful, but he'd learnt to live with it. Compared to all the other aches and pains, it hardly registered. Paolina smoothed things. Made excuses for him. She told their children over and over that he loved them. She tried to convince him to do things differently, but she didn't betray him.

'She defends you all the time, even when you're being an arsehole.' Nicki didn't understand her mother's loyalty.

He stretched his body long in the bed and watched Paolina. He loved her more than he'd ever loved anyone else.

'The phone, Nello,' Paolina said, shaking him awake. 'It's the phone.'

Antonello looked at the clock. It was 6.00 am. He hauled himself out of bed and raced to the kitchen, where the phone hung on a wall bracket above the bench. The ringing was insistent and demanding. Then it stopped and the house fell silent, but before he could turn back, the ringing began again.

Later, he'd speculate about his reluctance to answer. Was it a premonition? Not that he believed in premonitions; they were Paolina's domain. But there was a secret hope he harboured that not answering the phone might prevent whatever bad thing had happened from happening. As if bad things could be thwarted by his refusal to pay them attention. As if he didn't know better. As if he didn't know that tragedy could and would strike whether you were around to pick up the phone or not, that it would catch up with you and stop you in your tracks no matter how hard or how fast you ran, no matter how happy you were or how sad. No matter whether you'd had your share of tragedy or not.

'Hello.'

'Dad.'

'Alex, what's wrong?' Antonello heard the quake in his son's voice, the intake of breath.

'Everything is wrong, Dad, everything.' Alex paused and Antonello knew the panic was real. It wouldn't pass.

'There's been an accident. It's Ashleigh.' Alex's voice was cracking, broken.

'How bad? Is she okay?'

'No. She's dead, Dad. My Ashleigh, my baby girl, she's gone.' Alex broke into thick, heavy sobs.

Antonello heard himself gasp, but after that he wasn't sure what else they said, what he said, what Alex said, before they hung up. His body was limp. His arms dropped to his side. His legs buckled. Shaky, he leaned against the wall.

'Nello?' Paolina reached for his arm. He gazed at her. She was so old and frail that he thought for a second it wasn't Paolina at all but the ghost of his mother-in-law, Giuseppina, who had been reduced to half her size, wrinkled skin loosely draped over brittle bones, when she died in her nineties.

'Sit down.' He couldn't tell Paolina. He couldn't say the words out loud.

'No, tell me,' Paolina demanded.

'It's Ashleigh,' he said. 'A car accident.'

'Which hospital?'

'No, *è morta*.' Antonello shook his head, wrapped his arms around her, and pulled her close.

'No, no, please no,' Paolina wailed. She was trembling, a tiny tree in the wind. He stood, solid, and she leaned into him. They held each other. Since Paolina's diagnosis, they'd become used to finding themselves without words. Closing his eyes, Antonello stroked her short grey hair, and remembered her hair long and thick, and the way she loved weaving it into a plait, the tail reaching the base of her spine. And the way he'd taken pleasure in unravelling it, running his fingers through it until the strands separated. And how when Ashleigh was little, she measured the length of her hair against her grandmother's. The way they loved to brush each other's hair. Ashleigh. The tears flowed — silent tears he couldn't wipe away, because that would mean releasing his grip on Paolina.

'Ashleigh. Ashleigh,' he repeated her name to himself. *Little Ashleigh, princess, wild thing, pestie pest*: all his pet names for his first-born granddaughter, his son's daughter. Calling her up in his mind, as if he might be able to call her back to life. Ashleigh. The last time he saw her was only a few days ago — arriving with a copy of *Beverly Hills Chihuahua* and teasing Paolina that with her short hair, she looked like Jamie Lee Curtis. He remembered the way Ashleigh and Jane slid into bed on either side of their grandmother so they could watch the movie together on a laptop.

Ashleigh. Ashleigh. Loved so much.

Paolina was sobbing.

'We have to get dressed and go over to Alex's,' he said.

Paolina nodded, but didn't move.

'They need us. We need to help them through this.'

'I don't know if I can get through this, if there is a way through this,' Paolina whispered. '*Mia bellissima nipotina.*'

Antonello hooked his arm around her waist and guided her slowly to the bedroom, and there they both began to dress. He kept an eye on Paolina, as he'd fallen into the habit of doing, standing back, but not too far, waiting in case she stumbled, in case she was dizzy. Usually it annoyed her to see him hovering, but now neither of them spoke.

———

When they arrived at the house, Alex was alone in the kitchen. Paolina drew her son into her embrace and Antonello watched him spiral back in time to become her little boy again. He saw the unspoken hope between them that Paolina could make everything whole again. He wished he could hold his son. The desire was there: to pull Alex close, to give him a safe place to weep. But they so rarely touched. They shook hands at Christmas and on birthdays. While each kissed other men in the traditional one-kiss-on-each-cheek greeting that was almost impossible to avoid, especially at extended family gatherings, they didn't kiss each other. Antonello moved closer to mother and son and placed his hand on Alex's back, holding it there until Alex moved away from his mother's embrace.

Antonello and Paolina sat at the kitchen table as their son told them the details of the accident, pieced together from the police and the ambos. Over and over, he repeated the details of the night, of the last time he saw Ashleigh. He was frantic, a wild man in the grip of a fever, stomping up and down the length of the room.

'She came home from the library late afternoon with a stack of books. "For my Legal Studies essay," she said. I said, "You look as if you've brought home the whole library." And she said, "The old fart says no online references, can you imagine, as if we live in the Stone Ages." We both laughed even though I agreed with the old fart, even though I thought I shouldn't have laughed …' Alex swallowed and repeated, 'We both laughed,' as if the possibility of having laughed were the most shocking element of the story he was telling.

'And she gave me a kiss on the cheek.' This last statement was made in a squeaky small voice, a child's voice, and Antonello was transported back to an afternoon when Alex was seven or eight. The little boy racing into the house exhausted and sweaty, his nose bleeding, his school shirt torn and dirty. Alex's indignation coming out in the ceaseless prattle.

'Five minutes later,' Alex continued, 'she was out the door in her jeans, half her wardrobe thrown over her arm. "Going over to Jo's", she said. That's the last time I saw her. That girl's name was the last thing I heard her say.' He paused, sat down, and immediately stood up again. 'Later we had dinner. Rae took Jane to the movies, and I read my book, and I thought how great it was to have the house to myself — how could I have thought that? I don't want this fucking house to myself.' Alex gripped the back of a chair with both hands, his knuckles turning white.

Alex told them about the knock at the door in the middle of the night, and waking up in a panic and running down the stairs, and stopping and hesitating, and looking around and seeing that Jane and Rae were there, but no Ashleigh.

'Ashleigh?' Alex had called out her name.

'She's not home,' Rae said. 'I looked in her room.'

'I knew,' he told them, 'I'd known all the time as I was running down the stairs, but I kept thinking it's okay, she's slept over at Jo's, she's fine, she's asleep, she's fine, she's fine. Rae knew too. We both knew. I could see the cops through the glass panel, but I couldn't move. My body was numb, but my head was racing and I was running through all the reasons that might bring the cops to the door.

'I hoped that someone had broken into Jim's place — he's away and we have the key. And I hoped it was about you, Mum, you'd been rushed to hospital or you'd had a fall or something, or something at Rae's school, or something to do with work — maybe the Premier had been attacked and they needed me to go in to the office … I thought — no, I wished, as hard as I could, that it was someone else, that it was you or the Premier or … anyone. Anyone else, but not Ashleigh. I wished everyone else dead, everyone else, anyone else. Anyone. But I knew.

'When I saw the cops, a man and a woman, I knew it was bad news. They asked to come inside and we all sat down in the lounge room and there was a long pause where none of us said anything. The policewoman was almost crying even before she started talking. And I wanted to stop her. I wanted to gag her. I wanted to stuff something in her mouth to stop her from saying anything … When she said it, when she said "an accident", Rae asked, "How bad?" But I knew, I knew, because otherwise they would've rushed us out to the hospital. And then …'

Alex couldn't stop talking; a torrent of words spewed out of him. He described the policewoman and what she'd said, how she'd told them that his baby, his daughter, had been killed, moments from home, under the West Gate Bridge.

'The bridge?' Antonello whispered.

Alex didn't hear him and kept talking. 'They spun out of control …'

Paolina's hand reached out for Antonello's. He let her intertwine her fingers with his but he dared not look at her. *The bridge, the fucking bridge.* His granddaughter, his beautiful Ashleigh, had taken her last breath under the bridge, on the road where thirty-nine years earlier, they lined up the dead. Thirty-five stretchers cloaked with white sheets. A graveyard.

'There was silence. No one screamed, no one said anything. All the way to the morgue, we sat in the back seat of the cop car in silence. I didn't dare speak, I willed Rae not to speak. I was hoping and praying that it wasn't her, that they had the wrong girl. I didn't want to say Ashleigh's name. I didn't want Rae to say Ashleigh's name, as if we could keep her alive by not speaking, as if saying her name might make her death real when we knew it wasn't real, because it couldn't be.'

Antonello remembered the cop tapping him on the shoulder and telling him they'd found Slav's body. He stood by the stretcher hoping, praying, that it was not Slav, and then he saw Slav's arm, the only part of his body not covered by the white sheet, and the old gold watch, its glass face cracked. It was Slav's father's watch. Slav never took it off.

Antonello listened to Alex. It was important to listen. It was important to let Alex speak. It was important not to be sucked back into past by the bridge.

Alex was describing Ashleigh's body, his little girl, cold and still and covered in blood. He told them that Rae collapsed. He thought it was a heart attack, but he couldn't bring himself to do anything. He watched her fall, watched the police run to her, watched them call a doctor, watched Rae waking, heard the doctor saying she'd fainted and she was fine. He told them how shocked he was that Ashleigh was lying there dead but his heart and Rae's heart were still beating.

Antonello's heart kept beating its irregular beat — *atrial fibrillation*, an ageing heart, an old man's syndrome — but it too was beating.

'Jane was on the couch, waiting — she was wearing her tomcat pyjamas, and I wanted to yell at her to take them off. They're too happy, those pyjamas. She sat with her arms wrapped around her knees, she was sobbing, and she's so young and I wanted to say, "No, it wasn't her. Ashleigh's alright — it was another girl, Ashleigh's safe." But I had to tell her it wasn't a mistake, that her sister was dead. That we came home without her. All we have is a bag with her phone and the choker she was wearing. That's all we have left.

'Everything is lost and broken. I was meant to keep her safe. I'm her father. I was supposed to keep her safe.'

Antonello saw that his son's face was wracked with grief and fatigue and anger. Alex no longer looked like himself — his eyes were hard, his jaw tight, and deep furrows had formed across his forehead. He told them Jo was speeding and drunk. 'She's fine, though, a couple of scratches,' he said, his voice slow and heavy. 'She's home. She's okay. She's okay. All in one piece. Home in bed. And her fucking mother can stand at the door and watch her sleeping … They said Ashleigh was already — my baby — gone when the ambulance arrived, that they tried, but they couldn't …' Alex banged his fist on the table.

Ashleigh gone. Taken at the bridge. Antonello's head throbbed. He'd planned to destroy the bridge. After the collapse, he'd spent hours lying in bed, walking around his father-in-law's garden, imagining ways he might blow it up or tear it down. He should've destroyed the bridge. He should've stopped them from finishing it. If only, if only, then his granddaughter might be alive. Instead she was dead. So young, so beautiful. He expected to see her running into the kitchen, sneaking up behind Paolina and covering her grandmother's eyes with her hands and whispering *guess who* in Paolina's ear. And Paolina laughing as she guessed all the wrong people. He expected her to run into the kitchen and laugh at her father, teasing him for thinking she was gone when she was upstairs asleep all that time.

But Ashleigh would never run into the kitchen again. She had died at the base of the bridge. He didn't want to think about the bridge. Or Ashleigh. Or death. He wanted to stop thinking.

'Poor Jo,' Paolina murmured.

'How dare you say that, Mum?' Alex shouted, slamming his fist on the table again, his face flushed. Paolina gasped. He'd never yelled at his mother. Not even when he was a teenager. Never. But now, a middle-aged man, thickening around the waist, hair speckled with grey, he towered over Paolina. 'Don't you dare feel sorry for her,' he roared. 'She was driving and she was drunk and speeding and she killed Ashleigh. And she's alive.'

'They were best friends, Alex. They loved each other. She must be going through hell,' Paolina whispered. She put her hand on Alex's where it had come crashing down on the table, but he pulled it away. When Paolina reached for him again, he moved away from the table.

'Do you know what it's like to lose a daughter? I feel dead. No, I *am* dead. I want to be dead.'

'I'm sorry, Alex. Ashleigh is my granddaughter — I love her too. I'm sorry.' Paolina took the rosary beads out of her pocket and ran them through her fingers. 'Let's say a prayer.'

'Jo's alive and my baby, my *daughter*, is dead. And I don't want to hear any of your religious shit. No God, no forgiveness. I don't want to hear any of it. Do you hear me?' Alex snatched the beads out of Paolina's hand and threw them across the room, where they smashed against the wall. Paolina cried out. Alex yanked open the sliding door and slammed it shut behind him so hard that Antonello thought the glass might break.

Antonello picked up the rosary beads and handed them to Paolina. She kissed the cross and clutched the beads to her chest. His faith had collapsed with the bridge, pulverised into dust along with the concrete structures, along with the lives of his friends and workmates. If he went to funerals and weddings, he stood outside the church with the smokers, refusing to go inside. For years, Paolina avoided mentioning God or religion and rarely went to church, but she'd insisted the children be baptised, and they were, though unlike their cousins they didn't go to Catholic schools. She kept her faith to herself. But after her diagnosis,

Paolina prayed more openly, carrying rosary beads like a talisman everywhere she went.

They'd spent so many hours in this kitchen, and in earlier versions of it, watching Ashleigh and Jane grow up. They'd squeezed around the table with the whole extended family to celebrate all of Ashleigh's birthdays. They'd watched her blow out the candles, and each year, waited for Paolina to say, "Cut the cake now, but don't touch the bottom or you'll have to kiss the nearest boy." They were there all the years when Ashleigh screwed up her face at the idea of a boy and a kiss, until the last birthday, when she'd grinned and touched the bottom and kissed her boyfriend Kevin, who'd turned bright red.

'I meant,' Paolina whispered, 'the girls were always together, they were so close. It must be awful for Jo too.' It was true that when they were together they shut the adults out, that when Jo was around, Ashleigh ignored her parents, her grandparents, her sister. And now she was dead because of *that girl*, that girl Ashleigh loved and had often chosen above her parents. But hadn't they all, at some point, chosen other people above their parents? It was what young people did. It was part of growing up, wasn't it?

If Ashleigh was alive, she'd be telling them that they were overreacting, that accidents happen. She may or may not have learnt a lesson, and the accident would've been a lucky escape, all part of growing up.

Stupid, reckless girls, all of them. Stupid, reckless.

Ashleigh is dead. Ashleigh is dead. Ashleigh is dead. He repeated it to himself so that he didn't forget. Because all he wanted to do was forget.

Antonello understood Alex's urge to break, to smash, to hurt. Underneath that rage was grief, the grief that Alex didn't want to acknowledge, that he was trying to keep at a distance, the grief and the guilt, and the shame: 'I was meant to keep her safe. I'm her father.' That grief wasn't going to go anywhere; it would never go away. It would weigh him down, pull him under. Eventually he'd have to surrender to it.

'You're right, Paolina,' he said. 'Jo deserves our pity. She might be alive, but being the one left behind, being the one responsible, that's going to be hard.'

Paolina squeezed his hand. 'Yes. But we've all been left behind.'

They retreated into silence. Outside, birds chirped and whistled. Alex paced, ignoring Lewis, the family Jack Russell, who was nudging an old ball towards him.

'I was remembering Ashleigh's birthday,' Paolina said eventually. 'When they were planning the food and the music.'

Antonello remembered too. The two girls had sat on the floor organising a playlist for the party. They had a laptop opened, an iPad connected. They both wore headphones. Rae wanted Ashleigh to help plan the menu for the party — she was running through lists of finger food — but Ashleigh was ignoring her mother. Occasionally, either Ashleigh or Jo pulled the headphones out and loud music came crashing into the room. Several times Rae told them to turn the music down. Later she said to Antonello, 'Ashleigh's controls are stuck on high speed, high volume, and when she and Jo are together, it's impossible.'

'They laughed so much when they were together. I loved to see them so happy.' Paolina leant against Antonello. He stroked her head gently.

The mystery of friendship. The randomness with which the two girls, so different, had found each other and become friends. And a memory returned to him, of a Sunday afternoon after a soccer match, he and Slav and Sam caked in mud and sweat, sitting on a bench outside the clubrooms. They'd lost the game, but they were happy. Slav, the best player of the three, the one that a league coach approached and invited to try out for the state team, was the least concerned. 'I don't care that much about soccer,' he said. 'Otherwise I wouldn't play with you two.'

Sam hit Slav hard on the arm. 'What are you trying to say there, *mio* mate?' Having adopted 'mate', Sam used it to refer to everyone, but with an Italian emphasis: '*ehi* mate' or '*mio* mate'.

Slav pretended to be knocked over by the hit. 'Come on, Sam. I know Australians who can play soccer better than you.'

'Would you like a coffee?' Antonello asked Paolina. She nodded. He put the pot on and went over to the fridge for milk. On the door, there were photographs of Jane and Ashleigh, and one of Ashleigh and Jo, the two girls dancing at Ashleigh's eighteenth birthday party. Ashleigh was caught in mid movement, her arms swinging. Ashleigh, with her mother's pale skin and oval face. Jo's features were more Italian than Ashleigh's. Occasionally when they were out with the girls, people mistook Jo for their granddaughter. Ashleigh was thinner and more athletic. She was shorter too, and recently she'd started to wear those ridiculously high heels.

'Killer heels,' Antonello had teased Ashleigh at the party. 'Well, at least if you get into trouble, you can use them as a weapon.' The memory was so sad it choked him. But he didn't stop breathing. Paolina didn't stop breathing. Alex and Rae, they were still breathing. And Jane. Everyone else except Ashleigh was breathing.

Antonello removed photographs that included Jo from the fridge and shoved them in the back of a corner drawer, behind birthday candles and matchboxes, business cards and brochures, paper clips and picture hooks.

Chapter 10

Sharp slivers of light pierced the room. A yearning for darkness propelled Jo out of bed and to the window. Trembling, she yanked the curtains shut and crawled back under the bedcovers, eyes closed, knees to chin. Cocooned. She should be crying, weeping, sobbing, but she hadn't shed a tear, not one. Acid mouth. Stomach cramps. The night had been a series of runs to the bathroom, three or four times. Heaving and puking in the darkness. The stink of vomit and bile trailing her through the house. Her body rotting from the inside.

Her mother hadn't come to her. Not once.

Loud and ponderous and unstoppable, the world was awake. Heavy trucks, grunting and grinding, sped towards the refineries and the wharves, Coode Island, the West Gate. The sounds reverberated around the house. Boom-gate bells. Factory sirens. A ship's foghorn. Mrs Nguyễn's Alsatian, Wes, barking and Bob's mongrel Lupie responding. The rattle of a wheelie bin rolled out to the curb. Mr Johnson's hacking morning cough.

Shut the fuck up. Stop. The day was coming, unwavering, relentless. It didn't care about her or Ash.

Once, not long ago, she had joined her neighbours and the local environmental group to demonstrate against the truck traffic, the refineries, the *capitalist pigs who run big business and don't give a shit about community*. Fifty-three people, several children, and a dozen or so dogs camped on the footpath along Francis Street on a cold April night to highlight the uselessness of the truck curfew. They spread out sleeping bags and old foam mattresses, and every time a truck drove past they yelled and blew whistles and banged pots and took photographs of licence plates. Jo fell asleep. Mandy told Mrs Nguyễn, 'Jo can sleep through anything.'

On weekday mornings, Jo resented having to get up for school and not having enough time to sleep. This morning Jo wouldn't get up. She wouldn't get dressed. She wouldn't argue with her mother as they ate their breakfast. She wouldn't run all the way to Ash's house and knock on the door so they could go to school together. No more Ash. Not ever.

Ash dead. It was impossible. Not true. A bad dream. A nightmare. Clutching the twisted sheets, Jo ached for her mother, to crawl into the warmth of her mother's bed, to be embraced by her mother, encircled in her arms. For Mandy's welcome. *Did you have a bad dream, darling?*

All night sleep mocked her. Not sleep. A state of semi-consciousness, out of which she was jolted when she remembered Ash was dead. And a swell rising … a hard fist in the belly, and rivers of heat burning in her throat. The wheel slipping, the car skidding and skating and spinning and spinning. Body bounding and head whirling, and time slowing, and the screams. And more screams, and slamming the brake down hard. The car soaring. And crashing, amplified and vibrating and so close.

Again and again, the screams. The sirens. The police. The ambulance. The ringing in her ears.

'The young woman in the front seat didn't survive the accident.'

Dead.

Laura and Mani were yelling and screaming. Laura and Mani were sobbing. Smashed glass and metal strewn across the road. The fluttering lights on the bridge. The half moon. Men talking, calling out, yelling. The clang of chains. Flashing orange lights. Horns and sirens. Alarms.

And darkness, black and thick.

'Open your eyes.' A paramedic. Lying still. 'She's fine. Nothing broken.'

'Concussion?' Emergency Room lights, rolling corridors.

The memories coming in a rapid stream. Surging. Spilling. Spewing. A cubicle. A nurse pulling the curtains across, glaring at her with scorn. 'She can wait. She's fine. To look at her you wouldn't know there'd been an accident.'

Police, doctors, nurses, questions.

'You understand the test is to check your blood-alcohol concentration. You have to consent to the test. Do you understand?'

'You understand that the young woman who was in the front seat, Ashleigh, is dead. Do you understand?'

No, I don't understand. No, she isn't dead.

Was it possible to erase everything, to make it not true, a lie?

Blood test. A syringe. Drawing of blood.

'To look at her you wouldn't know there'd been an accident.'

'Drunk?'

'Looks like it. Smells like it.'

Mandy holding the curtain aside. Standing half in and half out.

Nothing. Not a word. Mandy silent, refusing to meet her eye.

Please yell at me.

How did they get home? Was it the back of a taxi? A police car? Falling, falling into her bed. Her head drowning in memories and nightmares.

'The passenger in the front seat is dead.'

'Your friend is dead.'

'You killed Ash.'

Ash is dead.

At 7.00 am, the alarm triggered the radio. Jo hit the off button with a hard thump. At the café they'd be opening up soon. Ted and the staff … did they know about the accident? News travelled fast in Yarraville. The morning regulars arriving with their dogs, their iPhones and earplugs, on their way back from boot camp at the park or their Pilates class, lining up even before the coffee machine was fired up. The sweep of gossip between orders, patrons picking up fragments. Soon they'd hear about the accident. Just a story to them. There would be shock, horror. There would be pity and fury.

It would be impossible to go back.

Ash would never again come into the café, arriving in her safety jacket, covered in the smell of the dogs she'd been walking, and ask for a strong macchiato to go.

Ash would never again sit in a classroom in the school where they had been students for the last six years. And Jo would never again sit next to Ash with Laura and Mani, gossiping when they should've been working. Never again giggling at silly jokes.

An accident. *Accident.* The word didn't seem right. *Accident* was too small and slight. Accidents: a broken plate, a ball through a window, spilt milk …

If only. If only. If only.

If only she hadn't been drinking.

If only Kevin had come along. If only he'd driven.

If only they'd stayed home studying. Isn't that what VCE students were supposed to do?

If only they didn't know Rosie.

If only they had left the car at the party and caught a taxi home.

If only she hadn't read Ash's journal.

If only she'd left good enough alone.

If only they had never met, never been friends.

If only she'd read the signs … There must have been signs.

If only … if only she'd died too.

Ash was going to do things with her life. Ash was smart and ambitious and going to make a mark in the world. Ash was beautiful. Everyone liked Ash.

Jo should be dead. She should've been the one to die.

Everyone would be thinking, *It should be Jo dead.*

But Jo wasn't dead. Her heart was beating. She was breathing.

Across her belly and chest there were a few bruises, purple and black blotches spreading. No broken bones. No permanent damage.

'Jo?' Mandy called through the closed door. 'The police are here. You have to go with them to the station for an interview. They're waiting.'

Jo listened to Mandy walk back up the hall to the lounge room, tracking the creak of the loose boards under her mother's feet.

'You can sit if you want,' she heard Mandy say. 'Would you like a drink? Tea? Coffee?'

'No thanks, Mrs Neilson, we're fine.' It was a woman's voice.

To find her clothes, Jo switched on the bedside lamp. There was an untidy mound on the floor next to the bed. On top was the red dress, ripped and stained with blood. Jo threw the dress onto the floor and grabbed a pair of crumpled blue jeans, giving them a shake. Her belly and chest ached when she moved. She unbuttoned her pyjama top and pressed her fingers, hard, into the translucent purple bruises. The pain intensified; she pressed again. She gasped, then pressed harder. But the pain eased. It was bearable. She'd have to finish dressing and come out. She slipped her feet into her thongs, ran a brush through her hair, and tied it into a ponytail. She noticed her phone on the bedside table. It was turned off. She didn't remember turning it off — she didn't remember bringing it home. She hesitated at her bedroom door, then went back and slipped the phone into her pocket. All she wanted was to go back to bed and never have to get up again.

'Are you coming, Jo?'

'Yes.' The bathroom smelt of disinfectant and vomit; the acid, the bile, the memory of it was in her throat. She brushed her teeth and washed her face without looking in the mirror. Maybe she didn't exist at all and there would be no reflection in the mirror. Maybe she was dead. She wished she wasn't alive. She wished she didn't exist. Was that the same as wishing she was dead?

The hallway was a clutter of shelves and dressers, of books and ornaments. It was her job to dust the hallway once a week. To pick up each thing, each book and vase and crystal animal, to lift each doily ... on those days the hallway seemed so long, but ten steps, that's all it was, ten small steps and she was in the lounge room: one couch, two beanbags, a television set, and a coffee table squeezed against the wall under the window. The two cops sat side by side on the couch. The man's legs stretched halfway across the room; the woman had hers tucked back.

Mandy sat on the edge of a chair she'd dragged in from the kitchen. The cops were familiar, both of them. But Jo couldn't place them. School? Or were they customers at the café?

'I'm Constable Lumina,' the woman said. 'This is Constable Peters. We met at the hospital.'

She remembered their voices. *You understand that the young woman in the front seat, Ashleigh, is dead. You understand the blood test is to check your blood-alcohol concentration. You have to consent to the test.*

They managed to go home, to sleep, to spend time with their families, and get up and put their uniforms back on, and their guns and batons, and go back to work.

She didn't meet their eyes. Shame, guilt, grief, sadness — she couldn't describe her emotions.

'You might want to grab a jacket,' Constable Lumina said. 'It's cold outside.'

Jo noticed her feet. Thongs. It occurred to her that thongs and jeans might be inappropriate for a police interview. She stood up to go back to her room, and came face to face with her mother. Mandy's face was milky white. The hollows under her eyes were deeper and darker, and her lips were thin and pale. Mandy handed Jo a jacket. It was the black windcheater with a broken zipper — she only ever wore the jacket to the gym, on cold mornings. It was old. It was the jacket she threw in the locker and on the floor of the car.

No one cares about your fucking jacket.

Jo turned to look at her mother, but it wasn't her mother's voice. The cops were outside now. There was no one else in the house.

Voices came and went, especially in her early adolescence; her head overflowed with voices as if it were a tiny cell filled with people. *You're fat. You're ugly. You're stupid. You'll never be popular. You don't get anything. Your friends are only pretending.* But those voices were her own voice, playing her doubts back at her like a chant. This wasn't her voice. *No one cares about your fucking jacket.* This was Ash's voice.

Ash's voice: how was that possible?

———

The cop car was parked on the nature strip. Constable Lumina held the back door open. Mandy slid all the way across, buckled her seatbelt, and rested her head against the door. Jo followed. As soon as the car started moving, the nausea returned. Jo's mouth was dry. She worried she might be sick. She took a deep breath. Her mother passed her a water bottle, and she took a sip and handed it back.

Jo scratched at her nail polish: blue satin, Ash's. The floating blue flakes fell like coloured snow and then disappeared. Her nails were now a mix of blue and purple, the colour of the night sky on smoggy Melbourne nights.

The cops discussed rosters, forms, schedules, the weather (a 70 per cent chance of rain). Constable Lumina complained about the number of semi-trailers on the road, and Constable Peters said his father had been a truckie for twenty years. Life on the road was tough. As a boy, when he'd gone on a road trip with his father, he counted fifty-six abusive drivers. The two cops talked as if they were alone in the car, as if the back seat were empty, but Jo sensed their restraint as tight around their throats as a noose. She imagined they longed to turn around and tell her exactly what they thought. She focused on their conversation, on their words, on imagining herself in the cabin of Constable Peters' father's truck, between the man and the little boy.

'Dad never talked about stress. I don't think stress had been invented yet.' Constable Peters laughed. He had an unexpected laugh, loud and jolly, the sort that might land a man a job as a Father Christmas in a crowded department store. When he stopped laughing, his voice softened. 'At least, not in my neighbourhood. He'd be away for days, even whole weeks, and we were so excited because he was home, but he couldn't keep his eyes open. By the time his energy came back, and he started chasing us around the backyard or playing cricket with us in the street, it was time for him to go away again.'

When they arrived at the police station, there was no one standing on either side of the counter. The row of plastic chairs under the waiting area sign was empty. The walls were plastered with posters promoting the

Police Ethnic Unit, the Neighbourhood Program, Defensive Driving. Jo had been to this station twice before: once when Mandy's wallet was stolen, and another time to have a statutory declaration form signed. On both occasions they stood at the counter, facing the mirrored glass and their own reflections. Now, sandwiched between the two cops, they went past the counter, through the door, down the hallway, and into the interview room.

'Your lawyer's running late. We can't start the interview until she gets here,' Constable Lumina said. 'You can wait here.'

'I have a lawyer?' Jo asked.

'Court appointed,' Constable Lumina replied.

Both cops left the room. Mandy and Jo sat next to each other at the table. This was the first time they'd been alone since the accident. Neither of them spoke. Mandy's anger, her disappointment, her sadness — these were the ocean of emotions that Jo didn't want to disturb. She sat still and quiet, as if she were seawater prey and her mother the predator. As if being quiet and still would save her from her mother's wrath. But Mandy sat next to Jo without touching, without speaking.

The interview room reminded Jo of a small classroom at school, D3. The room had the same furniture. The same blue-vinyl steel-framed chairs. The same dull laminated tables, small and square. D3 had been Literature with Mr Russell, a thirty-something poet.

'I'm a poet,' Mr Russell had announced at the beginning of the year as he handed out a sheet with a list of titles and dates. 'My published poems. You might want to read them … out of interest, of course, no obligation.' The students giggled and sniggered. English Literature was a small group of thirteen.

Liam, one of the three boys in the class, called out, 'Read us a poem, sir.'

'You can read the poems for yourself. I'm giving them to you to rebut the myth "those who can, do; those who can't, teach".'

'What? What do you mean?' Liam asked.

'Never mind. We've got mounds to get through.' When he said it, Jo had thought about the prisoners in *The Great Escape* — she'd watched the movie on a Sunday afternoon when she was supposed to be studying. In the movie, the prisoners dug a tunnel under the prison wall; they dug and thought about freedom, and they dug even though there was no end in sight.

Mr Russell materialised each week in skinny black jeans and one of a series of black t-shirts with images of various punk bands or their albums. He pushed the tables together, *for discussion*. Jo avoided joining the discussions. Occasionally he picked on her, caught her eye or called her by name, asked her what she thought about the poems they were reading. They were studying Auden: 'This Lunar Beauty', 'To Ask the Hard Question is Simple', and 'Lullaby'. She was supposed to have memorised the poems for the exam, but now the only poem that came to mind was Blake's 'The Tyger' — she and Ash memorising it together, challenging each other, one stanza a week. *Tyger Tyger, burning bright / In the forests of the night / What immortal hand or eye / Could frame thy fearful symmetry?* Their laughter and giggles after each stanza. But that was Year 11, a whole year ago now. *Tyger Tyger, burning bright / In the forests of the night / What immortal hand or eye / Could frame thy fearful symmetry?* She kept repeating it, wishing the rest of the poem would materialise, closing her eyes and concentrating. *Tyger Tyger, burning bright / In the forests of the night / What immortal hand or eye / Could frame thy fearful symmetry? Tyger Tyger, burning bright / In the forests of the night / What immortal hand or eye / Could frame thy fearful symmetry?* If only the rest of the poem would come back to her, if only she could recite it in its complete form.

When the door opened, Jo's body tensed. A large woman came rushing into the room, banging the door shut. Jo jumped. The woman was at least six foot tall, and fat. The room shrank as she dropped a bulging satchel to the floor, swung her heavy black cape off her shoulders, and rummaged through her bag until she found her phone and turned it off.

'Sorry, apologies,' she said. 'The trains were a bloody mess this morning. Stolen copper. Can you believe that? Stolen copper? People steal copper from the railway line and that stops the trains. Unbelievable.' And then, abruptly, as if taken by surprise by where she was, she stopped, apologised again, held out her hand to Jo and Mandy, and introduced herself. 'Sarah Cascade. I'm your lawyer. From Victoria Legal Aid.'

To be Sarah's size was Jo's worst nightmare. A vague memory grew clearer: her father and stepmother showing her photographs of fat women. Her father saying, 'This is how fat people can get, as big as a side of a house. People this fat die young. People like this are lonely and miserable. They don't have any friends. They don't have any life. Not one worth living.' The people in the pictures were huge — 'obese', her stepmother called them. She'd screwed up her face when she said the word, as if their fatness were contagious.

If Jo had let herself get fat, would Ash still be alive?

Jo's grandmother Mary often bargained with God and with the Virgin Mary — for her knee to improve or for Jo to do well in VCE, and promising that in return, she'd volunteer to clean the church or buy the flowers for Easter Sunday or make a donation to the church fund or stop eating chocolate. Could Jo make a bargain with God? She wasn't Catholic. She wasn't baptised. Did God care? Was he open to making bargains with all comers? Mary did say, 'We are all God's children.'

If she was willing to be fat, would God turn the clock back?

'Now, I'll get settled before we call them in,' Sarah said, sitting down across the table from Jo. Sarah's body was a series of soft rolls and folds; the top she wore was tight, and distorted red and yellow tulips stretched over the bulges and into the folds.

Jo closed her eyes.

'Are you okay?' Sarah asked.

Jo opened her eyes and nodded.

'Sorry, stupid question,' Sarah continued. 'Look, sorry I'm late. We'll talk more later. The police are going to ask you questions. They want you to make a statement. They want you to tell them what happened in detail. Step by step.' Jo was mesmerised by Sarah's bright red lips, her double chin, her pale neck.

'I'll be here. If I think they're asking you a question that you shouldn't answer, I'll tell you. But otherwise I won't interrupt. I'm here to make sure you are treated as you should be, within the law. Okay?'

'Yes. But what if I don't know … don't have the answers?'

'Let's see how we go.' Sarah turned to Mandy. 'It's best if you don't interrupt, either.'

'Are they going to ask me questions too? Will they interview me?'

'Not now, not today. Maybe later.'

Sarah opened the door and called out, 'We're ready.'

The cops came back in. Constable Peters was carrying a box, from which he took a small digital recorder. As he set up the microphone, Constable Lumina settled at the table with her notepad and pen.

'If we're ready,' Constable Peters said, and turned on the recorder. 'It's 10.10 am on the twenty-first of September 2009. Footscray Police Station. Interview with Joanne Neilson. Conducting the interview, Constable Peters and Constable Lumina. In the room, we also have Ms Neilson's lawyer, Sarah Cascade, and Ms Neilson's mother, Mandy Neilson.' He looked up. 'Jo, please state your name and your address.'

'My name is Jo Neilson. I live at …' Her voice was small, distant, a whisper.

'Can you speak a little louder? And say your full name,' Constable Peters interrupted.

She repeated her name and her address. In Jo's head, her voice was booming. She waited for them to reel back, but no one moved. The two cops were staring at Jo. Sarah glanced up from her notebook, and even Mandy shifted in her chair so that she was facing Jo. To stop herself from fidgeting, Jo slipped her hands under her legs, like she had as a child. Back then, her legs didn't touch the ground and she could swing her feet. She pressed down on her hands with all her weight.

'What is your birth date?' Constable Peters bent closer to the microphone every time he asked a question.

'Eighth of June 1990.'

'You are older than the other girls.' This seemed like a statement to Jo, but when she didn't answer, Sarah nodded in her direction.

'The others are eighteen, or almost eighteen. I started school late.'

Jo waited for Mandy to explain, to say what she usually said about keeping Jo back from school: 'It's not that Jo was slow or anything. Her grandfather was sick.' But Sarah shook her head and Mandy slumped back in her chair, eyes fixed on her lap.

Constable Lumina wrote notes with a fountain pen, the blue ink staining her thumb and her index finger. *Running writing.* Jo's Grade 4 teacher, Mrs Morris, called it *running writing.* The students had to conquer the style before they were awarded a pen licence. Jo was bad at *running writing.* She recalled the shame of being the second-last person in the grade to qualify for her pen licence. A boy, Macka Smith, was slower, but he was a brat who couldn't read, let alone write. Jo wasn't good at reading upside down. She wasn't good at reading people's *running writing.* Her father and her great aunt — the aunt who lived somewhere in Canada, somewhere cold, where it snowed in the winter — sent her handwritten letters and cards. When they arrived, Mandy translated them. Not that they ever said anything interesting. *Have a good birthday. Hope you have a nice Easter. All the best for Xmas.* Her father wrote Christmas with an X. Her aunt spelt the whole word out. Her father's script was small and squashed; Mandy called it 'stingy writing'. He wrote about Jo's brothers: *Michael is the captain of the cricket team. Ed is going to start high school this year.* Lists of impersonal details. He didn't use adjectives. Her aunt wrote about gardens and travelling. In her letters, nouns were weighed down by adjectives, though her vocabulary was limited, and everything good was *fabulous* or *stunning* or *so, so beautiful,* and everything not so good was *disappointing* and *unsatisfying.*

'Jo, tell us about that evening, before the accident.' Constable Peters reached out to steady the microphone.

Jo hesitated. Where to begin? The party, the house ... or further back? Did they want to know about her nerves, her anxiety, the panic she felt before Ash arrived? Or the relief when Ash agreed to come over in the afternoon to study? Or later, when she came back with champagne and her clothes: 'Party time.' Her warm hug. 'A strong beginning is what catches the reader,' Mrs Hunt had told them. *The beginning is simple to mark* was the first line of Ian McEwan's *Enduring Love* — it didn't catch her, she wanted to give up on the novel, and in fact she did several times, wouldn't have continued reading it if it weren't for the exams. Those exams.

The beginning is simple to mark.

'Jo?'

'Where do you want me to start?'

'What time did you get together with Ashleigh?' Constable Lumina asked. Her voice was soft, and she leaned in to ask her questions, as if they were friends exchanging intimacies in a café.

'Ash was at my place all afternoon, we were studying. Then she went home to get her clothes and came back at 7.30.'

'Did you go out straightaway?'

'No. It was too early. We did our make-up and dressed, and Mum cooked us dinner.' Jo's body craved her mother's: to curl up on the couch against her mother's body, to be held in her mother's embrace. Mandy's grip would be strong, her hands warm. Mandy was her anchor. But Mandy's hands were on her lap. She had a tissue in one hand, her fist tight around it. With the other hand, she gripped her phone as if someone were threatening to snatch it.

Jo stared at the vinyl tiles, at the metal-framed chairs, at the notices on the noticeboard, at the poster for Victoria Legal Aid.

'What did you have for dinner?'

'Mum made eggs and toast.'

Sarah scribbled notes. Her fingers were slender, long, and fast. Her nails were short, but not shaped or filed. Sarah's nails were like Mandy's nails. No manicures. Ash had given Jo her first manicure when they were thirteen. They followed the step-by-step instructions in a *Dolly* magazine. They bought nail files and clippers, and pinched Ash's mother's hand creams.

How could Sarah and Constable Lumina have so much to write?

'Did you have a drink with dinner? Alcohol?'

'Yes.'

'What did you drink?'

'We had a Cruiser each when we were getting ready. Later we opened a bottle of champagne that Ash brought —'

'How much did you drink?' Constable Peters was asking his questions in quick succession now, one after the other. His arms were folded and his eyes fixed on the digital recorder.

'A glass each, I think.'

'Were you drunk?'

'I only had a couple of drinks.'

'Then what happened?'

'At about nine we headed off for the party.'

'You were driving?'

'I'm the only one with a car.'

'Did you know you were going to be driving?'

'Yes.'

'But you still drank?' Constable Lumina interrupted. In the ensuing silence, she dropped her pen. It rolled off the table onto the floor and she stood up and chased it across the room.

'I only had a couple of drinks.' Jo tried to count how many. A Cruiser and a glass of champagne at home. At the party she drank another Cruiser or two. A glass of champagne. Another champagne with cake, maybe two … she could count the drinks up until the cake. After that she wasn't sure.

'We all drank. I drove because I'm the only one with a licence and a car. I wasn't drunk. I don't drink that much. It's not like I was … I don't get that drunk. I knew what was going on.' They didn't believe her. She didn't believe herself. It was true that she didn't drink much, not compared to some. If only they knew how much some people drank.

'You have a probationary P1 licence, is that right?' Constable Peters asked, his eyes on her now.

'Yes,' Jo whispered, looking away.

'You are aware of the conditions of that licence? You know you must have zero blood-alcohol content when driving? In other words, no drinking at all?' He was almost shouting at her now. 'You do know that, don't you?'

Jo flinched.

'I think we should take a break,' Sarah said, and stood up. 'A coffee break.'

Constable Peters turned the recorder off, picked it up, and left the room. Constable Lumina offered to make them tea and coffee and followed him out.

'You don't have to admit you were drunk.' Sarah shoved her chair out of the way as she stood up.

'I wasn't drunk. Not when we left the house.'

'Okay. But later. When they ask about later, don't lie — you can tell them how many drinks you had if you remember — but don't admit you were drunk.'

'We were all drunk.'

'Jo,' Mandy hissed, and both Sarah and Jo turned to Mandy, but she didn't say anything else.

'You were the one driving.' Sarah's voice was soft but stern. 'It doesn't matter whether Ashleigh or the other girls were drunk.'

'But we ... we usually drank together.'

'Yes, but the person driving is the person responsible,' Sarah said.

'It's my fault. Everything is my fault?' Jo pleaded. *Fat cow*, Jo thought. Anger was rising in her. 'It wasn't only my fault. Fuck. It was Ash's fault too. It wasn't ...'

All your fault. All your fault. Killer Jo. That voice again, spitting and hissing in her ear. *You want to blame me?*

'According to the law, Jo,' Sarah said in the same soft voice. 'I know it's hard, but that's the law. Unless there is something else you're not saying. Unless someone forced you to drive the car, unless they held a gun to your head, unless Ash took the wheel or put her foot on the accelerator, unless someone cut you off on the road ...'

'Don't call her Ash,' Jo said. 'She hates other people calling her Ash.'

'Okay.' Sarah rose from the table. 'But you drank too much. You're a P-plate driver. No drinking. No more than two people in the car. You know all this.'

Jo didn't respond.

'You do know this, Jo, don't you?'

'Yes,' Jo whispered. 'Yes.' She tried to remember if she'd thought about it on that night. When she first got her licence, she had been so careful. No alcohol at all. But she often felt on edge and tense when they went out, so worried about what everyone was thinking. A drink or two helped her relax. What was the harm in that? She rarely got drunk. She hadn't felt drunk at the party, had she? Had she driven knowing she was too drunk? 'I said I'd drive. Taxis are so expensive. My mother doesn't drive, and Ash hates asking her parents. We were tired. Ash wanted to go home. She was working the next day. She wanted to go home. How were we supposed to get home? I'm a good driver. I don't drink much. I've driven home from parties before, plenty of times. I don't know what happened, it was an accident.'

'Did you drink less because you were driving?'

'Yes.' She always drank less because she was driving. She teased the others, told them that when they had their licences they'd owe her, they'd have to drive her everywhere, that she'd be the one getting drunk. But she didn't mind. She liked being the one with the car, the one they counted on.

'So you drank less that night because you knew you were driving.'

Jo didn't say anything.

'When they did the blood test you were over 0.07.'

'Was I? I didn't feel that drunk.'

'You were drunk, too drunk to drive,' Sarah said. She gripped the back of the chair. She waited for Jo to meet her gaze. 'You need to admit, at least to yourself, that you did the wrong thing. That you shouldn't have been driving. It doesn't matter what the others did. They shouldn't have gotten in the car with you. They should've stopped you driving. The people whose party it was, the people at the restaurant, they should've stopped you driving. Your mother, she should've stopped you taking the car in the first place. She should've taken the car keys and thrown them away. But they won't be charged because you're an adult now and you drove the car. You,' Sarah said. She rummaged in her bag, pulled out her tobacco, and headed towards the door. Before she opened it, she turned back to Jo, her hand on the knob. 'For God's sake, Jo, show that you know what you did was wrong. And apologise and keep apologising and don't stop.' She opened the door and left the room.

'Fuck,' Jo heard Sarah mutter as the door closed behind her.

Jo imagined what Sarah might've been thinking: *That girl is an idiot, a stupid, dumb bitch ... a murderer.* But what would Sarah know, or Mandy or the cops? How could Jo make them understand? Of course she was sorry. So sorry. So fucked up. She wished Ash was alive. She wished she hadn't been driving. She shouldn't have been driving, of course. Her body was slack in the chair, as if she were a rag doll, as if the stuffing were seeping out of the unstitched seams, as if she might collapse on the floor and disappear.

Too many drinks, was that what it came down to? The Cruiser with Ash while they did their make-up, the champagne afterwards. 'Let's have some champagne with dinner,' Ash had said, popping the cork.

Did they drink the whole bottle?

Jo willed herself to think about something else. Anything else. School. The English essay, due Friday. The presentation for History, with Bec, who was distracted, private, who hated group work. How would she get these done? Would she be expected to get them done? Would she be allowed to go back? She almost asked her mother, 'Do I keep going to school?' But that was a stupid question. What was the point? No need to concern herself with these things.

Go directly to jail, do not pass go.

Jo shivered.

Would she go to prison? Even if they didn't lock her up, she couldn't go back to sit in a classroom, to give a History talk. Ash was dead. There would be no more school. No more work in the café. No more life. She didn't deserve to have a life. There was more than one way to be dead. She could forget VCE. She could forget work. She could forget friends.

Who'd want to be friends with a killer?

Who'd want to go out with a murderer?

Jo cupped her ears. Now she was sweating; her face was damp and hot. 'I didn't mean to hurt Ash. I didn't mean to,' she cried out.

She killed Ash. This is what the cops and Sarah were really saying; they were telling her, 'You killed Ash. You're responsible.'

'I know.' Mandy's response surprised Jo. They were both staring ahead, at the wall with the posters, but until now it was as if they were in separate rooms, as if between them there were a thick, impenetrable wall.

'They think I did it on purpose.'

'No. No, I don't think they do,' Mandy said quietly.

There was silence for a few minutes and then Mandy, in a low voice, her resigned voice, the voice she'd used when she told Jo that Grandpa Tom wouldn't survive the cancer, when she told Jo her father was getting remarried, when she told Jo she couldn't be bothered arguing with her anymore, said, 'You shouldn't have driven while you were drunk. That was wrong and irresponsible. And I shouldn't have let you take the car that night. That was wrong too. Stupid mistakes, bad mistakes —'

'People do it all the time,' Jo said automatically.

'Stop it, Jo,' Mandy said. Her voice remained low and restrained. 'You aren't ten years old. You haven't broken a toy or come home late … Yes, people do stupid things and get away with it sometimes, but sometimes they don't. And then —' She paused for a moment and then said, 'What's the point?'

'The point?'

'Yes. What's the point of anything? Of this conversation. Too late now.'

'You couldn't have stopped me,' Jo said, but she didn't feel any of the old resentment towards her mother.

'But I didn't try,' Mandy whispered.

Chapter 11

In the hallway outside the interview room, Sarah leaned against the wall. Lately, her anger was getting the better of her, and being on a strict high-protein diet wasn't helping. She craved sugar. She needed a cigarette. She needed a less stressful job. She needed to work with clients who weren't idiots. Who took some responsibility for their actions.

'Ready to go back?' Constable Lumina asked, handing Sarah a coffee.

'Give me a minute? I need a smoke.'

'Sure. I'll come out with you,' she said, and went across to a desk that had a solitary but high stack of papers and files, opened the top drawer, and took out a packet of cigarettes. Sarah trailed after the constable, through the back door and into a small courtyard where two other cops, both men, sat on a bench smoking. The men nodded at them, and continued their own conversation.

'These car-accident cases are tough,' Constable Lumina said.

'The worst,' Sarah said as she rolled herself a cigarette. 'So much bad stuff that happens is the result of thoughtlessness and bad luck.'

'Not bad luck, negligence.'

'We're all negligent; we're all irresponsible from time to time. Apparently, we're being negligent right now.' Sarah pointed to their cigarettes. Some people, like her mother, thought she was negligent because she was fat. 'You'll regret it when you're older,' her mother said. 'When your knees go, when you have diabetes and high blood pressure, it'll be your own fault.'

'Smoking isn't illegal.'

'No. Not yet. Worth too much in taxes. But we know the risks,' Sarah said, and the constable nodded in agreement. In some jobs, smoking gave the sort of comfort it was impossible to get in any other way. Lots of the cops Sarah knew smoked, and plenty of the legal aid lawyers too.

Constable Lumina was in her early twenties, Sarah guessed. Her uniform was a size too big and it fell from her shoulders like it might from a hanger, eliminating all curves. Sarah expected that in civvies Constable Lumina would look adolescent.

'I guess you've seen a lot of these accident cases?' Sarah asked.

'Too many, unfortunately. And ...' Constable Lumina sat down next to the table with an ashtray overflowing with butts.

'And? You were going to say something else.'

'Not sure why I'm telling you, but something about Jo reminds me of my brother. He was sixteen when he died. A few too many mates. A few too many beers. And a stolen car. They wanted to have a good time.'

'That's tough. I'm sorry.'

'It was a long time ago. I was a kid.'

Sarah didn't ask questions. She knew the answers. Of course the family was broken; recovery was impossible. Of course people went on with their lives. Of course the grief was ever-present, sometimes seeming to recede, but returning, waves of it swelling at unexpected moments, destructive, erosive.

The two male cops finished their cigarettes and went back inside, their boots thumping down the corridor, the sound audible long after the door banged shut behind them. At the nearby railway station a train arrived, and Sarah heard, *Stopping all stations to Flinders Street.* The courtyard was a concrete square, surrounded by a tall fence. As well as a wrought-iron table and two chairs, there were a couple of wooden benches, and in the corner a supersized barbeque. Sarah had been here once, when she'd gone to the station's Christmas drinks. 'Fraternising with the enemy,' one of her co-workers called it.

'We take it in turns,' her boss said. 'Your turn this year. No point pissing off the cops.'

Sarah had gravitated to the corner with a group of community and youth workers. They discussed low funding and the lack of emergency beds, and they whispered to one another about the problems they'd encountered with particular cops, sharing strategies for handling the worst of them, naming the ones to stay away from, the ones to call. Sarah told them that when she was sixteen, she'd wanted to be a cop. It was high on her list of possible careers. 'No way,' one of them said. 'Lucky escape,' another one added. 'So instead you became a lawyer?'

They told each other lame lawyer jokes and laughed. She didn't tell them that her mother said, 'With your brains, being a police officer would be such a waste. You should do law.' Her mother had meant corporate law. She pictured Sarah — a slimmer Sarah, of course — in pencil skirts and fitted jackets, earning *six figures*. But Sarah believed she could make a difference, change things, bring a little justice into the world. 'Hippy nonsense,' her mother said. 'We should never have sent you to that school.'

'That school' was an inner-city government high school. Her mother had planned to send her to a private school — Melbourne Girls Grammar, Camberwell Girls Grammar, or perhaps Methodist Ladies' College. Schools with history and character and reputation. Sarah's brothers went to private schools, but Sarah refused to go. There were fights and arguments, but her father supported her decision: 'If she has a brain on her, it won't matter what school she goes to.' For such a successful and intelligent man, Sarah's father was naïve. Of course, even Sarah knew she would've done better academically if she'd gone to a private school, but she was glad she hadn't. At her high school, she'd had a different sort of education. Of her friends, only Jess came from a white middle-class family, and Jess's parents were artists, living just above the poverty line. They worked part-time in cafés so they could buy art materials to make their 'work': large collaborative installations that involved hours of collecting from tips, hard-rubbish collections, op shops, and markets. At Jess's house, Sarah slept on a mattress that Jess's mother picked up from a roadside hard-rubbish collection. Sarah didn't tell her mother, because she would've demanded to know if the mattress had been fumigated, but Jess's mother *never, ever used chemicals to kill living creatures.* Sue, a refugee from Cambodia, lived in a small housing commission flat, with peeling paint and dripping taps, with one television for the whole family and not enough money to spend on the after-school art lessons for her talented younger sister. Ada's family was Greek — seven people in a small three-bedroom terrace. Ada's father worked on the docks and her mother was a cleaner. They had three children and two widowed grandmothers to look after. The grandmothers grew vegetables in the front garden, cooked big hearty meals, spoke only broken English, and argued with their grandchildren, who refused to speak to them in Greek.

When Ada's younger brother was arrested for stealing a car, his parents panicked. They didn't have the money for a lawyer. Sarah went to her father for advice. He gave her a brochure about legal aid. The legal aid lawyer represented Ada's brother. He was found guilty, but they didn't send him away; they gave him a good-behaviour bond. It didn't save Nick. He was often in trouble — drugs, stealing, assault with a weapon — and ended up going to prison anyway. But the idea of a lawyer giving free help and advice to people like Ada's family was a revelation for Sarah; there were people working to make an unfair world fairer. She was so impressed she decided to become a legal aid lawyer.

Constable Lumina took a final drag on her cigarette. 'Let's go back in,' she said.

'Sure.' Sarah butted out her cigarette and picked up her bag. This case was going to be tough. She'd have to keep her own feelings out of it. Focus on Jo.

Constable Peters came back, followed by Sarah and Constable Lumina. The two women were carrying half-empty mugs. They smelt of nicotine and mint. Constable Peters set up the recorder and turned it on.

'So,' he said, 'tell me what you and Ashleigh did once you left the house.' His voice was softer now. It reminded Jo of Grandpa Tom, of sitting on the back verandah with him when she was little, of him saying, 'Tell me what's wrong.' Grandpa Tom never betrayed her, hadn't told their secrets, not even to Mandy. With him, she'd been safe. Here, they'd take her words and use them against her. What could they do to her? What would be worse than the accident? Than Ash's death? If she knew what they wanted from her, what they wanted her to say, she could say it and then she could go home.

Would it ever be over?

'We drove to Mani's place to pick up Mani and Laura, and then to Willy. We parked the car on the Esplanade and walked to the party.'

Constable Peters asked a series of questions about the party, including the contact details for Rosie's parents.

'I don't remember the number — but they live in Stephen Street.'

'We need the phone number.'

'Okay, I have it somewhere ...' Jo took her phone out of her pocket and turned it on. There were several messages from Ash. How was that possible? Was Ash alive? Was this all a mistake? The phone slipped from her hands and hit the floor.

'Are you okay?' Sarah asked.

Jo's hands were shaking as she picked up the phone. Did Ash send the messages before the accident? From the party?

'Jo, do you have the number?'

'Yes, sorry.'

She ignored the messages, opened up her contacts, and read out the phone number. She needed to focus, to keep a clear head. The messages would have to wait. She turned the phone off before she put it back on the table.

'Did you keep drinking?' Constable Peters asked. With each question, Sarah and Constable Lumina paused their note-taking, resuming only as Jo began to answer.

'Yes.'

'What else did you do?'

'We talked. We danced. We laughed.' She stared at the phone on the table. When did Ash send the messages? 'We always laughed together.'

It was true. They made each other laugh. Ash singing 'Bart the General' from *The Simpsons* in their English class: *In English class I did the best. Because I cheated on the test.* Jo telling Ash about Mandy's outrage at the *Australian Idol* auditions. Ash and Jo dressing up as Fred Astaire and Ginger Rogers for a dance party and no one knowing who they were. And having to dance every time someone asked, and giggling so much that Jo had to run to the toilet, and then having to call Ash to help her out of Fred's pants, because they were so big that to keep them from falling Ash had used half a dozen safety pins that in her haste Jo couldn't locate. She remembered laughing so hard that they were crying. How could she have doubted their friendship?

'You were good friends?'

'She's my best friend. We met at school —' She stopped. Ash wasn't her best friend anymore. Ash was dead. This was history. Constable Lumina passed her the box of tissues that had been sitting on the window ledge. This was the point when a best friend would be crying, but she wasn't crying.

Over the years, she'd shed so many tears over Ash: when Mandy wouldn't let her go and play with Ash, when Rae came to pick Ash up early, when they fought and 'broke up'. That afternoon, after reading Ash's journal, after Ash ended her phone call with Kevin, Jo held her tears back for hours. When Ash left to go and get her clothes for the party, Jo went to her room and cried. Torturing herself with various end-of-friendship scenarios, running them in a loop until they gained so much momentum they spun on their own.

But now there were no tears. She was wounded, damaged, ashamed, alone, guilty, sad … A string of words, but they weren't how she felt. She didn't feel like herself. She'd heard people say that before, *I don't feel like myself,* but what did it mean? She longed to curl up into a tight ball, tighter and tighter. To shrink. To be invisible. To be able to run away. But where could she go? There was nowhere to go, not now. Wherever she went, Ash was dead. And she would never be herself again.

'What time did you leave?'

'I'm not sure what time it was. Ash wanted to leave.'

'You didn't want to go?'

'Not really. Well, kind of, but we were talking and I wanted to talk.'

'But she didn't?' Constable Lumina asked. 'Were you fighting?'

Sarah put her pen down.

'Friends have problems sometimes, they have fights sometimes. Were you fighting that night?' Constable Lumina asked again.

Jo wanted to say, 'Ask Ash. Ask Ash, please ask Ash.'

'We were singing in the car,' she said.

'Laura and Mani said that you and Ash were arguing.'

Laura and Mani. Jo kept forgetting that they were in the car too.

'You were fighting, Jo?' Mandy asked, her interruption surprising everyone in the room.

'Mrs Neilson, please don't ask questions during the interview,' Constable Lumina said.

'Sorry, I just … I didn't know.'

'We were singing,' Jo said. Laura and Mani, singing and giggling, and rolling down their windows, and singing to the river, to the road, to the bridge. She'd been singing too. But not Ash.

Finally Constable Peters asked, 'You'd been drinking at the party but you didn't think about getting a taxi or ringing someone to pick you up?'

'I felt okay. We didn't have money for a taxi. I don't know … we got in the car.'

'Did the other girls tell you not to drive? Did they ask you if you were okay to drive?'

Sarah dropped her pen on the table. 'I think we need to have another break.'

Constable Peters sighed and turned the recorder off again.

When the two cops left the room for the second time, Sarah stood up. Jo noticed that the skirt she was wearing was in fact a pair of pants, long black pants with wide legs. Under the pants were red suede boots. Sarah's feet were tiny, her body tethered on such a tentative base she reminded Jo of a stilt walker, though it would be impossible, she imagined, for someone Sarah's size to walk on stilts.

'You have to be remorseful,' Sarah commanded, and Jo felt like a child who had done something wrong and was now being asked to apologise.

Say you are sorry.

'I *am* sorry. I didn't mean to have an accident. I didn't mean to hurt Ash …'

'I know,' Sarah said. 'I know, but you need to make sure they know too. And you need to face what happened. You caused an accident that resulted in Ashleigh's death. These accidents happen too often. So many families ruined. Everyone knows someone who's lost a sibling or a child or a friend in an accident like this one. There's no sympathy for people who drive when they're drunk — even Constable Lumina lost her brother in an accident like yours. There's lots of anger in the community. The police, the courts, the media. Everyone wants drunk drivers punished, they want to stop it. You're not some drag-racing adolescent boy, but you need to show you know that what you did was wrong, really wrong, or they'll lock you up and throw away the key.' Sarah was now bending over the table. As she inched closer, Jo leaned back. 'Do you understand?'

'Yes,' Jo said. 'I understand.' But she didn't care. She hoped they'd lock her up and throw away the key.

While Sarah went to call the police back to finish the interview, Jo picked up her phone and held it in her hand. As she turned her phone on to look at the messages, Constable Peters walked in the door and she had to turn it off again.

Constable Peters resumed the interview with questions about the accident itself.

'I can't remember what happened,' Jo said. 'The car started to skid. I remember thinking, *don't put on the brake.* The mechanic who serviced the car said that because the car didn't have power steering, braking too fast would make it skid. But it was like, my foot, I couldn't control my foot, and I slammed on the brake, but the car … I lost control of the car. I heard screaming. But I don't know who was screaming. And then nothing. I don't remember anything after that until someone, a woman, was standing next to me and telling me to open my eyes. I didn't want to open my eyes. And someone speaking, someone saying, "She's dead." I didn't know if they were talking about me, if I was dead …' Jo stopped; it was as if she'd been running and hit a wall. And it was as if she were back in the car, with her eyes closed. And it was as if the paramedic were shouting in her ear to wake up. Sweat dripped from her temples, slipping down the sides of her face.

If only she hadn't woken up, if only she hadn't kept her eyes shut. If only she'd refused to leave the car. Was it possible to stop time? To go back. Could she trade her life for Ash's life?

When the interview ended, they charged Jo with culpable driving. She was surprised that they let her go home.

'You're on bail,' Sarah said as they were leaving the police station. 'There are conditions. You can't leave the state. If you move house, you have to notify the police. No driving — your licence is suspended. And no drinking, of course.'

Chapter 12

There were four messages on Jo's phone from Ash. All of them sent after the accident.

You should be dead.

You're a killer.

You killed Ashleigh. You killed her.

Murderer, scum of the earth, it should have been you who died.

Was Ash's mother or her father sending those messages? Jo couldn't imagine it. Maybe Jane? *Feral Jane,* Ash often teased her sister because she wore tight jeans with rips in the knees, and men's checked shirts, and went everywhere on her skateboard, her hair flying. They fought a lot, the two sisters. Jane rummaged in Ash's room when she wasn't home. She pinched Ash's make-up without asking. Jane and her friends skated up and down the driveway. Loud rumbling and thumping as the skateboards rolled over or crashed into the obstacles Jane and her friends set up to jump over, to slide off, to mount with their boards. 'It's torture,' Ash complained. She screamed at them, and if they didn't stop she chased them with the hose on full spray. The sisters fought and made up and Ash would promise to take Jane out — to the movies or shopping — and forget and make other plans and they'd fight again. Sometimes when they were younger, Jane would say to Jo, 'I wish I was *your* sister.' As loud as she could to annoy Ash.

Jo deleted the text messages.

There were other messages. From Laura: *I hope you are okay. I can't believe that Ash is gone. I wanted to come and see you but my parents said no. Stay strong Jo. xx*

From Mani: *I'm so sad and so angry.*

Kevin wrote, *Jo, are you okay? Call me. Let's talk.*

'Kevin is too laidback,' Ash had complained recently. When Jo asked what she meant, Ash said, 'He's a softy, doesn't stand up for himself. He wants to do film or photography, be an artist, but his parents convinced him to do architecture. I told him, *If you want to make films, make films.*'

When the three of them went out together, Jo was jealous. All the kissing and touching between Ash and Kevin, and Ash forgetting she was there. It pissed Jo off. But now she wished desperately that Ash had invited him last night. If Kevin had come to the party, Ash would be alive.

From Bec, her partner for the History presentation: *So sorry to hear about Ashleigh. Worried about you. Do you feel like a visit from a friend?*

Jo began texting back, *Ash was my friend.* But she deleted the message and began again: *I killed my friend.* And then deleted that too. She switched the phone off and buried it under her socks and tights in the bottom drawer of her dresser. She shut down the computer and disconnected the power. She didn't want to look, she didn't want to read Ash's Facebook page or hers; she didn't want to know. She didn't want to talk to anyone. She didn't want to read the accusations or the sympathies, the tributes to Ash.

There would be no more friends. She couldn't be trusted with a friend.

'We are in limbo,' Mary said. She was sitting at the table, a cup of tea in hand. The pot of chicken soup she'd spent the morning making remained untouched on the stove. The aroma of it wafted through the house, but it hadn't enticed Jo out of her room.

'I don't know anything about limbo. This feels like hell to me,' Mandy said, as she leaned against the kitchen bench. Ever since the police had knocked on her door the morning of the accident, she'd been resisting the temptation to pack up everything, to leave the house and Jo and all of the sadness and not come back.

'Stupid, stupid girls,' Mary lamented into her cup of tea.

Mandy didn't respond. She wished she was some other woman in some other life. A single woman, childless and disconnected, not related to anyone. A woman without a daughter. What kind of a mother made those kinds of wishes? What kind of mother was too weak to stop her drunk daughter from driving? Too weak to even try?

'I can't go anywhere now,' Mary continued. 'This morning at the supermarket, everyone was looking at me and whispering. Some people feed on this stuff, and now the gossips will be out, and they'll be looking at us and blaming us.'

Mary's wrinkled face, caked with foundation, showed no physical evidence of the impact of the accident or its aftermath. That morning, as well as making soup, she'd put on a full face of make-up, soft pink lipstick, eyeliner. She'd dressed for going out, in her green woollen jumper and brown jersey pants, and put on the green topaz earrings her grandfather had bought her when she turned twenty-one. Last year, Mary had found the earrings after years of thinking they were lost. When she wore them, she often touched them as she talked, rubbing the topaz as if it were a good-luck charm. Mary had been to church that morning, and to the supermarket. Most of her life was spent within a couple of blocks of the Yarraville shopping centre; she'd lived in the same house since she was married, more than forty years. Mary was right: everyone already knew about Jo's accident. Mandy tried to control the sudden urge to grab her ex-mother-in-law by the shoulders, drag her out of the chair and into the street, and tell her not to come back again.

'It's best if we stay close to home and don't go out too much,' Mary said. 'At least for a few days. Especially Jo. I rang David and told him about the accident. He said he'd phone and talk to Jo. You should send her away for a while. She could go and stay in Adelaide with her father. It'll be hard for her now, around here.'

'Well, let's wait and see if he rings; nothing yet.' Mandy couldn't imagine David inviting Jo to hide out in Adelaide.

'He probably thinks she isn't up to talking yet,' Mary said. 'I'm sure he'll call.'

'We have to find a way through this, Jo and I,' Mandy said. 'I have to find a way to steer myself and Jo through this. It's up to me. It's always up to me.'

Usually she was a chatty mother, talking to Jo even when Jo was being surly and dismissive, but now she couldn't bear to be in the same room as her daughter. All those hours in the police interview, she was ashamed. She was useless to Jo. To comfort or reassure Jo was impossible and wrong. It was wrong, wasn't it?

'Mandy, that's not true. I'm here to help, and David too. Poor David, it was a big shock for him.'

Poor David, Mandy thought. Poor fucking David, living in another state with his clever wife and his two sons, not even offering to come and see Jo, not offering anything. Relaxing back on his couch in Adelaide, he could pretend it was happening to someone else's daughter. He didn't have to worry about dealing with this shit. 'I know you want to help, Mary, I know.'

Outside in the backyard, the strong wind had transformed the ancient Hills hoist into a spinning wheel. It creaked, whirling erratically, like the wheels at local fundraisers run by stocky, middle-aged Rotary men.

'It's about luck — it was bad luck. Every night young people like Jo and Ashleigh are careless and stupid, and most of them get away with it. But Jo and Ashleigh didn't get away with it. They should've known better. Should've …' Mandy began to cry. 'I can't stop crying, even though I know it's useless. My life — as if it'd been a piece of cake up to now — is a mess. I'd hoped for another kind of life for Jo.'

'It'll get better,' Mary said. 'People'll forget. Life'll go back to normal.'

'For fuck's sake, Mary,' Mandy yelled.

'Mandy, please. I didn't mean —'

'Ashleigh is dead. She was eighteen years old. A child. Jo loved her. *I* loved her … Her parents have lost a daughter, and Jo is responsible.' Mandy shook her head. 'It's never going to be normal again, for any of us. I can't see any possible recovery from this.' She sat back in the chair and put her head down on the table. Would there ever be a normal again? Her daughter was alive, but less than five minutes away Rae was making preparations to bury Ashleigh. Life wouldn't go back to normal, not for her and certainly not for Jo.

Mandy was exhausted, spent. How could she go to work after this? How could she walk through Yarraville to Coles and stand behind the deli counter while the locals, people she'd known for years, came in and bought their olives, their bacon and cheese, and chatted about the weather, school, the council, the new development, while she measured and sliced? But she needed to work. They had no savings. They lived week to week, and if she didn't work they wouldn't be able to pay their bills. She'd have to ask for a transfer, to another supermarket in another suburb, somewhere where she'd be anonymous, where she wouldn't be a constant reminder to Ashleigh's family and friends that she was Jo's mother, and that Jo was responsible for Ashleigh's death.

'Mandy. Mandy.' Mary was calling her gently. 'Are you —'

'Am I what?'

'I thought you were off somewhere.'

'I wish.'

'What are we going to do?'

'What can we do? We are going to sit and wait. Wait until the police and the lawyers do whatever it is that they do. Like you said, limbo.'

'They won't send her to prison. Not for an accident.'

'She'll go to prison, Mary.'

'We can't let that happen.' It was a plea.

'There's nothing we can do to stop it.'

Mary could be hurtful and thoughtless. She blamed Mandy for getting pregnant young; she blamed Mandy when David moved to Adelaide. But Mary and Jack had supported Mandy with Jo. They babysat and lent her money, and in return all they asked was to be included in Jo's life. And so Mandy included them. It had been more difficult since Jack died, but Mary loved Jo and Jo loved her grandmother. Mandy hoped that their love would survive and be strong enough to help them deal with the grief and the guilt, with the bloody nightmare they were trapped in.

Chapter 13

Sarah weighed her piece of chicken and put on the steamer. What she craved was a vindaloo curry, saffron rice, a garlic naan, and lots of hot mango pickle from the Curry Vault in Bank Place. And a glass or two of merlot, on the balcony.

The pale chicken breast was bland. She sprinkled sea salt and ground pepper on it, along with a squeeze of lemon, and served it on a plate with broccoli, mushrooms, and carrots. Protein and three vegetables, Weight Watchers–style. No potatoes. *Potatoes aren't a vegetable.* Fidelity to this diet would be rewarded. If she *shed* a kilo a week, over the next three months she would've *shed* twelve kilos, which wasn't enough but would inch her closer to her goal weight. If she lost the weight, she could wear the clothes she bought last time she went on a diet, which were now shoved to the back of her wardrobe: expensive bootleg jeans that even then required lying down on the bed and sucking in stomach muscles to get the zipper up; a silk designer dress from a boutique in Toorak Road that the shop assistant said was 'so fashion forward' but that she'd only worn once. If she lost the weight she'd be normal, and her mother might finally see beyond her body. If she lost the weight, she could sit comfortably on the train, on aeroplanes — if she ever managed to save enough to go travelling again.

She spread the contents of the Joanne Neilson file on the table. She was meant to give eating her full attention. No reading at the dinner table. *Mindful eating,* they called it in the diet books. This *mindful eating*

162

somehow, magically, translated into weight loss. But if she concentrated on eating her tasteless dinner, she'd get depressed. When she was depressed she ate more, and thought more about weight and being fat — it was such a waste of time. If she added up all the minutes and hours and days over her thirty-four years that she'd spent worrying about her weight, it'd add up to half her life. This is how they kept women in their place: imagine what women could achieve, what she might've achieved, if she didn't spend so much time hating and obsessing over her body and trying to transform it to match some unrealistic ideal.

She read through Jo's statement. Jo was driving. She was drunk. It was Jo's attitude that concerned Sarah. During the interview, Jo was too controlled. There was no visible sign of remorse or contrition. She didn't cry, not even when the questions focused on her relationship with the dead girl, Ashleigh. This worried Sarah, because people were always judging women and making judgements about them.

The evidence from the other two girls — Mani and Laura — was damning. They'd made an effort to be fair: 'She's a good driver,' Mani had said. 'I felt safe with her. Maybe there was something on the road, oil or something.' But in the end, their answers to the police questions said it all: Was she drunk? Yes. Was she driving too fast? Yes. Was she arguing with Ashleigh? Yes. Did anyone tell her to slow down? Yes. Did she slow down? No.

Sarah mapped the preparation needed for the case: identifying people to interview and those willing to give references and testimonials. Her aim was to uncover Jo's story. If there were some extenuating circumstances, something in Jo's background — poverty, abuse, or illness — that would explain, if not justify, her drinking, Sarah would track it down. She hoped that there was a long line of respectable people who were prepared to speak on Jo's behalf. To say she was polite and friendly, that she helped little old ladies cross the street, that she had a bright future.

It was the storytelling part of the law that fascinated Sarah. The challenge of finding a way of turning the 'accused' into a person, someone real and vulnerable; someone that the judge (and jury, if there was a jury) would warm to and empathise with. There was a way of presenting the evidence, the arguments, that gave the court a sense of the person beyond the crime, before the crime. Storytelling was what made the difference between a good barrister and a mediocre one. The prosecution would produce victim impact statements from the dead girl's parents and her sister, the grandparents, the aunts and uncles and friends. These would be sad accounts. Narratives that would fill the courtroom with grief and with anger, that would make no sentence seem long enough.

Of course, some clients lied. When Sarah was a child, her mother would say, 'Don't bother, Sarah, I can tell when you're lying to me.' It wasn't a bluff — no matter how elaborate or straightforward, no matter what voice or tone Sarah used, her mother picked the lies. Sarah had inherited the gift, but there were times when she wished she hadn't. Greg, one of her clients, a young guy, robbed several stores and bashed a teenage girl who was working at the petrol station in order to save enough money to go to Bali with her girlfriends at the end of the year. The girl spent six months lying in a coma in a hospital. At the hearing, the doctors said that even if she lived, she would be paralysed, and might not be able to read or write. 'She loved to travel,' her mother told the court. 'There's a big map of the world on her wall. With pins marking the places she's planning to visit. Should I pull it down before she comes home?' In court, Greg cried; he apologised; he was remorseful. Sarah knew he was lying. There was no evidence in the stories other people told about him that he had any redeeming qualities. It made mounting a defence difficult. She had the skills and the training to argue on his behalf, to plead for the minimum sentence, but she hoped he'd get the maximum and no one would let him out again. He had a 'good' story: a tough life. His parents were addicts, rarely conscious enough to bring up a child. They tried but failed to look after him. Society owed him, but she knew that he'd re-offend.

Jo wasn't Greg. Jo wouldn't go out and deliberately hurt someone. She wasn't evil or malicious. But Sarah knew there wouldn't be many people lining up to tell her the sorts of stories that would convince the judge to keep Jo's sentence to a minimum. Jo was an ordinary young woman from a working-class family. She had been irresponsible, negligent, thoughtless; she'd driven while she was drunk and had a fatal accident. Luck, good and bad, was responsible for so much, but the law wasn't interested in arguments about luck. If Jo had been stopped by the cops that night, before the accident, she might've ended up with a fine and lost her licence, she might've been charged and ended up on probation. The difference was what — a spill of oil on the road? The difference was a life. Ashleigh's life.

Sarah read her notes on Jo's police interview again. 'Best friends,' Jo had said, 'since Year 7.' Was there a story in that? Sarah didn't have a best friend. People drifted in and out of her life, rarely staying long enough for any real intimacy to develop. She saw some of her university classmates a couple of times a year. Her ex-girlfriend, Laine, was living in New York. If they were both in the same city, they might've continued to see each other, but it was clear now that Laine didn't intend on coming back, and the emails and Skype calls were becoming less and less frequent. Occasionally Sarah went to Friday-night drinks with her colleagues, but she could hardly call them friends. Of course, there had been Ada; Ada was the closest Sarah had come to having a best friend.

What made Jo the kind of person Ashleigh would have as a best friend? What made Jo the kind of person that would have a best friend? What was Jo's story? And what if Jo didn't have a story? Were some people only ever secondary characters in other people's narratives? If Jo didn't have a story, how would Sarah give the judge insight into her life, create empathy?

When she was working on Greg's case, she'd been confident that the right story, told effectively, could shift the court — not just the jury, but the judge too. There had to be evidence and precedence, sure. But stories had power.

That was the danger of a good story: you could elicit pity and empathy for even the worst sociopath — for his rotten childhood, for the abuse and the bullying — and if it impacted on the verdict, on the sentencing, then a killer could be set free to go on killing. People often said, 'Just tell the truth,' as if there was a truth and it could be told by one person, as if it could be contained in one story. Sarah believed telling good stories, the ones people listened to and were swayed by, was a responsibility. It worried her that some people did not take it seriously enough.

———

From the large window over the sink, the sunlight, bright and glaring, beamed into Mandy's kitchen and exposed its flaws. The white gas stove, wedged into a brick alcove that had once housed a wood-fired oven, was scarred black with scratches and scrapes. The boarded-up chimney had cracks in its brickwork and a black-soot coating that someone had unsuccessfully tried to cover over with dark-blue paint. The sink under the window was stained and dented, and the red formica table, with its four matching chairs, was just *old*. The chairs needed reupholstering, their vinyl seats faded to a dull pink. On the wall opposite the stove hung an old print of a basket overflowing with bread. Underneath it, on the bench, there was a chipped crystal bowl with some oranges and apples. Even though everything was spotless, the room looked weary and worn out.

'I only have instant coffee,' Mandy said to Sarah. 'Not much of a coffee drinker. Jo says no one drinks instant anymore.'

'It's fine,' Sarah said. 'My mother's a coffee nazi, but I drink anything and everything.'

The latte set to which Sarah's mother and most of the legal fraternity belonged thought drinking instant coffee was sacrilegious. Sarah's mother gave long lectures to anyone who would listen on the dangerous chemicals used in the process of making instant coffee. She rarely drank coffee and bought only organic blends. For Sarah, instant might not be coffee, not in the same way that espresso was coffee, but she drank it with milk and sugar, in her clients' kitchens, in weatherboard houses in the western suburbs of Melbourne. The coffee, served in big thick mugs around which she wrapped her hands, opened up the way into difficult conversations.

'How long have you lived here?' Sarah asked.

'All my life, except for a couple of years when Jo was a baby. My mother was born in this house.'

'Guess you would've seen a lot of changes,' Sarah said.

'My father used to say, "Yarraville's getting too big for its boots," and the changes were only starting when he died. If he was alive now, he'd hate it. He was a boilermaker, worked in the local foundry. When I was a kid all our neighbours were workers — factory workers, rail workers, wharfies, or labourers. A couple were tradies. A few worked in shops. I remember the Kokinos family, who owned the fish and chip shop. Mrs Kokinos's arms were covered in burn scars from the splattering hot oil, and the kids, especially my friend Helen, were always falling behind at school because they worked in the shop most nights.'

'Very different now,' Sarah agreed.

'A lot of those people have left. The rents are too high, and you get sick of being looked down on. Some people can't hide their contempt. We're bogans, losers, trash. It's tough on our kids — they go to school with kids whose families can go overseas twice a year and buy all the new gadgets before they're even in the shops.'

'I'm surprised the wealthier families send their kids to the public schools,' Sarah said.

'Most of them bus their children to private schools in Werribee or Geelong or South Yarra because the local schools aren't good enough. But the lefties, like Ashleigh's parents, who are so *committed* to public education that they send their children to the local high school, take over the school councils and expect everyone else to toe the line. Jo doesn't want to be like me. She wants to be like them.' Mandy sighed. 'I can't blame her. I want her to be ... to have a better life.'

When Sarah was growing up, she knew that there were people in her street who were poor and she knew her mother was a snob who avoided some people. But she hadn't thought about how much those poorer neighbours might have resented her and her family.

They continued talking about the social problems arising from gentrification while Mandy set out the mugs, put the milk, full fat, and the sugar, white, on the table, and leant against the bench, waiting for the kettle to boil.

The previous day at the police interview Sarah had not had a chance to pay much attention to Mandy. Now she noticed how much Mandy looked like Ada: the same shoulder-length straight brown hair, with a fringe that covered her eyebrows. It was the sort of shapeless haircut that

Sarah's hairdresser would've despised, but Sarah couldn't imagine Mandy sitting in Christina's chair for three hours at a time and paying $200 for the privilege. Like Ada, Mandy was a plain dresser. Like Ada, she was average — average height, average build. Mandy probably didn't belong to a gym or go on diets. But Mandy was older than Ada — her hair was threaded with grey streaks, and the first fine wrinkles were developing around her eyes. Ada wasn't going to get old.

'Where is Jo?' Sarah asked as Mandy placed the mugs of coffee on the table and sat down opposite Sarah.

'In her room. Just lies in the dark. She's come out to eat a couple of times when I've called her. Not that she eats much.'

'How are you going?' Sarah asked.

'I'm struggling. I'm worried about Jo, about money.' Mandy's voice quavered. 'Sorry, it's not what you came to talk about.'

'Mandy, it's a tough thing you're going through,' Sarah said, realising that Mandy was working hard at being stoic and composed. 'You're grieving for Ashleigh and for the life you imagined for Jo. The legal system is slow, and it may take months before the hearing. It leaves everyone hanging. Most people need some support. I can organise a counsellor or a social worker.'

'Thanks, Sarah, but I'm not much of a believer in counselling. Life is tough, and paying someone to listen to you talk about it isn't going to make it any easier. But you came to ask me some questions?'

Sarah opened her notebook and wrote the date on top of a new page. 'I'd like to know more about Jo.'

'What kind of things?' Mandy asked.

'Your relationship, her childhood, her relationship with Ashleigh. I need to get more sense of who she is.'

Mandy told Sarah about falling pregnant at seventeen, about her short-lived relationship with Jo's father, David, and about the decision to move back into the family home as a twenty-year-old single mother. 'Dad was a great help, and David's parents too. Living here with Dad made it easier for me to work — he loved Jo and they got on well. In those days, she thought I was the best mum in the world,' Mandy said, and shook her head. 'Not anymore. I was a young mum, I thought it'd always be like that … For years and years, when she saw me standing outside the classroom door with the other mothers at the end of the school day, she'd race out and I'd scoop her into my arms; she was so happy to see me.'

'And then she changed?'

Mandy shrugged. 'I guess it's just, she grew up. Became a teenager, started to see that there were other ways of living, other kinds of mothers.'

Sarah was relieved she didn't need to do much prodding to get Mandy to talk. Mandy seemed to be in a reflective mood, scouring through the past as if they were on an archaeological dig, on the brink of a major discovery, as if by unearthing the moment when her relationship with Jo changed — as if it were possible to reduce it to one moment — she'd have a chance to make things right, to undo the accident, Ashleigh's death, and the bleak future that lay ahead for Jo.

'In hindsight I can see there were things that happened in Jo's childhood that I should've … I tried to deal with them as best I could. I didn't think long term. I didn't think, *This might affect her forever.* I didn't know what a mother was supposed to do.' Mandy's voice was thin and tight.

'It's like that for every parent,' Sarah said.

'I'd no idea what I was supposed to do, especially after my father died. Sometimes I resented Jo so much … At the end of her primary school, I sent her to stay with her father for two weeks. He had two more children and I thought it was important for her to get to know her brothers. And to be honest, I wanted a break,' Mandy confessed.

'That's understandable,' Sarah said.

Mandy told Sarah how that summer, she'd had a relationship with Theo, the manager of the storeroom at the supermarket, who was newly separated from his wife. He was the first man she'd met in years that she wanted to spend time with and he'd invited her to go away with him for two weeks. It didn't last long; in the end he'd gone back to his wife.

'Jo and I had never been apart for more than a couple of nights before that. I'd even gone as a volunteer on most of her school camps. And both she and David were keen. It was unusual for David, but he sent the money for her ticket. When she came back, she'd lost weight. She was a chubby kid — not fat, just not skinny ...' Mandy hesitated. 'I'm sorry. Do you mind me telling you this?'

'No, I don't mind,' Sarah said. People were awkward saying the word *fat* when Sarah was around. As if the mere mention of the word would be offensive. And in a way they were right. *Fat, obese, chubby, overweight* — even when the speaker wasn't talking about her, the words slapped Sarah right back into her fat body, to the edges of the chair cutting into her thighs, the tight cling of her trouser waistband, the clammy stickiness of flesh rubbing against flesh between her thighs.

'Anyway, she said she was on a diet. Her father had put her on a diet. I was furious. She was too young for diets. She didn't need to be on a diet. I told her she was perfect the way she was, you know, said all the right things.'

'Of course,' Sarah said.

'It turned out that her father and his wife had told her that she was fat. Apparently they're super fit, gym junkies. I didn't know. David played some football when he was at school, but most of the time he was in trouble with the coach for not turning up to training. Or turning up late and drunk. I had a big fight with David on the phone, but I didn't find out exactly what happened. Later, all this stuff came out about how she didn't have many friends and it was because she was fat. And that the reason she didn't do well at school was because she was fat. And the reason her father didn't want to see her was because she was fat.'

'So they'd made her feel like her weight was a problem and she had to do something about it?' Sarah asked.

'Yes, and I was to blame. She'd been a normal eater, but she stopped eating properly. I worried about anorexia and bulimia and hassled her about eating and we had some big fights. She didn't become anorexic. She lost more weight over that summer and she didn't put it back on. Since then she's controlled her eating. She pecks at the food on her plate, leaves meals unfinished. When she's done, she pushes the plate away, as if the remaining food might be toxic.'

If only, Sarah thought. Of all the diets she'd been on, for more than twenty years now — since her mother put her on her first diet when she was fourteen — if anything her love of food had intensified. She dreamed about food. She planned what she was going to eat days in advance, thinking about treats and food-related outings. *Eat to live, don't live to eat.* Another of her mother's annoying sayings. Sarah made a few notes, but she doubted that she could make much of a story out of an obnoxious father and a chubby childhood.

Mandy's hands were wrapped around the Bulldogs mug. She continued, 'Not long after that, in Year 7 or 8, their teacher invited some of the kids' mothers to come and talk about their careers. Ash's mother was one of them. Rae talked about being a school principal. They invited a lawyer, a woman who worked for Greenpeace, a journalist — professional women. Jo asked me if I'd talk to her class about working in the supermarket. I didn't think, just said yes. But Mrs Kintle said they had enough speakers. One of the other girls told Jo, "They only want educated women with important jobs. They don't want us to work in supermarkets." I should've known. I should've warned her and saved her the embarrassment. Motherhood is a litany of mistakes.' There was a slight crack in Mandy's voice. But she didn't cry. Instead she put down her mug, stood up, and poured herself a glass of water. 'Water?' she asked Sarah.

Sarah shook her head.

Mandy drank slowly and sat back down. 'It's that moment you realise the child who adored you, the child you adore, has turned into someone else. Your worst critic. She banned me from school pick-ups. Not long after that, we fought about something minor and she yelled, "I hate you. I wish you weren't my mother." It was the first time Jo said that to me. We didn't speak for days. And when we did speak again, everything had changed.'

Sarah never dared say those things to her mother, though she'd wanted to many times. Some nights, especially in her early adolescence, she'd shut herself in the bedroom, Talking Heads or AC/DC up loud, and instead of singing the lyrics, chanted, *I hate you, I hate you*, like a mantra.

'It was hard,' Mandy continued. 'I didn't have anyone else. I know it happens to all mothers, but it's bloody hard. From then on, everything I did was wrong: my clothes, my friends, my teeth … She came home one day insisting I get my teeth fixed — apparently the dental care nurse at school had said, "Some people don't have their priorities right and dental care is like putting money in the bank." As if we had money in the bank, as if we could afford to spend thousands of dollars we didn't have on my teeth. Of course, in Ash's family everyone had beautiful white teeth. She kept telling me that she didn't want to be like me. That was fine, I wanted her to have a better life … We fought about everything. She wanted to buy clothes we couldn't afford, she wanted to go out late, she didn't do her homework. Her schoolwork suffered and there were complaints from the teachers and poor reports. It was so tiring, so exhausting. After a while I gave up.'

Mandy rose from the table and wandered over to a wooden sideboard that took up one wall of the kitchen. From the top drawer, she took out a photo album. As Mandy brought over the spiral-bound album, with a horse galloping through a meadow on the cover, Sarah stifled a sigh. She had scheduled an hour to interview Mandy, but she knew from experience that once the mother took out the photo album, the present world and its demands became meaningless. It was the past that mattered. It was there that stories dwelled, and the only way to get a story was to allow people to tell it. This meant abandoning her other commitments so she could give herself over to the storyteller. It meant trusting that Mandy had a story to tell. Sarah checked her phone.

'Do you have to go?'

'It's fine. I have another meeting but I'll reschedule,' Sarah said, typing a message to her boss.

'Everyone has their photos on computers now, but I like looking at the albums,' Mandy said.

Sarah nodded. The album was old, the edges a nicotine yellow. The plastic acetate sheets had lost most of their stickiness. Some of the photos had shifted out of their place, covering other photos, leaving empty spaces. Sarah's mother's photos were in thick, elegant albums — archive quality — and now of course backed up on CDs. 'Precious memories,' she called them.

'The problem with photos on computers is no one looks at them anymore. We snap at everything and then store the images away,' Sarah said.

The photos in the first few pages were of the baby Jo and a young Mandy. There was one photograph of a young man with shoulder-length blond hair, standing next to the bed as Mandy held the baby. They were both smiling.

'Jo is older now than I was when I had her, and I can't imagine how she'd look after a baby,' Mandy said, lifting the acetate sheet to adjust the photograph. 'I had a perm before Jo was born. Mary, David's mother, insisted it was dangerous to have a perm while you were pregnant. She was furious. But I did it anyway, to spite her I think. I hated it. I looked like one of those scary clowns that make children cry.'

'Jo's father?' Sarah asked, pointing to the photo.

'Yes.'

'Is he still in Adelaide?'

'Yes. With his wife and sons.'

'Will he come down to Melbourne to see Jo? I'd like to talk to him too.'

'He won't come. Not sure why you'd want to talk to him, but it might have to be by phone.'

'When did you separate?' Sarah asked as she wrote in her notebook.

'We weren't married, we were *living in sin* … Does anyone say that anymore? My mother died when I was fifteen and I went off the rails, I didn't know what to do with myself. David was a distraction. We were young and infatuated, *in lust*. Then I was pregnant, and we were both in school. His parents hit the roof, but my dad helped David get an apprenticeship with the local electrician. I left school. Suddenly we were parents. We had no money and a baby. We lived in a one-bedroom flat in Braybrook, on Ashley Street, surrounded by factories and warehouses, not many neighbours. I felt so isolated. It's amazing that it lasted as long as it did.'

'It must've been hard on your own with a little baby.'

'It was easier after we split up. He gave us some money — not much, apprentice wages were hardly enough for one person to live on. His parents helped out. Dad helped out. And there wasn't the fighting.'

'So you're on good terms?'

Mandy grimaced. 'I wouldn't say good terms. He doesn't want to have any involvement in Jo's life — he pays child support and occasionally he sends her money, pays her off. His father left Jo that bloody car and money for driving lessons. That's how she got her licence.'

The doorbell rang. Mandy looked up and hesitated.

'Should you get that?' Sarah asked.

'Sorry. I don't know who that could be,' Mandy said as she stood.

There'd been a couple of abusive phone calls since the accident. No one had come to the house, but still Mandy felt nervous. Slowly, she made her way down the hall. At the door she waited for several seconds before she opened it.

'Rae,' Mandy said, shocked to see Ashleigh's mother standing on her doorstep. Rae flinched at the sound of her name.

Mandy could see the visceral impact of the grief on Rae. Her eyes were red and swollen, her face pale, her hair uncombed. She looked fragile and adrift; half woman, half ghost.

'I'm so sorry, Rae, so sorry about Ashleigh —'

'Stop,' Rae interrupted. Her voice was brittle. 'Please stop. Please don't say my daughter's name.'

Mandy held her breath. She waited in silence for Rae to continue, but she didn't say anything, so finally she asked, 'Do you want to come in?'

Rae shook her head. 'No, no, I can't, I don't … I don't want to be anywhere near you or your daughter.' She was wearing pyjamas bottoms and a thick old cardigan that Mandy recognised as Ashleigh's. She felt the urge to reach out and touch it. To stop herself, she pulled her arms back behind her and interlaced her fingers. Rae pulled the cardigan tight around her waist and rocked back and forth, as if she were balancing on a narrow beam. She shivered, and Mandy saw the goosebumps, rising like tiny bubbles, on the skin of her neck. The weight of Rae's grief was an impending tempest; Mandy felt the weakness in her knees, the ache in her belly. She could hear her heart thumping. She slid back and leant against the door frame.

But the tempest didn't come. Instead, Rae began to cry, the tears streaming silently down her checks, rivers of sorrow that she wiped with the sleeves of her cardigan. 'Your daughter … your daughter is alive and my beautiful daughter is … my daughter is dead,' she said.

'I'm sorry, Rae.' Mandy was trembling; her hands were shaking. Behind her she heard the scrape of a chair being pushed away from the table, followed by footsteps coming up the hall. But Sarah didn't come to the door.

'Yes. Everyone's sorry. So sorry. What use is sorry to me?' Rae's voice was barely audible, as if her throat were being strangled, as if she'd run out of air.

'It's a tragedy. Ashleigh —'

'Don't say her name. Don't you *dare* say her name.'

'Please, Rae. I loved her. We, you and me, we looked after each other's daughters, we watched them grow up together …' An image came of the two girls at thirteen, racing down the path and into the house. Tossing their schoolbags on the ground, Jo calling out to her, 'Hey, Mum, we learnt the Nutbush today, I told Ash you have the song on tape.' They had put the tape on and danced around the lounge room and Mandy joined them, and Mandy watched them dancing and laughing and filling up the room with their energy, their happiness. She wanted to share that memory with Rae, but she couldn't — never again would she share an anecdote about the girls with Ashleigh's mother. Every pick-up for years, they'd told each other a story or two about the girls. Never again. To avoid looking at Rae, she stared at the front yard — a mess of trees and bushes she'd planted as a filter for the dusty, dirty, oily air and to block the view of the oil tanks across the road, of the trucks and semis, of the bridge.

'My daughter isn't going to grow up. My daughter isn't going to go to university, or fall in love, or have children. Ashleigh wanted to work in New York. She wanted to travel the world. I was so worried about all the things she wanted to do and the risks and how I wouldn't be able to protect her, because I thought she was safe here with me. But she wasn't and she's gone and she won't ever fulfill those dreams …' Her eyes were tearing up again, and Mandy moved out of the doorway towards her, reaching out to touch her shoulder. Rae recoiled and retreated, almost tripping over the wooden step that led from the small porch to the path.

'No, stop, don't touch me. People keep trying to hold me, to touch me, to put their arms around me. I don't want anyone near me. It makes it worse. It makes me … reminds me that I will never touch Ashleigh again, never hold her … Sometimes she'd nuzzle up to me on the couch. I loved the smell of her. And just when I started to fall asleep, she would tickle me —' The wail that came from Rae was deep and long, and she doubled over with the force of it.

Mandy was crying too now — she could feel the tears running down her cheeks — but she had no right to cry. She needed to give Rae the time to say what she needed to say. She owed her that much.

When she had composed herself again, Rae said, 'I trusted you with my daughter. I loved your daughter. I invited her to all our family celebrations, I included her in everything. She has her own coffee mug in my cupboard, her own drawer in Ashleigh's room, her own towels.'

Mandy nodded in acknowledgement.

'I blame you. You … why didn't you stop her driving?' Rae asked. It was the question Mandy had been waiting for, but she didn't have an answer, just a series of useless excuses. 'The police said they were drinking before they left the house, before they even went to the party. I want to know why you let your daughter drive. What kind of mother are you? They were drunk and you let them take the car.'

'I'm sorry. I thought they'd be alright. It wasn't that far and Jo said she was fine … I'm sorry.' Mandy felt as if she might collapse. The effort of holding back sobs made speaking difficult. 'I should've stopped them. I should've.'

'It's parents like you that are the problem. It's your fault. No responsibility. You're a bad mother,' Rae said.

It hit Mandy with the force of a slap. *You're a bad mother.*

'I feel terrible …' she muttered faintly.

'What does it matter how you feel? What about your daughter? Is she sorry?'

'Of course. Of course, she loved Ashleigh. They were friends, they loved each other. Please come into the house, Rae.'

'My daughter is dead. Your daughter killed her. Why would I come into your house?' Rae's gaze was fixed on her, and her voice was imbued with contempt and disgust. Mandy was trapped. A bad mother, an irresponsible mother, worse than a monster. She felt shame and sadness, and anger too. Rae didn't understand how hard she'd tried to be a good mother. But Mandy knew there was nothing she could say to make things better for either of them.

'I am so sorry,' she said yet again. 'I wish I could —'

'What do you wish, Mandy? What? That you could go back and do things differently that night? Is that what you wish? Do you know what I wish? Do you know what I lie in bed wishing?' Rae had dropped her arms by her side, her hands in tight fists. 'I wish it was your daughter and not mine. That's what I wish, Mandy. That's what I wish.'

There was more despair than anger in Rae's words. Of course. Of course: a life for a life.

'But mostly I wish I was dead too. Because this pain will only stop when I die.'

Mandy could not speak. There were no words.

'I want my daughter's things. Everything. I don't want Jo to have anything. Do you understand?'

Mandy took a couple of short sharp breaths so she could speak. 'Of course. I don't know what she's —'

'Do you understand? Everything.' Rae turned around to head for the gate, but then she turned back. 'I trusted you with my daughter — all those years, I trusted you. My daughter trusted your daughter. I don't want any of you at the funeral. I don't want any of you near us.' She stared at Mandy, waiting for a response.

'Of course,' Mandy said.

Rae walked down the path and through the gate. On the footpath, she hesitated. She looked up at the bridge and began to walk towards it, changed her mind, and headed the other way, back into Yarraville.

Mandy shut the door and began to sob. She felt herself collapsing — she couldn't keep upright and let herself slip to the ground.

'Jesus. Mandy, are you okay?' Sarah asked as she came towards Mandy, offering her hand.

'No. No, not really,' Mandy said, burying her head in her arms. She remembered the moment long ago, sitting on her mother's bed as Sal took her last breath. She remembered the despair, the overwhelming sense of loss, of knowing her mother would never again open her eyes, would never again speak to her, hold her, that her mother was gone. She'd climbed onto the bed next to her dead mother and hours later, when her father tried to move her, she'd raged and howled and her father had to call the doctor. The doctor, an older man, had tried to coax her out of the bed. 'People die,' he'd said to her. 'Your mother was in a lot of pain, and she is not anymore.' It had struck her as such a stupid thing to say. 'How the fuck do you know?' she yelled at him. She remembered that he'd given her an injection and she'd woken up the next day in her own bed and the house had never ever felt like a home again.

She understood that Rae was crumbling under the weight of her grief. She understood that it was her fault and Jo's fault and that they were responsible for Ashleigh's death and they always would be, and there was nothing either of them could do to change that. Death was shocking and unjust. So hard to give up those we love. Rae and Alex would go on living, but they would carry with them the loss of their daughter — an unbearable loss from which they would never recover.

Chapter 14

When Mandy finally calmed, she and Sarah went back to the kitchen. Sarah put the kettle on and made Mandy a cup of tea.

'She was so sad. Ashleigh is — was — a beautiful young woman. She was so clever and talented. I loved her too, I did. She was a little wild sometimes, but … She was Rae's daughter. To lose a daughter: it's impossible.' Mandy's voice rose again in a sob. 'I feel sad and angry and ashamed and guilty. And all those feelings, they're just my feelings, and she's right that they don't matter.'

'Of course they matter, Mandy. They matter, but not to Rae. She has her grief to deal with and you have yours. You didn't do anything wrong. You thought they'd be okay. It was a misjudgement.'

'That cost Ashleigh her life.'

Sarah sighed. 'No point continuing down that track, Mandy. It doesn't lead anywhere you want to go.'

'I don't know where I want to go.'

Mandy remembered the months after her mother's death: the drinking and the partying with David, all of it to escape. To forget. But it had been impossible to forget.

'Rae doesn't want us at the funeral,' Mandy continued. 'I've been thinking about the funeral and what to do, whether we should go or not. I thought that Jo would want to go, but I haven't asked her.'

'It's best if neither of you go, don't you think? Everyone will be angry at Jo and it could get out of hand.'

179

'No, we can't go if Rae doesn't want us there, of course. But I … Ashleigh was Jo's best friend. I know Jo is responsible, but she needs to say her goodbyes too. But it can't be at the funeral.'

'No.'

'Jo will have to gather everything that she has that belonged to Ashleigh. Do it now, today. Rae doesn't want us to have anything that belonged to her daughter.'

'What does Jo have that belonged to Ashleigh?'

'Lots of things, I guess. They swapped clothes and jewellery and make-up and left them at each other's places. They kept things at each other's houses so that we — Rae and I — wouldn't find out about them. Silly things, expensive clothes they thought we'd disapprove of. Ashleigh came in track pants and a t-shirt that night, with her other clothes thrown over her arm and in a bag. I ironed her skirt for her while they did their nails and make-up. She wore Jo's top to the party, so I guess her clothes are here.'

Mandy pulled the album closer and flicked through several pages until she reached photos of Jo and Ashleigh at high school. The photographs of Ashleigh printed in the newspapers after the accident had been taken at her eighteenth birthday party. Ashleigh's long auburn hair was braided. She'd worn dangling silver earrings and dark red lipstick. In the album, there were photographs of Ashleigh and Jo in school uniform, on rollerskates, at a picnic, at birthday parties and school camps.

Mandy lifted an acetate sheet and picked up a photograph of the two girls, aged thirteen or fourteen, already young women. They were wearing running gear and red t-shirts, each with a number pasted across their waist. 'They fought sometimes, but they made up. Whatever else they were battling against, they seemed to be solid. I mean, Ashleigh was like part of our family. I watched her grow up. I took them both shopping for their first bras. I took them to swimming lessons and watched them sing silly songs at too many school concerts.'

'Mandy, do you think their friendship was as solid recently?'

'I don't know, Sarah. Ashleigh was more confident. More popular. Jo is … She needs reassuring; I'm not good at that. She's not as strong.'

She paused. 'Friendships are like marriages — they look different from the outside. That night — it seems so long ago, but it's less than a week — it was a lovely night, it was, and they were happy and having fun.' Mandy continued taking photos out of the album, arranging them and rearranging them on the table until they formed a large collage. There were more photographs of Jo with Ashleigh than of Jo with Mandy.

'I took a photo of them when they were dressed. They were so beautiful. It was on Ashleigh's phone. She promised she'd send it to me. They were drinking. I remember thinking *they're old enough* and even though I thought I should tell them to slow down, I didn't. I didn't want to have a fight with Jo. I wanted her to enjoy herself. So instead, I fed them. I hoped the food would soak up some of the alcohol. They ate, but not much. They were twirling around in front of the mirror, asking each other, *Do I look okay in this*? Sarah, they were being young. Young and stupid. Weren't we all young and stupid? It's so unfair.'

Sarah reached over and put her hand on Mandy's hand. 'I'd like to talk to Jo, get to know her a bit better,' Sarah said. 'I can talk to her about the funeral and about Ashleigh's things, if you like.'

'Okay. I'd appreciate that. Her room is at the front,' Mandy said, getting up to lead Sarah back along the narrow hallway, towards the front of the house, past the lounge, where the television was projecting to an empty room. Past an old stereo and a bookshelf with an odd selection of books — novels, science and history textbooks, the rules for netball — and on the top shelf several crystal animals and a set of china-and-glass bells, all sitting on a long white doily.

'That's Jo's room.' Mandy pointed at a closed door. 'I don't know how she'll be about the funeral, about Ashleigh's things.'

Mandy waited as Sarah knocked on the door.

'What?'

'It's Sarah. She needs to talk to you.'

'Sarah?' Jo said.

'Sarah, your lawyer.'

After a long pause, Jo replied. 'Okay. Give me a minute.'

Sarah heard Jo getting out of bed and moving around the room. She

181

gestured at the ornaments on the shelf. 'When I was in high school, a friend's mother had ornaments like these on the mantle. We called the mantelpiece Ada's zoo,' Sarah said.

'I've never been much of a collector of anything. I think I must've admired some ornaments like these once and Jo decided I was into them, so she's been buying them for me for Christmas or my birthday. She says I'm hard to buy for.'

'You don't like them?' Sarah said, picking up a tiny mouse and holding it up to the light. Miniature rainbows formed on the wall.

'They're okay. I like the way the light hits them. Does your friend collect them — like her mother?'

'My friend died a few years ago,' Sarah said quietly. She didn't know why she was telling Mandy.

'I'm sorry.' Mandy reached her hand out to touch Sarah's shoulder. She held it there for a moment, and then, as if realising she'd overstepped some invisible boundary, moved her hand away.

'I haven't been to her house for a long time,' Sarah continued. 'Last time I went was after the funeral. Her mother had cleared all of the ornaments off the mantle, and in their place was a framed photograph of Ada, a crucifix, and a wick burning in a glass half-filled with oil.'

This house isn't a home, Ada's mother had told Sarah. *How could she do this to us? How am I supposed to go on living?*

'I don't usually talk about Ada.' Sarah paused, surprised at how raw and close her grief remained even after all this time.

When Sarah visited Ada's mother, they'd sat together on the couch; Mrs Haris held her hands and they both cried. Sarah was so angry at Ada, but also angry at herself — maybe there was something she could've done to save Ada. She was angry at Ada's mother too: wasn't a mother supposed to know? Sarah remembered noticing that the crystal ornaments were no longer on the mantel. And wanting to ask about the black Greek urn that Ada's grandmother had brought with her when she came to Australia, about the framed cross-stitch with a map of Greece inside a map of Australia, and the wind-up clown on a unicycle that was the first thing Nick had pinched. 'Mum thinks it was a gift from one of his friends,' Ada had told her.

Those ornaments were so different to the objects Sarah's mother collected; the only objects allowed in her parents' house were original. *Original.* Her mother loved that word. 'These are *original, one of a kind,*' she said, and gave the history of the object, when it was made, by who, and where. She never said, 'Of course it cost a packet' — to talk about money was crude — but it was implied, and everyone understood.

'It must be nice to be surrounded by beautiful things,' people had said to Sarah when she still lived at home. Sarah didn't tell anyone except Ada how much she hated it. If you were lucky enough to have so much, the least you could do was be grateful.

Sarah shook one of the glass bells; the Christmasy tinkling echoed down the hallway, too light, too frivolous. She felt the urge to keep confiding in Mandy, to tell her how much she hated walking around her parents' house — how she seemed unable to estimate the size of herself and was constantly knocking into tables and couches. She had a series of bruises on her hips from the sharp corners of her own table. But at her parents' house, everything was worth money, a great deal of money; everything was irreplaceable. If she broke something, which she'd done from time to time — an English vase from the 1800s, a fine china teacup from a set like the ones in the Lodge — her mother would scream, get on her knees, and pick up each piece as if it were gold. She'd give Sarah that look: *How in the hell did I end up with a daughter like* you?

Mandy's bell was cheap, replaceable. There were hundreds of them in bargain and gift shops, at the big trash-and-treasure markets. *It's the thought that counts.* But for Sarah's mother it wasn't the thought that counted. 'That's what people say,' she'd told Sarah, 'when they are too cheap to buy a worthy gift.' Sarah put the bell back on the doily.

The door opened. 'You can come in,' Jo said.

The blinds were pulled down. The curtains were drawn. The only light in the room came in through the opened door behind Sarah. It took a few minutes for her eyes to adjust and for objects in the room to emerge. A desk with a computer. A dresser. Two chairs. There were clothes and a stack of books on the floor. There was a wardrobe and a bed, on the edge of which Jo tentatively perched. In the kitchen the outside world had been silent, but in the bedroom there was no escape: cars and trucks driving past, the click of the traffic lights, the voices of cyclists and pedestrians.

'Sorry, it's a mess,' Jo whispered.

Sarah left the door slightly ajar and walked around the clothes on the floor to sit on the bed next to Jo. Jo's hair was a mess of tangles. 'Do you mind if I open the curtains?'

'I prefer the dark,' Jo said quickly.

'Okay.'

A melancholia pervaded the room like a fog hovering low over a valley.

'I heard the doorbell earlier?'

'Ashleigh's mother.'

'She came here? Why? I didn't think she'd come here.'

'She doesn't want you or your mother at the funeral. I know it might sound harsh,' Sarah said.

'I didn't know if I could go. Whether I'd be allowed to go. I don't know if I could go even if they let me. I can't … I can't imagine …' There was a tremor in her voice. She paused. 'I can't believe she's dead.'

'It's sad. It must be difficult for you. We don't expect young people to die, it's always shocking.'

'I never, ever thought about Ash dying. I thought about my mother dying, my father, my grandmother, all sorts of people, but never Ash. I keep thinking I should run around to Ash's house to tell her about this bad nightmare I had, about her dying. And Ash would tell me off for killing her in my sleep, and we'd be laughing about it.'

'That's tough. There's one other thing. Ashleigh's mother wants the stuff you have that belonged to her daughter.'

'Does she hate me? I'm sure they all hate me.'

'She's grieving for her daughter. She's sad.'

'What does she want?'

'Anything that belonged to Ashleigh.'

'Her clothes are here … and her make-up, and other things … We're always leaving things.' Jo's voice softened back to a whisper. 'I keep thinking she'll race through the door, she'll be laughing. Telling me it was some joke.'

'That would be a cruel joke. Did Ashleigh play jokes on you?'

'Do I have to give her everything?'

'Yes. Yes, Jo, you do. Legally, everything belongs to Ashleigh's mother. I know you were friends. I'm sure that Ashleigh would like you to have something of hers, but I doubt she had a will, and at this point, it's better if you do what her mother asks.'

'So I have to do it now.'

'Yes. I can help you. Can we turn on a light? The bedside lamp.'

'Okay.'

The small fluorescent lamp radiated a yellow light that gave the room a jaundiced pallor. Even in the dimness Sarah could see Jo's face was pale, the shadows under her eyes deep purple. They both turned to scan the untidy piles of clothes on the floor, in front of the wardrobe, at the end of the bed, hanging over both chairs. Picking up a backpack that was leaning against the desk, Jo opened the zipper. 'This is Ash's,' she said. 'We can put things in here.'

Sarah held the bag open as Jo moved slowly around the room. She picked up a pair of track pants, shook them, folded them, and dropped them into the bag. She did the same with a t-shirt and jacket. Rummaging under the bed, she emerged with a plastic bag, in which she put a pair of white thongs.

Numerous bottles, tubes, and containers were scattered across the top of the dressing table. 'We shared our make-up. Not sure what is hers and what is mine.' Selecting one of the two make-up bags, the green one, Jo gathered lipsticks, eyebrow pencils, brushes, tubes of shiny cream and foundation, and stuffed them into the bag until it was overflowing. She crammed in as much as possible and did up the zipper and passed it to Sarah. She picked up two pairs of earrings and a ring. Sarah slipped them into the side pocket of the bag and zipped it up.

Jo slid the wardrobe doors open and pushed aside dresses and shirts; clothes fell off hangers and onto the floor. 'They only had one in the shop,' she said, holding up a black jacket with a row of silver studs on each shoulder. 'We both wanted our own one. We bought it half each. Do you think I should give her this?' Jo brought the jacket up to her face and closed her eyes.

'You could keep that one.'

Jo didn't move. 'It's so soft. And it smells like Ash, her perfume: Be Delicious.' But she folded it and handed it to Sarah, who put it in the bag.

'Is there anything else?'

'I don't know,' Jo said. 'I can't think what else now.'

'Okay, this will do.'

'I didn't mean to hurt Ash. Please tell them I'm sorry.'

'Have you thought about school? I could arrange for you to sit the exams,' Sarah said.

'No. Oh no, I couldn't do that,' Jo said.

'Well, you could come out for a while and have a cup of tea with me and your mother. I wanted to ask you a few things.'

'Not today, please,' Jo pleaded, and turned away from the door.

It took less than a couple of minutes to find the house. There were cars parked on either side of the street, so she had to double-park. The house, a large weatherboard to which a second storey had been added, was set back on a large block. There was a small rose garden along the front fence and several well-established Japanese maples on either side of the central path.

When Sarah knocked on the door, a teenage girl answered.

'This is for Ms White. She asked Mrs Neilson for Ashleigh's belongings.'

Silently, the girl took the bags and shut the door.

Sarah suspected that whatever Ashleigh's mother hoped to find in the bags, she'd be disappointed.

Just as she stepped off the porch onto the path, she noticed someone — a man standing at the window, holding the curtains open. Ashleigh's father, Sarah assumed. As he stared at her, she felt both his rage and his restraint emanating through the glass. She paused to meet his eyes. His gaze, intense, didn't shift. She turned and walked down the path and to the car, and as she pulled out she peered in the rearview mirror. The man was still standing at the opened window, his gaze following her as she took off down the road.

Chapter 15

Antonello headed towards Francis Street. At the lights, he waited and watched as a long line of semi-trailers — fully loaded with tanks and containers, plastered with 'hazardous chemicals' signs — headed towards Williamstown Road to make their way onto the West Gate Bridge.

The trucks flew past the dusty weatherboard houses, their motors roaring as the road opened up in front of them, seemingly oblivious to the large red signs demanding *CUT TRUCK TRAFFIC — PEOPLE LIVE HERE* nailed to front fences. Some drivers were drinking coffee or Coke, while others smoked cigarettes and flicked their ash out of their windows. Antonello imagined that to the drivers, peering down from their high cabins, the cars wedged between them looked like a series of moving Lego blocks.

Antonello had been teaching Ashleigh to drive along this stretch of road. He warned her to keep her distance, to stay back, to give way to the trucks as they swung into a right-hand turn. He insisted it was a serious exercise, and was easily annoyed with her tendency to be distracted by activity on the street, other drivers, and her phone, which beeped constantly to announce another text message. She'd laughed at his seriousness, teasing him, telling him to lighten up, trying to make him laugh with silly jokes. He hadn't relented. Being one of her driving instructors was a responsibility he took seriously. It was his duty to make sure she was a competent and safe driver so that she wouldn't have an accident. So that she wouldn't die on the road.

To avoid the risk of seeing Jo or her mother, Antonello kept to the other side of the road, with his head down and his eyes on the footpath. But he sensed Jo's presence, and several times he thought he heard their squeaky front gate and the rustle of the trees and bushes that hid her house from the street. Behind the cyclone fence, under the blue sky, the tanks soaked in the morning sun.

Back at Alex's, family and friends were still gathering. As more people had poured into the house that morning, Alex and Rae and Jane had retreated, shrinking into corners, disappearing. The ordinary rooms were becoming unfamiliar. There were too many flowers, the bunches of blooms garish and overwhelming. Too many voices. Too many people.

Nicki had arrived with food, and together with Rae's sister Rebecca, covered the kitchen benches with platters of sandwiches. But no one ate. Rae's parents, who'd arrived straight from the airport, in their holiday shorts and t-shirts, wanted Antonello to give them answers to questions they couldn't ask their daughter, questions Antonello hadn't even thought to ask. Their grief made them interrogative, as if the answers to queries about time, about speed, about states of mind would bring Ashleigh back.

'*I morti non tornano,*' he whispered.

'Sorry,' Rae's father, Gary, said. 'What did you say?'

Paolina nudged his leg under the table.

'Nothing. I'm sorry, I'm too sad, I can't speak,' he said, giving the other man a conciliatory pat on the back. He didn't want to witness his own grief reflected in the eyes of the other grandfather. There was a time when the two men had been rivals for Ashleigh's attention and her favour, childish behaviour that manifested itself in too many toys and outings and the invention of silly games.

When the funeral directors arrived, two women in grey suits lugging folders and suitcases on rollers, Antonello followed the others into the lounge room. Alex and Rae struggled under the weight of decisions — the coffin, the chapel, the cemetery, flowers, songs, prayers, eulogies. Jane snuck out of the house, into the garden, her skateboard under her arm, the dog at her heels. Antonello should've stayed. He should've stayed, but instead he'd absconded. He made excuses to himself. There was too much talk of God and prayers and hymns; he was so overwhelmed by the desire to echo Alex's outburst on the night of the accident, to shake each of them as they sat around the room — yes, even Paolina — until they understood there's no fucking God.

What he needed was a mate, someone who would listen to his rage and his grief, who would let him empty himself of it, so that he might be of some use to his son and daughter-in-law, of some help to his granddaughter. In the past, Paolina had been his only confidant, but since the cancer, he'd taken to hiding his rage, his dark thoughts and moods, from her — she had enough to deal with. He didn't trust his brothers with his emotions. He could trust both of them, Vince and Joe, with his life, with the lives of his children and grandchildren; they were better fathers, better men. But Joe would tell him to calm down, pat him on the back, and expect him to be able to do what he had to do. And Vince wouldn't know what to say. He would be a stream of platitudes: *You need to be strong, gather yourself up, it gets easier …*

Under the bridge, the thirty-five red and grey stone pillars, the sculptures that were part of the memorial, threw long dark shadows. The wind howled, and overhead the traffic was a constant clatter as cars and trucks sped over the ridges and joins that stitched the bridge together. Antonello longed for Sam and for Slav, for their friendship. It was futile to try and push the memories back; they had a force of their own.

'Hey *paesano*, come and sit with us,' Sam had called out to him at smoko on his first day, and when Antonello slipped into the bench seat next to Slav, Sam whispered, 'No bloody *Australiani* here. Dagos only.'

After that most lunchtimes, they sat at the same table. On sunny days they took their cuppas out to the same spot on the river, and after work, exhausted, they settled at the same corner of the bar at the Vic. They were his first real friends in Australia. At school, it had taken him most of the first year to learn enough English to hold a conversation, and even the sons of Italian migrants who could speak Italian stayed away. Once he left school, working on the building sites with Bob, he tended to keep to himself. He spent his spare time with Joe and Vince, and on the weekends, with some of his cousins who lived across the city in

Richmond and Collingwood, but he was lonely, yearning for friends his own age and missing his childhood companions, the boys and girls he'd grown up with in Vizzini. A couple were in New York. Several were in Australia, one or two in Melbourne, but he only saw them occasionally, at weddings and big religious celebrations. Away from the village, it was too difficult to connect.

'How long have you been in Australia?' Antonello asked Sam. 'Your English is good.'

'I've learnt English from Australian girls,' Sam said, giving Antonello a wink. 'Only Australian girls, that's my rule. Italian girls are locked up by their parents until they get married and it's too much trouble, all the sneaking around. Australian girls are friendly and sexy. They help me improve my English.'

Sam was short and muscular, and a charmer; women loved him. He was kind and compassionate, with a good sense of humour and a hearty laugh, and on the site, where there were often problems between the *real* Australians and the wogs, everyone liked Sam. He could turn the worst situation into a joke, and disarm the most racist and aggressive of the men.

He loved being a rigger, loved being up high. 'You could've been a tightrope walker,' Antonello said to him one day when they were both working on one of the spans.

Sam hurled himself in the air, somersaulted, landed on both feet, and took a bow.

'*Disgraziato!*' Antonello cried out. 'You are a bloody clown. I don't want to be scraping you off the ground.'

'Oh, don't get so wound up. I wanted to be a gymnast when I was a kid. I used to do somersaults all the time. Planned to run away to join the circus.'

Slav was the tallest of the three and the most serious. 'I'm not Italian,' he told them on that first day. 'I was born in Yugoslavia, in the north, in a small town near the Italian border.' He could speak several languages, including Italian and English. The son of primary-school teachers, he grew up in an educated, bookish household, but when his parents were killed in a ferry accident he, their only child, was shipped to Australia to live with his aunt. She took him in and loved and cared for him as she did her own children, but she and her husband worked long hours on the assembly line at the Ford factory and came home too tired to talk. There were no books in the house and little money; they expected their children and Slav to contribute to the household as soon as possible. In Yugoslavia, Slav's parents had wanted him to go into medicine or follow his love of literature. In Australia, those options slipped away, so he took up a carpentry apprenticeship. He wasn't a bad carpenter, but he wasn't a passionate one. He spent his money on books — novels and poetry. Sometimes he recited poems to Sam and Antonello, especially those of the Australian poets he made it his task to become familiar with: A.D. Hope, Bruce Dawe, and Judith Wright. Poets who wrote about the nature of life and death, who documented the lives of ordinary people and often used poetry to take up issues that troubled them — war, consumerism, and Indigenous land rights.

It was Sam who first called them the Rat Pack, one night when they were all dressed up in their suits, on their way to the San Remo Ballroom. 'Handsome and always together. We have each other's backs.'

In a parallel universe, they would've grown old together, and their friendship would've made him a stronger man, a better man.

As Antonello made his way back along the path, he caught sight of the roadside memorial for Ashleigh. There was a white cross, roughly made from two planks of wood. In thick black pen: *Ashleigh Bassillo-White 20/09/2009. RIP.* There were flowers — roses and lilies, already decaying. Tied and taped to the cross were several cards and notes, but Antonello didn't bend down to read them. He assumed the memorial had been built by Ashleigh's friends: the girls that were in the car, or maybe Ashleigh's boyfriend, Kevin, or even Jo. Roadside memorials were common enough, along the freeways, on the sides of roads, attached to poles and posts, to cyclone fences, to roadside barricades. He avoided them, unless he was with Paolina; then, avoidance was impossible. To Paolina, these temporary altars were sacred places. She was compelled to stop, and if they couldn't stop, she'd say a short prayer as they drove past, as if they'd passed the cemetery or a funeral procession. She said that some people believed the dead person's spirit lingered where they took their last breath.

Did the dead exist anywhere? Were they watching? He'd grown up with heaven and hell and had discarded the idea of both, but Bob and Slav were often with him, and now Ashleigh too. Were they ghosts? Not the kind that appeared as thin, ethereal apparitions in movies, not the kind he'd imagined as a child, draped with white sheets and the ability to walk through walls. But the kind that lodged themselves in your heart, and in your memories, the kind that came to you in dreams, that you could see when you closed your eyes and sometimes even when your eyes were opened, when a moment came back to you, their voices whispering in your ear, calling out your name. He felt the weight of their unlived lives, of all they might have been; he felt his own inadequacy.

He turned to look up at the bridge. He whispered to Bob and Slav to look after his granddaughter Ashleigh. Wherever she was, he hoped she was with them.

The Ashleigh portrayed in the newspaper articles after the accident bore little resemblance to the real Ash. They quoted the school principal: 'Ashleigh was an exemplary member of the school community.' In Ash's school reports, none of the teachers called her *exemplary*. They quoted Mrs Zapatero, a neighbour, who cried during her interview: 'She was quiet and kind.' This was the same girl who had talked Jo into hacking Mrs Zapatero's roses one night after the woman had complained to Rae about Ash's bad language.

One of Ash's uncles was quoted saying, 'Jo was a bad influence on Ashleigh.' An unnamed neighbour: 'I hope that girl gets what she deserves.'

Ash wasn't a saint. Jo longed to run up and down the streets of Yarraville screaming at them all, *She's no fucking saint.*

Jo tore the articles out, shredded them into small, unreadable pieces, and stuffed them under her mattress. Ash wasn't a bad person — she was funny, she was clever, she was never lost for words — but sometimes she was a bitch. Sometimes she was a cow. She could be nasty and mean. Say hurtful things.

But Ash was dead and Jo was alive, and even though she wished and wished, nothing could change that. She remembered the text messages sent anonymously the day after the accident: *You should be dead. Murderer, scum of the earth, it should have been you who died.*

The sender was right. She was a murderer, a criminal. Because of her, Ash was dead. Nothing would ever, ever change that. She could climb mountains, she could win medals, she could save the world from alien invasion, but she would still be a murderer.

You, climb mountains, win medals? Give me a break. I'm dead, and you want sympathy.

'No, I'm not asking for sympathy,' Jo said out loud, even though she knew Ash was not in the room.

The buzzing of a car alarm woke Jo. There was a moment or two in which she was only aware of her irritation at the relentless squawking. Every morning, she woke into her old life. For that first moment, Ash was alive. And then the anxiety, rising, swelling, erupting … remembering Ash. Ash dead. Ash dead.

Was every morning like this for Rae?

Rae was the only woman Jo had ever seen naked. It was during a sleepover at Ash's house. She had stumbled out of bed in the middle of the night to go to the toilet and almost collided with Rae.

'Oh, sorry, Jo,' Rae said. 'I forgot you were staying over. Forgot to put on the dressing gown.'

'Oh, just going to the …' Jo said, embarrassed and not sure whether to backtrack to the bedroom or keep going.

'Go, no problem,' Rae said. Even though Mandy and Jo were the only occupants of their house, neither of them ever left their rooms without clothes. Rae was lean and fit, with large breasts; she wasn't embarrassed to be seen naked. When Jo had imagined herself as an adult woman, she imagined herself as Rae.

What was Rae doing now? What were Rae and Alex and Jane and Ash's grandparents and aunts and uncles and cousins doing? How were they making it through the days, through the nights? How would they keep going with their lives? Would they return to work, to school?

Jo's room was dark and stale. Her head throbbed. She walked over to the windows, but she couldn't bear to open the curtains. Instead she sat on the floor and leant against them. Blue velvet curtains. Mary had bought them when Jo was going through a blue phase. They were soft and lush, and so much wider than her window that they formed waves.

Mary had been proud of her find. The curtains were in the Salvos op shop in Barkly Street, Footscray, folded and labelled: $4. 'They're new. Only rich people would be getting rid of curtains in such good nick. Curtains fit for a princess.'

Jo and Mary took down the old blinds — somersaulting clowns that Mandy had bought when Jo was three — and hung the velvet curtains. They were too long, and Mary took them up while they were hanging. Mary wasn't much of a seamstress, and so the rough stitches in the wrong shade of blue ran across the hemline like scars. Drawn, they were a thick and solid wall that no light could penetrate. Drawn, the room shrank. They blocked out the street. The tanks. The bridge. But not Ash. It was as if Jo were strapped in a seat at a twenty-four-hour cinema, and on the screen images of Ash played in a never-ending loop. Ash sitting in Jo's computer chair, twirling and spinning and talking about winning a ribbon, about wanting her own horse, about riding in the Olympics. And Jo laughing, 'The Olympics, give me a break.' Ash wearing the blue top and the red skirt with a glass of champagne in her hand.

Jo opened her eyes to stop the memories. As she started to get up, she noticed a flash of red under the bed. It was Ashleigh's Moleskine notebook, her journal. Jo slid her hand under the bed and grabbed the notebook. She felt the weight of it in her hand and remembered the betrayal.

My journal. Spy. Snoop.

I trusted you with my journals. I thought I could trust you, but you can't be trusted.

Jo shuddered. Ash's journals were still in the safe in the far corner of Jo's room, hidden behind an old chest. Grandpa Tom had bought the safe after a spate of robberies in the neighbourhood, long before Jo was born, before Sal, the grandmother Jo hadn't met, died. Sal only owned one thing worth stealing: her great-grandmother's blue pearl necklace. There were several different stories about the origins of the necklace. Sal told Mandy that her great-grandmother was from a wealthy family and the necklace was the only thing she took with her when she eloped with Sal's great-grandfather and the family disowned her. Grandpa Tom said that he was sure his great-grandfather-in-law took after his convict parents and had stolen the necklace: 'He was a thief in and out of prison all his life.' Sal wore the necklace in every photograph that Jo had seen. When Sal didn't wear it, she worried that someone would break into the house while they were out and find where she hid it — wrapped in a cloth at the bottom of the biscuit tin on the top kitchen shelf — and steal it. When a factory in Stephen Street closed down, they put up a sign: *Everything for sale*. Grandpa Tom came home with a hammer, several boxes of rusty screws, and a safe. A whole safe for one necklace might have seemed excessive, but not to Grandpa Tom. 'It was a bargain. It gave your grandma peace of mind.'

Jo didn't have any jewellery to keep safe, and Mandy had inherited the pearl necklace but was happy for it to sit on her dresser with the rest of her jewellery — a few dress rings, the odd strings of beads picked up at the local op shop. When Ash arrived one day with all her journals, a boxful, furious because she'd caught Jane reading one of them, Jo offered her the safe. When Ash filled a notebook, she slipped it into the safe. Until the red Moleskine, Jo had never once violated Ash's trust.

What was she supposed to do with the journals? It was obvious Rae would want them, not a bulging make-up bag or an old pair of pants. She was sure it was the journals that had propelled Rae to their front door.

She dropped the notebook, switched on the lamp, and opened the safe. The code was Ash's birth date, 100891. Jo pulled the journals out one at a time and threw them on the bed. A large diary with a reproduction of the birth of Venus on the cover, the yellow edges battered. A small square notebook with Homer and Marge on a motorbike. A purple velvet journal. Emily the Strange and her cats. A New York skyline, with the Empire State Building in the foreground. The first ever journal, a ballerina on the cover, sealed with a gold lock. Soon her bed was covered with Ash's journals, scattered and random, forming a crazy quilt. Laura's grandmother had made Laura a crazy quilt, the pieces of fabric cut from Laura's baby clothes and cotton blankets, creating haphazard shapes. Laura hung it on the wall. Each piece of fabric came with memories and stories that Laura said made it impossible to sleep under.

'Fuck, Ash. What am I supposed to do with these?' Jo said.

So many secrets shared. So many asides and sniggers about other girls, about teachers, about their mothers.

I'm dead. I'm dead. And it's all your fault.

Jo turned full circle twice. Of course there was no one else in the room; she'd know that voice anywhere. 'I never meant to hurt you.'

We were both there.

Jo backed away from the bed and the journals and slipped back down to the floor. Sitting up, hugging her knees to her chest, she said, 'I thought we'd be friends forever. I thought we'd always be friends. Because of you, I didn't make other friends. Because of you, Ash. I avoided getting closer to other people. I had my best friend. You can have only one best friend.'

Who else would put up with you?

'I love you. You're my friend.'

Was. I was your friend. You still suck at tenses.

'We were friends for so long.'

It's not enough. Ash's voice was sharp and shrill. Ash was dancing around the room, mocking her. *A shared history isn't enough. I was over you. I wanted to move on. I was just being nice. Pretending. Kevin said, Don't be mean. My mother said, Don't be awful. My father said, You've been friends forever. Good friends are hard to come by. I bet they fucking regret that now.*

'Stop, please stop.' Jo cupped her ears.

I'm not here. I'm dead.

On top of the pile was the Bonnie and Clyde notebook, the one she bought Ash for her seventeenth birthday. On the cover, a photograph of Faye Dunaway wearing a beret and a yellow jacket over a pencil skirt, and Warren Beatty in his 1930s chalk-striped suit. Faye had a gun in her hand. She and Ash dubbed each other Bonnie and Clyde after stealing a pair of earrings from a shop in the city. The shop assistant, a middle-aged woman in a long, flowing dress, had taken several pairs out of the cabinet for Jo. Jo was the decoy. She tried on a pair of short silver and black earrings, then a pair of long dangling earrings in red and pink and orange, admiring herself in the mirror on the counter. She asked the woman's advice while Ash slipped the first pair of earrings off the counter and into her pocket. 'I'll leave you to it, Jo. See you at the café,' Ash said, and left the shop. Jo continued looking at earrings until there were pairs spread over the whole counter. She told the shop assistant that she needed to have a coffee and think about it. When Jo walked into the café, they burst out laughing. 'We are totally Bonnie and Clyde. From that old movie your mother likes to watch,' Ash said, wrapping her arm around Jo. 'We ain't good. We are the best. BFFs.'

They might not have stayed best friends forever; they might've gone their separate ways. But now Ash was dead and Jo couldn't tell her to fuck off. She couldn't be the one to stop returning calls.

As if.

She'd never know if Ash was going to drop her, if their friendship was a lie. When had the lying started? If she read all the journals from beginning to end, would she discover the truth?

Crazy Jo, the answer's not in my journals. You can't be trusted with anything, with anyone.

She could not read the journals. She gathered them up, shoved them back into the safe, and shut the door. She would never have another best friend.

Chapter 16

By the time Sarah returned to the office, it was after six. She parked the car next to the rest of the office fleet, locked it, returned the key to the drawer behind reception, and left without talking to anyone. She caught the 6.40 to Flinders Street. There were less than a dozen passengers: a couple of groups of male workers with bright orange-and-green safety jackets; an elderly couple, both reading novels; a gaggle of teenage girls in school sports uniform, carrying hockey sticks and still analysing the game: why they lost and whose fault it was, coming to the conclusion that if they had a better coach they might have won. One of the workmen elbowed his mate and nodded in the girls' direction. The other guy grinned. 'That would be cradle snatching.' Sarah was tempted to tell the men to stop ogling the girls, all under age, but the girls seemed oblivious, the men too old to be on their radar, and she didn't want to spoil their afternoon.

The accumulated litter of the day's commuters was scattered around them: abandoned newspapers, soft drink cans, and paper cups carelessly dropped, staining the floor with their sticky dregs; half-eaten food abandoned in scrunched-up paper bags and plastic takeaway containers. The carriage smelt of fried food and sweat. Sarah thought about Ashleigh's father, standing at the window unable to move, about Ashleigh's mother knocking on Mandy's door, about Mandy pacing in her kitchen. She picked up the *mX* and flicked through pages of city news: drugged-out footballers, reality-television celebrity makeovers, alcohol-induced fights in the CBD.

Sarah loved living in the city centre. It was five years since she'd bought the apartment and the thrill hadn't worn off. For most people the city was an artificial place, all concrete and steel, somewhere they went to for work, for entertainment, for shopping. It wasn't the *real* world. At the end of each excursion, they returned to the *real* world, to the suburbs, to their homes and their gardens. At night, while thousands vacated the city, like birds flying south for the winter, Sarah came home to it.

In Swanston Street, the air throbbed with voices. On the edges of the footpath outside McDonald's, a group of young people strutted and smoked and ate hamburgers and fries. Three cops, wearing pistols and batons around their waists, slowed their pace as they reached the group. Sarah was reminded of the standoffs in the old Westerns her father'd watched when she was a child, and how she hadn't understood, still didn't understand, why men chose to walk towards fights instead of away from them.

Further along Swanston, two young Japanese women were setting up a jewellery stall. Sarah slowed but didn't stop. The earrings and rings were made by embedding torn magazine images between resin — cherry blossoms, Mount Fuji, the Eiffel Tower, an open book, letters of the alphabet. Next, there was another stall, a long table spread with trinkets and bright woven scarves from Nepal.

Several beggars sat in the doorways of closed shops. One, a young woman who looked about Jo's age, had a pleading note on cardboard — *Nowhere to sleep tonight, no money for food* — and was sharing her square of cardboard with a black-and-white cat. There was a collar around the cat's neck from which hung a long leash. Sarah dropped several coins in the woman's plate. She rarely talked to any of the beggars, but they were as familiar to her as neighbours might be to those living in the suburbs. People rushed past them in a hurry to get home, to cook dinner, to sit in the living rooms of their suburban houses to watch endless hours of television. To avoid seeing the beggars, to avoid the reminder that life could turn bad and go wrong, that everything could be lost. The stench of misfortune and tragedy clung to the beggars. Most people found it repulsive. Sarah was used to it; her clients were generally the kinds of people other people shunned.

In front of Gopals, the aroma of hot curry wafted onto the street. She made a quick decision and climbed up the stairs. *Bugger the diet.* There was a queue at the counter, mainly international students from India, Sri Lanka, and Nepal. Sarah lined up and waited. When it was her turn, she ordered pumpkin curry, dhal, rice, and a mango lassi, paid for her food, and took her tray to one of the bench seats overlooking Swanston Street. Across the road the town hall sparkled under blue lights. Two doormen in dinner suits (or were they well-disguised bouncers?) stood on each side of a narrow red carpet that stretched up the steps.

Swanston Street was closed to vehicle traffic in the early 1990s, the footpath widened to encourage more pedestrians. As far as Sarah was concerned, they could ban all cars. A city with no cars. Venice, without the canals and the sinking buildings, without the decay and the damp. When Sarah was six years old, her parents took the family to Europe. Her memory of Venice was of pouring rain and rising water, of lines of people on narrow trestles above the flooded piazza, of travellers taking their shoes off and running through the murky water, of locals in thigh-high gumboots and the persistent stench of soggy socks. Of her mother's refusal to leave the hotel room.

Sarah pulled Jo's police statement out of her bag and opened it. *All of us were drinking.* Jo wanted to share her guilt and blame with the others. Sarah sympathised. The guilt must be overwhelming, and to some extent all four girls were implicated. The other three had climbed into Jo's car knowing Jo had been drinking. But the law didn't care: Jo was the one driving, so she was culpable and she'd have to pay. Even though she was already paying. Even though she would be paying for the rest of her life.

The restaurant was full now. Did all those people know their world could change in a moment, in an instant, with one wrong move? There were some days when Sarah thought she should've chosen another profession, where at least occasionally she'd meet people who were happy, who she, in the line of her work, could make happy. A travel agent, say — organising people's holidays, helping them plan their visits to exotic places, to get away from their lives.

Working in a supermarket and raising a child alone didn't leave Mandy with spare cash. If Mandy and Jo went on holidays, Sarah assumed it was to the popular beaches of Rosebud or Rye, maybe to Lorne or Anglesea. A weekend camping in a caravan park or by a lake or a river. These were the sorts of holidays Sarah's friend Jess had gone on. While Sarah was in Europe, Jess slept in tents, ate baked beans and sausages, and went fishing and surfing. When they came back to school and compared holiday stories, Jess said she was jealous of Sarah. Jess begged her parents to take her overseas, but Sarah hated the hotel rooms, and having to share with her parents and brothers. Massive churches populated by frightening statues of Gods and saints, and so many museums and galleries, and her mother telling her she was *such a lucky girl* to be learning about history and art, and was she savouring it? She preferred school to holidays. Even when her father declared a 'rest day', usually so he could take her brothers to a soccer or cricket match, she'd be stuck shopping with her mother, who found antique stores in every city and town, no matter how small or remote. Sarah would've been a terrible travel agent.

By the time she left Gopals, the rush hour was over and the workers in a hurry to get home had been replaced by couples holding hands, friends going out to dinner or for a drink in one of the expensive bars hidden down laneways or on the top floors of converted commercial buildings. Sarah loved to walk, especially at dusk; she could walk around the city for hours. But she was a faller and had to be cautious. Raised footpaths, cracked bitumen, and loose gravel often caught Sarah unawares. A tendency to trip, slip, spill. Falling to the ground. Missing steps and failing to take gutters into account. Cobblestones, slate, any uneven ground. Her ankles twisted. *Weak foundations.* It wasn't a chronic condition, but it required attention. She had to watch her step. Over the years there had been multiple scraped knees and twisted ankles, bruised arms and hands. She'd split her lip, cracked a couple of teeth, and broken her left arm in two places. So the walking she loved was laced with fear and foreboding.

Even as a child she'd frequently fallen. Her falls drove her mother — netballer, runner, and, more recently, golfer — mad. A woman with excellent balance, she didn't understand Sarah's lack of it. 'You don't take after me or your father.' This was one of the only times Sarah heard her mother say anything positive about her father. 'When he was young he could run so fast that everyone wanted him on their team.'

'Watch your feet,' was Sarah's grandmother's advice. She was a faller too.

It was the blood that bothered Sarah's mother. When Sarah came home in tears, with blood dripping down her leg or arm, her mother tried to be sympathetic. If Sarah came home long after the fall, her clothes torn and stained with dry blood, crusty scabs forming on her skin, sympathy was impossible. 'Not again.'

'It's not my fault. It was an accident.'

After each fall, Sarah undressed in the bathroom and sat on the side of the bath while her mother washed the sores with cottonbuds and hot water, and dabbed them with Dettol. Sarah ground her teeth, clenched her fists, and bit down hard on her tongue, but she didn't cry, not even when the sting seemed unbearable; it was her fault, after all, for being careless, for taking after her grandmother.

Sarah walked with too careful a step for a woman her age. Her eyes were on her feet. Walking this way, it was possible to cover kilometres and see nothing. Nothing but the cracks and stains of the bitumen. Nothing but the litter: cigarette butts, lolly wrappers, crushed soft drink cans, and flattened bottle tops. If the fear took control, and it did sometimes, the possibility of falling would rise like a fever, like a blush, like a panic. And walking took a force of will.

Sarah had been avoiding the West Gate for years. But Jo had crashed under the bridge, and for Sarah to understand what had happened and the details in the police report, she needed to visit the accident site.

The next morning, Sarah headed for the bridge. She left the car across the road. It wasn't possible to park under the bridge — the scaffolding for the maintenance works was a complex web, metal towers rising to grip concrete piers. A crippled bridge: cracked, overloaded, tired. Built in the

1970s to take the city into the next century, it was now carrying a volume of traffic that many said was beyond its capacity.

'They're not adding on,' said her engineer brother, Paul, at one of their fortnightly family dinners. 'You can't add on to a bridge. They're narrowing all the lanes to create an extra lane each way.'

'Robbing Peter to pay Paul,' her mother said.

'But won't that make driving on the bridge more dangerous?' Sarah asked.

'No evidence of that,' he said. 'It's like airlines reducing the space between seats.'

'That's proven to be dangerous — what about thrombosis?' Sarah's other brother, Jake, said.

'It might be dangerous,' her father announced, 'but they won't publish any of those findings.'

'Engineers aren't the enemy,' Paul said. 'We give you what you want. No one wants to be stuck in traffic.'

The dinner-table banter went on and on, as it usually did. But Sarah was haunted by her brother's comment: *We give you what you want.* Did anyone ever explain the consequences of giving people what they wanted? Would people, would whole communities, cities, countries, reject progress if they knew the consequences? Was that what engineers and scientists were afraid of?

It was after ten and the traffic on the bridge was flowing. It was sunny, but not yet hot. Under the bridge, the mangroves were alive with birds. A group of older cyclists flew past, their voices as loud and bright as the lycra pants and shirts they wore. In the distance a couple were jogging, their Irish wolfhound, the size of a small pony, galloping towards a fisherman sitting on the banks of the river. The fisherman laughed and patted the dog as if they were old friends.

Sarah gazed up at the bridge and thought about Ada falling. Driving her mother's brown Nissan to the top, pulling over to the emergency lane, making sure the note was on the dashboard, stepping out onto the roadway, climbing the barrier, and falling. Falling into the river.

There are two types of jumpers, Sarah had read in a report about suicides off the West Gate: those who hesitate and those who don't.

Ada didn't hesitate. The cops told the family that the VicRoads security staff weren't able to reach her in time.

'They don't jump,' a cop told her once. He didn't know about Ada. They were in a meeting at police headquarters in the city, and the chairperson had called for a short tea break. She wanted to run away from him. 'Everyone uses that expression, "jump off the bridge", but they don't jump. They sit or stand on the barrier and they let themselves fall.'

Sarah imagined Ada as an eagle diving.

Finally, after years of resistance, the government had installed safety barriers, and now the authorities declared it was impossible to jump, to fall, to suicide off the bridge. Sarah didn't know if that was true or not. People found ways to scale walls. The Berlin Wall. Prison walls. You couldn't lock the passage to the underworld. Too late for Ada. But Ada would've found some other way to die.

'Most days,' Ada told Sarah a few weeks before she died, 'I wish I didn't exist.'

For over an hour, they'd been sitting outside the European restaurant in a patch of sunshine, drinking coffee and watching a group of animal-rights activists demonstrating on the steps of Parliament House. They'd talked about work — the challenges of legal aid and the perils of nursing — and about friends. Jess, who was in London, 'making ethereal installations'. Sue, who was doing her PhD in Sydney. They'd been gossiping and laughing before Ada made the comment.

'Go back to the psych,' Sarah pleaded. 'When you were seeing the psych you were better. The medication helped.'

'I'm never better, no matter how many pills. It's an illusion.'

Three weeks later, Nick had rung her. 'Ada's dead.'

Nick responded to all her questions, as if he were in the witness stand and she were the prosecuting lawyer. But knowing all the details was useless; it was sad and distressing and tragic. Even after eight years, there were moments Sarah forgot that Ada was dead and thought, *I must tell Ada …*

Sarah passed the mangroves and the backwash and headed for the memorial. She read the plaque erected in memory of the men who died when the bridge collapsed in 1970. She read through the list of names and occupations. She noticed the roadside memorial for Ashleigh. A wooden cross with her name painted in black. *Ashleigh Bassillo-White. 20/09/2009. RIP.* There was a bunch of red roses and several cards. Sarah picked up one of the cards. It was from Laura and Mani; on the front, a girl riding a horse; inside, *We love you, Ash, and we miss you.*

After a week of leaving messages, Mani's mother had returned Sarah's call. 'The girls have given their statements to the police. They're doing VCE. They've lost a close friend. We don't want you to talk to them. Please don't call again.'

'I thought they might want to help Jo. She's their friend too.'

Mrs Cruz's voice was shaking with anger. 'She was drunk and driving. And she was fighting with Ashleigh, and she might've killed all of them.' And then she hung up.

The girls almost made it home. A minute or two and everything would've been different. How long had it taken for the guards on the bridge to notice Ada: to notice her stop her car, to notice her getting out and making her way to the rail? How long did it take them to run out of the office, to get in their car, to make it to the top of the bridge? Was it a matter of minutes?

The debris from the crash had been cleared. There were several skid marks on the road. The police estimated that Jo had been doing 90 kilometres an hour in a 60 zone. The car spun out of control. Cause unknown. Mani had mentioned oil on the road, but there was no evidence here. If Jo had been sober, alert, not speeding, not arguing, it was unlikely there would've been an accident.

When Jo was young, Mary sometimes took her to St Augustine's on Sundays for the 11.00 am mass. Mary insisted Jo wear a pretty dress and nice polished shoes, *for God*. Mary wore her best dress too, and sometimes gloves and a hat. She told Jo that women were no longer obliged to cover their heads, but God appreciated it if they did. Jo hated the dressing up, but she enjoyed going to church with Mary, watching the priest in his white gown, and the altar boys — tough kids who played football and cricket on the street — so demure and pious in their lace-trimmed cotton tunics, their hands, washed and scrubbed clean, joined in prayer. Jo loved the way everyone stood up, hymn books in hand, and joined in the singing. She was intrigued by how compliant the adults were, how they sat silent and earnest, nodding in agreement during the priest's booming sermons on sin or love or forgiveness. And all the sitting and standing and kneeling, and then sitting and standing and kneeling again, reminded her of some of the games they played at school. When her grandmother lined up for communion, the body of Christ, Jo sat alone and watched as the priest placed a thin wafer on each person's tongue. After church, they went to the bakery to buy fresh bread, and Mr Maxim gave her a wink — 'All pure now' — and a warm and crusty dinner roll.

It was at St Augustine's that she learnt about heaven and hell. She found it comforting to think of Grandpa Tom in heaven, smoking his rollies and telling stories. Mandy let her go with her grandmother, but she squashed all notions of a God: 'There is no God. There's what there is, and if we aren't good to each other there is only misery.'

Since her early teens, when she'd stopped going to church with Mary, Jo hadn't given much more thought to heaven or hell or God. But now she remembered those sermons. *Blessed are those with faith.* If only she was as sure as her grandmother that heaven existed.

Did they let killers go to heaven? Would Ash be standing at heaven's door? Would she put her hand up in protest: *She doesn't belong here?*

From the bedroom, Jo listened to Mandy moving around in the kitchen. Running water. Banging pots. Rattling cutlery. The aroma of bolognaise sauce, fried chicken, and lamb curry, all mixed together. Since the accident her mother spent any free time cooking; the freezer was crammed full of plastic containers of food, waiting. Jo longed to be with her mother in the kitchen, to sit with her at the table, to watch her dish out the pasta, to yell at her for putting too much on her plate, to eat and talk and argue. To have nothing else to talk about except the weather and the news and the loonies at the supermarket and too much homework. This ache for her mother was physical — it was a throbbing pain, laced with regret. Overwhelming regret for all those years she had shunted her mother aside.

Your mother wishes you were dead.

Did her mother wish she were dead?

The night before Ash's funeral, Jo dreamt she was teetering at the edge of a high cliff. Under her feet the ground cracked, and loose rocks crashed into the surf below. Behind her, people were gathering. If she didn't jump, they'd push. Had her mother been among them?

She woke, unable to lie still, and paced the room. The torn red dress was still on the floor. She snatched it, scrunched it into a tight ball, carried it out of the house, and dumped it into the wheelie bin. Back in her room, she thought about Ash and how particular she was about clothes. Rae was particular about clothes too, but their tastes didn't match. Jo knew what Ash liked. She shouldn't let Ash be buried in just anything. Ash had picked out a dress to buy to wear to their Year 12 formal. It was in a designer shop in a laneway in the city. She wanted to pay it off in $50 installments, but the manager had refused to put the dress aside for her. Rae would hate the dress. It was so short you could see the feather tattoo on Ash's upper thigh. So short that when Ash lifted her arms, the dress rose above the trim of her white lace knickers. The seams were on the outside. It was black silk with three roughly cut question marks, emerald-green, sewn to the front of the dress. The price tag was $455.

Was that too much to pay for Ash's last dress?

Should she tell Rae about the dress? Send a text or an email, slip a note under the door?

At midnight, the wind changed and a heavy gust blew the front gate open. The loose windows rattled. The neighbourhood dogs barked and howled, and their owners called out to them. All night Jo was dizzy and nauseous and went back and forth to the bathroom. She knelt on the floor and dry-retched into the toilet. Hanging her head over the bowl, liquid bubbles rising and turning into acid in her throat.

Just before sunrise, she dozed off and dreamt that Rae was running towards the house, wielding a knife, swinging it frantically. When Jo woke up, the dream seemed real. If it was real, soon she'd be as dead as Ash.

She imagined Rae with a gun. Alex hurling bombs through the window. *My parents aren't killers. Only one killer here, and that's you.*

If someone else was driving, if someone else killed Ash, Jo would've been furious. If it'd been Mani or Laura or Kevin driving, if they'd been drunk, Jo wouldn't be able to forgive them. She'd be sitting in the kitchen of Ash's house with Ash's parents, with Jane, and she'd want the driver dead. Death deserved revenge. 'You killed Ash. You killed her. Die. Die now.'

You owe me that dress.

St Nicholas, the Greek Orthodox church, was several streets away, but the ringing of the bells could be heard in Mandy's kitchen. Mandy sat in front of a cup of coffee gone cold. It was the morning of Ashleigh's funeral. But the bells weren't for Ashleigh. The dead man, Mr Anton, was a customer at the supermarket. Mandy knew him well enough to ask after his health, his wife, and his grandchildren. She knew his taste in cheese — 'don't tell the other Greeks, but Bulgarian feta is best' — and his weakness for expensive prosciutto; she knew which bones he bought for his dog, Misha, and that his diabetic sister craved the Turkish delights they kept on the deli counter, and that he snuck them into the nursing home at least once a week.

Mandy had planned to go to the funeral as a sign of respect for an old man who had a smile and a polite word for the woman behind the counter. He called her 'darling' and flirted with her, and even though he was well into his eighties, his harmless flirting made her happy.

But she wouldn't go. Today she wouldn't leave the house. Today, while the Greeks gathered in the church on Murray Street to celebrate a long life, several kilometres down the road, at the chapel at Altona Crematorium, another group of mourners would be farewelling Ashleigh. Young and vibrant; too young, a life cut short. What would Ashleigh have done with those extra seventy years?

Ashleigh's family and friends would drive past the house on their way to the funeral. She remembered Rae's words: 'I wish it was your daughter and not mine.' She imagined rocks through windows; she imagined gunshots. Rae and Alex could turn violent. When Rae had come to the door, she was spent, falling apart, despairing, a woman collapsing into her grief. It had shocked Mandy to see her so depleted. But fury might rise — it might be the only way to stop grief from becoming all-consuming. The death of a daughter was surely enough to turn any parent into a monster. Mandy remembered her gentle father after her mother's death, the way he crept around the house, his quiet steps, his silence. And then one day, a week after the funeral, she'd come home to find him in the kitchen, smashing plates against the wall in a violent and terrifying rage.

Mandy locked the front door and the windows, pulled down all the blinds, and turned off the radio. She lit the long white candle, the one she kept in the emergency drawer along with matches, a torch, and the first-aid kit. She'd never lit a candle to mark a death — candles had no special significance for her — but the flame was strangely comforting.

She knew she should go to Jo. They should be together. She should be holding her daughter, giving her comfort. But it was Jo's fault Ashleigh was dead, and the anger was overwhelming. The anger and the sadness. She was weary and bruised and unable to move, so she continued to sit at the table with her cold coffee and weep.

No one hammered on the door. No one came to yell at Jo. Or at Mandy. The day was listless. The candle flame flickered, the clock on the kitchen wall marking every second.

Jo finally fell asleep exhausted. She woke hours later, disorientated.

Why aren't you going to my funeral? You can't even stay awake.

When they'd slept at each other's houses, Ash fell asleep first. Many nights Jo lay awake watching Ash sleep, watching her toss and turn. Ash kicked her legs until all the covers were tossed off, onto the ground or, if they were sharing a bed, onto Jo.

Jo closed her eyes, crossed her arms over her chest, and tried to imagine being Ash, lying in a coffin. No more movement, no more tossing and turning, no more kicking.

I am dead, not you. Let me at least have that.

'I'll be dead too, one day.' The thought gave Jo comfort.

Chapter 17

Ashleigh's family gathered at the house and waited for the funeral cars. The men, dressed in their suits and ties, paced around the garden; the smokers lit cigarette after cigarette and the non-smokers envied them. The women wore dark dresses or dark pants and jackets. Normally a boisterous crowd, they were lost for words.

Jane wore a plain blue dress. She hadn't worn a dress since she was a toddler. 'Don't ask that, Dad,' Alex reprimanded him once when Antonello asked his granddaughter why she didn't wear dresses.

'This is Ash's dress. Is it okay to wear it? I asked Mum, but I don't think she heard me,' Jane had asked Paolina earlier. Paolina had nodded.

Jane was taller than Ashleigh and skinnier, so the dress was too big. She wore it with purple Doc Marten boots that reminded Antonello of his mother, on those winter days in Sicily when they all went out to the vineyards to pick the grapes. Emilia always wore a dress, and over the dress, an apron. She didn't own boots, but for the harvest she borrowed a pair of his father's old shoes. They were too big, and accentuated her narrow ankles and her strong calf muscles.

Jane was avoiding her parents, keeping out of their way, out of their sight. With Ashleigh, they'd been a family, a tight unit, but now they'd been yanked apart; they were separate entities, detached, floating. They were lost and broken and it seemed impossible that they could become a family again. 'Never,' Antonello heard Rae say. 'We will never be whole again.'

Gone was the spontaneity that Alex and Rae encouraged, that Antonello had disapproved of. Gone were the in-jokes that he didn't get, the giggling laughter, and the eye-rolls when he or Paolina did something old-fashioned, something too Italian, something they didn't approve of.

Ashleigh was the more affectionate of the two girls. From the time she learnt to crawl until she was eleven or twelve, she'd climbed onto his lap asking for stories, curled up next to him on the couch and fallen asleep, begged to stay over and inched between them in bed. He'd never let Alex and Nicki sleep in their bed, but he didn't say no to Ashleigh. Jane was a fussy baby, and hated being left behind by her mother. Skittish. She slipped off laps and out of grasps. She refused to spend nights anywhere but her own bed. She hated to be touched; she squirmed when they moved in to give her a kiss, a hug, to run their fingers through her hair. Jane was more aloof than Ashleigh, and he hadn't persisted. He'd let her be. Now he put his hands tentatively on her shoulders, and she leant into him.

There were two funeral cars. Jane said she wanted to go with Antonello and Paolina. Rae's parents went in the other car, with Rae and Alex. Nicki and her son, Thomas, and Rae's sisters and their families, made their own way to the chapel at the Altona cemetery. No one said anything about which route they might take, but someone must have alerted the funeral directors, and so they avoided Whitehall and Hyde Streets, the freeway, and the West Gate Bridge.

Paolina wore a black dress, black stockings, and shoes. If Ashleigh were alive, she would have teased her grandmother about being dressed in black. 'You're a goth,' she would have said, 'just missing a tattoo and a few piercings.' And if it weren't Ashleigh that was dead but some elderly relative, Alex, Rae, and Nicki would've all said something — *Oh, Mum, no one wears all black for mourning anymore* — like they did when Paolina's mother died and she insisted on wearing black for three months, as was the old Italian tradition, even though Paolina was born in Australia and for most of her life had rebelled against the old ways.

Now Paolina might never wear colour again. She might dress in black until she died. Antonello envied her. She wore her grief, took it with her, and wherever she went she was a reminder to everyone, to the whole world, that someone much loved had died.

All week people had mistaken Antonello for a normal bloke. They didn't notice that his whole world was crumbling and that he was having trouble keeping upright; that his body was loose and unstable, unanchored. He wasn't sure about anything, not walking or breathing. He'd lost the ability to operate in the world, to stand at the street corner and give directions to the cinema to a mother with a carload of ten-year-olds. Or listen to a young man wanting to sell a new phone plan. He didn't have the energy or the words to tell them, he couldn't bring himself to say, *My granddaughter died, my beautiful granddaughter died.* If he'd been able to wear black, all black, they might've read the signs and left him alone.

Paolina wound her rosary beads around her fingers. At some stage she'd swapped her everyday blue ones for the black rosary beads that had belonged to her mother. Her funeral beads. At regular intervals she raised the silver cross to her lips. She chanted prayers in a low whisper. In the early days, when they were first married, he found this irritating. Why, he wanted to know, could she not say the prayers in silence? 'I am,' she'd insist.

They slid, all three of them, into the back seat, Jane in the middle, with her headphones on, eyes on her phone, and her body pressed into her grandmother. Only a few weeks earlier Antonello had asked her why she spent so much time on the phone, and Jane, surprisingly forthcoming, showed him several music and game apps.

At the chapel, the funeral directors led them up the centre aisle to the front pews. Alex and Rae and Jane. Rae's parents. Antonello and Paolina. And then all of Ashleigh's aunts, uncles, cousins, and then more people, until the chapel was full.

The coffin was a plain white box, sustainable wood. Antonello was bewildered by Alex and Rae's ability, in their grief, to think about the planet. The coffin was covered in flowers, including one large wreath of red roses. A selection of photographs of Ashleigh were mounted in frames and sat on a small table next to the coffin. In every one of them she was smiling, a big smile that forced the dimples to go deep into her cheeks. Antonello stared at the photographs and tried not to think about

213

the coffin, about Ashleigh's body inside, broken and bruised and lifeless. He wanted to remember her living. Alive, laughing, dancing, teasing. He couldn't shake the wishful part of him, the hope to see Ashleigh running into the church, screaming, *It's a mistake. I'm alive, alive.*

Alex sobbed through the service until he got up to speak about his little girl, his first-born — Ashleigh as a toddler he'd spun in the air, as a little girl who loved playing dress-up, whom he'd chased in circles around the backyard. He spoke of Ashleigh as if she'd never reached adolescence. Rae had planned to speak too — public speaking was part of her job; every day for thirty years she'd stood in front of hundreds of children, teachers, and parents — but when the time came she didn't stand up.

There were other speakers. One of Ashleigh's high-school teachers. Her Aunt Michele, Rae's oldest sister. No one mentioned Jo or the accident. Rae and Alex had forbidden mention of *that girl*.

Two days earlier, Alex had said, 'Rae and I plan to speak at the funeral, but we don't know if we'll be able to or what we'll be able to say. I want you to, Dad — I want you to tell them about my baby.'

It was impossible to refuse. Later, at home, he said to Paolina, 'Why did they ask me?'

'Because they think you're strong. You look strong, Antonello. You look strong.'

The night before, he'd sat at the kitchen table, after Paolina had gone to bed, to write the eulogy. But hours later, the sheet of paper in front of him was covered in small sketches of Ashleigh's face. The sight of them shocked him. He'd spent his youth drawing. As a child in Vizzini he'd drawn the old stone houses that ran along both sides of the main street; the young women in their bright floral dresses, and the older women in black dresses and scarves, walking up the stone roadways to the market. He'd been good at quick, funny sketches of his friends. At school in Australia, he'd created sketches of his classmates and cartoon characters, of the streets and the houses in his neighbourhood, of the birds that lived in the swamp by the Yarra River or along the creek in Cruickshank Park — especially the rosellas and finches, birds he'd never seen before, with feathers of dazzling colours, but also the seagulls and the crows, which gathered whenever he and his brothers went fishing. His ability to draw had helped him at school. The Australian boys who picked on the wog kids who couldn't speak proper English didn't pick on him; instead, they lined up at his desk with their comic books and their demands, and he acquiesced, drawing them pictures of their favourite superheroes. That way he managed to avoid being bullied.

Drawing was something he did; it had been as natural as eating and sleeping, as playing soccer with his brothers after school. His hand taking up the pencil automatically and without hesitation or thought. He sketched without any plan, and the image made itself on the page as if it might have been there waiting, a kind of retracing; a kind of sorcery. And then he'd stopped.

When it was Antonello's turn to speak, he made his way to the lectern. He hadn't written a eulogy. On the sheet of paper in front of him were the sketches of Ashleigh: her face, her long hair, her wide eyes. At the bottom of the page there were a couple of dot points — Paolina's suggestions — Ashleigh's love of writing, her sense of humour, her determination to be a lawyer like Geoffrey Robertson, whom she'd hero-worshipped since she saw him on a *Hypothetical* on television. How they were so proud of her, and that she was an attentive granddaughter.

He began. 'Ashleigh was ...' He couldn't bear to look up. The chapel was full of friends and family and so many people he didn't know. The living — many of them old and sick — while his granddaughter was dead. But he told them about the day Ashleigh was born and how both sides of the family rushed to the hospital and filled the waiting room, how excited they were when they saw Ashleigh, the most beautiful baby in the world, and how that only seemed like yesterday. The first-born grandchild. He told them about her sense of fun. About the pleasure she took in reading and singing, in writing and debating, in having a *good* argument, and in sport — she'd tried everything at least once, he told them, including fencing and judo and horse riding. 'She was a loving daughter and granddaughter, and a loyal friend,' he said. And he told them she was a blessing and that he would miss her forever. He planned to say something about forgiveness, to remind them that the dead are dead and the living need to go on living. To remind them that the cliché was true. He wanted to tell Alex and Rae and Jane that if they didn't move on they wouldn't be able to build a life worth living. He wanted to shout, 'And you may as well all be dead too.' He wanted to tell them not to make the same mistakes he'd made. But when he looked up, he saw Sam, and he stopped mid-sentence. He was sure it was Sam, no doubt, even after all these years. He was older. He'd lost most of his hair. But it was Sam, sitting in the middle of the chapel, his eyes red from crying. And it took all Antonello's effort not to call out to him, but he did catch his eye for a moment. After that he could muster only the strength to thank everyone for coming, for their support, and make his way back to his seat.

Outside the chapel, Antonello was subsumed in the crowd of mourners. Men shook his hands, women kissed him, unknown hands patted him on the shoulder; friends, acquaintances, cousins he hadn't seen for decades expressed their sorrow. Strangers cried before him.

And then there was Sam, standing in front of him. 'I've missed you,' Antonello said, and they embraced.

Not wanting to bring attention to herself, Sarah sat at the back of the chapel. She listened to the eulogies: the Ashleigh they spoke about was *bright* and *spirited*. A little wild and prone to taking risks, but no one said that directly. Overall, if you believed the stories they told, she was a *good kid* — kind, considerate. But in Sarah's experience — and she'd been to her share of funerals now — people didn't speak ill of the dead, especially when the dead were young.

No one had mentioned Jo, but when Ashleigh's grandfather said something about friendship during his eulogy, a ripple of whispers had run along the seat in front of Sarah. Not even the celebrant mentioned Jo directly; he spoke about love and forgiveness, about tragedy. He talked about the risky nature of youth and families left devastated.

Outside the chapel, the young girl who had answered the door at Ashleigh's house, who Sarah assumed was her sister, was standing in the middle of a group of teenagers. A boy gave her a cigarette, and she took it with the confidence of a girl who knew that her parents were no longer watching. Sarah hoped to catch a glimpse of the two girls, Mani and Laura, but their photographs had been kept out of the newspaper and there was no way to distinguish them among the mourners. Moving to the edges of the crowd, where the smokers were gathered, she lit a cigarette.

'Where is that girl, what was her name — Jo or Joanna — you know, they were always together?' an older man asked a small group of smokers who were standing in a circle not far from Sarah.

'She was driving,' another bloke said. 'Plastered, apparently. Not a scratch.'

'I heard they'd all been drinking,' the woman with him whispered, leaning in as if she was sharing a secret.

'Yeah, but the other girl was driving.'

'God. They don't think, and everyone else has to pay for it. I can't see Alex and Rae getting over this.'

Did any of these people know Jo or Ashleigh? It was likely they were work colleagues of Rae or Alex's, who'd never met the girls.

'No. Nothing worse than a kid dying. Let's face it, we all did dumb things when we were young. Only difference is we survived.'

'Has the girl been charged?'

'Yep, culpable driving.'

'So they still have the court case to get through?'

'Apparently there's a backlog of cases and it might be months yet.'

'I hope the judge is tough. The message has to get through to these kids.'

Sarah sighed and butted out her cigarette.

The days after Ashleigh's funeral were empty, breathless days. Voices seemed to go missing, to be lost. Even Jane, a noisy, boisterous, uncontainable adolescent, had withdrawn. She rarely spoke, and when she did her voice was barely audible. Rae cried, sobbed, and paced, but refused to be comforted, wouldn't eat, wouldn't be touched, pushed her sisters, her parents, even Alex away. Alex raged. Banging his fist on the tables, throwing things across rooms. He cleared the whole of the vegetable garden, pulling out plants that hadn't yet matured. Soon all that was left was a lemon tree pruned to a stump and the Hills hoist spinning in the wind.

'He's like a bear in a cage,' Gary, Rae's father, said to Antonello, as the two men stood on the verandah looking over the back garden, watching as Alex stuffed the green waste into the bin, pressing down with his hands before climbing into the bin and stomping and stamping on the broken twigs and branches, on the leaves and grasses, like his ancestors once stamped on grapes to make wine.

There had been no contact with Jo or her mother. No card. No apology. Antonello considered going to Jo's house and knocking on her door. But he doubted an apology would make any difference. Would it make any difference to anyone? Dead is dead. What is done is done.

Would it have made any difference if the companies had apologised after the bridge collapsed? Would it have made any difference if they'd come knocking on their doors and begged for forgiveness? Most of the men went back to work on the bridge the week after the collapse; they needed the income. Antonello hadn't gone back, but Sam had rung him, to tell him that the men had been gathered together, that one of the engineers had spoken, thanked them for the great work they had done during the rescue operations, acknowledged that they had saved lives. But the Royal Commission was underway, he told them, and so there was no work; they were all sacked. A week's wages. No compensation. The site was closed. There were no jobs.

The companies, the company directors, the engineers should've done more. They should've gone to the funerals and begged the widows, the parents, the children for forgiveness. They should've taken care of the families and kept the survivors on the payroll instead of sacking them within days of the collapse, while they were still going to funerals, still burying their mates.

Some of the survivors, including Sam, were called to give evidence by the Royal Commission. They relived the moments before and after the collapse in detail. Antonello wasn't called. He hadn't been up at the top; he hadn't witnessed the events that lead to the accident. The papers reported on the hearings regularly. One witness, an inspector, was quoted as saying the bridge was put together like a patchwork quilt. When she read the paper, Emilia said no patchwork quilt she made would fall apart so easily. For Antonello, the newspaper reports were infuriating, the men were often portrayed as naïve, easily betrayed — by the companies, by the engineers, by the unions, and by the bridge itself.

For months he didn't work. He refused to see any of the other men. He didn't return Sam's calls. Twice Sam came to the bungalow and knocked on the door, but Antonello didn't let him in. He spent hours sitting on the doorstep looking out across the garden. Sometimes he sat with Giacomo and they smoked a cigarette, not speaking. When Paolina came home from school, she talked and he listened. He stopped reading the papers. Turned off the TV and radio at news time. He didn't want to hear about the bridge or the Commission hearings or the world going on as if nothing had happened.

Two months after the collapse, Antonello's father took him aside and said, 'You have to go back to work. There's a job at the factory. I asked the foreman, you can start tomorrow.' Antonello agreed without even asking what the job entailed. The men at the factory treated him as if he were a returning war hero — they patted him on the back as he passed, they shook his hand as they introduced himself. He worked in the storeroom and he spent his days loading boxes on and off trucks. He lived and worked in silence. While others around him talked and laughed, he was mute.

The Royal Commission interviewed fifty-two witnesses, the investigations took nine months, but the report when it was released didn't make a difference to him. Not to Sandy, either. Not to the other widows and orphans. The thirty-five men stayed dead. The Commission found the companies hadn't paid enough attention. ... *There were errors of judgment, failure of communication and sheer inefficiency ... Error begat error.* Careless. The bridge had mattered more than the men. The men were expendable. *Events moved with all the inevitability of a Greek tragedy.* Antonello remembered reading those words. A Greek tragedy? Was all life a Greek tragedy? As soon as the report was submitted, the government made plans to complete the bridge. Many of the survivors continued to feel betrayed by the companies and the government, but they went back. To finish the job. To honour those killed. To make the city whole. Antonello couldn't go back.

'It takes more courage to live,' said the old Greek widow he encountered at Footscray Cemetery after the collapse, 'more courage to keep going.' Giacomo had given him the same advice before he left Australia in his fifties, after twenty-five years of depression, to live in Vietnam, with the hope that hard work helping rebuild the country he felt guilty for destroying might give him purpose.

Seeing Sam at Ashleigh's funeral was both a shock and a relief. So many times over the years he'd longed to see his friend again but didn't have the courage to seek him out. So many nights, Sam appeared in his dreams. They should've helped each other after the accident. Sam tried. But Antonello hadn't been able to face him, to talk to him. Thirty-nine years — was it possible, could it be that long? There was so much that he remembered about those years. Watching Sam run around the soccer field — hopeless, no ball skills, but he and Slav and the rest of the men all keen to be on Sam's team because he made them laugh, made them roll on the ground with laughter, laughing so much they couldn't kick the ball. Rising early on Sunday mornings, even though it was their one day to sleep in, so they could sit together by the river and fish and talk about their futures, about the houses they'd buy, the girls they'd marry, the families they'd have … the holidays they'd take together, maybe even back to Italy.

And he remembered his excitement on his first day at the bridge, arriving early and standing on the viewing platform, sketching the outline of the twenty-eight piers, thick, solid concrete towers rising out of the water in a snaking curve from west to east. After a week of rain, it had been a perfect autumn morning, clear and fresh. Everywhere, even in the most industrial pockets of the west, where warehouses and factories butted up against one another, the lawns and the trees and of course the weeds that poked through cyclone fences and in-between cracks in paths were all a deep green and overgrown.

He remembered his mother cooking him a big breakfast of scrambled eggs with *cavolo nero* she'd collected the previous day, along with brassica, pigweed, and wild fennel on one of her scavenging excursions around Cruickshank Park. 'Lucky for us,' she said to Antonello, 'the *Australiani* don't understand these plants. There are plenty, especially after good rain.'

'Big job, building a bridge,' she said as she spooned more eggs onto his plate.

'Hey, some for me. I work too.' Franco winked at Antonello. 'She thinks you're building that whole bridge on your own.'

'There they are,' Bob had said later that morning, stepping up on the platform. 'Those piers are our giant stilts and we'll be heaving the girders onto those stilts. Hard to imagine that those piers are going to hold all that weight, all that fucking concrete and steel, a whole fucking roadway, and the traffic, the cars and trucks. It'll be bloody amazing driving across the bridge.' He elbowed Antonello and pointed at the tallest pylon. 'Hey Nello, imagine that, your first bridge, mate, and it's a beauty. We'll be so high up; we'll see the river and the bay, and the whole bloody city. The views will be great from up there. To die for.'

They had both stared across at the city centre on the other side of the river, and Bob added, 'Hope you're wearing your woollies, it'll be cold up there. Freeze your balls off if you're not careful. It'll be worth it, though — we are gonna make history here. Bloody hell, son, you and me, part of history.'

And he remembered a warm afternoon when the breeze came from the sea, and Slav recited A.D. Hope's 'The Death of the Bird' as they sat on Sam's front verandah, waiting for Sam's mother to call them in for dinner. He could remember the whole poem, even though he hadn't read it in all those years. The poem opens with a bird's migration towards summer and love, but it is the bird's last migration and when, finally unable to keep flying, the bird falls, nature is indifferent.

'It's such a sad poem,' he remembered saying to Slav. 'Why do you like it so much?'

'For everyone there will be a last migration, but in the meantime, let's enjoy the view, the experience, the flying.'

'Cheers,' said Sam as he poured them each another wine, 'let's drink to that.'

Chapter 18

For Jo, the funeral had been a marker, a rope across a finish line. An end and a beginning. After the funeral, she planned to think about what was next. About the court case and prison and life after that. But the funeral was over and she wasn't sure that any future was possible. Did she have the right to a future? To a life? Could she spend the rest of her life in bed, in the dark, avoiding everything?

Before the accident, she'd imagined going to university. Some kind of job. Marriage. Children. Six children. A big, busy family. Enough children to fill all the spaces in the house. Enough children so that each child had several siblings and wouldn't be lonely. The kind of family that filled a kitchen at dinner time; a noisy house. But there would be none of that. No husband. No children. Who would want a killer for a wife? For a mother?

At the hospital, on the night of the accident, while she lay in bed in the Emergency ward, her mother had stood in the gap in the curtain, half in and half out, and said, 'We, you and me, we are going to have to learn to live with this.' Live. Jo didn't want to live. She wished she didn't exist, that she'd never existed, that there was a way of travelling back in time to wipe herself out.

One morning a couple of days after the funeral, Jo switched the computer on for the first time since the accident. Avoiding her email and Facebook — all those places where someone might try and contact her — she googled 'suicide' and 'suicide methods' and found over 42 million hits. So many people thinking about dying, about ways to die; so many people wanting a way out. For the first time in days, she was calm. There was a sense of relief. A way out was possible.

Pills. Poison. On one site there was a list of twenty-four poisons, including water. Eight litres of it would be enough. She would have to drink and drink and drink … Carbon monoxide was another, but there was no car. She hadn't even thought about her car — no one had mentioned it. She assumed it had been destroyed, compacted into a thin sheet of metal, thrown into landfill and buried.

Alcohol. She could drink herself to death. She hadn't touched alcohol since the party. She went to the cupboard in the hallway where they kept wine and spirits. But it was empty. She went outside and opened the recycle bin: it was full of empty bottles. The stench of wine was a slap, and she reeled back from it. She hated the taste of wine, of spirits. She drank sweet mixed drinks when she went out, and only then to suppress the anxiety. So much drinking. All of them — Ash and Laura and Mani, everyone they knew: why did they drink so much?

There were websites that explained, step by step, how a person could hang themselves. Sites giving advice on guns. On how to get them. On how to use them. There were sites listing places high enough to jump off. The West Gate Bridge was still on the list, even though with the barricades it was almost impossible. But the bridge would be the perfect location — what if it were possible? What if she snuck onto the bridge at night, climbed the fence, and let herself fall? Jo was a good swimmer. A good diver. What would it take to stay under the surface? To refuse to take in air? *Fill your pockets with stones*, one post said, *like Virginia Woolf.* Jo read Woolf's suicide note posted on another site — her fear of going mad, the voices in her head, the inability to keep going. The belief in death's release, the peace of a long deep sleep. No more anxiety. No more sadness.

If she died, everyone would understand how much she loved Ash. They'd realise she hadn't meant to hurt Ash. They'd know she was sorry. 'Show that you are remorseful,' Sarah had said.

You want to do everything I do, even die. Really?

———

Mandy stood outside Jo's room, listening for signs of life. Jo hadn't been a quiet child. Before the accident, they had fought constantly about the volume of the music and the television. Now it was the silence that woke Mandy in the middle of the night. It was the silence that vibrated through the house, the silence that drew her to Jo's room, listening for her daughter's breathing. To make sure she was alive, that she hadn't killed herself. Suicide. Two of Jo's classmates had suicided when they were sixteen. They had seemed like normal kids living normal lives.

Mandy remembered arriving at the hospital on the night of the accident — there had been a moment when she thought Jo was going to jump out of the bed and run into her arms. But Mandy had kept her arms folded, deliberately shutting Jo out. Standing half in the cubical and half out, she'd barked at her daughter, 'What have you done?' Now she felt guilty, a *bad mother*, but still she could not bring herself to open the door, to go to her daughter, to forgive her.

Jo didn't talk to Mandy about suicide. But the signs were all there: Jo's despair, her silence, her refusal to leave her room. Mandy knew that Jo was struggling to imagine a life in the aftermath of the accident. How did people keep living when grief was weighed down by guilt? So at night, she kept vigil at Jo's bedroom door, sometimes for hours at a time, shivering in the cold hallway, afraid to go to bed until she heard a murmur or a sigh, signs of life. Suicide watch.

Mandy had gone back to work. What choice did she have? She had requested a transfer and they moved her to a store in Glen Waverley. At least when she was at work she had people to interact with and things to do, and some days she forgot about Jo, about Ashleigh, about the accident, for whole hours at a time. It took her an hour and a half to get home, she didn't hurry, hesitating each time before she opened the front door and called out, 'Jo, I'm home. Jo, are you there?' Jo took her time to respond, and sometimes not until Mandy had called out a second or third time. 'I'm here. Where else would I be?'

With some coaxing, Jo began to come out at dinnertime, and they sat at the table together. Mandy talked about the weather, about people at work. She was careful not to complain about travelling to Glen Waverley, or about missing her old workmates. Neither of them mentioned the accident or Ashleigh. Mandy planned to talk to Jo about getting a job or going back to school, but she couldn't stand the idea of Jo out in the world where she might run into Alex or Rae or Jane or some of her schoolfriends. And she was worried, ashamed, and so sad. She didn't think they'd ever be able to see anything, do anything, in any other way. Plus there was the trial to get through. 'It might be six months or longer,' Sarah had told them.

Sarah was collecting character statements from people prepared to say Jo was a good person, that Jo wasn't the sort of young woman given to being irresponsible, but Mandy worried that Sarah wouldn't find enough people willing to make positive statements. Not that Jo had ever been a bad kid. But who did they know? Jo didn't belong to any clubs or community groups. Mandy didn't have influential contacts. 'I don't know any politicians or business managers, anyone like that,' she had told Sarah. 'My neighbor, Mrs Nguyễn, likes Jo and she's happy to sign a statement. But she doesn't want to go to court. Those kinds of places make her nervous. She asks me to go with her if she has to talk to someone at the bank or Centrelink. My other neighbours — well, Bob has been in and out of prison most of his life, and the rest are renters I don't know.'

'I want you to promise me,' Mary said, 'that you won't do anything silly.' She was sitting opposite Jo at the kitchen table.

'Too late for that, Nan, don't you think?' Jo put her sandwich down. She hadn't eaten peanut butter and honey sandwiches since she was a fat twelve-year-old. But her grandmother had made them, and spent a long time coaxing Jo out of her room. White bread, in neat triangles, and a pot of tea. The sandwiches were comforting.

'What's done is done,' Mary said. 'But I mean, you won't do anything to hurt yourself?'

Jo didn't tell Mary she'd spent the morning googling suicide methods.

'Things'll get better,' Mary said.

Your grandmother is a Pollyanna. It was one of Mandy's more common complaints about Mary. It was true, Jo thought, but maybe it was a special gift, to believe that things would turn out alright.

'You think that's possible, Nan?'

'I know it seems like it's the end of the world. But bad things happen to everyone. Everyone makes mistakes. Slowly life will get better. I know that from experience. You're young. I'm old, you have to trust me.'

'I can't imagine anything ever getting better. Ever.' Jo knew that Mary's early life had been difficult. Mary's father had died when she was a child, and her mother had spent years in psychiatric hospitals. Jo had heard some of her grandmother's stories about the poverty, the loneliness, of growing up in a house with elderly grandparents who never stopped grieving for their son. 'How poor were you?' Jo and Mandy often teased Mary when they could see she was about to tell a story they had heard before. But Mary told the stories anyway, and talked about God and strength and carving out a life.

'I haven't told you how my father died,' Mary said.

'No. Was he sick?' Jo sensed a story coming. Listening to Mary was better than listening to Ash's voice or her own circling thoughts.

'I don't know if he was sick. These days we'd say he must've been.' Mary hesitated. 'This is a story I thought I'd never tell you,' she said. 'I was five years old and playing in the backyard with my baby doll and an old pram, taking the doll for trips down the path that ran around the lemon tree, through the lawn, past the barbecue, and to the vegetable patch. I was singing "Rock-a-bye Baby" and watching the doll, pretending I was its mother.'

Jo pushed the plate with the remainder of the sandwich away from her. Mary frowned and pushed it back towards Jo. 'Eat,' she said. Jo grimaced, but didn't respond. It seemed to Jo that her grandmother hadn't aged in the last twenty years — she'd been an old woman when Jo was little and she was an old woman now. Her hair was a soft cloudy white, and she still wore it in the same short bob. It was difficult to imagine Mary as a little girl pushing a doll in a pram.

'I can still remember my mother's scream, a high-pitched cry, and I knew it was bad, so I ran into the house, calling, "Mummy, Mummy, where are you?" She didn't respond, and I couldn't find her until I heard the door of my parents' bedroom bang shut, and there was my mother standing against the door and yelling at me, "Go away, go back into the backyard. Go now and don't come back. Go." She was so angry, she didn't look at all like my mother. My mother had the most beautiful blue eyes — "smiling eyes", my father called them — but the woman at the door had dark, bulging eyes, and she wouldn't look at me.

'I was a little girl, so I don't remember everything. But I remember I was scared. I hadn't heard my mother yell before. I stopped and my mother shooed me away like she did our old cat, Ginger, when she came too close to the table at dinnertime, waving me away with her hand. She opened the door and slid back into the room, slamming it shut and yelling. I cried. I called out to her. I wanted her to come back out and pick me up.

'My grandparents said they found me sitting on the back doorstep pulling the farm animals off my dress — I loved that dress. My mother had made it on her treadle Singer sewing machine. Around the hem, she'd sewn felt farmyard animals. They held hands and paws to form a ring-a-rosie. I must've heard the sirens, the ambulance and the police. It was a couple of days before my grandmother told me that my father was dead, and that my mother was very, very sad.'

'Suicide?' Jo asked.

'Yes.'

'Why?'

'I still don't know. Maybe my mother knew. Maybe my grandparents, but no one ever talked about it. He was a coward. Let himself off the hook, and killed everything for the rest of us — for my mother, for his parents, for me. My mother changed. She hated music, especially the radio. She hated seeing me playing with my friends. We couldn't live in our house, so we moved in with my father's parents. My mother spent the next ten years in and out of hospital. My mother became stuck. If you get stuck, it can be impossible to get unstuck. I don't want you to get stuck.'

But Jo *was* stuck. She didn't identify with Mary's mother in the story. She wanted to know more about Mary's father, and the desire to make life stop.

'Please promise me,' Mary pleaded, interrupting her thoughts, 'that you won't hurt yourself.'

Jo promised.

Cross my heart, hope to fly, stick a cupcake in my eye. Ash's singsong voice in her ear. So many pinkie promises, little fingers locked together.

After Mary left, Jo went back to her room, to the list she'd made of suicide options. She longed to fall into a long deep sleep, for all the anxiety and pain to disappear. But though she might not deserve to live, she knew she wouldn't be able to kill herself. And not just because of what it might do to her grandmother and her mother.

Jo screwed up the list and threw it in the bin. And then took it out, unscrewed it, and ripped it into tiny pieces and threw them in the bin. To live — what would that mean? Prison, first, but after that? She couldn't keep living in her mother's house, down the road from Ash's family. She'd have to leave. Run away. She'd change her name. To Smith or Jones or Brown. An ordinary name. A name that no one would remember. Anna Smith. Kate Jones. Live alone in some remote place as far away as possible.

You can't run away from me. You can't run far enough.

Where did the missing go? People disappeared; they disappeared for a lifetime with no trace. Jo had written an essay on missing people for a school assignment in Year 9. She'd discovered that it wasn't a crime to go missing. The police refused to spend too much time looking for adults who went missing unless there were suspicious circumstances — blood, abandoned cars, break-ins. Some people just stepped out of their lives. Sometimes without even leaving a note. More than 35,000 people a year, in fact. Some came back or were found after a couple of days. But others kept going, leaving everything behind. At the time, she'd imagined the fear of being discovered would be unbearable; a lifetime of looking over one's shoulder. Now, she thought of the relief of being anonymous and unattached.

She didn't think about forgiveness. She didn't believe in God. Before Ash died, she believed the dead were dead, gone. She and Ash made fun of the religious people — Seventh-day Adventists, Jehovah's Witnesses — who came door to door, *selling God as if he was a vacuum cleaner,* as Mandy would say.

'God forgives everything. You have to be sorry and be prepared to do the penance,' Mary often said.

What penance would make up for killing you, Ash?

Are you kidding? Penance?

Ash had big plans and all kinds of ambitions. She was going to be a renowned lawyer. She was going to fight for human rights across the globe. She was going to work for the United Nations.

Did she owe Ash a life?

Did she owe the world Ash's life?

You owe me.

Sarah and Mandy were sitting on the back verandah, looking out at the backyard. At the tall gumtree, at red bottlebrushes in full bloom, at the kangaroo paws — orange and yellow — and the clumps of native grasses. It was a mild spring evening. The bridge, visible over the back fence, was a dark line against a pink-and-grey sky.

Mandy brought out two glasses and a longneck.

'No thanks, I still have to drop the car off at the office,' Sarah said, shaking her head at the offer of a beer.

'Just in case you change your mind. It's the only thing I have. I threw out all the alcohol in the house last week. A friend brought this around, homemade beer, her father makes crates of it. It's not great, but it's not too bad. Drinkable.'

Sarah rolled a cigarette. She'd been on her way back to the office from a meeting in Williamstown when she decided to drop in on Mandy. She was still working on developing Jo's case and wanted to get more sense of the relationship between the two girls, and also the two families.

'We come from different worlds,' Mandy said when Sarah asked about Ashleigh's family. 'Sometimes I felt like I wasn't good enough. Early in the girls' friendship, Rae and Alex made lots of suggestions.

About sending Jo to this class or that, but those classes — I mean, they're for kids, but they cost a packet … But we were civil and polite to each other. We're not friends, never socialised, but we trusted each other with the girls.'

'What about Ashleigh and Jo?' Sarah asked.

'Rae and I, both of us thought they wouldn't be friends for long. Ashleigh was at the top of the class. Jo isn't academic. I mean, she's fine, you know, she gets through, but I think Rae thought Jo wasn't smart enough to be Ashleigh's friend — not that she ever said that to me, but I could tell that's what she thought. She would say things like, "Ashleigh helped Jo with her homework", "Ashleigh is so quick at maths, so much better than me, my God", "Ashleigh reads so fast".'

'Do you think Ashleigh used that against Jo?'

'Jo's not dumb.' Mandy shrugged. 'They're both readers, but Ashleigh finished a book every couple of days, whereas it takes Jo weeks. But, look, Rae and Alex didn't interfere — they've been good to Jo. I guess they were used to having her around: they invited Jo to all the family events, even holidays. And I invited Ashleigh to ours, but of course we don't do as much. Got so we didn't go anywhere without Ashleigh.'

'Did Jo like going to Ashleigh's house? Did she feel comfortable there?'

'Yes, at least as far as I know.'

'Jo said Ashleigh wanted to be a lawyer?'

'That girl wanted to change the world …' Mandy choked up and couldn't finish the sentence. 'I'm sorry.'

'Don't be. It is sad.'

After Mandy composed herself, Sarah continued. 'Mandy, have you talked to Jo about why she and Ashleigh were arguing in the car?'

'No.'

'Was Ashleigh ever mean to Jo?'

'I don't think so, no.'

'Do you have any idea what they were fighting about?'

'No. You're supposed to know your kids, what's happening in their lives, but I don't know much about Jo's life, not much at all. One minute you know everything there is to know about your child, and suddenly they have a separate life and the parent has no access. Most of the time I have no idea what Jo is thinking or feeling. How is it possible that I have no access to my own daughter?' There was despair and regret in Mandy's voice. Sarah reached out and put her hand on Mandy's arm and they sat together in silence for several minutes.

Chapter 19

The week after Ashleigh's funeral had been unusually warm for spring, but suddenly the city had turned grey. Dark clouds appeared late morning, and by early evening there were storms — lightning, thunder, and heavy downpours. On the street, neighbours discussed Melbourne's volatile weather, the predictions for a long, hot summer, and the ongoing fears that climate change was increasing the risk of bushfires. At home the conversation was minimal, reduced to the organisation of meals and Paolina's doctor's appointments. Most afternoons they made their way to their son's house and sat with whoever happened to be there — Alex, Rae, Jane, Rae's parents, neighbours, friends, extended family — in the kitchen or the front living room, keeping company. But all Antonello wanted to do was to be alone.

Some visitors spoke at length, didn't stop speaking, told their stories about Ashleigh or avoided mentioning Ashleigh at all and instead recounted car accident after car accident, tragedy after tragedy, the horrible things that happened to other people. Alex came into the room to greet each new visitor, his face expectant, but after a few minutes, unable to sit still, he wandered off, into the garden or the garage or the shed. If Rae was in the room, she was the focus, the one they hugged, the one they wept over. Rae let them. She was an experienced school principal; she understood how to keep her emotions contained. In the gaps and silences, she talked about going back to work (*maybe tomorrow, maybe next week*) and she talked about the court case (*we need to make sure that girl pays for what she's done*).

In the bleakness, some visitors sprang at these statements, adding their own commentary: *Drunk drivers should be locked up for a long time, throw away the key I reckon, they have to be taught a lesson.* Those that might've spoken for Jo, who might've empathised with her, kept silent.

During these afternoons, life was in a holding pattern. Beyond it was the future, what people referred to as *getting back to a normal life* or *moving on*, something none of them could imagine. And so they continued gathering, as if by coming together they could stop time. Or spin it backwards.

When Sam rang, Antonello was listening to Rae's mother sharing her memories of Ashleigh as a toddler. Beverly was a stocky woman in her seventies. Everything about her was large — her breasts, her belly, her head, with its crown of unruly grey hair — except for her legs, which were slender and shapely. She sat on the sofa next to her daughter, holding Rae's hand, patting her arm. Her legs were stretched out across the rug. Antonello sat opposite and stared at her feet, at her strappy sandals, at her toenails painted a soft yellow.

'Who was that? I heard the phone,' Alex asked as Antonello came back in.

'Sam. An old friend.'

'I've never heard you mention him,' he said.

'We worked together once. It was a long time ago.'

Alex shrugged and left the room.

As a child, Alex was enthusiastic and overly energetic. He'd had lots of friends. Once, when he was six, three of his friends demanded he pick his *best, best* friend: they wanted him to choose and he couldn't decide.

'Dad, who is your best friend?' Alex had asked him.

'Your mother.'

'But what about a boy, a friend who is a boy?'

'Your Uncle Joe. Your Uncle Giacomo.'

'No, someone else,' Alex insisted. 'Outside the family? Why don't you have other friends? You know, like from work? Or from football?'

'I've got responsibilities and I've got you and your sister and your mother, and my mother and father, and I don't have time.' Antonello wanted to say, *Stop asking me all these questions, you little pest.* But he knew that even Alex could see the flaw. What kind of man has no friends?

The following afternoon, when Antonello arrived at the Vic, Sam was already sitting at a table, a beer in front of him. On Antonello's side was a glass of red wine. 'I took a punt — ordered you a merlot.'

'Thanks. Still my drink of choice. I used to pretend I liked beer, I thought it'd make me more Australian, but I gave up that a long time ago.'

'Unfortunately, I like it too much. More ocker than the ones born here.'

They were the sole customers in the bar. A middle-aged waitress carried a tray of salt and pepper shakers and placed a pair on each table. The barman and the chef played pool. From the games room next door, there was the constant beep and chime of the pokie machines, the clink of coins against the metal trays, the jackpot jingles and old-time tunes, vaguely familiar. Flashing lights reflected on the mirror above the bar.

It was a gloomy pub. Poorly renovated several times since the 1970s, the layers of change were visible, one on top of the other. Like make-up clumsily applied over scar tissue, it failed to camouflage its faults.

'Don't remember the bar ever being this empty,' Antonello said.

'No more factories around here, no more punters,' Sam said.

It was difficult not to drift off into the past. Antonello had spent so many nights sitting at the bar with Sam and Slav, watching Bob play pool. Bob had a knack for it and there was usually some younger bloke willing to challenge him to a game. They'd throw a coin or two on the table, but no one ever took Bob's money. Antonello remembered gathering around the bar after every shift. The pungent mix of sweat and beer, the arguments — mostly about football — and the yelling, the stupid jokes and the raucous laughter. The dead were back, sitting at the bar. They swung around to face him and raised their glasses.

'Just a few compulsive gamblers now,' Sam said, nodding towards the pokies. 'Don't come here anymore? This would still be your local?'

'This or the Blarney. But I don't go to the pub much. Paolina dragged me here one night about ten years ago — she wanted to have dinner and play the pokies. I couldn't stomach it. I kept expecting to see Bob or Slav at the bar. I could hear Bob's laughter ... We didn't even stay to eat.'

'Should we go somewhere else?' Sam asked, picking up his beer and taking a long swig. Sam had put on weight, but he wasn't fat; there was just a hint of a beer belly under the blue Australian Workers' Union windcheater. Antonello stared at his face: there were a few frown lines, some wrinkles, the flesh around his cheeks sagging, but he was still so familiar, with the broad Roman nose, the bushy eyebrows, and those luminous hazel eyes.

'No. I was going to suggest somewhere else, but nowhere else seemed right, either.'

'I'm surprised you're still living in the area,' Sam said. 'I thought you might've shifted away. A lot of us did.'

'Where are you?'

'Geelong. I work out of the office there and live in a flat — small place, with a view of the bay from the bathroom window.' Sam smiled, bringing his hands close together to show the narrowness of the view.

'Paolina wanted to move. But I couldn't imagine living anywhere else.' He didn't tell Sam that the further from the bridge he was, the worse the nightmares. After Alex and Nicki had moved out of home, Antonello and Paolina went on a trip to Europe. They booked a twenty-day tour and spent time in Sicily with their extended families. Every night he was away, Antonello dreamt of the bridge. Not the falling bridge he'd witnessed, not the half-constructed bridge, but the finished bridge crowded with peak-hour traffic. He watched the piers crumbling, the roadway collapsing over and over again, cars and people dropping into the river like dead birds. He had those nightmares at home too, but he could get up, go outside, and see the bridge. Calm himself down. Away from it, the anxiety clung to him, and there was no reprieve. He was bound to the bridge, bound to living under its shadow.

'I thought I might never see you again,' Sam said, and Antonello heard the reproach. What kind of man refused to see his best friend?

'I'm sorry, Sam. At first I needed to be alone, I didn't want to see anyone. And then it seemed too much time had gone by.'

Antonello remembered watching Sam coming up the driveway and shaking hands with Paolina's father, who was digging over the soil in the vegetable patch. Sam knocked and pounded on the door while he stood inside the bungalow, gripping the back of the chair to stop himself from falling, from caving into himself, his head throbbing. His body shaking.

'I gave up after Alice left,' Sam said. 'I had my own shit and I thought, *bugger you.*'

Antonello nodded. 'I know for some of the blokes it helped to get together, working on the plaque and the memorial, and even on finishing the bridge, but for me …'

'It was fucking hard for all of us,' Sam said, pushing his empty glass aside.

'Another round?' Antonello asked. His own glass was still half full.

Sam nodded, and Antonello called out to the barman, 'Same again.'

'A couple of times I set out to come and see you,' he continued. 'Once I got as far as your gate. And then I thought I'd come back to work on the bridge and I'd see you on the site, but the week we were due back I got so sick I couldn't get out of bed. They call them panic attacks now. I had the shakes so bad that at one point they did tests for Parkinson's. Paolina was pregnant and we had the mortgage and I had to work. My father organised a storeman's job at Bradmill's. Most days the only sunlight I saw was through the gaps between the storeroom door and the containers. I stayed there for a couple of years, until Sandy organised the job in the library. So I took it and went back to school to retrain.'

'White-collar.' Sam grinned and ran his finger around the inside of his own collar. 'Bit of a change from rigging.'

'I miss the rigging. The library's okay, but I miss being outside. Even miss the height work, even those freezing mornings.'

'Great view, though, across the whole city. I loved the heights.'

'You sure did.' Antonello smiled. 'No bloody fear.' The barman put the drinks on the counter and Antonello stood up, paid, and brought them over.

'I was young and silly. I thought I was invincible. Becoming a union organiser knocked some sense into me. Sometimes it feels too much like a desk job, so I hit the road and visit workers around the region.'

'You've done a lot of good. I've seen you on the telly, at the rallies. You're …' Antonello was choking up and had to stop and take a breath. 'I'm proud of you, Sam, proud of you.' Over the years, when he'd seen Sam on television, he'd had the urge to shout out, *that's my best mate.*

Sam shrugged. 'It hasn't been easy. I was a fucking mess for a long time and did a shitload of drinking. *The survivors*, we had permanent spots at the bar. Alice and I fought every day until she left. I blamed her, but it wasn't her fault. Not mine, either.'

'You were crazy about her. I thought you guys'd be together forever,' Antonello said.

'Still a bit crazy about her,' Sam said, shaking his head.

'I'm sorry, Sam.' Antonello sighed and remembered Alice, a nonstop talker who loved going to the San Remo and being the only Australian girl there, and dancing all night with Sam, and plotting to convince Sam's mother it wouldn't be the end of the world if he married an *Australiana*.

'She's happy, married with a couple of kids. And I'm happy too — I met Judith twenty-years ago now, and we're good together. She already had two boys, so it was an instant family. Alice and I'll always be friends.'

'We needed help, but no one offered,' Antonello said.

'No, I thought going back to the bridge would help, but it was tough. There were days working on the bridge when it shook, when I was sure I'd fall … I could hear Bob's voice calling me and I wanted to fall. There were times I considered, just a step, just a step, and I'd be gone too.'

'It's surprising no one did,' Antonello said.

'Blokes died in other ways: heart attacks, strokes. But yeah, these days they'd have us all on suicide watch. I believed if the bridge didn't get finished, Bob and Slav and the other blokes would've lost their lives for nothing. As if the fucking bridge was something. And I thought I owed it to 'em to get the thing done. I wanted to see it finished. Alice and my mother were furious. Finally, they agreed on something … But I went back. Most of the time, I was either drunk or hung-over, but it was the only way I could keep going. And the bloody companies were as bad as ever — as if they hadn't learnt anything from the accident, nothing. So of course there were strikes and stopworks, and money was tight. Alice was trying to get pregnant. She had two miscarriages and I wasn't around. It was the last straw. After she left, I lost the house and had to move in with my parents. Now, that was hell.'

Antonello nodded, and they both laughed at the memory of Sam's bossy mother.

Could he have made a difference to Sam's life? If he'd let Sam into the bungalow, if he'd picked up the phone, would life have been better for both of them? The sharp yank of regret: another trap.

'Things got worse until Gary Willis gave me a job.'

'Gary Willis, I remember him. He was a racist bastard,' Antonello said before he could think to censor himself. Gary had been their shop steward on the bridge. He was a tough guy, prepared to stand up to the bosses, but often that put him off side with the men as well. In hindsight, they knew Gary had been right about so many of the problems on the bridge: the asbestos in the welding blankets and gloves, the damage to hearing caused by constant loud noise, the lead and chromium in the paints, the need for scaffolding and guards, and of course the problems with the structural design and the construction processes. There had been so many accidents. The men who survived were still paying the costs years later, but no work meant no pay, and that meant not enough money for the mortgage or the rent, to buy food or pay bills. So even for the committed unionists, it became difficult.

'He wasn't all bad,' Sam insisted. 'He taught me a lot.'

'He hated us wogs,' Antonello said. 'He never referred to any of us by name — we were the *dago bastards* or *a pack of bludgers and scabs*, even when we were out on strike.' At one meeting, after the workers voted against Gary's proposal to strike, Gary had let loose on the *fucking dagos*, who shouldn't have been allowed in the *fucking country*. Antonello and Sam and Slav had been in his line of vision. He stood only inches from Antonello's face with his fists raised: 'You should fucking go back to where you fucking come from.' Antonello wasn't a fighter; even as a child he'd avoided boyish tumbles. But he'd wanted to hit Gary that day. Sam and Bob had to pull him away. In Gary's eyes, he was scum, he could see that.

'The day I started working, my father said to me, "You never step onto a work site without union membership. Otherwise, the bosses will screw you. When everyone stands together, that's when workers can have some power." So I'd expected the unionists to be the good guys,' Antonello said.

'Okay, yes, Gary can be a bastard, but he was right about Freeman Fox and World Services — they didn't know what the fuck they were doing. He was right about a lot of things, including Milford.'

With the mention of the Milford Haven Bridge, Antonello winced; he felt as if Sam had taken a swipe at him. Milford should've been the warning that saved them. Four men had been killed. The Milford and the West Gate had the same design, by the same company. Gary organised a meeting and urged them to strike. Then the engineer, Michael Shields, came to talk to them. 'I'm one of the best engineers in the world. I've worked on more bridges than most of you have had hot dinners,' he said. 'The West Gate is safe. If I didn't think it was safe, I wouldn't be working on it.' Of all the engineers, Michael Shields had been most like them, down-to-earth, a father of young children. He sounded confident. 'Our bridge isn't the same as the bridge in Wales. We have a stronger bridge — it's better designed, it's better built.'

They believed him, and made naïve reassurances to their families. They were unwilling to believe that the bridge, their bridge, could be faulty, capable of that kind of betrayal.

'I wake up in the middle of the night sometimes,' Antonello said, 'thinking, *why the hell did we believe that man?*'

'Because he believed it,' Sam said. 'Bloody fool, cost him his life.'

'And he took thirty-four other men with him.' Antonello took off his jacket. It seemed to have gotten hotter in the pub and he could feel a sweaty dampness in his armpits. Why had he agreed to meet Sam? Why now? He knew they'd talk about the bridge — that's where their friendship lived, as if it were still trapped under the debris of the collapsed span.

Sam lifted his glass up. 'Another?'

'No, but you go ahead.'

Sam went to the bar.

Antonello remembered the overwhelming feeling of pride when he started working on the bridge. But as they fell behind schedule, further and further, it turned into shame and embarrassment — *that bridge is taking longer than Rome to build, are you guys building it with tweezers?* He remembered the mounting pressure to complete the project, to ignore the problems.

Sam came back with a beer and some salt and vinegar chips.

'Haven't had these for years, they're so salty.' Antonello opened the packet and took a chip.

'You need to drink beer with them,' Sam said, pushing the packet closer to Antonello. 'Anyway, Gary was the one who convinced me to get more involved in the union when we went back to finish the bridge. We ended up on strike straightaway because they didn't want to let the shop stewards on the job. Can you imagine: they wanted us to forget the accident and work on the bridge as if nothing had happened?'

Antonello didn't say anything, and Sam continued, 'Okay, maybe Gary was racist — things were different then — but he's been a good mate, and together we've done important work.'

Antonello frowned. Was that kind of racism defensible? Sam was defending Gary, a man who had been awful to all the Italians, to the Greeks and the Yugoslavs. Had Gary's good work compensated for it? Could everything and anything be forgiven?

'So many workers are killed each year in industrial accidents, and the companies can't be trusted to do the right thing, and we pay for it with our lives. The accident on the east side in '72, another death — it was the last straw. This work is my legacy, my way of taking what happened on the bridge and doing something with it. It's given me a purpose, a battle to fight. '

'I still have nightmares,' Antonello said. He hadn't told anyone about the nightmares, not even Paolina, though of course she knew. 'And sometimes a noise — a bolt of thunder, a car backfiring, a jackhammer — and I'm back under the bridge looking up, and I can see the whole fucking thing moving and the men falling ... and it's as if Bob and Slav are saying, "Don't forget us. Don't fucking forget us."'

'Look, mate,' Sam said, leaning across the table, 'I don't think Bob or Slav or any of the other blokes would want you to spend your life suffering. They'd want us to be happy, like we would've wanted them to be happy if things were the other way around. We paid for that memorial, the unions and the blokes — the government and the companies wanted to forget the whole fucking thing, but we wouldn't let them. We haven't forgotten them. Fuck, we'll never forget them.'

'I should've died that night. It was meant to be my shift. I was supposed to be up there and Ted was supposed to be on the ground. We did a switch.' Antonello had mostly kept silent about the switch in shifts. He'd told himself it would only make things worse for Ted's family.

'Nello, it's been thirty-nine years. None of those blokes deserved to die, and if we'd died we wouldn't have deserved to die. It was the fault of the companies. Not your fault. Not my fault.'

'But I saw stuff that was wrong and I didn't —'

'Yeah, we all did. That's what we are trying to change — workers' and bosses' attitudes, both. Trying to get workers not to ignore problems, to stand up and say when things are wrong. But it's tough. Who wants to risk losing their job?'

'Or lose faith? We were all so committed. We loved that bridge. We thought we were big bridge builders, some kind of heroes.'

'We were proud of what we were doing. Nothing wrong with that.'

'We were fools, Sam. Fodder for the companies, for the government. The bridge, that was the important thing — the bridge and joining the bloody city together and progress. And they used us and we fell for it, for the whole thing. We fell for it.' Antonello had forgotten where he was and his voice had risen. The chef and the barman stopped playing pool and stared at him. He wanted to yell, at Sam, and at the two young men who probably had no idea that thirty-five men had died building the West Gate.

'Sorry,' he said, and the chef went back to play his shot. Antonello watched him lean across the pool table, the cue aimed at a ball in the far corner. He was focused on the game, taking his time, shifting to the right and back, and again, as if nothing else existed. It took him three shots to finish the game. The barman laughed. 'At this rate, I'll still be paying for your drinks into the next century.'

'And now Ashleigh,' he said to Sam in a quieter tone.

'How is your family coping?' Sam asked.

'They're struggling. Alex is a mess. My daughter-in-law hasn't left the house for weeks. She's obsessing over the court case and Jo — the young woman who was driving — and making sure that Jo pays. As if locking the girl away will make everything better.'

Sam reached out and put his hand on Antonello's shoulder.

'I was an absent father even though I was home. Even when I was playing games with them, I wasn't there. But now, watching Rae and Alex, I see how obvious it is when parents aren't coping. My granddaughter Jane is so sad. She misses her sister and now her parents are falling apart. She stayed with us a couple of nights, and with some friends too, but it's tough. She's closest to her mother.' He paused. 'I was a poor role model. Paolina has been the strong parent. She's held the family together, but now she's sick, so she can't do it.'

From the gaming room the loud beeps and bells of a slot machine jackpot broke out, followed by exclamations and laughter. Antonello felt like a man waking up in the middle of the night to a neighbours' party, and realising that while he was sleeping other people were living.

On 15 October, the thirty-ninth anniversary of the collapse, there was a small gathering at the memorial under the bridge. Sam rang and invited Antonello, but he made excuses and didn't go. Instead, he waited until late afternoon and went to the bridge on his own. He tried to remember the days, the weeks, the months after the bridge collapsed. There were so many funerals he couldn't distinguish one from the other. He hadn't slept for days, until he went to a doctor who gave him sedatives. There were weeks of hiding out at home, of not being able to get out of bed. In his memory, the time after the accident stretched out long and black.

He remembered, too, going through the bungalow — it must have been a month or so after the collapse — and searching for sketchbooks and his drawings of the bridge. Paolina refused to tell him where she'd hidden them. When finally he found a couple of them, he built a fire in the metal drum his father-in-law kept for boiling sauce bottles and threw them in. Paolina tried to stop him, pulling at his arms, at the sketchbooks half eaten by the flames. Defeated, she cried, and the ash and smoke choked the backyard. He never sketched again, not even with his children and grandchildren.

For whole days he sat at the kitchen table or on the back doorstep and smoked cigarettes, one after the other, the panic and fear so overwhelming, the sense of looming disaster unbearable. On those days, he didn't want Paolina to leave the house; he pleaded with her to stay home. When she left, he worried about her all day, and if she was late, he paced up and down the driveway until she arrived.

Only his brother-in-law Giacomo understood. 'It doesn't matter how far away you go. Moving away is pointless. The ghosts are everywhere.' Giacomo's ghosts stalked him — they were relentless and mocking, and he was tormented. He didn't talk about the war, and he didn't ask Antonello about the bridge. The two brothers-in-law, both talkers as children, had lost their tongues, but sometimes in the middle of the night, when they couldn't sleep or their nightmares were unbearable, they found each other in the garden. They sat on the old chairs Paolina's father kept under the fig tree, or on the bungalow doorsteps, and reminisced about their boyhoods: Giacomo's in Yarraville, Antonello's in Vizzini. Those long-ago memories of the time before the war, before the bridge collapse, when the life that stretched out in front of them was seductive.

Almost two months after the accident, they'd discovered that Paolina was pregnant. His insomnia worsened. The surging panics became more frequent. The sense of impending doom followed him everywhere. He changed his shift at Bradmill's so that he could walk Paolina to work and be there in the afternoon to walk her home. He didn't tell her that sometimes he didn't go home at all, that he sat in the park and watched the school. He didn't go to work unless he knew that Paolina's parents or Giacomo were home. Before he left the house he checked that the gas stove was turned off, that the windows were locked. Often, he had to turn back at the front gate and check everything again.

When Alex was born and the nurse handed him their little baby boy, all clean and wrapped up in a blue blanket, Antonello took him reluctantly. The panic rose in waves. His hands shook. The sensation was like the vertigo he'd experienced that first time he went up high on a building site; it left him numb and unable to move. His mother noticed and took the baby. 'I can't wait any longer to hold my grandson,' she said. Relieved, but still trembling, he handed his son to Emilia. Surrounding him in the waiting room were all the fathers who had died on the bridge and all the children they'd left behind.

When the bridge works were completed, all the survivors were sent an invitation to the opening and a toll pass for an initial trip across. They came together in a Victorian government envelope with a letter from the Premier that he couldn't bear to read. He ripped it into tiny pieces. He swore he'd never drive across the bridge.

For years, the strongest, most persistent impulse was towards death; a desire to stop living. Now Alex and Rae wanted to stop living. But life didn't stop. It went on whether you lived it or not. *You have to choose life.* This is what he needed to tell them — *you have to choose life*. If you stop living, you may as well die. If you stop living, you aren't going to be able to love again, and everyone you know will pay for that, everyone.

Chapter 20

Long days and long nights, no relief at the end of either. No difference. No beginning and no end. There was nothing to mark time, and yet time passed. Sarah rang to tell them that the hearing would be in the new year, probably not until June. The courts had a backlog of cases and Jo wasn't considered a risk to the community.

Could she spend all those days in the dark room, waiting in limbo?

Summer was on its way now — set on its course like the container ships that slid into the bay from the sea, slow and languid. In the two months since the accident, Jo had left the house twice, and only to go to the police station. Once for the interview. A second time to sign her statement. Before the accident, she rarely spent a whole day at home. She'd been busy — work, school, the gym, hanging out with Ash.

On the days Mandy was at work and Mary didn't visit, Jo dragged herself to the back verandah and sat looking out at her mother's garden. She avoided looking over the fence at the bridge. She was meant to be doing something: at least preparing herself for what was to come. But the world was a blur. She tried to shift the angle, to stand in a different light, but the picture refused to come into focus.

Ash was everywhere. Jo knew ghosts didn't exist, but Ash's voice was clearer than her own. She rarely slept, but when she did Ash appeared in a recurring dream: Ash, kneeling in a garden bed in the centre of a large kitchen, her face pasted with dirt. Rivers of dried mud wound around her legs. No sense of inside or outside.

'What is it like to be dead?' Jo asked.

Ash was digging. Mud caked into her fingernails.

'What is it like to be dead?'

The morning light was streaming in through the kitchen window. Ash was wearing the blue top and skirt she'd worn to the party. The flowers in the garden were dying: yellowed stems, rotting petals.

Jo marked all the would-have-been milestones from her bed — the school formal, their graduation, the beginning of their VCE exams. English would have been her first, Geography her last. Were Mani and Laura going on with their lives as if nothing had changed?

On the morning that would've been the first day of the Schoolies Week holiday at Byron Bay they'd planned a year ago, Jo, unable to bear the house any longer, waited until Mandy left for work and got dressed. Like a small-time criminal in an American detective series, she put on a pair of sunglasses and a cap as a disguise. She opened the front door to a hot wind and a heady cocktail of diesel and petrol as cars and trucks hurtled down Hyde and Francis. Next door, Mrs Nguyễn was listening to morning television. Across the road, behind the cyclone-wire fence, there were several men in safety jackets and helmets. The tanks, still and defiant, shrugged them off. The men reminded her of the plastic characters her Grandpa Tom used to buy her as a child. In the evenings they'd build tall towers with her blocks, a world for the miniature men and women, and her grandfather would make up the stories.

She locked the door. At the gate she hesitated, unsure which way to go. Against the clear sky the bridge was monumental, a towering monolith. The sight of it made her want to crawl back into the house.

If she went into Yarraville, no more than five minutes away, it was likely she'd see someone she knew. She couldn't imagine that. For almost two months now, her mother, her grandmother, Sarah, and the police were the only people she'd seen.

If Ash were alive, they might've gone to Williamstown for a swim on a warm morning like this. They might've spent the day sitting on towels on the crowded beach, surrounded by families with picnic baskets and beach shades, playing spot-the-cute-guy, reading novels, falling asleep in the sun, and speculating about their VCE results.

Hyde Street was empty, so she headed north, towards Footscray Station. Anxious someone might see her, she found it impossible to walk, and so she ran, sweat building before she'd reached the next intersection. But she kept going, into the station and onto a train seconds before it left. She scanned the carriage. There was a woman with two young children: one, a baby sleeping in his pusher; the other, a little girl in a fairy costume with her face pressed up against the window. The mother was sending a text with one hand, the other lightly touching her daughter's back. Two seats down there was a man in an orange workman's jacket, reading the newspaper. At the other end of the carriage, four women, all of them in their sixties, talked in low voices to each other. Jo didn't recognise any of them, but she sat as far away as she could.

Only two people got on at North Melbourne. A young woman and her boyfriend. They were having conversations — separate ones, into their mobile phones. The girl was speaking in Vietnamese, at a rapid pace. The boy was speaking in English, and his conversation was clipped. The other person was doing most of the talking. *Yep … Sure … No … Maybe …*

At Flinders Street Station, she followed the other passengers up the escalators, lined up to scan her train pass, and only stopped when she was standing next to the flower seller. Bunches of gerberas and roses, lilies and orchids. Their perfumes, too sweet, shrank against other smells: car fumes, fried chips, cigarette smoke. Ash's mother, whenever they came back through Flinders Street, would buy flowers. Sometimes two or three bunches. 'Mum, can't you get flowers in Yarraville?' Ash would complain. She hated sitting on the train with her mother, with the flowers, with her mother talking about the flowers, with her mother taking up an extra seat with the flowers, especially on the busy trains when people would kill for a seat. No one ever asked Rae to move the flowers.

From the steps, under the clocks, Jo glanced across at St Paul's Cathedral. She scanned the crowds standing at the intersection, waiting to cross Flinders Street, waiting to cross Swanston, waiting at the tram stop, walking up and down the steps, walking along the path in front of Young and Jackson.

Jo and Ash had gone into Young and Jackson once, with a man they met on a tram. 'I'm here on holidays and don't know anyone. Can I buy you a drink?' he asked.

'Yes,' Ash said. And all three of them jumped off the tram and headed for the pub. 'I'll show you a real tourist sight. A real piece of Melbourne history — the naked *Chloé*,' Ash said, winking at Jo.

The man, whose name they didn't know, was in his thirties. He seemed excited, his wide mouth spreading into a broad grin. Two young girls, a painting of a naked woman, alcohol — what more could he want?

The publican took one look at them and asked for IDs. They didn't have any. Ash and Jo ran out of the pub giggling. They didn't see *Chloé* and lost the bloke. Ever since, they'd planned to go back together one day.

So you'll never go in to see Chloé? *Promise.*

'Promise.'

Laura and Mani would have finished their VCE. She and Ash would never finish theirs — all that work, all that angst, for nothing. She couldn't move out of home and find an apartment in the city without Ash. She couldn't go to university without Ash. She couldn't travel — to Japan and South Africa and New York — without Ash. She couldn't get married without Ash. Or have children and become a mother.

Jo walked down the steps and joined the mid-morning crowd waiting to cross Swanston Street, the bulk made up of a group of schoolboys carrying heavy backpacks and talking about getting takeaway. She made her way past the pub, past Dangerfield, with its gothic outfits in the window, past Flora and the smell of hot curries, past a second-hand bookshop, and into Degraves Street. Cafés lined both sides of this laneway and tables took up the centre. But she remembered another Degraves Street. Smoking cigarettes in school uniform. Brazen girls with too much time on their hands. … And suddenly there was Ash, swinging her bulky backpack over her shoulder. And her long red-brown hair tied in a ponytail, stray hairs floating in the breeze. It couldn't be Ash, she knew that, but she followed the girl, desperate to catch her, to see her face.

'Please turn around.'

Catch me if you can.

Past offices, a beauty school, a university, boutiques, and more cafés; past groups of students standing in doorways smoking cigarettes; past men in suits; past shoppers carrying large bags; past young people in neat office attire, plain and conservative; past young people all in black, with multiple piercings; past young people in jeans and too-short t-shirts slipping between cars and taxis. Everyone was going somewhere. Everyone had somewhere to go.

At the corner of Flinders Lane and Queen Street, Ash disappeared, on a tram or around a corner. One moment of looking away and Ash was gone and out of sight. Jo had nowhere to go. There was nowhere to go but back. Jo leaned against the concrete wall of an office block. Her head swirled. She closed her eyes. She took a few deep breaths. Could she go back far enough to change everything? Could time be unspun? Back to that afternoon, the table covered in books, a red journal not opened, not read? Back to the first day of high school, resisting the urge to become Ash's best friend? Back to her birth in a hospital in Footscray, where the baby wasn't born to a woman living with a boy not ready to be a father? If she went back far enough, would Ash come back to life?

All those teenage years, telling each other stories of an adult life lived together, imagining it into being. All those years of feeling so lucky because she had a best friend. Looking down at the lonely girls in the schoolyard, so pleased not to be one of them, so pleased all her wishing had come true.

Her grandmother said that wishing for too much was bad luck. The sort of bad luck no one could shake.

On the way back home, Jo couldn't avoid the West Gate. Surrounded by scaffolding, it looked wounded, unable to hold itself up. An old soldier buckling under the weight of history, of trauma. As she came closer to it, she remembered the wheel slipping. The car spinning. The screams. The air was grainy, dirty. The dust was coating Jo's skin, getting into her pores.

'Jo. Jo.'

At the sound of her name, faint and in the distance, she shuddered. It wasn't Ash's voice. When she looked up she caught sight of a man walking a bicycle. He was waving. It was Kevin. He was heading towards Jo. She could not face him; her heart was racing now and she was trembling. She ran across the road and into the Stony Creek Reserve. Once she was sure he had not followed her, she sat under a tall river red gum. There was a cool breeze and it took her a while to calm down.

The first time Jo had met Kevin, it was at a club at the beginning of the year. Ash and Kevin were already there. Jo spotted Ash in the middle of the crowded dance floor.

'That's Kevin,' Ash said, pointing to a nerdy-looking guy sitting on his own. 'He's not much of a dancer.'

Jo longed to talk to Kevin about Ash, to ask him, *Is she really dead?* She wanted to ask if Ash was talking to him. She wanted to ask if Ash had been trying to push her away. She wanted to tell him about all the things she and Ash had done together over the years. About the shoplifting, about going into Young and Jackson, about sneaking out at night to graffiti the walls of the underpass, about climbing out of their bedroom windows to go to parties their parents had forbidden them from attending, about sitting on the roof of Ash's house at midnight and smoking their first joint and the way the city had swayed under the moonlight, and about the nights they spent sleeping together in each other's rooms, about waking up with Ash's arm wrapped around her waist … about the fear, the anxiety, that Ash would find someone better. Did Kevin know that feeling?

Sarah strolled past the building where her meeting was scheduled for ten and down the road to a small café in a laneway: five empty tables along the wall, and a counter behind which two women in white gloves were constructing mountainous sandwiches. Sarah ordered a coffee and took out her notebook.

'I can't think of anyone,' Jo had whispered when Sarah asked for a list of people to contact.

'Come on, Jo. There must be people you'd go to for a reference.'

'Who'd give me a reference? For what?'

'Before the accident, though?' Sarah prodded and pushed, cajoled and coerced, and Jo finally relented and offered a few names — the manager at the café, her school principal, Mrs Chang, Ian Williams. 'If they remember who I am, they might say I was okay.'

'There have to be more.' Sarah had turned to Mandy.

'How many more?' Mandy asked.

'We want it to look like hundreds of people would speak for Jo, even if it's only three or four who we offer as character witnesses. It has to be the right three or four.'

'They let you do that?'

'Yes.'

Mandy had emailed Sarah a list of all Jo's teachers over the thirteen years of primary and high school. She said she couldn't remember all the teachers, that she wasn't one of those friendly mothers who chatted with the teacher as if they were old friends: she'd combed through all the school reports and class photos to find their names. She said she had asked Mary for the names of the two priests at St Augustine's — she wasn't sure if they would provide references, though, given Jo hadn't been to a service for years and she wasn't baptised, and so not one of *them*.

Sarah had interviewed Ted, the owner of the café. 'Reliable enough,' Ted said. 'Came in on time. She was okay with the customers. Not great with numbers, but quick enough on her feet. Got on okay with the other staff. Didn't suffer fools — and we get our fair share — but neither do I,' he said, laughing. When Sarah pressed him to explain, he shook his head and leaned in closer. 'I was sorry to hear about the accident, sorry about Ashleigh, great kid, sorry for Jo. Bad for everyone. These young people' — he said it as if he were in his fifties, but Sarah would have guessed he was in his late twenties or early thirties — 'they drink and drive, they don't think, but neither did I when I was their age. Really, a sorry business. Everyone here feels real bad.'

'Was Jo friendly with anyone? Other staff, I mean — anyone in particular?'

'Oh, not sure about that. They hang out together in their breaks, sometimes have a coffee after their shift, they chat when it's quiet, but nothing more that I've noticed. Occasionally, Ashleigh would arrive as Jo's shift ended and they'd head off somewhere together, but you can ask Ruby or Sue. They worked the same shifts as Jo.'

'Will you write a character reference?'

'Not much on writing, but if you want to write something up, along lines of what I've said — you know, reliable, hard worker, got on well with staff and customers, I'll sign it.'

'Would you rehire Jo?'

They were sitting at a corner table. Next to them, four real-estate agents, wearing grey suits and company ties, were discussing 'the list'. Ted paused. He was tall and broad-shouldered. There was something of the working-class bloke about him — the kind of man you might imagine working in the mines or on a road gang. 'Well, it's tough. I mean, everyone knows her and Ashleigh. And one of Ashleigh's aunts is a regular — was, anyway, haven't seen her since the accident — but her friends, they come in here and have their breakfast and I don't want any trouble. I didn't think she wanted her job back. Her mother rang and said she quit.'

'Yes, I know. I meant generally speaking.'

'It's not that I wouldn't employ her. I'd like to give her a chance, but not here. Not yet. All too raw.'

Sarah would write up a letter for Ted to sign, but she was afraid it wasn't going to make much difference.

'What about Jo's friends? Her other friends?' Sarah had asked Mandy.

'Mani and Laura, of course,' Mandy said. 'If there were other friends at school, I don't know them.'

'No one has come around, rung?'

'Not that I know of. She has her mobile, she has her email, but I don't know if she's even turned her phone on since the accident. Her father left a message on my mobile, said he tried to ring her but her phone was off.'

At 9.55 Sarah sipped the last of her coffee. Worried she was now running late, she sprinted back down the street to the Department of Justice building. Halfway, she caught her foot on a raised section of the footpath and tripped, unable to catch herself; she landed hard on her hands and knees. *Shit.* Her knee hurt. Her right hand stung. A couple of people stopped to help. Embarrassed, she struggled to her feet. 'I'm fine, fine, thanks,' she said, picking up her bag and limping towards the entrance of the building. She headed straight for the toilets, locking herself in a cubicle. Once alone, she took several deep breaths and brushed the scuffs from her trousers. Fortunately there was no damage. In the past, she'd ruined clothes, shoes, even a handbag. *Stop feeling sorry for yourself.*

After a couple of minutes, she left the cubicle and washed her hands. Her palm was scratched but there was no blood. She brushed her hair and retouched her lipstick, but didn't linger with the reflection in the mirror. *It's fine.*

She took the lift up to the fourth-floor meeting room. Even though she was late, she was the first to arrive. She poured herself a glass of water from the dispenser — she was supposed to drink eight glasses a day; that was part of the diet. This would be her second glass. She opened her notebook and wrote 1/12/2009 and put two ticks. Yesterday she'd only managed four glasses. At this rate she wouldn't lose the weight.

'Water,' her mother said, 'makes all the difference.'

She would've ignored her mother, but the nutritionist had given her the same advice. 'Eight glasses a day. More if you can manage.'

If she drank eight glasses of water a day, she'd spend most of her time walking between the tap and the toilet — the extra exercise might result in weight loss, but she wouldn't get any work done. Some days it was hard to find time to go to the toilet at all. But if she lost weight, she might not fall as often. If she lost weight, she might turn into a light, wispy creature, who floated elven-like through the day, through the city, through life. She shook her head. If only she lived in a society where people respected her for her skill in the courtroom, her ability to work with people no one else wanted to work with, her passion for justice, and didn't judge her on the size of her body. Maybe then she could be fat and it wouldn't matter.

Law reform was a part of the legal aid lawyer's job. Each of the lawyers in her office was assigned particular issues. This meant serving on committees and working groups, going along to meetings, organising events — demonstrations and information nights and campaigns. She hated the meetings, but she went to them. She was committed to political action. *Collective political action is the only way to create a more just world*: it was her mantra, repeated numerous times, at school talks, during committee meetings when she could see the mood dipping down towards despair or lethargy. She venerated activists. There was a time when she'd aspired to be one, a real activist on the frontline, demonstrating, yelling abuse at the politicians and the police. Not the kind of activist who went on boats with Greenpeace, fighting the whalers, or tied themselves to a tree in the forest, to challenge the loggers; she wasn't a greenie or an environmentalist. Climate change was happening — there was no doubt about that — and something should be done, but she couldn't summon up the energy to take it on. Her causes were tied to the unjust living conditions of the people she worked with: poor public housing, inhumane refugee policies, increasing rates of Indigenous deaths in custody, deteriorating conditions for female prisoners, violence against women. But in reality being a full-time activist didn't suit her. She preferred having a job, a routine, and working one-on-one with her individual, sometimes crazy, clients.

Mandy had asked Sarah what prison would be like for Jo the last time they spoke. It was a question she dreaded. *It'll be fucking awful* was the unutterable truth. She couldn't bring herself to tell Mandy that most women who went to prison ended up going back, time and again. That women prisoners suffered from high levels of depression and anxiety, that suicide attempts were common, and that it was rare for women to come out unscathed.

'It will be hard,' Sarah had said. 'She'll need all the support you can provide.'

By the time the committee members (several legal aid lawyers from across the city, including from the Victorian Aboriginal Legal Service and Women's Legal Service Victoria; a social worker; two police officers; a couple of bureaucrats; the representative from the Victorian Law Reform Commission; and representatives from various prisoner support groups) gathered, it was quarter past ten. Sarah's knee ached, and she became increasingly annoyed with the chair, a long-haired middle-aged lawyer who was *happy to wait for a couple more minutes until everyone gets here.* The agenda was long — and included the discussion of the submission that Sarah's working group had drafted on discrimination against women in Victorian prisons. Writing and researching the submission had taken five months: it included substantial evidence that women prisoners faced more health problems (especially diabetes and heart disease, not to mention the mental-health issues) and were given fewer educational opportunities, which resulted in many of them being unable to cope once they were released. The outcomes were even worse for Indigenous women. But Sarah and the other members of the committee were proud of the report. They wanted these issues highlighted, they had recommendations that would make a difference; now they needed the support of the committee to lobby for change.

An hour later, Sarah thought about Jo as she walked out of the meeting towards the station. The work they were doing had a real chance of improving the conditions of women in prison, and the whole committee was behind it, thankfully. They'd allocated funds to implement the recommendations. But it was unlikely anything would change in time for Jo.

Back in her office, interned by files that required action, Sarah gazed out the window. Across the road, a group of boys in their teens were smoking outside the 7-Eleven. She wasn't worried about them — they weren't drinking alcohol. Lately, the majority of her cases were alcohol- and drug-related. Kids as young as twelve and thirteen were already alcoholics and addicts. The judges were frustrated. In the courtroom, the judges, the lawyers, the probation officers, the youth workers, and the cops sat in different sections and acted as if they had something against one another, but in truth they were all in it together. They were all throwing their hands up in the air. As the judges pronounced their sentences, they made grand statements — *It shouldn't be this way; there should be more support and help* — but, generally speaking, they locked them up because the parents and the community needed some relief.

Her clients often complained about being picked on by the cops, about being moved on from shopping centres and kicked out of venues for being young, or for not being white and 'Australian', or for hanging out together, having fun. And they were right to complain, and she'd often taken up the cause of young people wrongly accused. Because they were a *gang* — which meant three or four kids standing around together — or looked *like trouble*. Because they were Sudanese or Vietnamese and weren't speaking English. Because they were too loud. The problem was that sometimes it was difficult to tell if a group was going to be trouble or not. Sarah was a reasonable judge of character, but sometimes the young people she represented committed crimes that shocked her, even after more than eight years working in legal aid. Still, you had to make an honest case, as honest as you could — you were obliged to even when you wanted to say to the judge, *You should lock this one up and throw away the key.* You never did — they knew you never would.

The boys in the street were throwing something around. Sarah couldn't see what it was. Not a ball. Something small and square. On the bench, a younger boy was crying. Sarah considered opening the window and yelling at them to give it back, but that would be a bad move — both for her and for the kid on the bench. She kept one eye on her files and one eye on the boys.

The day before, she'd interviewed Ashleigh's boyfriend, Kevin. He hadn't hesitated when Sarah had asked to meet. 'Sure. Ash and Jo were mates. Whatever I can do to help.' Now she read over her notes.

She had interviewed Kevin at his home in Brighton. The house was about as different to Jo's as a house could be; it reminded Sarah of her parents' place. Kevin's mother and her mother probably bought their floral silk-screened curtains from the same South Yarra decorator. They probably went to the same dinner parties, the same theatre productions. The house, set back behind a high fence on a corner block, was what her mother would call *substantial*. A period home (Sarah had no idea which period) surrounded by a lush lawn and well-established trees — grey and ghost gums. Standing on the doorstep waiting, she pondered how Kevin had met Ashleigh. Sarah's parents and their friends didn't go to the western suburbs; they said things like, *I never drive across the bridge unless we are going to Lorne.* Recently, Sarah's Aunt Sophie, her mother's youngest sister, told them that a friend had dragged her out to Yarraville. 'I was kicking and screaming, I kept saying, "No, why would I want to go there?" But, you know, I was pleasantly surprised. There are some nice boutiques and cafés. I bought the perfect little clutch bag for Annie.'

Kevin had been alone when Sarah arrived. He led her through the hallway and the kitchen to a small table in the garden. The view, like the house, was expansive. There was no sense of the surrounding suburb. The backyard sloped down to a tall hedge, beyond which Sarah could see a golf course. He offered her a tea and she accepted. When he brought it out, she could see he was shaking, and she reached out to take her cup. He was lanky and tall, dressed in black jeans and a white t-shirt. His black hair was wet, and since there was no pool, Sarah assumed he'd just had a shower.

'Thanks for letting me come and talk to you,' Sarah said.

'No problem. I can't concentrate on anything. Can't study. Can't work. Just been hanging around the house all day.'

'I'm sorry.'

'What do people do?' he asked.

'Grief takes its own time.'

'I want to talk about Ash all the time, and everyone's getting sick of me. They don't say anything, but I can sense it.' He stopped speaking to pour the tea. 'I don't usually talk much, but now I can't stop.'

'You and Ashleigh were going out? You were her boyfriend?'

The garden was quiet, the only sounds coming from the rustling of the leaves in the breeze. Sarah poured milk into her tea and took a sip. English breakfast, her mother's favourite.

'Yeah, we met at the beginning of the year but had been going out for about six months.'

'And you know Jo as well?'

'A little. She's Ash's friend, but we get on okay and the three of us go — used to go — out together.'

'Was that a problem?'

'It was fine, not a problem. We go out in groups, with friends. Ash liked to party.'

'Is Jo a party person too?'

'I guess so. She likes to go out and dance and have fun. Ash is — was — more outgoing, though. She could talk to anyone. Made friends with people quickly. Jo's shyer.' Kevin seemed close to tears. 'It's hard to believe Ash's gone. I keep expecting her to turn up.'

Sarah apologised and offered to leave. When she rang to make the appointment, she had spoken with Kevin's mother before she talked to Kevin. There had been no hesitation on Mrs Tang's part. 'Of course,' she said. 'I'm sure Kevin will talk to you.' But now Sarah wondered if it'd been such a good idea for her to interview Kevin without at least one of his parents present.

'No, it's fine. I guess I've just been lucky up to now. No one I know has died. No friends or family members, not even grandparents. So I don't know what … how to be.'

'I don't think anyone knows what to do or how to be, even if they've had lots of experience with grief. It's tough, especially when it's an accident and so unexpected. Especially because Ashleigh was so young.'

'My parents are angry at both Ash and Jo. Even though they don't say it.'

'Did Jo and Ashleigh drink a lot?'

'They … Everybody drinks. Ash and Jo didn't drink much during the week — hardly at all. Only on the weekend, when we went out.'

'Did Jo often drive on those nights?'

'I usually drove.'

'But when you weren't there?'

'Yes, I guess she did. Obviously she did. I'm sure that wasn't the first time.'

'What kind of person would you say Jo is?'

'She's a good person. I mean, I don't think she would've done anything to hurt Ash on purpose, if that's what you mean?'

'What else can you tell me about her, her personality?'

'She's a bit clingy and anxious, and sometimes it pissed Ash off.'

'So they fought.'

'I don't know. I never saw them fighting. I was shocked when I heard they were fighting that night. Ash would vent sometimes, but not at Jo.'

'About Jo?'

'Ash was happy-go-lucky, positive.' Kevin paused and put his cup down. 'Not much worried Ash. But Jo got anxious. I understand; I do too. Ash would get pissed off with her. She'd say Jo was needy, annoying. She'd say stuff but then send Jo a text to tell her what we were doing — like, a hundred texts a day, as if nothing was real until she had told Jo. I don't know, I never understood. Girls have different kinds of friendships to guys.'

'Have you talked to Jo since the accident?'

'No.'

'You haven't tried to see her or talk to her?'

'I sent her a text message after the accident. I wanted to talk about Ash. She didn't reply ... But I saw her. Last week I rode my bike to the bridge. It was an insane thing to do, it took me an hour and a half, and I was so stuffed I had to take the train back. But driving there didn't seem right, and I wanted to go there. It's weird, but I thought I could talk to Ash there. When Jo saw me, she turned around and raced off into the reserve, couldn't get away fast enough. So I figure she's not ready to talk. It sorta sucks, because it'd help to talk to Jo about Ash.'

Sarah sighed. When she thought about the impact that Kevin's statement, if he were prepared to make one on Jo's behalf, might have on the sentencing judge — if any — she wasn't sure it was worth putting him through the pain of having to write one.

There were now two groups of men on the golf course, and their voices wafted across to the garden. 'So you didn't get to talk to Jo at all, that day?'

'No. I didn't follow her. I stayed awhile. I read the names of the men who died when the bridge collapsed. They're engraved on a plaque down there. There are lots of workmen on the bridge at the moment, doing some major reconstruction. How do you reckon they feel, working on the bridge knowing all those other blokes died?'

259

'It was a long time ago,' Sarah said. 'Most of the guys working on the bridge now probably don't even know about the collapse.'

'Ash's grandfather was working on the bridge when it collapsed. Did you know that?' Sarah shook her head. 'He was there when it collapsed and he lost mates … the weekend before she died Ash told me about it, and about how her grandfather won't drive across the bridge. She'd only found out recently, when she asked him if they could go over the bridge for a driving lesson and he refused. We talked about how a tragedy might change people, how it might be worse for the ones who survive. It's so weird that we were talking about it and then for Ash to … for the accident to happen there.' He paused. 'It's been two months since her funeral. I haven't been to work or out with friends. I can't think about anything else. I can't concentrate on anything else. How did the men who survived move on? How did they go on living their lives?'

Kevin said he wasn't a talker. He was the shy and nerdy type, the kind who preferred to read or play computer games. But he couldn't stop talking. Sarah understood that impulse. After Ada died, she wanted to tell everyone about her. She said Ada's name over and over again. She inched her into every conversation. She wanted to tell everyone she talked to that this wonderful woman was gone. She wanted others to experience the loss — everyone she knew, everyone she met, especially all those people who hadn't known Ada and now wouldn't have a chance to meet her. She'd been zealous. Driven by anger and grief, but also by guilt. The truth was, she'd known Ada was depressed, that she was descending into a dark and narrow place, that she was lost and alone; she knew Ada was heading for a fall, and she'd done nothing.

Chapter 21

The Portarlington bus made its way through the centre of Geelong, past the hospital, and onto the highway. Jo loved driving in the country. She and Ash had talked about taking road trips along the coast. But Jo would never drive again. Never.

The other passengers were locals. The driver greeted each by name and asked after kids and elderly parents. He talked about the last Cats game and what they needed to do to make sure they were in the finals next season. He told them he found his ten-year-old son and a friend playing with matches in the field at the back of the house, about the dry grass, about getting angry and yelling at them and remembering his childhood attraction to fire and how he'd almost burnt down his father's shed. Some of the passengers laughed.

One of the older women said, 'Sounds like he's taken after you.'

'Problem is, fires catch too easy,' said a woman in a nurse's uniform.

Jo slid down in her seat at the back. The sky was dark grey, but inside the bus it was hot. She took her jacket off and stared out the window. Once they left Geelong, the highway was sandwiched between farmland. There were several wineries along the way, and even from the bus she could see the vines were heavy with fruit.

Earlier that morning she'd woken up with Ash's voice in her head. *No one, not even your mother, loves you.* And a beam of morning light coming in through the gap in the curtains, hitting the wall and exposing the faint outline of the jungle mural that layers of paint hadn't been able to cover.

'What is underneath the paint?' she'd asked Grandpa Tom when she first saw the outline, the hints of green and yellow.

'A mural painted by your mother and your uncle. I've painted over it half a dozen times, but it keeps coming back.'

'What kind of mural?'

'There were trees and monkeys, and I think a giraffe — your Uncle John was obsessed with giraffes. Your mother, she must have been about five at the time, and John, he would've been seven. They were right little rascals.'

'Did it have birds in the trees?'

'There were birds sitting in the branches, and rabbits running around the base.'

'Did it have snakes?' Jo had recently seen her first snake on a walk along Stony Creek. Mandy had spotted it. 'An eastern garter snake,' she had whispered. The snake was striped, grey and yellow, and coiled so that its head and tail were almost touching.

'No snakes that I can remember,' Grandpa Tom said, shaking his head.

'Were you angry?'

'I laughed, but your grandmother almost blew a fuse, and I was in the biggest trouble of all for laughing.'

That morning, staring at the wall, with Grandpa Tom's voice in her head, she'd been overwhelmed with despair. Wherever he and Pop Jack were, they were ashamed of her now.

When she heard Mandy leave for work, she had dressed and packed a few clothes. She turned her phone on for the first time in weeks and put it on to charge. Almost immediately, insistent beeping announced new messages: from Laura, from Ruby at the café, from Mrs Hunt, from her father, from Ash … from Ash's phone …

You are a murderer.

You fucking killed Ashleigh. You stupid bitch, you should be dead.

Her stomach churned. She felt her heart beating faster. Someone in Ash's family wanted her dead. Maybe everyone wanted her dead. She read the messages again, and a third time. It was true, she was a murderer. She understood, she agreed. She should be dead. But she wasn't. She turned the phone off, pulled it off the charge, and threw it onto the bed.

She took her bag and left the house without turning back.

At the station, the next train was headed for Geelong, due in six minutes. That was where she'd go, then. On the train she spent the whole hour staring out the window into the backyards of the houses lining the railway track as they sped through Yarraville and Newport, through the flat open fields on either side of Werribee, through Little River and Lara, until they finally reached the outskirts of Geelong. She tried not to think, but her head was swarming with the voices.

When the train arrived at the Geelong station, she was relieved to be able to move. At the bus terminal, several vehicles were waiting. She took the St Leonards bus. Portarlington was a vague childhood memory from a holiday with Grandpa Tom when she was four. They'd stayed in an old caravan and fished off the pier. They'd eaten chips on the beach, surrounded by squawking gulls; she'd been frightened at first, but he'd shown her how to chase them away. Mandy hadn't come with them — she didn't remember why. Probably working. She remembered the smell of his tobacco floating in through the open door of the caravan. The overly sweet hot chocolate he made her at night. Paddling barefoot along the water's edge, her feet freezing. Sitting next to him on an old deck chair outside the caravan and counting the stars. Giggling at his silly stories.

By the time they arrived at the Portarlington shopping centre, it was raining heavily. Jo raced across the road to shelter under a row of shop awnings, but even with her back pressed flat up against the supermarket window, she was getting wet.

'Torrential, this rain. But it'll be great for my garden,' announced one of several older women lined up next to her. She reminded Jo of a too-cheerful politician wanting to convince her constituents that recessions, unemployment, and increasing taxes all had a silver lining.

'Yes, we need it,' responded an old man, leaning on a walking stick. Beside him there was another elderly woman sitting on her electric scooter, and a couple with their shopping and a scruffy terrier. Jo couldn't see another person under sixty.

The woman kept talking about the importance of a good soak for the garden, the amount of rain it took before moisture penetrated to the roots, and the pleasure it was to see all the trees, especially the older trees, refreshed.

'We might need the rain,' the woman in the scooter said with a hoarse laugh, 'but I don't have to be grateful when it comes, especially when it's bucketing down.'

Sheets of rain were closing in on them. From the road, the bay was covered in a fine mist; there was no horizon, no city, no mountains. The pier had dissolved. The town was adrift.

Jo was weighed down with a desire to curl up and sleep, knees to chin, head buried in the folds of her arms. Since the accident she rarely slept, and when she did it was broken, shattered by nightmares, the nights more tiring than the days, and no relief in sight. But standing under the canopy, surrounded by people her grandmother's age, the possibility of sleep, its inevitability, was seductive.

'Are you alright, love?' The woman with the garden inched a little closer and placed her hand on Jo's arm.

'Sorry?'

'You look pale, like you might faint.'

'Oh no, I'm fine. I never faint,' Jo replied.

'My husband's gone to get the car. Can we give you a lift somewhere?' She had grey hair and wrinkles, but she wore jeans and heavy work boots. Her skin was tanned and weathered, and she reminded Jo of the colonial women in Australian movies, the ones who lived in isolated rural shacks and chopped their own wood. She might've been the same age as Mary, but was as unlike Jo's grandmother as two women could be — no make-up, no lipstick, no earrings, no pastels.

'No, not sure where I'm staying.'

'Just arrived, have you? Are you looking for somewhere to stay, love?'

'No … umm, yes.' Jo had been driven by adrenaline all morning. By the inkling of an idea, to run, and then to run to Portarlington. But she had no plans, no sense at all as to what she might do now that she'd arrived.

'We live next door to a hostel, it's a backpackers'. They have a dorm and you can walk to the beach and into town. They'll have a bed for sure. It's early, not the tourist season yet. We can give you a lift, save you getting wet.'

'I'm not ... I haven't decided —'

'It's nice here. You young travellers prefer the ocean coast, Lorne and Anglesea, but they're much more expensive, and the natives aren't as friendly.' She laughed.

'Hear, hear,' said the man with the walking stick.

'It'll get busier here soon, love, and there'll be work in the cafés and the restaurants.'

In the woman's presence, Jo was transformed into a young, carefree traveller looking for work, and the sleepiness passed. She straightened up and met the woman's gaze, returning her smile. 'A job, yes,' Jo said. 'Any leads would be great.'

'My son's the manager at The George,' said the old man. 'It's there.' He used his walking stick to point down the street, but through the teeming rain, it was impossible to make out the individual buildings. 'It's a restaurant and a motel. One of his waitresses up and left. She fell in love with a young bloke from Canada, and now they're gone north together.'

'Was that Bella?' the woman asked.

'Yes, yes.'

'Lovely girl, but a little rash.'

'More than a little rash,' the man said. 'She only knew the Canadian guy for a week and was packed and gone.' He turned back to Jo. 'Have you done any waitressing?'

'Yes,' Jo said, feeling herself swept up in a current that was out of her control. Did she want to stay in Portarlington? Did she want to get a job? Was she allowed to leave Yarraville? She'd have to check the conditions of her bail with Sarah. She didn't want the police to come looking for her.

'Well, why don't you go down to The George and tell them I sent you. Bob's my name.' The man held out his hand for Jo to shake.

'Thanks.' Jo took his weathered hand. His grip was surprisingly strong.

'Your name, love?' the woman asked when Jo didn't introduce herself.

Jo didn't want to tell them her name. She didn't want to be Jo Neilson the murderer, the girl who killed her best friend, the person who was on her way to prison. She wanted to be the carefree traveller, this new girl the woman had conjured up.

'My name's Ashleigh,' Jo said. The words spilling out before she could stop them. Before she could push them back.

'Well, Ashleigh, I'm Susan, Sue. My husband, Laurie, and I, we'll drop you off at the hostel. You can book in and then come and have a bite of lunch with us. After lunch we'll drive you back up to town.'

'Oh, but I can't …'

'Sure you can. We love young company.'

Laurie drove a silver Holden Commodore. Before Jo could say anything else, she was sitting in the back seat of the car. The seats were black leather. There was a strong new-car smell, a cocktail of glues and plastics. It reminded Jo of Ash's parents' four-wheel drive. That was the first new car she'd ever ridden in, and the smell was overpowering. Within minutes she was nauseous, and Rae had to stop the car so Jo could jump out and throw up. When Jo passed her driving test and Mary gave her the keys to Pop Jack's car, Ash gave Jo new-car-smell spray. It was a joke, and the label, handmade by Ash, covered a normal lavender air freshener.

'Laurie,' Sue said, 'this is Ashleigh.' At the sound of Ash's name, Jo cringed. Was it too late to take it back? Too late to tell them it wasn't her name? Too late to stop the car and get out, go back to the city?

'Hi, Ash,' Laurie said.

Startled, Jo jumped in quickly. 'Ashleigh,' she said. 'I don't like being called Ash.'

'Sorry. Bad habit I have of shortening everything.' He wasn't what she'd expected; he seemed too frail to be Sue's husband. Laurie wore a crisp white shirt that called out for a tie and jacket, and frameless glasses that sat too low on his nose. His hands shook even as they gripped the steering wheel. He was the sort of man you expected to find behind a desk: a bank manager or an insurance agent. When Mary and Jack had fought, Mary would sometimes say, *I should've married a gentleman*. Laurie was exactly the kind of elderly gentleman Jo imagined her grandmother meant. He wasn't at all like Pop Jack, who only ever wore a suit to funerals and weddings and was never comfortable in them.

'We'll drop her off at Bernie's. And she's stopping in for lunch. We'll have those pasties and later we'll take her down to The George. Bob says they need a waitress.'

The town's centre was one long strip with a dozen or so shops and cafés, the supermarket and the pub, and a couple of restaurants, including The George, which was a substantial white building on the corner. Across the main road and down the hill there was the bay beach and the pier.

The hostel was a weatherboard house with a wide bullnose verandah and a rusted corrugated-steel roof. When Jo rang the doorbell, a blonde woman in her early twenties opened the door. She had a strong German accent. Once Jo explained that she was after a dorm bed, the woman introduced herself as Diane and led Jo through to the kitchen. On the table was an opened laptop, and she sat in front of it. 'To register I need your ID.'

'I only have a bank keycard,' Jo said, realising as she pulled it out of her purse that she would have to come up with some story to explain the name difference.

'You said your name was Ashleigh — what's the J?'

'Joanna Ashleigh Neilson,' she said. 'But I hate Jo, so I go by Ashleigh.'

'Do you have any other ID?'

'No,' she said, 'just the card.'

'I'm supposed to get a couple of IDs. A driver's licence?'

'I don't drive. But I can take some money out of my account and give you a deposit. Okay?'

'Sure. I guess if you know the pin, it must be your card.'

Sue and Laurie lived in a large two-storey brick house on the hill at the back of town. From their living room, there was a view of the wide expanse of the bay, of the south part of the township and their own extensive garden, divided into several sections — herbs; vegetables; an orchard with apples, oranges, figs, and plums; and a large section of native bushes and flowers. That first afternoon, they sat on the balcony and ate hot pasties with Sue's homemade chutney. Laurie asked endless questions — what are you doing in Portarlington? How long will you stay? What work do you do? Did you finish school? Are you planning to go to university? Jo was as evasive as she could be. *I needed a break. Not sure how long I'll stay. I'm a waitress. I haven't finished school, but I plan to one day. Not sure about university …* Finally Sue said, 'Laurie, enough with the inquisition. Lunch doesn't give you the right to pry. If she has secrets, she's under no obligation to tell us.'

Was she transparent? Could everyone see she was hiding something? And if they could sniff out her lies, how long would it be before she was exposed? A welt of panic rose and she blushed. But Laurie dropped the questions and they spent the rest of the meal talking about the town and Sue and Laurie's decision to retire by the sea.

Later, when Laurie left to play golf and Sue and Jo were alone, Sue said, 'Laurie was a lawyer in another life. He can catch the whiff of a secret from the other side of the bay.'

They were still sitting on the balcony. The rain had stopped and the smell of damp grass wafted up the hill. A mist hung low to the ground, but the sky had transformed into a broad expanse of blue, with only a smear of the finest white clouds. Jo gazed out at the bay, the pier and the fishing boats, and the now clear outline of Melbourne. Her mother would arrive home to an empty house. She'd call out, frustrated and angry at the lack of response, until she discovered Jo gone. Mandy would be worried, of course, but she would be relieved too. Surely she would be relieved. 'I don't … I want to have a break.'

'Sure,' Sue said. 'You can't run forever, but sometimes we all need a break.' She raised an eyebrow and smiled, and Jo knew she wouldn't pursue the issue — at least not for now. 'How about I take you to town and introduce you to Justin.'

While she followed Sue through the house and down the steps to the car, there was a moment when Jo thought about telling Sue everything. Mary went to confession regularly — she said it made her lighter. She said, *God wipes the slate clean if you are truly sorry.* Sue wasn't God, but maybe God didn't exist at all and priests were just ordinary men dressed in fancy clothes; maybe the lightness came from the act of confession itself.

But Jo didn't tell Sue. No one could forgive what she'd done. Killing your best friend was unforgivable.

Sue took her to The George and introduced her to the manager, Justin, who was sitting drinking a beer and peering at an open laptop.

'I'll wait for you outside,' Sue said.

Justin was much younger than Jo had expected. She guessed mid-twenties.

'So Dad offered you a job,' Justin said.

'He suggested you might.'

Justin grinned. 'Don't worry, Portarlington is a small town. It's the way things get done here. And I do need a waitress.'

Jo sat down opposite Justin. She was nervous, expecting him to ask for references or the names of past employers. She'd already decided she'd make an excuse for not having them — a stolen bag on the train. But Justin only asked her a few questions about her waitressing history. 'Do you have a Responsible Service of Alcohol certificate?'

'No, I've been working in a café and I didn't serve alcohol,' Jo lied, and wondered if she'd be allowed to work in a licensed restaurant without one. She did have an RSA — she'd completed the training earlier in the year — but she thought the police might have cancelled it and she didn't want to take the risk.

'It's fine. You can help in the kitchen and serving the food. We'll work around it. The barman usually looks after the drinks anyway. We're so short-staffed at the moment, I need you. Fill in the employee details,' he said, handing her the form. 'If you can start tonight, that'd be great. I had to call one of the waitresses in and she's struggling to find a sitter for her kids.'

'Really? Tonight.'

'Sure.'

'I was expecting you'd want a CV, which I didn't bring, and I lost my phone so I don't have a phone number.'

'It's a waitressing job. If you drop plates on the customers' laps we'll have to let you go, otherwise no problem. But you will need a phone. You might be able to pick up a cheap one in Drysdale.' He was grinning, taking pleasure in the moment, as if sitting talking to her were all he wanted to do, as if work were not stressful at all. Her shoulders dropped, the tension easing. Grandpa Tom as a young man might have looked like Justin: tanned and hair bleached blond from spending too much time in the sun. She couldn't imagine Grandpa Tom wearing the bone earrings or leather strap bracelet around his wrist, but they suited Justin. 'Come in at four, and I'll show you around.'

On the way back to the hostel, Sue gave Jo a guided tour of the town centre, which wasn't much more than the main shopping strip, made up mostly of cafés and restaurants. Jo said she needed a black skirt or pants and white shirt to wear to work and Sue took her to her favourite op shop, in a small garage that backed onto the car park at the rear of the shopping strip. The elderly woman behind the counter was leaning on a walker and chatting with a slightly younger woman, who was sorting through a box of recent book donations. Behind them, racks of clothes stretched the length of the shop. The women greeted Sue by name and she joined their conversation about the council proposal for controlling the jet-skiers over the summer.

Jo had spent her childhood in op-shop clothes, living with other children's smells, their stains, their rips and tears. She hated it. As soon as she could afford to buy her own clothes, she refused to go into another op shop. But here, in a small change room, an old brown curtain drawn across, surrounded by the odours of other people's lives — stale perfume and sweat — she could transform herself into a girl called Ashleigh, who worked in a restaurant in a small country town by the sea, a world away from the girl who killed her best friend, the girl with an impending court case, who lived in a city where she was too scared to walk out the front door.

Chapter 22

It was 'free-for-all' night. That's what the lawyers called the evening sessions they ran three nights a week. Anyone could come along and get free legal advice. They had three or four volunteers — law students and recent graduates — and one of the legal aid lawyers. There was a roster, as one of the permanent legal staff needed to be on the premises each night. For Sarah, that meant she was scheduled at least once a fortnight.

Sarah both hated and fought in defence of these nights. They were tough to organise, long and challenging, especially at the end of an already full work day. And they were busy. There was rarely time to reflect on anything. There were nights when the cases were straightforward — accumulated parking fines, shoplifting — but other times the cases were more complex, and on the same night they might give advice on a custody battle, a burglary conviction, what constitutes dangerous driving, whether a case of aggravated assault could result in jail time, and a dispute with a neighbour about a tree or a fence (there was always at least one of those). *Solve what you can on the night* was their motto. Those that couldn't be dealt with became cases, and already the staff were overloaded with too many cases.

Tonight, a baby was crying in the waiting room, and the receptionist was trying to get Tanu, a regular, to take his cigarette outside.

'It's non-smoking in here,' Sarah heard Helene say.

'Nobody minds, do you?' Tanu said. Sarah couldn't see into the waiting room, but she knew Tanu was now swinging around, eyeballing everyone and daring them to object. Most people would turn away to avoid answering. The locals knew Tanu. He spent his days marching up and down the main street. Once he fixed his sights on someone, he was relentless.

'Please, Tanu,' Sarah heard Helene pleading, 'you'll get me into trouble.'

'Okay, okay, for you, my lovely, because you asked me nice. Not many people are nice to me.'

Helene was in her mid-thirties, a local woman with two kids. Her husband ran the post office and coached the under-elevens footy team. Her mother volunteered at Vinnies Sunshine in Station Place. Her father, now dead, was a well-known trade unionist, active in the fight for compensation for the workers exposed to asbestos at the Wunderlich factory in Sunshine North. Everyone knew Helene and her family. She had a soft, childlike voice and a sweet smile, but she was a strong woman, and Sarah knew the pleading tone was a strategy. If she wanted to kick Tanu out, he would've already been on the street, and he knew it too.

Helene organised the bookings, and already she would have a queue at the counter.

'I want to see the big woman lawyer.' *Big, fat, large*: this is how clients described Sarah when they didn't know her name. No one said *obese*. Most said *big* or *large*, unless they were angry with her, and then they called her *fat* — 'Where's that fat cow?'

She shouldn't let it get to her. The clients who came into the office were usually facing some crisis. This was likely to be one of the worst times in their lives, and they were confronting prison or battling to keep their homes or their kids. And they described all of her colleagues by their physical failings — *the bald guy, the guy with the scar* — except, of course, for Lisa, who was *the pretty one*, and Alan, who was *tall* and, sometimes, *tall and gorgeous*. Unless he'd refused them something, and then he was a *wanker* or an *up-himself wanker*.

'I want to see the woman, the big woman lawyer.'

'Sarah.'

'I don't know her name, but you know who I mean.'

272

'Yes.'

'Is she here?'

'Yes, I'll put your name down to see her. Have a seat.'

'Hi, my name's Sarah Cascade.' Sarah held out her hand and the woman shook it. Her now sleeping baby was strapped to her with a halter.

'My mate Jody said I should see you. She said, "Go down to legal aid and see the fucking big sheila …" Sorry, it's what she said. She said you is an ace lawyer, though. She said, "She'll make the fucker pay" — sorry for the language — "make him wish he wasn't born."' She was a tall woman; her long brown hair was dyed with streaks of purple and green. She had several teeth missing and bruises on both her arms. Unable to stand still, she bounced from side to side.

'You can sit down,' Sarah said.

The woman took the baby out and spread the halter on the floor, laying the sleeping baby on it. 'When she's asleep, she can sleep anywhere. Love the baby halter. Fell off the back of a truck, hey.'

'What's your name?' Sarah frowned but ignored the woman's comments about the stolen halter now on her floor.

'Oh sure, sure. I'm Dawn, Dawn Angus. This is my baby Alberta. Stupid name, I know. Was his fucking idea. Fancy name. He said it'd give her a better start in life. I wanted to call her Stacey. I call her Bert, to stick it to him. Because fuck, he gives her a stupid bloody name and pisses off — won't give me no money, says it's not his baby, not his responsibility.'

'Is she his baby?'

'Bloody oath. He couldn't get enough of me.'

'Why does he think it's not his baby?'

'Says I was doing it with other blokes.'

'But you're sure?'

'Yes.'

'Have you had a paternity test?'

'A what?'

'A test to see who the father is?'

'What kind of test would that be?'

It took over half an hour for Sarah to work through the issues with Dawn and to start the process for a court order for the father to pay maintenance. Too long on a free-for-all night, with a waiting room full of other people. To the question of whether the father of the baby was abusive, Dawn didn't reply. When Sarah asked the second time, Dawn said, 'I come here for the child support. That's all.'

'Okay, but if he's hurting you it's wrong and you should go to the police.'

'Just the child support,' Dawn repeated. Sarah acquiesced and didn't pursue the issue.

After Dawn, there was a guy with a dangerous-driving charge — drag racing. Followed by an eviction. Two shoplifters. One had stolen a battery-operated dildo from a Sexyland store, and Sarah managed not to burst out laughing. Another driving charge. Followed by Tanu and his ongoing dispute with a neighbour.

It was only at the end of the night, on her way home, that she had a chance to think about Mandy's phone call, and about Jo.

'She's run off.'

'Where?'

'I don't know.'

'She might need a little break.'

'I'm worried.'

'I'll drop in tomorrow. We can talk about it.'

Sarah parked the car on the other side of Hyde Street and crossed Francis Street. The lights took so long to change, she considered running across. But she didn't. The trucks, some of them three containers long, sped past. If she slipped or fell, always a possibility, she didn't think they'd be inclined to stop for a fat jaywalking pedestrian.

Finally the lights turned green and Sarah crossed the road. Once at Mandy's gate, she hesitated. She was spending too much time on this case — if she put her actual hours down on the weekly timesheet, her manager,

Eric, would demand an explanation. But she hadn't been putting down her actual hours; after all, some of it was in her own time, and she was sick of the way Eric wanted them to calculate every hour of their day as if they were some corporate law firm dealing with multimillion-dollar contracts.

Sarah rang the doorbell, and immediately Mandy opened the door. Her eyes were red, and it was obvious she'd been crying; she led Sarah through to the kitchen. There were dirty plates on the sink. On the table, the newspaper was still in its sealed roll. There was a basket of dirty laundry near the back door. 'Sorry about the mess. I can't seem to do anything this morning. I don't …'

'It's okay,' Sarah said. 'You're worried.'

Sarah suggested tea and Mandy made it.

'Let's go outside,' Mandy said once the tea was made. 'Since Jo left I can't stand being in the house.'

The morning clouds had cleared and it was a sunny afternoon. Next door, Mandy's neighbour mowed the lawn and the whiff of cut grass floated over the fence. In the distance, there was the non-stop drone of traffic.

'Two days ago I came home from work and thought she wasn't here,' Mandy told Sarah. 'I could tell straightaway the house was empty. I looked out the back window and she was sitting under the gum tree — so still. I went out there and asked her if she was okay. "I locked myself out," is all she said. "You went out?" I said. I was surprised. But she didn't answer, and wouldn't tell me where she'd been. She walked past me and went to her room. She hadn't been out since the accident — as far as I know.'

'But you have no idea where she might have gone or why?'

'No. That night we had dinner. Or I had dinner — I called her, but she didn't come out of her room until later. I'd finished eating. I'd put her dinner away. She ate it cold. I tried a couple of times to have a conversation, but she didn't respond. Yesterday, when I came home from work, she was gone. She left a note, saying she's sorry and that she had to go. Telling me not to stress, she'll be back. That she'll let me know where she is in a few days.' Mandy passed the note to Sarah and watched her read it. 'That's it. I tried to ring her, but there was no answer. Later, I found her phone on her bed.'

'What did she take?'

'Not much. Some clothes. A small backpack, I think.'

'So long as she obeys the bail conditions, it'll be fine. She shouldn't leave the state, and she'll need to let the police know she's moved and her new address. And because she's moved out of here, she'll have to report to the police station once a week. Let's wait a couple of days and see if she contacts you. If she doesn't, we will have to tell the police.'

Mandy nodded. 'I'm so worried.'

'I know. If you hear from her, let me know. Get a number from her so I can talk to her.'

'Her grandmother is in a panic. She thinks I should go looking for her.'

'Where would you start looking?'

'I don't know. In the past whenever she's run off, it's been to Ashleigh's.'

'Let's wait a couple of days. Time away might even help. I hope she finds somewhere to go that'll give her a break. You know, in ancient Israel, they used to have several small cities outside the main city — they called them cities of refuge, and they sent people like Jo there.'

'People like Jo — what does that mean?'

'Sorry, I mean people who'd accidentally killed or injured someone. It was partly for their protection.'

'Do you think Jo needs protection?'

Sarah thought about Ashleigh's father at the window the day she dropped off the clothes. She thought about Ashleigh's mother at Mandy's doorstep. 'No, I don't think she needs protection, but getting away from Yarraville, for a while, might be good for her.'

'It's my fault she left. I can't seem to ... I feel like I fell out of love with Jo the night of the accident. I loved her more than I've ever loved anyone, more than I loved my mother, but it's a memory, it's gone, that obsessive, pure love, and I can't seem to get it back. I don't know how to love her anymore.' Mandy was sobbing. 'Jo knows. She looks at me, and she can see, she knows. That's not supposed to happen.'

It seemed to Sarah that Mandy was stuck, like a rabbit in the hunter's spotlight. She was stuck on her front doorstep on the night of the accident, overwhelmed with shame and anger that would not shift.

'I'm sure you love Jo. You're angry, you're grieving, all those feelings are getting in the way,' Sarah said. But in truth, she had puzzled over a parent's ability to give unconditional love — especially when in the case of some of her clients, the child was cruel, ruthless, vicious.

'I should've been glad to see she was alive and unhurt. She was alive, and she could've died. She came so close to dying. I should've run to her; instead, I didn't want to go to the hospital at all. I should've held her like I did when she was a baby and fell out of the cot or fell over, and she would sob, and I'd hold her to my chest and everything would be alright again. Those moments, the warm smell, the press of her body into mine — it was everything. But I didn't open my arms to catch her and she didn't run to me. I didn't hold her, I couldn't make everything right again. I wanted to run away.'

'You and Jo will work through this. It's still so raw.'

'The last four or five years she has been awful — she's been such a bitch to live with. But I kept on loving her, supporting her ... Driving drunk, the accident, was too much.' Mandy paused. 'I saw Ashleigh's grandparents walking down the street yesterday. I was on the other side of the road. I hid around the corner. I told myself it'd be painful for them to see me. But I'm a coward. I've no idea what to say to them. What can I say? "I'm sorry my daughter killed your granddaughter?"'

'Jo didn't ... you shouldn't say "killed", Mandy. It was an accident.'

'The point is, I am ashamed. Ashamed of being Jo's mother and ashamed of Jo. I can't help it. I used to envy Rae. She's so confident. Whenever I talked to her I felt like I was a child and she was the adult. Like I was back at school ... like any moment she might tell me off for not behaving like a lady. I'm not saying — I mean, she was nice and friendly and good to Jo, and I was good to Ashleigh. She was a little stuck-up, Ashleigh, I mean, sometimes, but I was good to her ...'

'I'm sure you were, Mandy, you're a kind person.'

'No, sometimes I'm mean. Sometimes I was mean to the girls. They got on my nerves, so irresponsible. Now I'm constantly going back and forth between wishing I was nicer to them and regretting not being more of a tyrant, not putting my foot down. Not stopping them. I should've stopped Jo from taking the car … I didn't even try. I didn't even say, "If you're going to drink, don't drive." I could've given them taxi money.'

'If we had the foresight, we'd all do things differently, but we don't. None of us knows what is around the corner.' Sarah hated platitudes, but she didn't know what else to say. Why hadn't Mandy — sensible Mandy, whom she'd grown to like — why hadn't she said anything? Why didn't she take the car keys and stop her daughter from driving?

'I heard a story,' Mandy said, 'of a man who was driving when he noticed the car in front of him was swerving from lane to lane and even into the gutter. The driver was drunk or drugged or falling asleep, so when they stopped at the lights, the man jumped out, ran over to the car in front, and knocked on the window, and, when the driver rolled down his window, he reached in and took the key and threw it as hard and as far as he could. And then he jumped back into his car and drove away without looking back. He probably saved a couple of lives that day.'

'You have to stop blaming yourself, Mandy. It doesn't help either of you. Let's hope you hear from her in the next day or two,' Sarah said. 'Try not to worry before then.' Sarah put down her cup and picked up her handbag. She hated to leave Mandy like this, but she was running late for her next appointment with a new client, a young man charged with drug dealing. He'd been caught outside a local school and his parents were in a panic. And there were only so many hours she could fudge before Eric would notice.

On her second day in Portarlington, Laurie and Sue drove her to Drysdale and she bought a cheap phone. She sent her mother a text letting her know that she was okay. Five minutes later, there was a call from a number she didn't recognise. She ignored it. A minute on, a text: *It's Sarah Cascade. I need to talk to you now.*

Jo hesitated before pressing 'call'.

Sarah wasn't angry. 'I need to know where you are. It's part of the bail conditions. The police need to be notified of your new address, and you'll need to go to the police station and report to them.'

Jo told Sarah where she was staying. 'Please don't tell my mother. I don't want her or my grandmother to come.'

'They're worried.'

'I know, and I'm sorry, but I'm fine. I need a break. I can't be at home at the moment.'

'You need to talk to your mother.'

'I can't, not now.'

'Okay, well, you're an adult. It's your choice. But you need to promise me that you'll send your mother a text every couple of days to let her know you're okay, can you do that?'

'Yes.'

'And you need to promise that if I ring and tell you to come home, you'll come home. Court dates can be shifted with little notice.'

'I promise.'

'Okay.'

'Can I work? I have a job in a restaurant.'

'Yes, that's fine.'

'I don't want anyone to know … I mean, will the police here tell people?'

'No, as long as you stay out of trouble.'

On her way to The George, Jo went to the police station. Nervous and shaking, she reported to the front counter. They were expecting her, and they had her sign a form with the date. Of course she signed *Jo Neilson*. Would they find out she was using Ash's name?

When Sarah walked, she watched her feet, waiting to avoid a fall. When she walked, she saw only what was caught in her peripheral vision, in side glances. She looked up momentarily in reaction to a car horn or a shout, to follow the smell of curry or pho, to move around oncoming pedestrians. She should wear a neon sign above her head — *obese woman walking* — so people knew to avoid her.

Even though she walked regularly, she didn't lose weight. *You walk too slowly*, her mother said, *and without purpose*. It was true Sarah didn't power walk like other women; their determined striding made her wince. They circled the botanical gardens, and sometimes even the streets of the city, in pairs, with leg and arm weights. She did wear her runners, and sometimes she took her iPod. But no matter what she did, she would never look like them. She walked because walking was how she thought, how she found her way around life. If she didn't walk, she became stressed and overly anxious and smoked and ate too much. Besides, her one-bedroom apartment was tiny. And the balcony was narrow — no room for a table, just one chair and one plant, a tall prickly cactus that survived both her lack of care and the city smog.

On the street, she was part of the city, not alone. As she strolled, she looked in windows. Sometimes she went into shops, or through parks. Sometimes she walked in circuits around the city centre. Occasionally she ventured down to Southbank, making her way along the Yarra towards the casino. The river, brown and thick, was a long stretch lined with restaurants and bars. She liked the city best at dusk, when the lights came on and the river reflected the city back on itself, when people transformed into indistinguishable silhouettes and holograms.

She thought about the phone call with Jo earlier that afternoon, and her reluctance to ring her mother. She liked Mandy; they were becoming friendly. It was the first time since Ada died and Laine left that Sarah had felt the possibility of friendship. But Mandy was Jo's mother, and Jo was a client. She'd considered passing Jo on to one of the other lawyers, but that felt like a betrayal of both mother and daughter. And it wasn't, Sarah told herself, as if she was sleeping with her client, which had happened before in the office — though not to her, of course. It wasn't even as if she was socialising with Jo or Mandy, not really; she and Mandy just talked. Mostly they talked about Jo and the accident, but increasingly they were confiding intimacies, stories and dreams. And Sarah had warned Mandy that Jo would likely go to prison and there was nothing she could do to prevent it, so it wasn't as if she was making false promises or setting herself up as some great lawyer who could perform miracles.

'There are lines,' an old boss had said once, when they discovered one of the lawyers they worked with was having a relationship with an ex-client. 'Sometimes it's hard to see where the lines are; other times the lines are clear but people ignore them.'

Sarah turned into Flinders Street and headed down towards the station. It was dark now, and the streets were busy. In Federation Square, there was a band playing jazz, their image projected on the large screen. A crowd had gathered, some standing, some sitting on steps and on the ground, others lounging in deckchairs. A group of children danced and laughed and chased one another in circles. Sarah crossed at Swanston Street, walked past Young and Jackson, and headed down to Elizabeth Street.

Outside Lord of the Fries, two teenage boys stood smoking and drinking. 'Look at that fat lump,' one boy said as she approached, loud enough for her to hear. 'She's bigger than your sister.'

'Shut the fuck up about my sister, arsehole.'

Both boys laughed. In their tight jeans, their legs were twig-thin. Sarah blushed and walked faster.

'Hey, you,' the boy with the sister shouted. 'You should try going on *The Biggest Loser*.'

'Hey, loser,' the other one screamed after her. 'They'd reject you 'cause you're so ugly.'

They laughed again. Sarah bent her head down and watched her feet persistently. They weren't following, but their voices were like heavy hands on the base of her spine, pushing her forwards. She remembered being with Ada once, long ago, when they were in their teens. A couple of boys much like these had called her names — *fatso* and *fat face* and *ugly bitch*. They were on a gravel path, and Ada had picked up a handful of rocks and thrown them at the boys, yelling, *dickheads, fuckwits, arseholes*. The boys had run away, laughing and calling them *ugly bitches*. Ada chased after them. But Sarah, terrified, called her back.

To shake the boys' voices, to shake Ada's disapproval, to shake her own shame at her lack of courage, she quickened her pace and crossed Flinders Lane. She was almost at Bourke Street before she slowed down again. In front of a judge and a jury, acting on behalf of her clients, she was strong and articulate, but on the street, she could so easily be reduced and belittled by a couple of drunk adolescent boys. It wasn't her body she was ashamed of, it was her inability to ignore the judgements and abuse, and to stop those judgments and that abuse interfering in her life.

To keep herself from spiralling into useless self-pity, she refocused her thoughts on Jo and Mandy. Jo was going to prison. None of them, Mandy, Mary, or Jo, were prepared for the moment when the judge handed down the sentence. None of them were prepared for being in the courtroom with Ashleigh's family, or the fact that their very presence would put pressure on the judge to hand down the longest possible sentence. For Ashleigh's family, no sentence would be long enough, and, of course, for Mandy and Mary, any sentence was too long.

Chapter 23

Portarlington was the quintessential sleepy town, even in the lead-up to Christmas and the holidays. Jo fell into an easy routine. In the morning she woke up early and went for a long walk along the Esplanade towards St Leonards. This way she avoided the other residents in the dorm. She was also worried about Laurie and Sue, whom she was finding herself gravitating towards as if they were her own grandparents. They were generous with their invitations to lunch and dinner on her days off. They invited her to go with them on their weekly shopping trip to Geelong and their occasional excursions to ocean beaches and wineries. But with the increasing intimacy, the guilt of what she was keeping from them, of the lies she was telling them, festered like a persistent sore.

Once a week she went to the police station, early in the morning when there weren't many people around. She signed in, and they rarely asked her questions. She thought about her mother and her grandmother, whose text messages and voicemails she answered with brief replies: *I'm fine, all good. Yes, I am eating — looking after myself.* And she thought about prison and what her life might be like after that. Her mood varied from day to day. There were times when she could walk to the water and smile at the joggers and dog walkers, at the workmen building and renovating houses on the Esplanade, go for a swim in the bay and think only about Portarlington and her present life — doing her laundry, updating the specials board at the restaurant, helping Sue with pulling some ivy off the back fence.

'When you're young,' Sue had said to her one day, 'you think about all the things you want to do. To achieve. You want to be famous. Or you want to change the world. But the years go by and the things you haven't done don't matter anymore. You're happy to plant a garden and watch it grow.'

There were some days when Jo convinced herself that she could go on living, and go on living this life, a day-to-day existence, like so many of the people around her. Granted, most of them were retired, but here it seemed possible to work, to garden, to walk, to eat and sleep, to repeat the whole thing again the next day and the day after. To live without aspiring to anything in particular, without planning for the future. But there were also the mornings after sleepless nights when Ash's voice invaded and wouldn't stop — *You can't keep pretending to be me. You've stolen my name. How long are you going to keep it up?* — when she thought about suicide again. When the desire not to be alive was urgent, and she stood at the end of the pier and imagined disappearing into the blue water, sinking into a peaceful, dreamless sleep. On those days, work provided relief. Often she worked both the lunch and the dinner shift, and volunteered to help clean up in the kitchen, to close up at the end of the night.

Jo and Justin worked the same shifts, so they often ate lunch together in the kitchen or on the balcony. A couple of times during her breaks, when she crossed the road and sat on the grass overlooking the bay, he came across and sat with her. They talked about Portarlington, mainly. Justin told her the bay produced most of the mussels consumed in the state, and that mussels had grown in these waters for centuries — there was lots of evidence that long before white settlement, the Wathaurong people fished here for mussels as well as other fish. Jo had seen people lined up to buy them off the boats at the end of the pier. At The George, mussels were always on the menu.

Justin told her the story of William Buckley, the escaped convict who'd lived around the area with the Wathaurong people for thirty-two years. He told her about the vineyards and the olive groves. He talked about his love of fishing. He told her he'd moved back to Portarlington after his mother died, to keep his father company. But she could see how connected he was to the place, to the preservation of its environment, to the acknowledgement of its Indigenous history. He was not an activist like Ian Williams: this was his home, where he belonged, and he would simply do his best to take care of it. Around him she found herself noticing the shape of the bay, the colour of the water, the species of trees.

Justin felt solid and comfortable. He did ask her personal questions, but he didn't press her when she didn't answer. She told him about Grandpa Tom and his stories. She told him about her house in Yarraville, across the road from the oil terminal, down the road from the refineries, and her fear that her mother would sell it and move and the house would no longer be theirs.

'Really?' he said. 'I lived in the west when I lived in Melbourne, in Sunshine. Most people couldn't wait to get out. Don't you worry about living so close to the refineries?'

'No,' she told him. 'You get used to it.'

From their vantage point, they could see the beach populated by shade tents and domes, by sunbathers and swimmers, by squealing children and the rumble of jetski motors and fishing boats.

'When I was a kid, I used to point to the signs — *Dangerous, Explosive* — and my mother would avoid explaining, try to change the subject, until one day, she was frustrated with my questions, and she said, "It means the whole place could blow up. One big fireball."'

'Gosh, did it freak you out?' Justin asked.

'It must've. I remember worrying we'd catch fire and our house would burn down. Mum tried to take it back, and said, "We'll run like the wind until we're far, far away." But after that, I had these repeating fire dreams: great walls of flames roaring towards the house.'

'There was an explosion once, on Coode Island,' Justin said.

'I didn't find out about the Coode Island fire until I was older. Apparently the smoke choked the neighbourhood and people were evacuated from their houses and schools and businesses. I was a baby when it happened and we were living in Braybrook. Mum said my grandfather was evacuated. He spent a couple of days on our couch in the flat. She told me Grandpa Tom used to say, "Lucky the wind was blowing towards the city that day, towards those rich bastards."'

All through her childhood and into adolescence, Jo had dreamt about the tanks exploding, and the flames chasing her and her mother. Often in these dreams she ran, exhausted and breathless, not knowing whether they would make it, whether they would escape, whether the house would survive. When her mother told her about the actual fire, those dreams stopped. She'd told Ash about the dreams and their sudden departure. Ash had laughed. 'My dreams are set in forests or deserts, places I haven't been, beautiful places. I can't believe you, anxious even in your sleep.'

'Portarlington must be a big change,' Justin said.

'It is, and I know it sounds strange to you, but I love our house and I miss it.'

'So why did you leave?'

These were the sorts of questions she couldn't answer. If she did, she wouldn't be able to stay. She became adept at changing the conversation, at steering it in other directions.

Jo regretted changing her name to Ashleigh. It was a stupid, spur-of-the-moment mistake. She lived with the dread of Sue and Laurie and Justin finding out. If a cop walked past the restaurant or if a patron seemed vaguely familiar, it sent her into a panic. But she liked the way Ashleigh, the name, transformed her into someone else. Not Ash, but also not Jo. It was liberating. Ashleigh wasn't a killer. Ashleigh could live. Ashleigh could laugh. Ashleigh could be funny. Ashleigh deserved to be happy, to be loved. At school Jo had avoided taking drama. Now she was playing at being Ashleigh, like an actor in a play, she could see the attraction. To be given a name, a personality, a life that isn't yours, and to be allowed to become that person. There were moments of exhilaration, when the world was open with possibility.

If only she'd chosen another name — she could've become Melissa or Annabelle or Chelsea or Jodie — then maybe Ash would've stopped plaguing her, stopped occupying her dreams, taunting her with nightmares.

You're not me.

I know.

You can't take over my life.

I know.

286

My family won't let you.
I know.
Well, stop using my name.

Jo volunteered to work Christmas Day. Sue and Laurie were in Melbourne, having Christmas with Laurie's sister. A number of the permanent staff wanted the day off, so no one seemed concerned that Jo wouldn't be spending time with family.

On Christmas morning, Jo sent her mother and grandmother messages, but didn't return their calls. The connection between them and Ashleigh, the girl rushing off early to set the tables and help with the carving of the roasts, was tenuous; she couldn't think what she might say to them.

Once her shift started, there was no time to think. The customers were large extended-family groups, mainly from the caravan park. There were balloons and tinsel, and the music — Christmas-themed — was loud and eclectic, including old Bing Crosby classics and songs by Billy Bragg and Coldplay. There were kids running around, and most of the adults were drunk before the entree was served. By the time they had cleaned up after lunch, they had to set up the dinner buffet. When the staff gathered for a quick meal at four-thirty, she sat quietly at the end of the table while the others told anecdotes about the silly, rude, ridiculous things some of their customers had said and done. It was then that she thought about Ash, and Ash's family. Last year, she'd gone to Ash's for pudding after Christmas lunch at Mary's house with her mother and an elderly couple who were long time neighbours of Mary's. She could hear Ash's family, their laughter, their animated conversations, from the end of the street. There was a cricket game in the driveway and people spread through the house and the backyard. Ash's father was playing the Eagles and singing along. And Ash and Jane were teasing him.

'Great, Jo's here,' Ash said when Jo walked in the door. And there was a boisterous *Merry Christmas, Jo* from Ash's family.

She felt a wave of sadness and grief. There would probably be no

Christmas lunch at Ash's house this year. No laughter or singing. No Ash. She could feel herself sinking.

Jo was relieved when Justin shouted across the table, 'Sorry to break this up, but we need to get back to work, guys.' He pointed outside and they could see that the first of the dinner bookings were lining up outside the door.

It was well after midnight by the time she got to bed, grateful to be too exhausted to think.

The week between Christmas and New Year, the stream of holiday-makers arriving in town increased severalfold; cars towing jetskis, caravans, or boats, or overloaded with bikes, toys, and children, clogged the main street. Every night the restaurant was full, and on New Year's Eve they were booked out again. By the time they finished cleaning up and Justin suggested champagne, it was 3.00 am and she was not the only one too tired to hang around. She walked home past houses where the parties were still going, music blaring, voices streaming out of open front doors, partygoers too drunk or too tired to stand sprawled on front lawns. 'Happy New Year,' they yelled out to her, holding up their glasses and bottles.

It was a new year. 2010. Twelve months ago she'd spent the night with Ash, Laura, and Mani. They'd made New Year's resolutions standing on the balcony of Laura's house, silly, ordinary resolutions — to study hard, to exercise, to lose weight — and danced until early morning. They'd been excited, and anxious too, as they looked forward to their last year of high school. One last hurdle. Around the corner, freedom and the beginning of their 'real' lives.

Jo crawled into her bunk in the dorm. 2009 had turned out to be Ash's last year. Everything had gone to shit. She curled up, knees to chin. She would not make any resolutions; there was no point.

Happy New Year.

Last year, she and Ash had seen the year out together, had woken up next to each other the following morning. By the time they'd had breakfast, it was mid-afternoon. The whole twelve months stretched out ahead of them.

On your own in 2010.

I miss you, Ash.

I'll always be missing.

No matter how bad 2010 turned out to be, 2009 would always be her worst year ever.

Before New Year's Eve, Jo had kept her distance from the other staff, making excuses not to join them for after-work drinks or excursions to Geelong on nights off to see a movie or go to a club. Partly it was to avoid the inevitable questions, partly to avoid the alcohol. She hadn't had a drink since the accident. Some nights the smell — of the beer especially — or the sight of a group of drunk young women made her nauseous. But in the first weeks of 2010, The George continued to be busy and, exhausted at the end of her shifts, Jo could not face going back to the dorm alone, to Ash's taunting voice, to the relentless memories of her life before the accident. So she gathered with the others in the courtyard after they closed. She drank Coke or lemonade and didn't say much. She let the talkers talk, she laughed at their jokes and deflected the occasional questions, but otherwise she was invisible, the quiet child in a big, boisterous family.

So she was surprised when one night Margaret, the other regular waitress, whispered in her ear, 'Justin has the hots for you.'

After that night, Jo became wary around Justin, more conscious of the way he sought her out, and of the way she anticipated her time with him. When she was with Justin, she forgot about Ash, about the accident, about the future. When she was with him, she was calmer. But if Justin did like her, who exactly did he like? A girl called Ashleigh he knew nothing about?

She didn't want to start a relationship with him, with anyone. She tried to avoid him after that. Took her breaks when he was out or busy. Found a new grassy spot to sit, away from the restaurant, so he wouldn't find her. But in the quiet times — at night in bed, on her long walks — she thought about him, she daydreamed a romance she knew was impossible, could only happen in a parallel universe where Ash was alive.

Justin wasn't at all like the boys she went to school with. Or like Ian, or Craig, the first guy she'd slept with, what seemed like centuries ago but was less than twelve months. Justin worked, he fished, he spent time doing odd jobs for his father, volunteering with the SES. He wasn't ambitious; he had no plans to study or travel. It was this quiet contentedness, plus his kindness and care, that drew her to him. This idea that life could be lived day by day, in a series of small movements, without climax or crescendo, without taking things too seriously.

One afternoon, Justin called the staff together between the lunch and dinner shift to discuss changes to the menu. Afterwards, they all sat at an outdoor table having a drink. The conversation turned to fishing, and one of the other waiters asked Jo if she liked it. 'I've only been fishing once,' she said. 'Down there, actually.' She pointed to the pier. 'I was little, and I came here with my grandfather. I think to give my mother a break. We spent most of the week on the pier fishing.'

'Did you catch anything?'

'I can't remember. I think a catfish, or something that we had to throw back. I remember it was fun, but maybe it was hanging out with my grandfather.'

'It was the fishing too,' Justin said, and the others laughed.

'According to Justin,' Margaret said, 'fishing is the cure for everything. He's worse than those religious fanatics. Come to Jesus, no, come to fishing.' Margaret was in her late twenties with two children, a ten-year-old and an eight-year-old. According to the others, her partner was a 'wanker who doesn't deserve her'. She was tall and skinny, with short blonde hair, and from a distance she could be mistaken for an adolescent boy. People gravitated to her, and she was often at the centre of their after-work gatherings.

Justin hit Margaret playfully on the shoulder and she called out, 'Harassment, did you guys see that? The boss is hitting me!'

'You wish,' Rob, the chef, said, laughing.

'You can make fun of it, Mags,' Justin said, 'but when life gives me the shits, I get in the boat and head into the middle of the bay and forget everything.'

'As long as you don't forget how to swim,' Margaret said. The others laughed.

Justin ignored her. 'I find it hard to imagine life without fishing.'

'That would be great,' Jo said. 'To have something that lets you forget everything else.'

'Come fishing with me. I'm going out tomorrow arvo, around four-thirty.' The invitation caught her by surprise.

'You should go,' Margaret said, giving Jo a kick under the table. 'I'll do your shift. Mum's visiting so she'll look after the kids.'

'I don't know. I don't want to spoil your fishing.'

'You won't. Come on, I'd love the company.' Justin smiled.

Jo wanted to go. She wanted to spend the afternoon on the bay, in a boat with Justin. What harm could it do?

The small aluminum boat was just big enough for the two of them, the fishing basket, and the rods. Justin gave her a life jacket and put one on too. When he started the motor, they flew out into the bay. It was too noisy to talk. Jo sat holding onto the sides, enjoying the sea spray and the wind, while Justin steered the boat into the middle of the bay.

It was her first time on a boat. Once, she'd been on the Blackbird ferry down the Maribyrnong River on a school excursion; it came with a history lesson and a quiz. On that trip, she, Ash, Laura, and Mani had talked about going on a cruise. One of those ten-day cruises to the Caribbean. What were Laura and Mani doing? She supposed they had finished their VCE and were now on summer holidays, waiting to hear about university and beauty school. In another world, their lives were moving on, gaining momentum, forging forward.

Finally, Justin stopped the boat, turned off the engine, and threw the anchor into the water. 'This is my favourite spot,' he said.

They were surrounded by water, and Portarlington was a speck in the distance. Melbourne, a faint outline dominated by skyscrapers, was a ghost city. The water swirled around them, grey-blue and then green-blue, as the setting sun appeared and disappeared behind the clouds.

'Does each fisherman have his own favourite spot or do you fight over the best ones?'

Justin laughed. 'The bay is big enough for all of us. Are you ready?'

'Sure.'

He picked up a fishing line and lifted the lid on the bait bucket. Once he had threaded a small prawn onto the hook, he reeled the line and sent it flying through the air and into the water. It was impossible to see the line's point of entry.

He gave Jo the second rod and then the bait. A fleshy prawn. Helping her hook it, he explained the process step by step. Jo made several attempts to throw the line. She struggled to get it out as far as Justin's.

'No matter,' he said after her fifth go, 'it's far enough.'

With the rods slotted into the small holds on the side of the boat, they sat back and waited.

'When I was a kid my dad took me fishing every day during summer. The first time, I was only two years old. I can't remember, of course, but that's what I'm told. After the first time, I was hooked — excuse the pun — and he couldn't get rid of me.'

'Is your whole family into it?'

'No. Mum hated fishing. My brothers both fish occasionally, but they get bored. My sister used to like fishing, but we had an accident one day when she and Dad and I were all out together. The weather was bad. The boat overturned. And I nearly drowned — we all nearly drowned, in fact, but I was in the worst shape. She saved me actually, but it put her off going out in the boat.'

'Understandable.'

'You'll be fine.'

'I'm not worried,' Jo said. She didn't worry about dying anymore, although she couldn't say that to him.

Justin was looking at her, his blue eyes fixed on her face. 'Tell me, Ashleigh, tell me about yourself. I don't know much about you.'

Hearing Ashleigh's name brought her back with a jolt. 'Telling lies is hard work,' Mandy had said to Jo when, as a child, she told fibs and Mandy caught her out. 'You have to have a good memory.'

'Not much to tell.'

'Oh, come on, Ashleigh. Give me something? This is like pulling teeth. How come you're in Portarlington on your own and not at uni or something?'

'Just needed to get away.'

'A dark past.'

'Something like that.'

Jo managed to change the conversation back to fishing and then there was a tug on her line. They caught a small snapper, but they threw it back in. 'Will it live?' Jo asked.

'Yes,' Justin said. 'Fish don't have as many lives as cats, but this one will have at least one more.'

Half an hour later, they caught two whiting. Justin said they should be fried lightly and served with a squeeze of lemon. 'I'll cook you dinner tonight,' he said enthusiastically. 'We can have the whiting?' He was holding the fish up for her to assess, as if the dinner invitation were a casual thing, and her decision based only on the quality of the fish. Jo hesitated. It was tempting to go home with Justin, to watch him cook, to eat dinner with him, to go to bed with him. So tempting to think she could be that girl, become that girl. The boat swayed. Justin waited, with his broad smile and his hopeful expectation.

'Sure,' she said. 'So you can cook?'

With the engine back on and the boat set towards the shore, Jo stared out at the horizon, avoiding looking at Justin. Ian was her last infatuation, and he'd been all fantasy. Justin was real, and he was attractive and fun and gentle. Maybe he was 'the one', her soulmate. Maybe he was her only chance to find love. How easy to move towards him, to fall into an embrace, to spend the night curled up against him. To make love.

Are you for real? A soulmate?

At the sound of Ash's voice, Jo felt the panic rising, the shortness of breath, the chill in her spine; she turned away from Justin, closed her eyes, and willed herself to breathe, to calm down. To act normal. But her body was a traitor, her heart racing, her head spinning. She gripped the side of the boat. It was impossible. It was impossible to keep spending time with Justin and keep lying.

By the time they reached the pier, her breathing was returning to normal, and she distracted herself by helping him unload the gear and the fish. 'Thanks, Justin, I had an awesome time. I didn't expect to enjoy fishing, but I did,' Jo said, already moving away, but Justin stepped closer, until he was so close his breath skipped across the surface of her skin. *No*, she thought, but even as her mind said *move away*, her body gravitated closer, and they kissed.

'I like you. It's been a long time since I met anyone I liked as much you, Ashleigh.'

Ashleigh. Jo touched her lips with her finger. The kiss lingered, but she moved away. Justin had kissed Ashleigh. Flushed and nervous, she wasn't sure what to do. She didn't want him to call her Ashleigh again. But she couldn't tell him about the accident. About not being Ashleigh. What would she say: 'My name's not Ashleigh. My name is Jo. I killed my best friend and now I've stolen her name'?

'I'm sorry, I forgot I promised to have dinner with Sue and Laurie,' Jo lied.

'Ring them, they'll understand.'

'No. Sorry, I can't.'

She saw his smile drop. She saw the disappointment and hurt on his face.

'Sure. Well, you better go then. I imagine Sue and Laurie don't have a late dinner.' He turned away, picking up the bucket with the whiting. 'You can have the fish. Give them to Sue.'

'Sorry, I'm running late,' she said. 'I have to go. Sue and Laurie, they'll have it ready ... They eat at the same time ...' She didn't wait to hear Justin's response. She ran the full length of the pier, past several groups fishing off the side. 'What's the hurry, love?' a man called out. He was part of a small family group, whose rods hung over the rail while they sat on chairs. Next to them, a toddler slept in a stroller. As she left the pier, their laughter ran up the hill towards the town.

She ran straight to the hostel. Slipping in through the back door to avoid the receptionist, to avoid being seen by Laurie, who was often in the backyard in the evening, she sighed with relief when she reached the dorm and found it deserted. She emptied the contents of her small locker onto her bed. The clothes she had brought with her from home, she threw into her backpack. The clothes she had bought in Portarlington — shorts, singlets, and thongs, and the white shirt and black pants — she stuffed into a shopping bag to drop back off at the op shop. They were Ashleigh's clothes, and Jo couldn't take them home.

Liar, liar, pants on fire.

Ash, please don't.

Serves you right.

She left a note for Justin. *Sorry, it's not you, it's me, but can't explain.* When she reread it, she heard Mrs Hunt's voice: 'Cliché, cliché, cliché. If you write in clichés, your writing is meaningless.' She circled their clichés with a red pen.

Jo rewrote the message: *Sorry I can't tell you the truth. I can't stay to watch your reaction. My name isn't Ashleigh, it's Jo. You are a good person and I enjoyed spending time with you, but please don't try to contact me.*

She wrote another note for Laurie and Sue. *Sorry, had to leave. One day I hope we will see each other again. I owe you big time.*

'You'll have to face it some time,' Sue had said one afternoon, while they sat together on a bench at the beach, surrounded by seagulls. It sounded like an invitation to confess. Jo considered it. Since the night of the accident, since Ash's death, there had been no reprieve. Even when other thoughts and memories came, they were quickly swept away. Everything returned to that night. She was worried that once she started to speak, once she started to tell the sorry story, she would not be able to stop, and the outcome would be bad for everyone. It would be a deluge from which there might not be any chance of recovery.

She set the alarm for 5.00 am. She planned to leave the notes in Sue's letterbox and catch the first bus into Geelong. She'd be gone before anyone she knew was awake.

2010

Chapter 24

It was twenty-eight degrees by the time the Geelong train pulled into Footscray. It would be in the high thirties before lunch, according to a man sitting opposite her on the Werribee train to Yarraville. 'The last heatwave of the summer,' he said in the authoritative tone that older men often used with young women, as if they were empty vessels with no experience of the world. She did her best to ignore him.

When Jo opened the front door, she hesitated. All her life this house had been her home, a refuge, but now it felt foreign and unwelcoming. She lingered in the hallway, reluctant.

'Mum?' she called out. There was no response. The house was empty. Jo made her way to the kitchen. There were dirty dishes in the sink. At one end of the table there was a stack of newspapers and catalogues, and at the other end a single cork placemat, a half glass of water, and a margarine tub. On the bench sat several unopened bills. Every surface was coated with a layer of dust, and along the front of the stove, crumbs congregated. There was a trail of ants from the crumbs to the door. Jo could feel the weight of her mother's sadness and despair, and the force of the connection that linked them together. She had ruined so many lives, including her mother's. Jo picked up the melting margarine, pushed the lid down tight, and put it in the fridge. The house was hot and stuffy. She opened the front and back doors and the windows in the kitchen, and then went back down the hall to her room. Jo threw her bag into the corner. She crawled into bed. She could smell her mother's scent on the pillow, on the sheets, on the doona. Or was she imagining it?

Jo fell asleep and dreamt she was in a warm pool. There were none of the usual lap swimmers jostling for lanes. There were no children jumping and splashing. The water was murky, and she couldn't see more than an arm's length in front, yet she swam easily. Back and forth. Back and forth.

At the bottom of the pool, a garden was growing. Plants rose out of the mist. *Impossible.* Rosemary. And parsley. Broccoli, eggplants, marrow. Garlic and mint.

Jo altered the shape of her swim to avoid the thorny arms of the cactus sprouting in the corner. She was swimming better than she'd ever swum. She could've swum forever if it weren't for the plants growing so fast, transforming the pool into a dense watery forest, and the long and snaking tendrils that reached up and wrapped themselves around her waist, her shoulders, and her throat.

'What have you been doing all this time?'

'It doesn't matter.'

Jo and Mandy were sitting in the kitchen, sharing the pre-packaged salad Mandy had brought home from the supermarket for her dinner. There was a quick-sale sticker over the original price. Mandy had divided it into two separate bowls. Though the salad — noodles and Asian greens — was soggy, they both ate it.

'Why Portarlington?'

Jo pushed the bowl aside.

'Jo?'

'Yes.'

'Why?'

'Why what?'

'Why Portarlington?'

'Because that's where I ended up. Grandpa Tom took me there once.'

'But all that time.'

'Yes.'

'What did you do?'

'Nothing.'

'For two and a half months?'

Jo didn't respond.

'Jo, I'm talking to you.'

'You're shouting at me.'

'Yes, I am, but you're not responding. You're not answering me.'

'What? What do you want me to say?'

'Tell me how you feel. What you're thinking. I'm your mother. I want to help.'

'Do you? Really?'

'I want to help.'

'Well, you can't.'

'Maybe I can, maybe I can't, but you won't give me a chance.'

Jo looked around the kitchen. Mandy had rules: don't leave dirty dishes in the sink, not even a cup or a glass; sweep up after meals, because *crumbs attract rats*. She wiped the benches, the stovetop, and the oven after each use. She vacuumed twice a week. Mopped the kitchen and bathroom floors every second day. Jo noticed that the fruit bowl that always sat on the bench was gone. 'Where's the crystal bowl?' she asked.

'What?'

'Nan's crystal bowl?'

'It's broken. I dropped it and it broke, so be careful. Don't walk around without shoes on. I don't think I got all the pieces.'

'You don't break things.'

'Accidents happen.' Mandy stopped. 'Sorry, didn't mean to say that.'

The air was brittle and sharp. What was broken couldn't be put together again. There was now a permanent crack in the world. It couldn't be mended with a little glue or a row of stitches. It couldn't be covered up, like her mother might cover a stain on the lino by throwing an op-shop rug over the top.

Mandy wrapped her hands around her mug and stared into it as if the answers to all her problems might be swimming there, under the milky surface. She wore her red supermarket shirt; it was too baggy and too bright. She looked pale and thin in it. Jo stared at Mandy's arms, fragile, protruding from too-wide sleeves.

'Didn't mean what? Didn't mean to say the word *accident*? In the hospital when you came to pick me up ...'

'Yes,' Mandy said.

'You didn't touch me.'

Mandy pushed back into her chair. 'No. I ...'

'You're ashamed of me. You didn't just look angry, you looked like you hated me.' Jo hadn't meant to say any of this. It was as if there were a leak — the words kept spilling out, and, unable to find the source, she was powerless to stop them.

'I was angry. I was in shock. I don't hate you,' Mandy said.

'It was the worst moment in my whole life. I wanted to die. And you came and I wanted to run into your arms, and for you to hold me, but you didn't want to have anything to do with me. The sight of me made you cringe. I understand. I hate myself. But you're ... you're my mother ... and I didn't expect that.'

'I don't hate you.'

'You don't love me. Not anymore. You've loved me all my life. Didn't you think I'd notice when you stopped?' The word *love* wedged itself between them, flaunted itself, as they sat defeated in the messy kitchen. After a while, Jo stood up and went to the sink. She stacked all the dirty dishes to one side and filled the tub with warm, soapy water. Mandy wasn't the same woman who promised unconditional love to her five-year-old daughter. Jo wasn't the same daughter.

She turned to face Mandy. 'I had a job in a restaurant in Portarlington. I stayed in a hostel. I worked long hours. Some days I went for a swim. Most days I went for long walks. I tried to avoid people. I kept to myself. But a couple of people, well, you know ... People get to know you and start asking questions. They wanted to know about me, my life, why I was in Portarlington. I couldn't tell anyone, so I left. I couldn't tell them, but I couldn't keep lying.'

'I don't hate you. I care about you. I was so worried. You didn't even ring for Christmas,' Mandy said.

'I'm sorry. I wanted to avoid Christmas. I sent you a text.'

'I care about you.'

'Of course,' Jo said. 'I know.' But Jo didn't believe it. She'd expected her mother's love to be unconditional — wasn't that what people said about parents, they loved you unconditionally? She'd learnt early on that her father's love was fickle and conditional and easily forgotten. Now she knew her mother's love had limits and there were things even a mother found difficult to forgive.

'I've no idea how to steer us through this,' Mandy said, getting up and taking a clean tea towel out of the drawer to dry the dishes as Jo washed.

'It's not up to you.'

'Can you explain to me ...' Mandy began.

'Explain what?'

'How you feel. What you're thinking?'

There were no tears on the night of the accident, as Jo sat trapped in the car. No tears when they told her Ash was dead. No tears at the police station, even with all the questions and the badgering. No tears the day of Ash's funeral, or on any of those long nights when she couldn't sleep and Ash's voice was loud in her head. She'd wanted to cry, but there'd been no tears; a dry, desolate tract, parched and barren. Now she was sobbing. And shaking. She had to stop washing the dishes and sit down.

Mandy passed her a box of tissues. She made her a cup of tea. She brought her a blanket and wrapped it around her shoulders.

Through her tears, Jo considered her mother, a woman she no longer recognised. Maybe she'd never seen her mother — for years they'd been two bodies circling around each other, not connecting, mostly antagonistic. She didn't know anything about this mother. All Jo's life, her mother had been doting and loving, ever-present. Other mothers would run late for school pick-ups, but Mandy was always on time. Other mothers went out at night and left their children with babysitters, but Mandy rarely went anywhere without Jo. And then there was the mother she avoided, found embarrassing, didn't listen to, couldn't confide in. Did her mother long for another life? A career? A relationship?

'Let's get out of here,' Mandy said.

'It's midnight.'

'I know.'

The silent, cold air hit Mandy as she opened the door. It had been a warm day and she was wearing short sleeves. 'I'll get some jackets,' she said, leaving Jo at the front door, walking down to her room, and grabbing a couple of old windcheaters. On her way back, Mandy took a moment to look down the hallway at Jo. Her daughter was back. Two and a half months she had prayed for her return — she, who wasn't religious, going with Mary to the Catholic church and lighting candles, sitting with Mrs Nguyễn in her Buddhist meditation group, praying and wishing and hoping. She was on antidepressants. Taking sleeping pills. Drinking more than she should. Working extra shifts at the supermarket. *Going crazy.* Her feelings for Jo were a poisonous cocktail — anger, grief, guilt, shame — but there was also the relief at Jo's return home. Was this love?

Mandy steered them out of the house and onto Hyde Street, across Francis Street, and into Stephen Street, away from the bridge. Planning to walk with her daughter as they had often walked when Jo was younger, when walking had loosened Jo's tongue and she had talked about school, about the teachers and the other girls … Only recently had Mandy begun to wonder if Jo, even then, had kept secrets, and censored her chatter even when it seemed mindless and Mandy thought she was divulging everything. Had she failed to read between the lines, to notice the gaps? Was it possible she didn't know her daughter? Had never known her? Did other people know their children? Some parents spoke with such authority — *my daughter is a deep thinker, my son's outgoing and popular at school, my child would never do that, he has the determination to get there, she won't last the distance …*

A three-quarter moon glowed behind a thin powder of clouds, giving the night a soft brush. The streetlights shone over the footpath and the road, their beams bouncing off the white trunks of the birch and the gum trees; in the shadows, the houses retreated. They seemed abandoned and neglected, as if their occupants had left under duress, with no time to gather toys or bikes, to pick up discarded jackets and hats, to close shutters, to pull gates shut. In this empty world, Mandy and Jo relaxed into an easy striding — fast enough to keep warm — along the footpaths of the neighbourhood that was now both familiar and unrecognisable.

When a car sped past, triggering a sensor light outside a converted warehouse, the resident dog woke and growled at them. Jo and Mandy returned to their bodies, to discover they were a block away from Ashleigh's house. Jo stopped. Approached from this direction, the house was partially hidden by several large trees, including an old elm that dominated that part of the street with its broad canopy. But they could see a light was on in Ashleigh's room, and they could see the rose bushes were gone.

'In Portarlington, when I first arrived, when they asked me my name, I panicked and said Ashleigh,' Jo whispered.

'What?'

'So the whole time I was there, they called me Ashleigh.'

'You miss her.' Mandy reached tentatively for Jo's hand, shepherding her gently back around the corner.

'I can't get her out of my head.' Her mother's hand was warm and familiar and almost unbearable. The tears were slow at first, but soon she was sobbing again. 'You know, when I was in Portarlington and people were calling me Ashleigh,' she paused to catch her breath, 'I didn't … I worried someone would find out. But I didn't feel bad. I mean, I felt bad because I shouldn't have used her name, but I also felt better, not so anxious. I felt better, like I was someone else.'

They retraced their steps back down Stephen Street and into Gray Street and then Hyde. There was little traffic, only an occasional car or truck. They passed a cat balancing on a front fence. It leapt to the ground as they approached. They passed a dog sleeping on the front verandah of a small brick house. When they reached the corner of Hyde and Francis, they crossed, walked straight past the house, and headed towards the bridge.

'Where are we going?' Jo asked, even though it was obvious.

'You know,' Mandy replied. Life required courage; the past needed to be confronted. For some people, lighting candles, meditation, and prayers provided relief. For some people, faith was their anchor. But Mandy didn't have faith, not in God. Mary always said, *blessed are those that have faith*. It sounded like criticism to Mandy, as if Mary saw her as one of the damned. She understood that Mary's faith gave her solace, and solace was what everyone wanted. For Mandy, solace came from facing problems head-on.

At the base of the bridge, they stopped at the small roadside memorial for Ashleigh. It had been carefully maintained; several bouquets of fresh flowers tied to the cross. Only the cards and notes had deteriorated: faded, crumbled, the words smudged where the ink had run.

'That night, I was so angry. So angry I couldn't speak. I wanted to yell at you and Ashleigh. I wanted to tell you both how stupid you were, how reckless, but I knew there was no point. I knew I should've been more supportive, but I couldn't …'

'We — no, me, me, I was driving, I shouldn't have been driving. So stupid. My fault, all of it, I know. We — not just Ash and me, but you and Ash's family and everyone — are paying for it. I'm so sorry, so sorry, but sorry doesn't make any difference.'

Above them, on the bridge, the traffic was sparse. The river caught and reflected the lights in bands of yellow and green and red, luminous waves of colour fluttering like flags on a carnival ride.

'I used to love the bridge at night,' Jo continued. 'But it's different now — the lights feel too strong, and I feel too exposed. I've been scared to come here, scared I'd run into Ash's parents. Or Jane. I want to get the accident out of my head. To get Ash out of my head. Even when I'm talking, I hear Ash. I can't think.'

'Jo, honey, she's dead. It's not her,' Mandy said.

'I know. I tell myself, I tell her, *you're dead, Ash*. But I can hear her voice. I tell her I'm sorry. I tell her I wish it hadn't happened. That I wish she was alive.'

'But she's not,' Mandy said, drawing her daughter into an embrace.

'No, but I don't feel alive, either.'

———

Memories of Ash were relentless. Some memories were like songs stuck in her head; they played over and over again. They were fifteen and sitting on a bench in the park, each of them with their iPods, their different music, in their own world. Ash pulled one of the earplugs out of her ear, and then she pulled one out of Jo's ear. 'We should do something.'

'We are doing something.'

'Something exciting. We should have an adventure.'

'Like what?'

'Let's steal a car and go for a joy ride.'

'Sure.'

'Come on, Jo, there must be something we can do. We're fifteen — our lives shouldn't be so boring.'

'I'm not bored.'

'But you're boring.'

'Fuck off. If I'm so boring, go and hang out with someone else.'

'Don't get your knickers in a knot.'

'Okay. So what are we going to do then?'

'I want to do some spraying!'

'Spraying?'

'Graffiti.'

'What?'

'My cousin Peter and his mates have been tagging the neighbourhood. Let's go with them.'

'We'll get into trouble.'

'Come on, don't be such a wuss. You can be too much of a fucking goody-goody, Jo, and you'll have plenty of time for that when you're old and have kids and a house, and have to spend every night sitting in front of the TV, wiping snot off your kids' noses and worrying where you are going to get the money to pay the bills ...' Ash kept at it until Jo felt her life was already over, and if she didn't do something soon she would get old overnight.

It took Ash ages to convince Peter and then it took him time to convince his mates. In the end they said yes because they were all worried Ash would tell Peter's mum about the graffiti. They agreed to meet at midnight in the goods yard at the back of Yarraville Station.

Sneaking out wasn't difficult. Mandy slept at the back of the house and Jo slept at the front, and there were several rooms in between. At eleven, Jo made a hot chocolate and went to bed. She listened to Mandy turn off all the lights and lock the front door. She listened to her walk down the hallway to her room. Then she waited until her mother was asleep and, with her shoes in her hand, she tiptoed down the hall, making sure to avoid the creaky floorboards and close the door carefully as she left.

Once she was outside, she started to worry. At the gate, she hesitated, considered turning around and going back to bed, but she didn't want to let Ash down. Across the road, the tanks shone under the lights, and the traffic across the West Gate was a series of speeding fireflies.

Jo ran all the way down Hyde Street, across and into Francis Street, down Stephen Street into Schild, and then Anderson past the shops, down Ballarat and Murray and into the goods yard. When she arrived, the others were waiting. There were four boys and Ash. Two of the boys were carrying backpacks.

'Now,' Peter said, 'if I say run, then you run as fast as you can straight home and don't stop, and if you get caught you don't fucking know us, never seen us before, don't know our names.' Peter was a pimply-faced teenager a year or so older than Jo and Ash. He'd been kept down at school so they were in several classes with him.

The boys led the way. They stopped under the Somerville Road overpass, where the council workers had recently painted over the last lot of graffiti with grey paint, leaving them a large blank canvas. The boys took out their spray cans and started tagging. Ash joined them. 'Come on,' she said to Jo.

'What will I tag?'

The boys laughed. 'Fucking amateurs,' Peter said. 'Your tag is your ID. You put it everywhere, as many places as possible. For fuck's sake.' He shoved a spray can in her hand. 'Here, hold it straight. And then write your tag.'

Jo's heart thumped and she thought she might throw up. But she was excited too. Alive. Full of energy. She wanted to tag. She pushed the nozzle down and wrote *Jojo*. The letters were fuzzy, only just readable.

'You're a fucking toy,' Peter said.

'Give her a break,' Rico, one of the other boys, said.

Peter thumped the boy on the arm, hard. 'What, you got the hots for her?'

Rico thumped him back and they began wrestling. Until they heard a car coming — then they all ran and hid in the shadows, behind trees, under the steps of the overpass. When one of the cars turned out to be a police patrol car, Jo thought she might wet herself. Adrenaline. Heart racing.

'Wasn't that great,' Ash said when the cop car had driven away and they came back to look at their tags. Ash insisted they all walk Jo home, and she was grateful. Along the way, Peter and Rico and the others stopped to graffiti fences and walls, and Jo and Ash giggled and laughed. But Jo was still trembling when she climbed into bed.

Were some people more alive than others? Was loneliness a kind of death?

Sometimes Jo had been lonely, even with Ash as a friend.

One of the things Jo admired about Ash was her willingness to reveal details about all aspects of her life. Until recently, Jo thought that this meant Ash didn't have secrets. She'd told Jo all about sex with Kevin, all of the intimate details. How it hadn't gone well the first time, *stage fright, he was a virgin*. She told Jo about her arguments with her parents and her sister. About the arguments her parents had, about her mother's affair with a teacher at school that almost ended up with her parents divorcing — family secrets no one was supposed to know. About an old neighbour who lured Ash into his house once when she was eight and showed her his penis. She described the penis and told Jo it wasn't the first one she'd seen because her father sometimes walked around the house naked, and so it hadn't been the sight of the penis that made her cry — *it was a small, shrivelled thing*. She cried because he wanted her to touch it. She screamed and ran, her neighbour giving chase, but she'd made it out of the house and told her parents and then watched out of the window as the police dragged him away.

Ash told Jo things that, if they had happened to Jo, she wouldn't have told anyone, not even Ash. She didn't tell Ash about the girls at primary school who said she was too fat to play with them. Neither Mandy nor Ash knew about her trip to Fitzroy, when she stood outside Ian's house. She hadn't told either of them about the anxiety, about the doubt, about the voices in her head telling her over and over that no one wanted to be her friend.

'Are some people's lives worth more than others?' Ian Williams had asked their Geography class once, during a lengthy discussion about poverty in India. He'd given them an article to read about a train accident in the rural south of the continent — hundreds had died, yet only the three white tourists were named. They talked about the way accidents or disasters overseas only seemed to matter if Australians were killed. Of course, they all agreed every life should be equal, but the world was unjust. Anyone weighing up her life and Ash's life, measuring their worth against each other, would agree they weren't equal.

Jo had been back for a week when Sarah rang to tell her the date for the hearing had been confirmed for 15 June, a week after Jo's twentieth birthday. 'Seems a long way off, but you need to prepare yourself,' Sarah said. 'It's not going to be easy.'

'No,' Jo responded. Listening to Sarah's advice — *prepare yourself, you might get as much as five years* — Jo didn't say much. *It will be no picnic.* Sarah actually said *picnic*; Jo almost laughed. She'd seen many films and TV shows in which prisoners were harassed, bashed, raped. Even if prison weren't as bad as that, it would be bad, in ways she couldn't yet imagine. Otherwise, what was the point of it?

For the next four or five years, her life wouldn't be her own. She would live in the confines of an institution with strict rules and no way out. Her life would be in the hands of other people, and they'd decide what she would be allowed to do or not do. For the last five or so years, she'd been resisting and resenting her mother's desire to exercise authority. She hated her mother's rules. She hated being confined in the house. Some people chose to be secluded. To be alone. To work in jobs where someone else made all the decisions. Could she be one of those people? Would confinement and the loss of freedom be a relief? Would it stop the endless and relentless voices in her head? Would she be able to give her life over?

Through a friend Mandy had worked with, Jo found a job cleaning a local office block. It was a big block and there were several cleaners. Each had their own floor, their own trolley of cleaning equipment and cleaning chemicals. Jo's shift began at 10.00 pm. At 12.30 she had a tea break, and at 2.30 a meal break. The other cleaners called the second break 'lunchtime' and congregated in the third-floor kitchen, which had a television set that was on all the time. By 'lunchtime', the only stations going were the shopping channels — fitness equipment, home gadgets, and beauty products that eradicated wrinkles and made people young again. Sometimes Grace, who was from Ethiopia, walked down the stairs to Jo's floor to ask her to read the label on a bottle, or the note left by Rob, the supervisor who organised all the communication with the people who owned the building. Grace was a gregarious mother of four, and she was embarrassed about her inability to read in English. The notes weren't difficult to explain: *The toilet wasn't cleaned properly; The cleaner needs to vacuum under the desk; A woman lost her diamond earring somewhere, please look out for it.* Grace always wore a headscarf and a long skirt. The building air-conditioning was turned off by the time the cleaners arrived, and Grace was usually sweating. When she stopped to talk to Jo, she wiped her forehead with the handkerchief she kept in an invisible pocket. She often asked Jo to join them for 'lunch'. Jo smiled and said, 'Maybe,' but she didn't go. Most of her co-workers were migrant and refugee women twice her age. They worked so their children could get an education. They were kind to her, but curious about why she, a young *Australian girl*, was working as a cleaner. 'My children all go to university,' Grace said, showing photos on her phone of her son in his graduation gown.

Only Rob mentioned the accident. He was a regular at the café where Jo had worked. 'I was sorry to hear about the accident,' he said to Jo one night. 'I guess that's why you left the café. Though it's not right, Ted sacking you.'

'He didn't sack me,' was all she said in response. They were standing outside. It was almost three o'clock. He was smoking and she was drinking a cup of tea.

'Well, if you need someone to talk to,' he said, inching closer.

'No, I don't want to talk about it.' She moved away.

He shrugged his shoulders, butted out his cigarette, and went back inside.

Counting your lucky stars.

I don't feel lucky at all.

You're alive.

I feel dead.

You have no idea what dead feels like.

Please, Ash, leave me alone.

It's you that can't leave me alone.

Chapter 25

It was a long narrow hallway with a row of doors on each side. From behind a red door, about halfway down, came the thunderous rhythm of instrumental music. Jo carried a heavy box full of notebooks. She pushed the door open with her body; it opened into a garden, and the music came to a sudden stop. There was a lush overgrown lawn, rambling bushes, tall gum trees, climbing roses. A garden shed. A park bench. A table. In the middle of a green patch there was a campfire, the flames contained by a small circle of grey stones.

Jo's shoulders and arms strained under the weight of the box, and before she reached the fire, it slipped out of her hands, landing with a thump as it hit the ground. She sat on the grass. The fire glowed and sparked. Her cheeks turned hot.

She straightened and opened the box and stared at the notebooks. Ash's first journal, pink with a ballerina twirling on the cover, was on top. This journal predated her friendship with Ash, was filled out long before they met. Stories of another life, of a girl young enough to want to be a ballerina. By the time they met, they were more cynical — they laughed at little girls dressed in pink, at little girls with tiaras and tutus, as if they hadn't been young themselves.

'Not good to burn synthetic materials. They give off toxins.' A man stood behind Jo. He wore a suit and a tie and carried a clipboard. He was standing outside of the perimeter of the light radiating from the fire, and she couldn't see his face. 'You'll have to rip the pages out and then throw the cover in the bin.'

'Who are you? Where did you come from?'

The man stepped closer, and Jo noticed that he had a long grey beard, wide and full at the top, finishing in a narrow point at his waist. The man ran his free hand down the beard, stroking it like one might pet a dog or a cat. 'The plastic. You can't burn the plastic.'

'But I can't open the journal. I don't have the key.'

'She trusted you with the journals, but not the key?'

'The others, the later ones, don't have locks.'

'So she did trust you,' the man said as he walked away. Jo listened to his shuffling footsteps and the crackle of the fire. A fruit bat flapped its wings as it flew back and forth between the next-door neighbour's apple tree and a peach tree in a garden several streets away.

'Will you burn them?' the man called from the other end of the garden.

'I don't know.'

'If you aren't going to read them, what's the point?'

'Once they're destroyed, they're gone. I've got no idea what I should do. What's the right thing to do?'

'No right thing here.'

'She never said what to do with them.'

'She didn't know she was going to die.'

'I can't keep them. And I can't give them away.'

The garden was rustling and shimmering. The fire was dying out. If it died out, Jo wouldn't be able to burn the journals. She had no idea how to start a fire. If she didn't burn them, she'd have to carry them with her forever. 'Would you take them?' Jo asked the man.

He laughed. 'What would I do with a girl's journals? They're full of girls' stuff, boys and bras and complaints about her parents who won't let her go out.'

A car alarm screeched. Jo woke.

Were the journals meaningless? Were Ash's journals full of drivel, of teenage angst? Of frivolous things that didn't matter?

Inside the pages was Ash's voice. Jo knew she had no right to read them, but should she give the journals to Ash's parents or destroy them? Would reading the journals intensify Rae and Alex's grief, their loss? Or was it possible that reading the journals could be an antidote to their grief?

In the weeks after her return from Portarlington, Jo continued her early morning walks, usually after her shift, in the hour of semi-darkness before the sun rose, when the horizon was powdered with soft reds and oranges, and in the sky the moon was reluctant to give the night away. Avoiding the bridge and the village shopping area, she devised walks that took her to unfamiliar streets, through the reserves that skirted the river — Donald McLean, Anderson, and Stony Creek — hoping to avoid memories, to avoid Ash, hoping to find a new and unrecognisable suburb in which she might see the possibility of living. Down past the tanks, along the river, sometimes towards Williamstown, glancing across Port Phillip and imagining she could see clear across to Portarlington, the pier, and The George. Some days she allowed herself to remember Justin and the kiss, even though she knew there was no point lingering on the impossible.

'You should wear a suit, something plain and serious,' Sarah said. She'd arrived early with some papers for Jo to sign. Her next appointment wasn't until ten, so she'd said yes to a coffee. It had been a hot night and the house was stuffy, so they took their drinks outside, Sarah and Mandy on faded canvas deck chairs and Jo on the wooden step. In the background, the usual rumble of the traffic had been joined by screeching calls from the local magpies. The garden was dry, the leaves of some plants curled and sagged, and the stems were brittle and ready to snap.

'What difference will what I wear make?' Jo asked. Of course she knew she had to wear something serious — it's not like she'd turn up in her jeans and t-shirt, or some frivolous little party dress. She understood the importance of looking respectful.

'It's hard to measure the difference clothes make — more when there is a jury, but even with a judge, it could have an influence. People think the law is set down, that it's all about the facts, measureable and solid, and that's true, but the law is also like anything else. There's the human factor.'

The talk of clothes and the judge brought the court case closer, and Jo floundered for the words to express what she was feeling, a sudden rush of emotion sweeping her up as if she were a twig in the path of a flooding torrent.

'What should she wear?' Mandy asked.

'A suit. A blazer and a skirt, dark blue, and a plain top underneath the jacket — something subdued, grey or smoky blue.'

Jo heard them talking about the suit and the shoes and where best to buy them as if she were drowning and their voices were faint murmurs from a distant shore. Those voices plunged her into the past, to the afternoon four months earlier when Ash was sitting on the same wooden step, talking to Kevin, her legs stretched out across the small gravel path that led down to the garden. Back to the afternoon she read Ash's journal. The smooth red cover. And the pages filled with Ash's writing, pages and pages about Kevin, about school, about Ash's dreams … If only she hadn't read the journal. Was reading it the act that changed the course of her life, of Ash's life? Or does every act, every moment, have the power to shift and change the course of life? She recalled a movie, *Run Lola Run*, that she and Ash went to see at ACMI one night during their 'arthouse film phase'. Lola has to take 100,000 deutschemarks to her loser boyfriend — Ash said the most unbelievable part of the film was that Lola would hang out with such a loser and want to save his life. Lola leaves the money behind on the train, where it's picked up by a homeless man. Desperate, Lola goes to the bank to borrow the money from her father. The film has three scenarios, beginning each time from the same starting point. However, each scenario develops in different ways and has different outcomes — for Lola and for her boyfriend and for all the people she bumps into along the way. If only Jo could rerun her life from that point when her hand moved across the table and picked up the journal. If only Jo could rerun her life from the moment she stepped into the car on the night of the accident.

The shriek of brakes and a loud car horn, followed by a man shouting,

'Fucking look where you're going!' came through the front door, down the hall, to reach them on the verandah. An accident avoided.

'We can go shopping on my day off,' Mandy was saying. 'There won't be so many people around. What do you think, Jo?'

'I don't know what the point is. I don't care how long they lock me up for, so anything will do.'

'Don't say that, Jo,' Mandy said. 'Don't say that.'

'You have to find something,' Sarah said. 'Something you can do in the world, something that makes it better for other people. If I didn't have my work, if I spent my whole time thinking about myself, I would've slashed my wrists a long time ago.'

'I'm not good at much,' Jo said.

'When I was a child, when I fought with my mother, I'd run to my nan. She used to say to me, if you want to be happy, don't think about yourself all the time. Think about leaving the world a little better than you found it. She didn't mean big things — for her it was looking after her family, keeping an eye on the older people in her street, helping out at the refugee centre once a week. She used to like to help the people there with their English.'

'Is she still alive?' Mandy asked.

'Yes, but she has dementia,' Sarah said. 'Last time I went to visit, she didn't recognise me, didn't know my name. Sometimes there's a little spark, and I think she remembers bits of the past, from when I was a child. My mother says I'm imagining it and that Nan has no memories left at all. I don't trust her perspective on Nan. They never got on.'

What would it be like to lose your memory and forget everything? Would it be a relief? Would the weight lift off your shoulders?

'When things aren't going well, when I'm worried about stupid things, like not fitting into size twelve jeans, I think about what Nan would say: *Pick yourself up, girl, and get on with it.* You'll have to get on with it, Jo, with life. There'll be a life after all of this is over, and you should plan for it.'

'I guess.' Jo shrugged. 'I'll see you later, Sarah. Thanks for the advice.' Jo left her mother and Sarah talking, put on her runners, and headed for the bridge. She hadn't been back for weeks, since the night she returned from Portarlington. Standing on the boardwalk under the eye of the bridge, she watched the birds — seagulls, sparrows, several cormorants, and other birds she didn't know the names of — as they flew in and out of the mangroves that were part of the Stony Creek Backwash, oblivious to the West Gate Bridge overhead, to the trucks and cars on Hyde Street. 'Pick yourself up, girl, and get on with it,' was Sarah's advice. As if she'd fallen over during a game of netball, scraped her knee, and was overreacting. Jo had no idea how to pick herself up, or even if it was possible.

When she turned back towards the road, she was confronted by the barricade that had risen out of the darkness that night, the barricade that had smashed into her spinning car. There it was, the spot where metal crushed and glass shattered. Memories surfaced, and she couldn't stop them. The loud, unbearable screams — all four of them screaming. Ash screaming. In the moment between her loss of control of the car, between the skidding and spinning and the final crash, Ash was alive, Ash was sitting next to her, alive, and Ash was screaming, her hand reaching for the steering wheel.

After the impact, silence. And then sobbing and crying, and the calling out of names. Voices and names. Ash. Mani. Laura. Jo. A round robin. Each one calling out. All except for Ash.

Jo crouched on the ground, against the rail of the boardwalk.

She heard the horns and sirens, and the voices of strangers — so many voices, *are you hurt, I think she's dead, this one is breathing, get these girls out* … And now it was coming back to her, her arm reaching out for Ash, and Ash slumped onto the dashboard, a long tear of blood running from her temple, down her neck, dripping onto the floor. She reached for Ash, to catch the blood, to stop the blood. Her hand on Ash's skin. Ash still. Ash not breathing.

'This one is dead.'

Eyes shut tight.

Knees to chest, the feel of the rail pressing into her back.

She had reached out for Ash. All these weeks, these months, she had blocked out the image of Ash dead, of the blood, of her hand on Ash's arm. The horror of seeing, the horror of knowing. Ash, gone.

A ship's horn roused Jo, and she uncurled herself and stood up. Tears rolled down her cheeks.

There was no glass or metal debris in the gutter. The bent pole had been repaired. The only reminder of the accident was the small memorial to Ash: a white wooden cross, a couple of bouquets of flowers, and the faded remnants of the cards. She bent down to touch the cross. 'Ash,' she whispered. 'Oh, Ash. I miss you.'

When Jo turned back towards home, she saw a man walking along the path to the bridge. He had a slight limp. There was something familiar about him. And then she knew, too late: it was Ash's grandfather. Panicked, she considered crossing the road, but he was already drawing close.

'Hello, Jo.' It was hard to meet his gaze. The sadness in his eyes made her shiver. She held her breath.

'I didn't see you until … I can go …' She nearly said his name. *Nonno Nello*, that's what she called him. She remembered him saying, 'You can call me Antonello, or Nello if you want, or Nonno, like Ashleigh here.' Only, he wasn't her grandfather, he was Ash's. What could a child call a man who was older than her own grandparents? Jo couldn't call him Nonno Nello anymore.

'You don't need to go.' There was sternness in his voice. Would he yell at her? She braced herself. She deserved it, and he was entitled to it.

Antonello stood between her and the path; she stood between him and the memorial. Overhead on the bridge, the traffic continued, immune to them — a breathy whirr, punctuated by the rattle as the heavier vehicles, trucks and semis, drove over metal strips and joins. The scaly underbelly towered over them, and Jo felt reduced, like one of the little people in fairytales about giants.

'I come here often,' he said. 'I've been coming for years. Usually I have the place to myself.'

'For years? Before the accident?' Jo said.

'Before *your* accident. Yes,' Antonello said.

'I'm sorry. I never meant to hurt Ash.' The words came out in a rush.

'You must hate me.'

'Ashleigh was so beautiful. And now she's gone, and —'

'It's my fault, I know it's my fault. I'm so sorry. Please believe me.'

'Stop. Stop, please. I don't hate you, Jo. I'm angry and sad, but I feel sorry for you too. You must miss Ashleigh. You were so close.'

'Rae and Alex and Jane hate me. They must.' The words, these words, she hadn't expected to be saying to Ash's grandfather. She knew they hated her. Nothing else was possible, nothing but hate.

'They're upset and sad and it's hard for them. We've lost Ashleigh.' He sounded angry, even though he hadn't raised his voice.

'It's all my fault.' Her face was burning; she was sweating, her hands were clammy.

'It was an accident, Jo. We'll all have to come to terms with that — you'll have to come to terms with that,' Antonello said, bending down slowly to pick up a discarded milkshake cup on the edge of the path.

'But I was drunk, and if I hadn't been drinking … Or if I'd left the car there … It's all my fault.' She should stop talking. Her voice was the pleading voice of a child, whimpering. She had no right to expect him to forgive her, no right to burden him with her guilt. She stole a look at him, but he was looking at Ash's memorial. She longed for Grandpa Tom and the strength of his arms when he had swooped her up from the floor when she was younger.

Antonello crossed the path to throw the rubbish into the bin. 'There isn't much point in going through what would've happened, if you hadn't done this or that, because in the end it won't make any difference. You have to find a way to live with what happened.'

'I don't know if I can.' What possible life could there be? How did people put something like this behind them? Was it feasible that once she'd been punished, once she'd gone to prison, she could live again? Redemption was at the base of Mary's religion — confess your sins, ask for forgiveness, do your penance, and then start anew. *Pick yourself up*, Sarah said.

'You can.' Antonello's voice softened. 'We're stronger than we think. And if we couldn't go on, if we couldn't move on, when someone dies, when bad things happen, the whole world would fall apart. Every day people die, and the people that love them — not all of them, but most of them — pull themselves up by the bootstraps and keep going.'

'But what about the people who killed them? Do we have a right to keep living?'

Antonello stretched his hand out to Jo, and she took it. His palm was cold but smooth. Not like Grandpa Tom's hands, rough, cracked, and cut — even after all these years, even though sometimes she couldn't call up Grandpa Tom's face, the memory of his hands came back. *Hands like sandpaper*. Lines and cuts, dips and hollows. Scars, each one a story.

'Come with me,' Antonello said.

Jo was thin, her features sharper than he remembered. She wasn't beautiful, not like Ashleigh. She was a plain girl. Plain and ordinary and alive.

It snuck up on him, the desire to take her throat between his hands and wring the life out of her, the desire to slap her hard, to knock her to the ground, to shake her; to yell at the girl, to make her flinch; to scream *you stupid, stupid girl*; to see her broken and bloodied. It wasn't a sudden, all-consuming rage — it was a slow monster swelling. The impulse terrified him; he thought his propensity for such evil thoughts, for such an overwhelming desire for destruction, had gone. He closed his eyes and pushed down on the emotion.

Jo winced. He'd tightened his grip of her hand, and she was trying to pull away. He let her go. 'Sorry,' he whispered. He saw the terror in her face and was immediately overcome with pity, with something like love, deep and paternal. He resisted the inclination to embrace Jo. She wasn't Ashleigh. Embracing Jo did not have the power to bring Ashleigh back to life.

Jo took several steps back, but she didn't leave. She was the girl who had called him Nonno Nello, who he and Paolina had included on their trips with Ashleigh to the movies, shopping, to dinner. Every year they bought her a Christmas present, a chocolate rabbit at Easter, and a birthday present. Her birthday was marked on the calendar that hung above the phone in their kitchen, along with the birthdays of their children and grandchildren, their siblings and nieces and nephews. Their album included photographs of Jo with Ashleigh. The two girls laughing and scheming, having fun together. The girl in front of him was pale and tired, not much more than a child.

He thought of Alex and what he might think if he saw his father talking to this girl, *Ashleigh's killer.* Alex would feel betrayed. And Rae as well. Alex had said he wished they had never met her. He'd said he never wanted to see her again. He cursed her. *I hate that girl. I hope she rots in prison.* It sounded like hate. It had all of hate's outside features, all of hate's intensity, but he didn't think Alex and Rae hated Jo. There was too much sadness and grief for any other feeling to find room in their hearts. That was the problem: grief was ravenous. It found its way into each pore, took residence in the body and the mind, making it impossible to distinguish any other feelings. Sometimes grief, unbearable and relentless, disguised itself as hate, as anger. Hate mobilised; grief drained. After the bridge collapsed, Antonello was broken and battered, like an animal left wounded by a clumsy hunter. He was suicidal; he saw no way out. *Time,* Paolina and his parents told him, *give it time,* but instead he buried the grief under hatred and anger, and then he spun it into a cocoon that kept him at a distance from everyone.

In Alex and Rae, he saw himself: the younger man who'd survived the collapse of the bridge but remained lost, unavailable to his family, as if he'd been buried under the debris. His son and daughter-in-law drifted through the house as if they were alone; they didn't recognise each other or Jane. They loathed any evidence of the world continuing in Ashleigh's absence. It was this girl's fault. It *was* all her fault, that was true, but of course he knew that it was also not true. Death and disaster were intruders — they barged in unexpectedly, and they didn't discriminate. There was no *God's will* or *God's grand plan.*

Maybe it was fate. Was that a contradiction, to do away with God and give fate so much power? Paolina said it was. That for there to be fate there had to be something beyond the human, something or someone that planned life out. Could there be fate without orchestration? Was Ashleigh fated to die young? And if she were, did that mean Jo was blameless?

Or was it the randomness of life? Meaningless. Unplotted.

Or was it the fault of the flawed individual? Of the reckless girl who didn't think of the consequences? Jo hadn't considered the possibility of an accident. The engineers hadn't considered the possibility of the bridge collapsing. Was it possible to create a world in which accidents didn't happen? This question had often kept Antonello awake at night, but he had no answer.

Was it fair to blame Jo for Ashleigh's death? The law thought so. And so did Alex and Rae. The accident was her fault. It was due to her recklessness. But Ashleigh wouldn't rise from the dead because Jo was locked up in prison. The Royal Commission had laid the blame for the bridge collapse on the companies, but Bob and Slav had stayed dead.

'Come with me,' Antonello said again, and Jo followed him until they were standing in front of the West Gate Bridge Memorial. He pointed to a list of names: the men and their occupations.

'I was there when they died,' he said. The day Antonello first set eyes on the memorial, had first allowed himself to visit the bridge to read the names of his dead friends — like a list of fallen soldiers on a war shrine — he'd been furious at the inclusion of their occupations. Carpenter, rigger, ironworker: these men were fathers, husbands, brothers, and best friends. They were soccer and football players. They were jokers and kidders. They were gardeners and car enthusiasts. Fishermen, pool players, and surfers. And then there was all they could've been — grandfathers and lifelong friends. They weren't only workers. Not fodder for the city, vehicles for its progress, fools and easy prey. But the memorial was put up by the survivors, not the companies. The men, his mates and co-workers, had raised the money. They chose the wording. He couldn't destroy their memorial, he couldn't blow up the bridge. He couldn't do anything except mourn his friends.

For almost forty years, the West Gate stood oblivious to the cost those men paid. Every day, thousands of people drove over the bridge and complained about the traffic and the delays, annoyed at the way it choked at peak hour. They sat in their cars and listened to music or talked on their phones, argued with their children in the back seat. They drove over it on their way into or out of the city. They didn't see the memorial or the names — most of them didn't know about the accident, and if they had known once, it was now long forgotten.

'I worked on this bridge and I was here when it collapsed, in 1970. I lost two of my best mates. Here, Slav, he was a bit of a scholar and a poet. And Bob, he was my boss, like an uncle. He taught me everything I knew about my job. I spent more time with him in the four years before the collapse than with any other person — more time than I'd spent with my wife.' He paused and sighed. Jo lifted a hand to the letters of Bob's name, tracing them like a child tracing letters of the alphabet.

'And these other blokes: men I went to the pub with, played soccer with, sat in the lunchroom with, men I saw every day. I didn't know some of them well, but when we saw each other down the street, we'd smile and say hello, and we'd nod towards each other as we explained to whoever we were with, *he works on the bridge too*. We were so proud of the bridge. We were building this bridge, our bridge, the biggest, longest, better than any other bridge ... we bragged about it. Some of our other mates were sick of us talking about it, but we thought we were doing something amazing. It wasn't our fault it fell. The government had an inquiry and they said it was the companies. We noticed things, saw things, we fought, we went on strike. Yet we didn't fight every single thing. We were tired of saying, *Hey, that's wrong*, or *That looks a bit dodgy to me*, because we didn't want ... we wanted to be the heroes who made this amazing bridge.'

Antonello stopped and glanced at Jo. Her eyes were shut tight, and he assumed she'd stopped listening to him, like his children, who rarely listened to him. But then he saw Jo's cheeks were red and glistening. She was crying.

'I felt guilty after the bridge collapsed. Guilty about all the things I hadn't said, hadn't noticed, refused to notice. Guilty because I didn't die, because I lived and they didn't and I wanted to be dead too. And part of me did die. Part of me has never been the same again, ever. It's taken the death of my granddaughter to see the futility of it.

'Some of the men who were there when the bridge collapsed, who survived, they were braver than me — they faced the tragedy, the deaths, the horror, and decided to make sure it didn't happen again. They've fought for better conditions for workers, they've worked their whole lives to make sure we don't have another tragedy ... they've lived and loved and made the world better. I wish I'd been able to do something.

'You know, I don't know why some people reacted one way and some another. Some survivors didn't recover at all, went on to have heart attacks, cancer, early deaths. Some went off the rails — depression and anxiety. Post-traumatic syndrome, they call it now, but for years some of us were only partly human, going through the motions, like ghosts. I wish I knew what made the difference because I'd like to give it to Alex and Rae and Jane. I'd like to give it to you. No matter what you do, no matter if you're sad and miserable your whole life, no matter if you make yourself sick, Ashleigh won't come back.'

'I know,' Jo said.

'And it won't make a difference to Alex and Rae and Jane and their grief.'

'But it doesn't seem right that I can keep living.'

Blindness, death, a desire to stop witnessing and living — he understood these urges. They were impossible to argue against. 'I loved my granddaughter. She was perfect,' he said, and could sense the tears coming. Soon he would be weeping in front of this girl. 'I wanted her to have a long and beautiful life. To be happy. To have a magical life, where everything worked. If I could, I'd give my life so that she could live hers. But it's not possible. If you die, that will cause more misery. It won't bring Ashleigh back. For the people you love, the best thing you can do is forgive yourself and allow yourself to live.'

'I hear Ash's voice all the time. She's in all my dreams,' Jo told him.

Antonello nodded. 'It's not Ashleigh haunting you, it's your own grief and guilt.'

'I need to tell you something,' Jo said. 'We were arguing that night.'

'Friends argue sometimes.'

'We argued because I was scared she didn't want to be my friend anymore.'

'If only we knew when we were going to die, when our friends, the people we love, are going to die, we could make sure we weren't fighting, that our last words are the right ones.'

'There's something else,' Jo said. Behind them, the council rubbish collection truck pulled up and a man climbed out. Jo paused. He was a council worker, in a green work vest and shorts, a stout man with a round belly and thin legs. He glanced in their direction but didn't say anything. They watched him take a wheelie bin from the back of the truck and roll it along the boardwalk.

'What is it?' Antonello asked, and then regretted it. He preferred not to be told secrets, even in his own family.

Jo sighed, and Antonello thought she had changed her mind. 'I've got a box of Ash's journals,' she said.

'Her journals?'

The council worker had exchanged the empty bin for a full one and was now rolling it back up the boardwalk. He hoisted the bin into the truck, hesitated again, and watched them for a few seconds. Antonello thought he might call out to them, but he didn't. He banged the door shut behind him, started the motor, and drove away.

'Yes, all her notebooks. She wrote in them every day.'

'Yes, I know,' Antonello said. Ashleigh and her notebooks, her journals. *Are you spying on us?* Paolina had teased her sometimes. 'I heard Rae say something about not having found the journals, about where they might be hidden.' He remembered that the day after the funeral when he and Paolina went to the house, they'd found Rae in Ashleigh's bedroom, crawling under the bed. The wardrobe doors were open and all Ashleigh's clothes were spread on the desk, over the chair. The chest of drawers was empty too. 'Rae, what are you doing? It's too soon for all this,' Paolina had said, assuming that Rae was packing up Ashleigh's clothes. Rae had avoided their questions. Of course: Rae had wanted the journals.

'I have them. She kept them in my room, in this old safe. I never paid much attention. Every time she filled one up, she came over and put the next journal in the safe. I mean, we didn't talk about what would happen to the journals, and I don't know what to do with them.'

'Why did she hide them at your house?'

'Jane found one of her journals and she read it and made jokes about what Ash wrote and told Rae, and Ash was angry. She said she had to keep them away from her family because she thought Rae would read them if she had the chance, so it was safer to keep them locked up in my room. But now I don't know, I mean, I haven't … I can't keep them there forever. Soon I'll go to prison and I think my mother might sell the house. But I can't leave the journals and I can't take them with me, and I can't leave them for my mother to deal with …'

'You need to give them to Alex and Rae.' Antonello tried to give her the time she needed. He'd demand she give the journals back if he had to, but he hoped she'd come to that decision herself. He glanced at the path beyond them, towards Yarraville, and waited.

'I think sometimes Ash wrote in her journals about how pissed off she was at her mum and dad and Jane. It might be hurtful now, and I don't know if she'd want her family reading them.'

'They'll have to make that decision for themselves, whether they read them or don't read them. But you have to give them the journals. They don't belong to you.'

Jo moved away from the memorial to sit on a nearby concrete block. Antonello followed her gaze across Stony Creek, the Backwash, and the Yarra to the outline of the city. He could still recall the view of the city from the half-made bridge almost forty years ago. Over the years, he had watched Melbourne expand in all directions. Often he'd wondered about the impulse that drove developers to build taller and taller buildings, and he'd thought about all the workers, especially the riggers, who put those buildings together. And he wondered if the bridge made all that growth possible.

'Do you think it will collapse again, the bridge?' Jo asked.

'I know it will,' Antonello said.

He waited for Jo to ask him about the bridge, but she obviously had other things on her mind.

'I understand that everything that belonged to Ash now belongs to her parents, of course. That's what the law says, that's what Sarah says. But I don't know if that's what Ash would've wanted. If I give them to you, am I betraying Ash? I keep asking her, but she won't tell me.'

'Ashleigh is dead, Jo. She can't tell you. And the Ashleigh you talk to is in your head, is you. You're hoping and praying and wishing so hard, she seems real. Give the journals to her parents.'

Antonello had his own doubts. Of course teenage girls wrote about their parents, about love and hate. He imagined there were sections of Ashleigh's journals that Alex and Rae might find difficult, sections that might make them even sadder than they already were. And maybe they'd be better off not to read them.

'If I give you the journals …' Jo said. 'Can I give them to you? Can you give them to Rae and to Alex? Because I can't take them there.'

'Sure.'

'Now?'

'Yes, now.'

It only took a few minutes to reach Jo's house. From the street the house was hidden by shrubs and trees. There was an old wire fence, leaning towards the footpath under the weight of several bushes, and an iron gate, rusted at the hinges, a little out of sorts, so that it scraped on the ground as Jo pushed it open. It wouldn't take much to fix the gate — Antonello had a couple of hinges in the shed that would do. He thought about this as they walked up the path. The house was a rundown weatherboard cottage with a small verandah. Jo opened the door and led him down the hallway, past delicate crystal ornaments on a small bookshelf, to the kitchen. Inside the house was a sharp contrast to the outside: it was old and worn but impeccably clean and ordered.

Jo's mother was standing at the sink chopping vegetables. In the background, the Eagles were singing 'Hotel California', and she was humming along.

'Mum,' Jo called, and when Mandy turned around, 'You remember Ash's grandfather?'

Antonello watched Jo's mother's face turn pale. 'Oh, yes, of course,' she said, hesitating and then holding out her hand for Antonello to shake. 'Please sit down. I'm so sorry for your loss … So sorry. Ashleigh was a lovely girl.'

'Yes.'

'I'm so sorry.'

'I know, Mandy, I know.'

'Maybe you can make a cup of tea, Mum? I'm going to get Ash's journals.'

'*Ash's* journals? You have them?'

'Yes,' Jo said over her shoulder as she left the room.

'Would you like a cup of tea?'

'No, thank you, I had coffee this morning. Not so long ago.'

'I didn't know about the journals,' Mandy said. She wasn't old, perhaps late thirties, but she looked exhausted. He'd once seen a row of trees after a bad storm, barely standing, refusing to collapse, but it was obvious that one more gust of wind and they'd topple over. That's how Mandy struck him. 'I mean, I know Ashleigh kept journals, but I didn't know they were here.'

'I don't think anyone knew. One of their secrets.'

'Did you know about the journals? I mean, you and Jo — I didn't know she was talking to you.'

Antonello recognised Mandy's anxiety. She was embarrassed having to ask a stranger about her own daughter. This is what children reduced you to. He knew that feeling; he was often surprised by what other people told him about his children. He remembered one parent–teacher night when a middle-aged woman dressed in gypsy clothes — a long, flowing skirt and a peasant top — had asked them if they had talked to Nicki about her sexuality. He had no idea what the woman was talking about, but when he glanced across at Paolina, he could see she wasn't surprised at all. He sat silently while the two women discussed the possibility that his daughter was gay, the possibility she loved women, as if it were something obvious that only the blind would have missed. It turned out Nicki was bisexual, but that came later, and was also a surprise. And there were other things too — Alex joining the Labor Party, and then a choir. His children were strangers who lived in the same house. Sometimes a look or a mannerism, the tone of their voices, reminded him that they were of the same stock, of the same blood, but otherwise their lives were outside his grasp. Paolina wasn't surprised by their children's announcements, by their children's interests and passions or their sexual choices, so he imagined that mothers noticed things fathers missed. But here was Mandy, looking lost. Her discomfort was palpable.

'I ran into Jo at the bridge. She was on the boardwalk. I don't think she saw me, otherwise I think she would've left before I arrived there. But then we were both there and we talked.'

'I'm sorry. I mean, her going to the bridge must be difficult for you.'

'It's fine, Mandy. I know she misses Ashleigh. I know she feels terrible and guilty and sad. I know. She loved Ashleigh too.'

'And the journals?'

'She told me about the journals, about having them and not knowing what to do with them, worrying whether to give them to Alex and Rae, what will happen to them if she leaves them and you sell the house while she's in prison.'

'She talked about prison, about selling the house?' Mandy said, turning away from Antonello. She filled the kettle and turned it on.

'She didn't say much — mostly it was about the journals. I said she should give them to Rae and Alex.'

'That's what I would've said, if I'd known.'

'She asked me if I'd take them.'

When the kettle boiled, she pulled out two cups. Antonello didn't remind her that he didn't want tea. He watched her fill both cups with hot water, dunk a teabag in and out of each, and place one cup and the sugar and milk in front of him. The tea was already stronger than he liked it. Weak and black was the only way he could drink it, when he drank it at all, which wasn't often. Coffee with milk for breakfast. Coffee, black, at morning tea. That was it. After that, if he drank, it was red wine, although not during the day. He used to drink during the day, when he was younger, when he was a rigger, when some of them went to the pub at lunchtime even though they weren't supposed to. Even though it was irresponsible and dangerous, especially for the guys who had managed a second drink and then went straight back to work and onto the cranes, into the lifts, hoisting steel and concrete. Of course, in the library, they did occasionally go out for lunch, for a birthday or a promotion, and he did have a wine or a beer, but when they went back to work, the only machinery they had to operate was a computer.

'How are Rae and Alex doing?' Mandy asked.

'Not great. They've sent Jane to spend some time with friends on a farm by the coast, which is good. But Rae and Alex aren't doing well at all.'

'I wish I could help, do something, but I think I'd be the last person they'd want to see.'

'They have friends and family around. You have Jo to worry about.'

'Yes. Everyone must be so angry at her.'

'Yes, we're angry at Jo and at Ashleigh and at the other two girls too. Stupid. How many times have we told them not to drink and drive, not to get in a car with a drunk driver ... But it's useless now. And we all make mistakes. My wife would say it's God's will, but I don't believe in God. I think it's more random than that. It's bad luck.'

'Bad luck ...' Mandy said, as if she were testing out the words.

'When I was young, we drank and then drove home,' Antonello said. 'There weren't all the ads and the warnings. I guess the laws were the same, but we didn't think about it. People died on the road, but we kept doing it. We could've been killed or killed someone else, but we were lucky, I suppose. Not that I'm saying it's okay — of course it's not; they shouldn't have got in the car, any of them — but they did and were unlucky and life won't be the same for any of us again.' Antonello paused. He was close to tears, but he didn't want to cry in Mandy's kitchen. The place was already infested with guilt and sadness; he wouldn't add to it. He took a sip of the bitter tea and continued, 'Jo is alive and she has to learn to live with it. She has to grieve and to face whatever the law decides is her punishment, and then she'll have to learn to make a life for herself.'

'That's the hard thing. The difficult thing. Even for me. I think, what right has she to a life when she's responsible for Ashleigh's death?'

Just as Mandy finished, they both noticed Jo standing at the door with a box.

'It's okay, Mum. It's what I think too,' Jo said as she put the box on the table. Mandy and Jo were no different to Alex and Rae. The accident had left them all with the sense of ruin, of good things gone irretrievably bad.

'That sort of thinking is useless,' Antonello said, too sternly, and then, regretting his tone, dropped his voice to a barely audible whisper: 'I know how useless it is. There's nothing fair about life. That kind of talk is useless, unless of course you want to be miserable for the rest of your life.'

There was a pause. 'Here they are, anyway,' Jo said, breaking the silence. 'These are all of Ash's journals. I hope this is the right thing to do. I hope this is okay with Ash.'

Antonello stood up. The cardboard box on the table had once held a dinner set — the image on the side showed blue-and-white-striped plates and bowls — and now it was filled with his granddaughter's journals. And for the third time in less than half an hour, he was almost crying. 'Thank you for the tea, Mandy. Jo, look after yourself.'

He picked up the box. Even though it wasn't heavy, his back twitched, but he didn't hesitate, moving along the hallway, out the front door, down the path through the rusty gate, and onto the street. He wasn't sure about the journals now he had them in his hands, but he knew he needed to take them straight to Ashleigh's parents, without stopping. Because if he didn't, he might change his mind. So many things people did in the name of protecting those they loved, but in the end you can't protect people; you have to give them what they have a right to. You have to let them deal with what there is to deal with.

When he arrived at the house, he went down the side drive and knocked lightly on the back door. No one answered. He called out twice before Rae appeared in her pyjamas.

'Nello,' she said, and opened the sliding door for him.

'Rae, sorry if I woke you.'

'Oh, I don't sleep,' she said, moving aside to let him pass. 'Alex is out. He told me where, but I wasn't listening. I don't know when he'll be back.'

'It would've been better to give this to both of you, but now I'm here ...'

'What is it? What's in the box?'

Antonello thought about delaying by asking for a coffee, by sitting down, but they were standing in the kitchen with the box between them, and what could he say that needed to be tamed, qualified, when the worst news a mother could ever hear had already been delivered and registered?

'Ashleigh's journals.'

He watched Rae reach out to a chair and steady herself. Such a strong woman, his daughter-in-law — she ran a school and a household, and lots of people were scared of her: some of her teachers, many of her students. He'd heard her described as formidable and fearsome. But she was weak now, drained of her strength like a sick athlete whose muscles have gone soft.

'Where?' was all Rae managed.

'From Jo.'

'You went to see Jo?' There was an edge to her question, an insinuation: how dare you? Or, how could you?

'I went to the bridge, and she was there.'

'All this time, she's had these.' Rae clutched the back of the chair, her eyes fixed on the box.

'She didn't know what to do with them. Ashleigh hid them at her house so no one would read them. She didn't know what Ashleigh would want.'

'How dare she keep them all this time? How dare she? I've been going mad looking for them,' Rae said, but she didn't touch the box. 'Have you looked at them? Read them?'

'No. I don't think I have any right.'

'Do I?' Rae said, and began to sob. Antonello extended his arms and she pressed into him. He couldn't remember ever hugging his daughter-in-law. They kissed on the cheek occasionally, but it was a habitual greeting, not a demonstration of affection. Antonello liked Rae — she was a loving wife to his son, an excellent mother to his granddaughters, a caring daughter-in-law. She was thoughtful, polite, and warm, but even though they'd known each other for more than twenty years, seen each other several times a week, loved the same people, this was the first time there had been any intimacy between them. He continued holding her until he heard her breathing returning to normal. Then he pulled the chair out so she could sit down.

'You don't need to read them now. Maybe later. Maybe never. But they're yours. They belong to you and Alex.'

They stayed silent for a while, and Antonello sat down next to Rae.

'I used to be able to deal with anything.'

'You're the strongest person I know,' Antonello said. 'This is the hardest thing, the worst thing, that could ever have happened to you. But, Rae, you have to decide to live and to continue, to love Jane, and Alex, and the kids at your school, and your life. Otherwise everything will die.'

'I don't know if I can do that. I'm scared I can't. I'm scared if I do that, Ashleigh will disappear, and it'll be as if she was never here.'

'Ashleigh will not disappear. Never. Rae, you and Alex and Nicki and everyone, you think I'm hard and detached —' Rae looked like she might protest, but he continued, 'We both know it's true. When the West Gate collapsed, when my friends died, I wanted to kill myself. If it hadn't been for Paolina, I would've done it. And then we had the kids, and suddenly I was a father. I loved them, but I couldn't get too close. I was so angry and sad and bitter about everything, about Bob and Slav, about all the men who died. I worried about the kids dying, about Paolina dying, about my dying and leaving them alone and fatherless. It wasn't rational. And what a waste, Rae, what a waste. It didn't make Bob or Slav's deaths any easier to deal with, it made it harder, and I made it hard for everyone, harder than it needed to be. You have to find that strength. It's there, Rae, somewhere. You have to find it, and use it so that you can save your family.'

'The family is broken. Ashleigh is my first-born. Before her we were a couple, but she made us into a family. It'll never be the same. Never. She'll always be missing.'

'Yes. Every day. There is a permanent gap. There'll always be sadness and grief. But there can be other things too.' Antonello stood up. 'What about a coffee? I'll make it.'

At this, Rae smiled. 'Really? Can you make coffee? I don't think I've ever seen you at the stove.'

'Italian men have a reputation to maintain,' he said, smiling back at her. 'My mother used to say it brought shame on the woman if the man was seen doing anything domestic. My zia, my mother's sister — you didn't meet her but you would've liked her, she was a strong woman with a sense of humour — she insisted once that my father make her coffee, but it was so awful she spat it out. I make good coffee, and since Paolina has been sick, I've learnt to cook too.'

'Of course,' Rae said. 'Coffee, yes. But I can make it …'

'No, please, let me,' Antonello said. He knew his way around Rae's kitchen, having babysat his granddaughters throughout their childhood.

Rae pulled the box of journals towards her, but didn't open it. 'Ashleigh wrote in her journal every day. I'd ask her sometimes: "what are you writing?" When she was younger, she'd tell me, even read bits out to me. They'd be about what she did at school or pony club. As she got older, she'd tell me to mind my own business. It used to make me so mad. I was her mother. I knew her best, and suddenly she had secrets from me. I was so stupid to get angry about it. I'm a teacher, I know all teenagers have secrets from their parents. We had so many stupid fights.'

When the coffee had finished hissing and gurgling, Antonello poured it into the small antique espresso cups that had belonged to his mother, Emilia. They were dainty and fine, with gold rims. Alex had claimed them when his grandmother died — each of the grandchildren came to claim a memento before the house was cleared and sold. Alex said that whenever he thought of his Nonna Emilia, he pictured her drinking coffee out of one of those cups. Rae had laughed when Alex brought them home, but twenty years later they continued to drink espresso from them.

Antonello passed Rae her coffee and sat down. 'I can't imagine what a young girl would find to write about — boys and boring grandparents,' he said, and Rae laughed. But the box remained unopened between them.

'I'm afraid … I'm going to leave them,' Rae said, 'until Alex gets back. And then we can decide together.'

When Antonello arrived home, he found Paolina asleep in front of the television. She looked serene, and he tiptoed around her. It was amazing, he thought, how hard she found it to sleep at night and how easily she slept in the daytime. She was in her gardening clothes, old jeans and a frayed t-shirt. Her gardening shoes, a worn-out pair of runners, were outside the door. She'd been up early, before him, weeding and pruning in the garden — small jobs she had the strength to do. The breakfast dishes were in the sink, so he washed those and made sandwiches for lunch from the leftover meatloaf in the refrigerator. The meatloaf had been a little dry, but he was learning. Meatloaf and relish — not homemade relish, not anymore, no one seemed to do that anymore. He poured two glasses of water and took everything out to the table in the backyard. When he returned, Paolina was stirring. He sat beside her and put his hand on her cheek.

'You decided to come home.' Paolina smiled.

'*Tu sei la mia casa*,' he said as he kissed her gently. 'And I have made you some lunch.'

'Handsome, and you can cook. I guess I'll keep you, Nello.'

Chapter 26

Some days are sprints: time races, and the day seems to end before it has begun. Other days drift, time stretching and expanding, with no end in sight. Mandy's days were long. Monotonous and repetitive. She longed for change, but the only change on the horizon was Jo's sentencing, and it would come soon enough.

Jo had spent the afternoon with Sarah, working on her statement for the court case. She could hear them working. When they finished, it was short, a brief apology. A public recognition that the accident was Jo's fault. A declaration of grief and guilt, of how much Jo missed Ashleigh.

Sarah had left, and Mandy and Jo were sitting on the edge of the back deck, looking across the bush garden, with its native flowers and plants, to the old ghost gum. 'That tree should be chopped down. One day, one of those branches is going to fall on me when I'm in the backyard, and it'll kill me,' Rod, their neighbour, said to Mandy whenever he had the chance.

'I'm not cutting that tree down,' she told him, after years of trying to placate him, of trying to convince him the tree was safe.

'You're a cruel and careless woman,' he had said, the last time they spoke about it. This was after the accident, and she understood his reference to it. He was furious, and she'd expected he might finally take legal action, but for months he hadn't said a word.

The tree was a beacon. Every evening when she sat on the back doorstep, or stood at the kitchen window, if she focused on the tree, on its white trunk illuminated under the moonlight, she could imagine another life was possible. A life away from the suburbs. A house surrounded by creeks and hills and a large garden. She remembered her mother's suitcase with the magazine clippings — hundreds of clipped images of country cottages, of places where the morning arrived with the sound of birds and where there was a front verandah on which a person could sit looking out for miles, seeing only green and blue.

She'd finally confessed to Jo that she'd made up her mind to sell the house a few years ago and that she'd been planning to put it on the market after Jo's exams. 'Are you angry?'

'No, I thought as much. You should sell as soon as you can,' Jo said.

'But you love this house,' Mandy said.

'Whenever I heard you talk about the possibility of moving, I'd get upset. I wanted us to have this house forever. Grandpa's house. But everything is different now, and I think moving away is a good idea.'

'I don't know anymore. I planned for so long to get as far away from here as possible and was so worried about how you'd react, but I don't think now is the time. We've got to get through the court case and the sentencing.'

'You should sell and move away.'

'I want you to have a home to come back to.'

'This doesn't feel like home anymore.'

Mandy could see that Jo was close to tears. Since she'd met Antonello and handed over the journals, Jo had spent a lot of time crying. Mandy felt like crying too. But they had to be brave for each other. She wrapped her arm around her daughter's shoulder. 'I will make sure you have a home to come back to.'

After Antonello took the journals, Ash's voice stopped. Now Jo was overwhelmed by the absence of Ash, by the black hole in her life without her friend. Now she was sobbing in her sleep, waking not with Ash's voice in her head, but with a longing to see her, to talk to her, to talk things through with her. Waking up thinking, *I'll ring Ash and tell her about Mum wanting to sell the house. I'll ring Ash and talk to her about prison, about going to prison.* These thoughts, small and momentary, were followed by the realisation again and again that there was no Ash, that she would never speak to Ash again. And then the regret that Ash wouldn't fulfil her dreams, wouldn't become a lawyer, wouldn't work for the United Nations, wouldn't have her own *Hypothetical*-style program on television … That Ash would never have a life.

Sadness was the dominating emotion. She was sad for Ash's family: for Jane and Antonello, and for Rae and Alex, who now had their daughter's journals but not their daughter. She was sad for Mandy and Mary and the lives they'd lost. And she was sad for herself. Sad for the house that would be sold and would soon belong to other people, people who did not know the story behind the mural that refused to disappear, or why there was an industrial safe in the front bedroom. Sadness lingered like smoke after a fire; it saturated everything.

She mourned her old life and her old self.

'Our world has collapsed,' Mandy said.

'I'm sorry,' Jo said. She'd apologised over and over again. She'd continue to apologise for the rest of her life, even though she doubted it would make any difference. It wouldn't change anything. Jo hoped that Ash's family would get some satisfaction, some resolution, from seeing her punished. Knowing she was in prison might give them a way through to something else.

'I hate thinking of you being locked up,' Mandy continued. 'How can I go on living, move somewhere new, when you'll be there?'

'I hate thinking of you here,' Jo said. 'I'll cope better if you aren't here, if you have gone somewhere else. And anyway, it's not good for either of us to wake up every morning and look at the bridge.'

'Lots of people around here have spent their lives waking up to the bridge, with all the memories, with all the connections. Maybe it's better to look at death in the face than to turn away from it.'

There was no escaping the bridge. It was impossible to see the ghost gum and not the bridge behind it. It was impossible to step out of the front gate and not be aware of its looming presence. It was a grey span across their skyline. It was embedded in the local community, had become a symbol of the west — Westgate Motors, Westgate Computer Care, Westgate Brewers, West Gate Pasta Supplies …

The only place on their small block where you could stand or sit and not see the bridge — though you could still hear it — was in the left-hand corner of the front yard, under the canopy of an old plum tree.

Mandy wasn't sure what she was going to do. Was it possible to make a new home somewhere else? What made a house a home, anyway?

There were times when Mandy was so besieged by their street, by the stench of the petroleum, of the car fumes, of the rattle and roar of the traffic, that her body seemed to dissolve. 'On some days,' Mandy said, 'living here, I feel like I'm drowning.' On those days, the smell was everything; it was as if she carried it with her wherever she went, even if she went away, miles across town. On those days, Mandy kept expecting the people sitting next to her on trams or trains or standing across from her at the supermarket counter to say something about the smell, to tell her off, to move away in disgust. On those days, the smell invaded everything, from her nostrils to the pores of her skin. It settled on her, made itself at home.

It was true there were other days when the smell was hardly noticeable at all and she'd be surprised when a visitor asked, *How do you stand the foul smell?* Or when she heard someone walking past on their way to the path along the river or to Williamstown say, *How anyone can live here?* and peer through the bushes, curious to see what kind of strange creatures were capable of surviving in such an awful place.

The tanks were their neighbours. Like most neighbours, there were days when they seemed friendly, benevolent, and then there were days when they appeared hostile, even frightening. Some days they could be ignored, some days they were hardly noticeable. But other days, they dominated the street and it was impossible to get away from them. On the worst days, the tanks, dirty grey and black, each with their own large red numbers, concrete and steel stained with rust, were monstrous and menacing, formidable, as they peered over the cyclone fence, leaning all of their heavy weight towards the house.

But there were times, especially in the soft light of a winter's morning or on days when the wind blew east and the scent of the garden permeated the air, when, even for Mandy, the sight of them was home.

'Let's wait,' she said to Jo. 'Let's see what happens after the sentencing.'

It was Jo's twentieth birthday and Mary had made a cake, but it was sitting uneaten on the bench, and Mary had gone home in tears when she realised her desire to make it like any other birthday was impossible. Mandy and Jo peered over the fence at the bridge. It was peak hour and the traffic was building. The cars were multiplying, like rodents during a plague. They drove with determination, with a destination in mind, with purpose.

Chapter 27

The courtroom reminded Antonello of a church. In place of the large crucifix that usually stood above the altar, there was an Australian coat of arms, etched in black on a silver panel. The emu and the kangaroo held on to the shield. Below them, the judge's wide bench, elevated on a platform, towered over the room. Below the bench there were two tables, separated by a small gap. On the right side, wearing wigs and long black gowns, the prosecutor and his assistant; on the left, Sarah and her assistant. Behind them, rows of chairs. On the left, the empty jury's seats; to the right, the witness stand; and at the back of the room, in an elevated section behind a gate, the dock.

The County Court wasn't what he'd expected. He'd imagined a grand building, like the Supreme Court and the old Magistrates' Court in Russell Street, but instead it was a modern office building, all concrete and glass. Inside, there was no ornate colonial furniture, no sculptured ceilings, no cedar or velvet.

As if they were going to church, Paolina had insisted he wear a suit and tie. He was hot, and the collar made his neck itch. The family filed in and sat on the right side, behind the prosecutor. He and Paolina, and Alex, Rae, and Jane, Rae's sisters and their husbands, and Nicki and Thomas took up the first two rows. When Kevin arrived with his mother, they sat behind them. Laura and Mani and their parents sat in the back row. Jo's mother, Mandy, was already in the courtroom. She sat on the other side, with Jo's grandmother. Like Paolina, Jo's grandmother held rosary beads in her hands, allowing each bead to slip through her fingers at regular intervals. There was no father: Antonello had a vague recollection of some story about a divorce and another family interstate.

The *proceedings* were scheduled for 10.00 am, and at 9.45 they'd been led from a small meeting room into the courtroom by a young man who referred to himself as 'the court clerk', but looked, in his suit, like a fifteen-year-old schoolboy. Then he announced that the judge was *unavoidably delayed*, but he didn't suggest they leave the courtroom, and so they stayed: the lawyers, on both sides, shuffled papers, made notes, and talked to each other in whispers.

When the door opened at 10.30, everyone turned to look. At the sight of Jo being led into the courtroom by a police officer, Jane began crying. Rae put her arm around her daughter, and everyone turned back to face the front. Only Antonello's gaze lingered as a policewoman opened the gate and led Jo into the dock, as she sat down and the policewoman pulled the gate shut. This Jo didn't resemble the Jo he'd watched grow up, not even the Jo he'd met at the bridge. She wore a blue jacket and skirt, and her hair was neatly tied back. If he hadn't known her age, he would've said she was in her late twenties. Paolina tapped him on the leg. 'Turn around.'

The prosecutor approached Alex and Rae. 'It won't be long now. The judge has arrived. She'll invite you to read out your victim impact statements. Do you have copies?' he asked.

Rae and Alex nodded.

'It'll be difficult. We can read them for you, if you don't want to read them out yourselves. The judge might also decide it's better for her to read them quietly in her chambers.'

All the family members had been asked to write statements. Antonello and Paolina wrote a joint one, in the end. The pain of losing Ashleigh was impossible to articulate. *Numb. Sad. Devastated.* All the words they wrote down were inadequate. *A gaping hole*, Paolina said. *Emptiness.* The loss of laughter, of the possibility of laughter. The loss of hunger, of sleep. Shivering even on warm days. Deprived of energy. No energy for the garden, the house. Plants dying from lack of water. Surfaces covered in dust. And the ache, worse than any cancer pain. The rush every time he caught sight of a young woman in the distance who might be, who could be, who looked like Ashleigh, and having to stop himself from following. Paolina's refusal to do more tests. Her refusal to go back to the doctor. Antonello's inability to convince her. The loss of hope. No solace anywhere. Spending hours at the base of the bridge. Memories of the men falling returning in dreams again and again and again. Fury. Anger. And nowhere to direct it.

'They want statements to justify putting Jo away for a long, long time,' Paolina had said as they sat in their kitchen with their scribbled notes. 'If we say how we feel about losing Ashleigh, Jo will go to prison for a lifetime. I can't do that. Prisons are terrible places, and she's only young.'

'We have to write something,' Antonello said. 'We have to — otherwise it's like we're not affected.'

'Nello, that's not true.'

'The court case is a public acknowledgement of the terrible loss of Ashleigh. That she was important. Important to a lot of people. To us.'

'But it was an accident and Jo's already being punished. She won't recover.'

'I know it was an accident and she didn't mean to hurt Ashleigh. I know it was bad luck. I know Ashleigh shouldn't have got in the car. But Jo needs to be punished by the law. I want the law, the community, to say it was wrong,' Antonello said.

'But we don't need to make it any harder for her than it has to be. You said yourself that you felt sorry for her,' Paolina said.

'You're right, she's suffering too.'

They had talked about it for a long time, and in the end they agreed to write a short statement about their granddaughter, about her beauty and her potential, her intelligence, the joy she brought to their lives, and about their sadness and grief at losing her.

On the way from the carpark to the courtroom that morning, Alex had said, 'I hope she gets a long sentence. I know I should be more forgiving. That I should be moving on, and that I should think about what Ashleigh might've wanted. I'm trying not to hate her, but she must be punished … and after this fucking court case, I don't want to see her again, ever. I want her to be banished. I don't want to walk around dreading that I might run into her or that Jane or Rae might run into her.'

Despite Alex's lingering anger, he and Rae were coming back to themselves, slowly. They were back to parenting Jane, and they were talking to each other again, occasionally touching, winking at each other when something Antonello or Paolina said seemed old-fashioned or tiresome or repetitive.

In the few months between his meeting with Jo at the bridge and the court case, Antonello had made several attempts to get closer to his son and daughter. This wasn't easy. There was no going back to the man he'd been before the bridge collapsed, young and naïve, a man who loved easily. Nicki didn't trust his approaches, but she let him make them, and he was grateful for that. Alex was more forgiving, more receptive. Together, father and son replanted the vegetable garden in Alex and Rae's backyard and, with Rae's blessing, a magnolia where the rose garden had been.

They spent hours in the garden, Paolina sitting on a chair in the shade, dozing and waking and dozing again, and Antonello and Alex digging and planting, getting hot and sweaty. At first, they only talked about the soil and the plants, the direction of the sun, or the kind of fertiliser they should use. Antonello's muscles ached at the end of those days, and his knees creaked and he made jokes about the joints needing oiling. In the evenings, he lay in a hot bath wondering if he had the strength to lift himself up, but the next day he went back again.

A couple of days before the court case, Alex confessed to Antonello that he'd sent text messages to Jo after the accident.

They'd been planting a row of olive trees along the back fence-line. It was a particularly warm day and, exhausted, they'd stopped to have a rest. Antonello was leaning on his shovel for support.

'I had Ashleigh's phone. She had a photograph on it, of her and Jo all dressed up — it was taken that night, before they went to the party. She was so beautiful … I was so angry, Dad. I wanted Jo to hurt. I wanted her to be dead. So I sent her messages. I called her a murderer and a killer and said I wished she was dead.'

'Alex,' Antonello said. 'When?'

'That day, that awful day, and then on the day of the funeral.'

It was not in Alex's nature to be cruel. As children, when Alex and Nicki fought, Nicki was the one who threw punches, who broke toys. Alex caved early, apologised, made amends.

'It's a shameful thing for an adult man to do,' Alex continued. 'I know that. I was so angry. I wanted to hurt her. I wanted her to feel like shit. I wanted her to feel so bad that she'd want to die. I remember thinking, *I hope this makes her want to kill herself.* I wanted to drive her to kill herself so her mother could feel the pain I was feeling.'

'Grief can drive us crazy, Alex. Makes us do crazy things.'

'I wanted to drive a young woman to suicide; people get locked up for doing stuff like that. If Ashleigh was alive, she'd be ashamed of me. If Mum knew, she'd be ashamed of me. Aren't you ashamed of me?'

'No, Alex. No, I'm not. And Ashleigh would understand. She'd forgive you. And so would your mother.'

'Please don't tell Mum.'

'I won't.' Antonello tossed his shovel onto the ground and put his arms around his son. 'You are a good man, Alex. A terrible thing happened to you, and it's hard.'

'I loved Ashleigh so much,' Alex said, letting himself lean into his father's embrace. 'When she died, I wanted to destroy everything — not just Jo but everything, myself included.'

As they moved apart again, Antonello said, 'I understand, Alex, better than you think. When the bridge collapsed, I thought about blowing it up. I wanted to obliterate it. And when I realised I couldn't do that, I thought about suicide.'

'Why didn't you ever tell us about the bridge?'

'The guilt, the grief, the anger ... I'm not going to promise you it gets better, but I can tell you that some things make it worse, so please don't do what I did. Don't shut down. Don't hold on to the anger. If you do, you won't be able to give Jane and Rae the love they deserve. If you shut down, everything will get worse.'

'I'm starting to see that,' Alex said. 'But when people say move on, it seems so cruel. Move on and leave Ashleigh behind — how can we do that?'

'No one wants you to leave Ashleigh behind, but there are ways to move on. When I look at my friend Sam, I see that he moved on, but he took the bridge collapse with him and he used it to make things better for workers in the future. I am not suggesting you need to get involved with the road accident campaigns or anything like that. But you need to go back to work, go back to being a father and a husband and a part of the community.'

'Yes,' Alex said. 'I've been thinking about going back to work. It's time.'

Jo sat at the back of the courtroom and waited. Sarah, in her fancy black cloak and wig, was barely recognisable. It covered her large frame like a superhero cape, but Jo didn't expect any superhuman feats; she didn't expect to be rescued from the inevitable. Jo's new suit, bought under Sarah's direction, hung on her loosely. *A skirt and a jacket like you might wear to an interview for an office job.* But she wasn't going for a job, she was waiting to be sentenced. Waiting to hear what the judge was going to say. Waiting, and trying not to look at Ash's family. Not to look at Mani and Laura. Or Kevin. Or at Mary and Mandy. Looking down at her feet, at her mother's plain blue shoes, tight around the toes.

Her father had rung the night before. 'It's too hard for me to get away.'

'Bastard,' Mandy said, but Jo didn't care.

'I never see him anyway. I don't need him to come.'

She prayed the judge would arrive quickly, that she would be sent away for a long time, that they'd take her straight from the courtroom out some back door to the prison and lock her away.

Everyone stood when the judge arrived. She came in through a side door, took her seat, and nodded, and everyone sat back down again. Antonello had a strong desire to ask them all to stop. *Wait!* he wanted to scream, *Stop. She's been punished enough. Let her live her life.* But instead he sat still, his hand over Paolina's, from which the rosary hung like teardrops. All of them acting out their parts.

The victim impact statements, read by the prosecutor, were relentless. 'The house is so dark,' he began, reading Jane's statement out in his deep, old-man voice while Jane sat in her seat crying. 'It feels like there is never going to be any light again. I'm sad all the time. I don't think the sadness is ever going to go away. No one laughs anymore. Ashleigh used to laugh all the time. The day Ashleigh died, I was angry with her. She promised to take me shopping, but she was home late and then went back out. I told her I hated her. I don't hate her, and now she's dead. But I'm angry at her because she got into that car with Jo when they were drunk. And I'm angry with Jo because she drove while she was drunk. She was my friend too and now I have to hate her. The counsellor keeps asking me to write letters, paint pictures, do all this crap so I can stop being angry, but I don't want to.'

At the end of Jane's statement, the courtroom was filled with the sound of weeping. The prosecutor read Rae and Alex's statement, and a statement from Mani and Laura; there were still statements from Antonello and Paolina, Rae's parents, and Kevin, but the judge said, 'I think I'll read the rest in my chamber. I don't think we should read them all out aloud.'

Antonello thought Rae and Alex might object, but later, during the lunch break, when they all sat in a café around the corner from the courthouse, Rae said she was relieved too. She was so exhausted, emotionally exhausted.

Rae hadn't spoken all day. In the courtroom, she sat gripping the sides of the seat. She fidgeted in the chair, and whenever they were sent out of the room, she paced the hallway. At lunch, she took a couple of bites of the sandwich on her plate and then shoved it aside. As she walked back, she said to Antonello, 'It will be over soon. This is the last thing. We've been waiting for this as if it meant something, and now I see her … I thought I wouldn't want to look at her but I can't help it. She's a scared kid. I see her and I see Ashleigh, I see them together, and I see she's lost too. And now I can't feel what I should feel, I can't … Now I think I should do something to stop her going to prison, even though I know she should go, she should go … But I can see Ashleigh … It could've been the other way around, thick as thieves they were, and how many nights I cooked them dinner, helped them with their homework, and I was happy to see them together, glad my daughter had a friend and they were so close …' She stopped to catch her breath. 'I can't say this to Alex.'

'I think you can,' Antonello said.

'No. No, anyway the law will do what it has to do. It's how it has to be.'

Chapter 28

Sarah listened carefully to the prosecutor's closing remarks. She and Robert had been in court together before, and they knew each other's styles. There was nothing surprising — the victim impact statements had been difficult to sit through, and there wasn't much more he needed to add. Jo was a probationary driver; she should not have been drinking at all. But, not only had she been drinking, she was drunk, too drunk to drive in any circumstances. The other girls asked her if she was okay to drive and she said yes. She drove them, even though she knew that according to her licence conditions she was only allowed one passenger under twenty-two years of age. She was angry and arguing with Ashleigh as she drove. He accepted that she was remorseful. Noted it was her first offence, that she was pleading guilty, but that this shouldn't and didn't change the facts of the case.

'As a parent, I look across at Ashleigh Bassillo-White's family, at her sister, her mother, and her father, at her grandparents, and at her friends. I see their loss and their grief and it's heartbreaking. If Joanne Neilson had done the right thing, what she knew to be the right thing, Ashleigh would be alive. She would've finished her VCE and be at university on her way to becoming a lawyer, her cherished dream. Ashleigh's family would be going about their lives. But their family has been torn apart and they are devastated. Joanne Neilson's responsible for that.

'Should the court be lenient? If sentencing were only about punishment, then we might argue that Ms Neilson has already been punished: she's lost her best friend and her life will never be the same again. But sentencing is about much more — it is about deterrence. Not just about deterring Ms Neilson from getting behind the wheel of a car when she's had too much to drink, but also about deterring others. It is about denunciation, about letting everyone know this isn't acceptable behaviour, that as a community, we won't put up with drink-driving. It is also about restorative justice. A young woman is dead, and Joanne Neilson, sitting there at the back of this courtroom,' he paused and turned to look at Jo, 'is the one responsible. Until she serves her time, she's not entitled to be part of the community. Ashleigh's family, Ashleigh's friends, are entitled to justice.'

Sarah made some quick notes in the margins of her closing statement as Robert sat down. Judge Ryan tapped her pen on the table and nodded.

Sarah had considered launching her statement with a claim for joint responsibility — after all, the other girls, Ashleigh included, had entered the car knowing Jo had been drinking. They let their desire for a ride home taint their judgement and made Jo feel pressured to drive. They could've stopped her and didn't. They should bear some responsibility for the accident. But she remembered Danny Maher, her law professor, an older man who'd spent his whole working life in legal aid: 'Don't forget that the family of the victim are in the courtroom.' She'd spent many hours gathered with other students around the coffee table in his office for feedback on essays, for informal tutorials, and, later, when she was working for him as a research assistant in the third and fourth year of her degree, for 'case strategy meetings'. He was a serious-looking, heavily bearded man, and the first-year students were terrified of him; she'd often find them, too frightened to knock on his door, loitering in the hallway outside his office. He was loud and brash, especially in court and in lectures, but one on one he was a kind and gentle man. 'Some lawyers think they have to treat the "other side" like the enemy. Even when that "other side" is the victim's family. Show compassion. Sometimes you have to say things that hurt the victim's family, sometimes it's inevitable, but some lawyers go too far.'

She thought about Danny now as she turned to look at Ashleigh's family and past them, to Jo. She had asked him once, 'How do you make sure you give your client the best chance, fight for them, if you allow yourself to feel sorry for the victims?' They were in his office. He was sitting in a leather armchair, in front of a large window with a view of the courtyard where students sat to eat their lunch, to read, to make out. The room, with its high bookshelves, had a desk that was larger than the kitchen table in the share house she lived in with six other law students. He smiled at her. '*Surgeons must be very careful / When they take the knife! / Underneath their fine incisions / Stirs the culprit, — Life!*' He often quoted Dickinson in response to her questions. Sometimes this was frustrating, but after a while she came to look forward to hearing the poems. 'Emily Dickinson: you could learn a lot from her,' he said, as if he were referring the students to a top criminal lawyer or an acclaimed philosophy professor.

Sarah glanced down at her notes. At the top she'd written, *A good story elicits empathy.* Her job was to tell a compelling story. This wasn't a lesson she'd learnt from Dickinson, whose poems were sharp observations, not narratives; from Dickinson she'd learnt the power of words to change a person's perspective. It was the hours spent watching Danny in court. He was thorough. Meticulous research and planning were part of the preparation for every case. He knew all the facts, understood every relevant law and precedent. Everything he needed, the answer to any question the judge might ask, was within reach. But it only made sense when Danny began to speak. Even when she disliked the client, even when she was convinced they were guilty, Danny made her see them anew, as human. *This is a person not so unlike you and me.*

'Jo was nineteen years old at the time of the accident, twenty now. She's young, even though the law considers her an adult. We might say she was old enough to know better. There is no doubt she made a mistake, a bad mistake. She exercised poor judgement. The results were fatal. Ashleigh was a beautiful eighteen-year-old girl. We've heard she had a bright future and a family who loved her. This is a tragedy that has impacted the lives of everyone in this courtroom, including Jo.

'My colleague has pointed out already that Jo has been punished, that she's lost her best friend, that her life will not be the same again. He's acquiesced that Jo isn't likely to be a repeat offender. It is also clear that even if the girls were arguing that night, they were friends, they loved each other, and neither of them would wish harm on the other.

'A young woman is dead and Jo Neilson is responsible; the community demands justice. But before venturing into this notion of what justice is and how justice can be restored, if it can be restored, it's only fair that we learn something about Jo's life. That before, Your Honour, you sentence her, you have some sense of who she is and how she came to be driving that car on that night.' Sarah stopped and took a few sips of water. Then she went on to give some background about Jo: Mandy's pregnancy at seventeen, the separation between Mandy and David, the death of Jo's grandfather when she was five years old. She talked about their struggles with money, and described their small, run-down house on Hyde Street, with the unbearable noise of the traffic, the diesel fumes, and the petroleum stench from the Mobil Oil terminal across the road.

'By all accounts, Jo isn't particularly outgoing or confident. Often shy, she didn't have many friends in primary school. She was a chubby child, and there was some bullying and taunting. She met Ashleigh on the first day of high school and they became close friends immediately. Ashleigh was the more confident of the two, and she did better at school. Jo isn't academic. But no matter their differences, they loved each other and loved being together. Both families attest to the strong bond between them.

'According to the statements submitted by the other two passengers in the car, Jo and Ashleigh were out of sorts that night, they were fighting. Who hasn't fought with their best friend? What were they fighting about? Jo says she thought Ashleigh didn't want to be her friend anymore. Is this true? I don't know. We don't know. Did the fight contribute to the accident? We don't know. Does any of what I've told you about Jo's life explain the accident? Did any of it contribute to it? Does any of this excuse what Jo did? Not according to the law. Jo made a mistake. She shouldn't have driven home from the party.' Sarah paused. 'Ashleigh, Laura, and Mani also made a mistake that night; they shouldn't have got in the car with Jo. If all four girls had survived the accident, we'd be angry at all of them. But Ashleigh, Laura, and Mani weren't the ones behind the wheel.

353

They might've been, but Jo was the only one with a licence and she drove her friends around. She was the driver and she was responsible. It was a bad decision — the worst decision she'll ever make, even if she lives to be a hundred. She's pleaded guilty and is waiting to be punished. In her statement, she writes: *I'll get the punishment I deserve, but it won't ever be enough.* I hope for her sake that's not true.

'The accident happened at the base of the West Gate Bridge. In a couple of months' time it will be the fortieth anniversary of the bridge's collapse. Thirty-five men died during the construction of the bridge. On the morning of the fifteenth of October 1970, a span of the bridge was hoisted to the top, but when they put the bolts in, the span didn't fit, didn't line up with the adjoining span. The engineer managing that day's work told the men to remove the bolts that were holding two spans together. It was a mistake. Bad judgement. Poor judgement. He wasn't drunk. He wasn't on drugs. He was stressed and under a great deal of pressure. The bridge was behind schedule.

'The Royal Commission set up to investigate wrote in their report, *The bridge collapsed because of acts of inefficiency and omissions by those entrusted with building a bridge.* It apportioned blame to several companies, the designers, even the unions. And the engineer who was on site that day. But too late — he was one of the dead. They finished building the bridge, but not before another man died. And we drive over it. Life goes on. It's supposed to go on. Why am I telling you about the West Gate Bridge? Because it was a tragedy. Because it could've been prevented. Because we're all human and we sometimes make mistakes, and some of us have had lucky escapes, and no consequences. We think, *Oh, that was close,* but we thank God, if we are religious, or our lucky stars, if we aren't, that nothing worse happened.

'Every night people, young and old, drive home drunk. They shouldn't, and we need to do what we can to stop them. Most of them, like Jo, think they'll be fine: *It's only ten minutes down the road.* Or they don't think at all. When you're young, death is something that happens to old people.

'The collapse of the West Gate is Victoria's worst industrial accident. Ten times more people die on our roads every year. We build bridges and tunnels and skyscrapers — projects that are dangerous and that put workers' lives at risk. We build faster and faster cars. We allow alcohol advertising and we perpetuate a drinking culture. If we want to reduce the road toll, we need to address these problems.

'The individual has to take responsibility for their actions. Jo has to take responsibility for her actions. The law says she's a criminal, and so she must be punished. Prisons are awful places — of course; they shouldn't be easy — but on the whole they don't lead to rehabilitation, they don't help people remake their lives. Jo doesn't belong in prison.

'Jo isn't a bad person. She isn't the sort of young woman we'd ever expect to find in a criminal court. She can make a contribution to the community, and I hope whatever sentence is handed down will lead her in that direction rather than away from it. Jo is an ordinary young woman from a working-class background. I could've tried to spin her story into one of drama. I could've made her family look dysfunctional and Jo disturbed. But though she didn't have the advantages many of us grew up with, she's been loved and cared for. There is no significant family drama. No dysfunctional family. She's no delinquent. She's an ordinary girl who was sad and lonely that night as she imagined losing her friend, as she imagined being alone, and she drank ... There is no one in this room who hasn't been lonely, felt anxious, who doesn't understand that feeling. All human tragedy is caused by the failure of someone to understand and conquer their own flaws. If Jo had been more confident, less anxious, if she believed in her own self-worth, things may well have turned out differently, but she's young, and most of us don't gain power over our fears in a lifetime.

'Your Honour, thank you for your time and attention. In your deliberations on the appropriate sentence, I urge you to consider Jo's youth, her remorse, and the terrible damage that our prison system can do to a young woman.'

Sarah sat down; sweat was dripping down her temples. She was exhausted. Behind her, she heard sobbing — Mary or maybe even Mandy crying. In the brief moments she'd turned around during her statement, she'd noted tears on the faces of several of Ashleigh's relatives.

For a minute there was silence. The judge made notes. No one spoke.

'In my experience,' the judge said eventually, looking up from her notes, 'most of the young people who end up here on culpable driving charges aren't the sort of people one would expect to find in court. But she's here, and I agree this is the tragedy. Her friend is dead, and Ashleigh Bassillo-White's family have lost their daughter in an accident that should never have happened.'

She didn't raise her voice; there was frustration, not anger, in it. Aretha Ryan was an experienced judge. She'd recently celebrated twenty years on the bench: a rare achievement for any judge, but especially a woman. The first female judge in Victoria was only appointed in the mid-1970s. By the time Aretha was appointed in 1990, there were women judges in most courts across the country, but even now they made up less than a third of all judges.

Judge Ryan leant forward, towards the bench, pushed her glasses back, and stared out across the courtroom. 'It's true that as a community, we're all responsible for the alcohol abuse, for the fatalities on our roads, but letting individuals off the hook isn't taking our responsibilities seriously; it would be negligent. Joanne Neilson, you were driving and you were drunk. That is something we can't dismiss, no matter what other good deeds you have done or were planning to do.'

Jo heard everything and nothing. When the hearing first began, she'd forced herself to listen to the words, terrified that the judge or Sarah — though Sarah had already told her she wouldn't have to say anything — would ask her a question, that they'd test her to make sure she was listening. But the more she concentrated on the words, on what Sarah and the other lawyer and the judge were saying, the less she heard. And then, halfway through the reading of Jane's statement, she lost all sense … Words, individual words, fell like stones from people's mouths. They formed hills and mountains, and they created valleys; they changed the landscape of the room, and she was lost.

'At approximately 12.30 am on Sunday, the twentieth of September

2009, you, Joanne Neilson, along with your best friend, Ashleigh Bassillo-White, and two other friends, Mani Cruz and Laura Roberts, left the eighteenth birthday party being held at Siren's restaurant in Williamstown. All four of you had been drinking for several hours …'

Jo gripped the edges of the chair. She'd expected the judge to talk directly to her, to point her finger and yell out 'lock her up', but the judge was reading from her notes and addressing the whole court.

'… At approximately 12.45 am you were driving along Douglas Parade towards Footscray. You were driving over 90 kilometres an hour. This was well over the speed limit. You were arguing with Ashleigh and you were distracted. Ashleigh asked you to slow down. You …'

Ash had asked her to slow down. Ash had switched the radio off. Jo had been so angry at Ash. She wanted to stop the car and hit Ash, to stop the car and throw Ash out. But she kept driving: *Focus on the road. Focus on the road.* She knew she wasn't in control … lights racing across the windscreen … the steering wheel slipping out of her grasp …

Loud sobbing thrust Jo back into the room. The jolt resonated through her body as if she'd been caught in the grip of a powerful tornado and then dropped. The judge paused. Ash's grandmother Paolina was crying. Antonello reached out to hold her hand.

Jo felt tears running down her own face. They were unexpected, and she was bewildered by them. She hadn't heard all of what the judge said, but she was getting what she deserved, so there was nothing to cry about. She didn't dare to lift her hands to reach for the tissues on the table next to her; she didn't dare move. Paolina's sobbing continued. Others were crying too.

The judge made a note in the margins of her papers before continuing. 'As referred to earlier, your conduct had catastrophic consequences.'

The end of the statement was coming — Jo sensed it in the changing tone of the judge's voice, the intake of breath.

'The penalty for this crime must involve a sentence of imprisonment so as to recognise the sanctity of life and the gravity of taking a life.'

Jo closed her eyes, but that only made the crying seem louder.

'Ms Neilson, please stand.'

Jo stood up. Her knees trembled. She gripped the rail in front of her and pushed her weight against it.

'On the one charge of dangerous driving causing death, you will be convicted. You're sentenced to be imprisoned for five years, with a non-parole period of three years.' Mary stood up, but Mandy pulled her back down into her chair. 'Do you understand, Ms Neilson?'

Jo nodded, though she knew she'd missed the details of the sentence. Five years. The sentencing came as a relief. She fell back into her chair.

The policewoman opened the dock gate and led Jo out through the back door, while everyone else remained seated.

'Will they take me away now?' Jo asked.

The policewoman shook her head. 'You'll be here for a while. Give your family a chance to say goodbye.'

Please, Jo thought, *take me now.*

Mandy and Mary were weeping when they came into the room, led by Sarah. Mary didn't make any effort to stop; she hugged Jo close to her and sobbed. Mandy drew in her breath, wiped away her tears. 'I'll come and see you as often as they let me,' she said.

Jo nodded. When Mary let her go, Mandy gave her a hug. 'I'll see you soon.'

Maybe it's better, Jo wanted to say, *if you don't visit at all.* But that seemed cruel.

'Five years,' Jo said. 'A lot can change in that time.'

'Less,' Sarah answered. 'We can apply for parole in three years.'

Up until recently, one year had seemed like an eternity. *Another whole year of school,* Jo had said to her mother at the beginning of Year 12, *not sure I can last that long.*

Chapter 29

The week after the court case, Mandy stayed home in bed. She hadn't slept for days and couldn't get herself across town to work. She'd spoken to Jo twice on the phone — the fear in Jo's voice was raw, but neither of them acknowledged it. They were both being stoic: what choice did they have?

'Have you put the house on the market?' Jo had asked.

'No.'

'Mum, what are you waiting for?'

'I'll do it soon. I'm planning to ring the agent today. I'll let you know how I go when I come to visit you next week.'

Mandy planned to visit once a fortnight. Jo said that was too often, too long a journey, but Mandy insisted. She didn't tell Jo that once she sold the house she planned to rent in Bendigo, only half an hour's drive from Tarrengower Prison. Once Jo was released they could decide on where to move permanently.

But Mandy knew she couldn't leave Yarraville without seeing Ashleigh's parents. To sell the house, pack up, and disappear without speaking to Rae or Alex — especially to Rae — was not right. She was being a coward.

Once the real-estate agent set a date for the auction, Mandy took out the photograph albums and carefully removed all the photographs she'd taken over the years of Ashleigh and Jo — during family outings, at birthday parties, when Ashleigh stayed over. She picked a dozen or so of them and put them in an envelope. She planned to give them to Rae and Alex in person, but they might not want to speak to her, so she wrote a brief note as well:

> *Dear Rae, Alex, and Jane,*
> *I have enclosed some photographs of Ashleigh that I took over*
> *the years that I thought you might like to have. Ashleigh was*
> *a beautiful young woman. She was bright and kind and a good*
> *friend to Jo. I am so sorry for your loss — and for Jo's part in it*
> *and for my part in it. I know that no apology will ever be enough.*
> *I understand that you may never be able to forgive me or Jo.*
>
> *These photographs represent memories that I hold precious.*
> *Memories of the girls together. Please know that when your*
> *daughter was with us she was loved and cared for, and that*
> *I'll always remember her.*
> *Mandy*

As she made her way towards Ashleigh's house with the photographs and the note, Mandy was nervous. If Rae and Alex were angry, she needed to let them vent their anger. If they sent her away, she would need to go.

When she reached the house, she saw that a magnolia had been planted where the rose garden used to be. It already had a spattering of white buds; soon it would flower. Mandy took a deep breath to stop herself from spiralling back into the past and the many times she'd walked up the path with Jo, and with Jo and Ashleigh. She went up to the door and rang the bell.

Rae opened the door. 'Mandy,' she murmured, as if Mandy were a ghost.

'Hello, Rae.'

She looked better than the last time Mandy had seen her, neat and well-groomed, but she had lost more weight and the suit she was wearing was loose. There was a fragility, an unsteadiness about her that Mandy recognised. She saw it each time she looked in the mirror.

'What are you doing here?'

'I wanted to see you and Alex and —'

'Alex isn't home.'

'It's … I wanted to give you these.' She held the envelope out to Rae, who didn't take it. 'They're photographs of Ashleigh — of Ashleigh and Jo. Photographs I've taken over the years that I thought you might not have. That you might like.'

Rae took the envelope but didn't open it. 'I went through a period of wanting to cut your daughter out of every photograph I had with her and Ashleigh. Jane said I was acting crazy.'

Mandy nodded.

'Seeing your daughter in court, I kept thinking that Ashleigh loved Jo, but Jo doubted that love, and that doubt ruined everything.'

'We all have doubts, but they loved each other. They did.'

'We loved your daughter,' Rae said.

They were both crying now, tears falling down their faces.

'I loved Ashleigh too,' Mandy said. 'And I am so sorry, so sorry.'

Rae wiped her eyes and cleared her throat. 'I can't ask you in. I can't have you in my house.'

'Of course,' Mandy said, 'I understand. I wanted you to know I'm selling the house and moving away.'

'Okay.' Rae nodded.

Mandy started to walk back down the steps, and Rae called out to her, 'How is Jo? How is she coping?'

Mandy turned. 'She doesn't say much when I talk to her. I think it's tough, but then it's meant to be. I think more than anything she misses Ashleigh.'

Rae shut the door. Mandy cried all the way home. She was glad she'd gone to see Rae; it had been the right thing to do. It was important, but she was not under any illusion that it would reduce the weight of Rae's grief or her pain.

Mandy hoped that Ashleigh would come to Rae and Alex in their dreams like her mother, Sal, came to her, surrounded by flowers in a garden that spread to the horizon. Mandy didn't believe in heaven or hell, in an afterlife. The dead only lived in our memories and dreams. And there, they could live forever.

Chapter 30

Antonello changed three times. First a suit: the navy-blue one he'd worn to Ashleigh's funeral. But the suit smelt of incense and grief, and in the pocket of the jacket, folded and refolded, he found his eulogy notes and the sketches of Ashleigh. He took the suit off and shoved it far back into the wardrobe.

'That's the suit I want them to bury me in,' he said to his reflection in the mirror. An old man — sagging skin, thinning hair — stared back at him. 'You're not dead yet. Not quite.'

'Who are you talking to?' Paolina called out from the kitchen.

'No one,' he called back.

'First sign of madness,' she responded.

When he came out of the bedroom in blue jeans and a striped shirt he'd owned for two decades, she sent him back to get changed again.

'Well, what should I wear?' he asked her, even though he hated those stories about useless men who didn't know how to get dressed without their wives. Paolina struggled to her feet. The last bout of chemo had pounded her like hail on a rickety shack; she was the ruin of her former self. Her hair had fallen out for a second time, and her skin hung loose on her brittle bones everywhere except around her belly and legs, where fluid had built up and refused to shift. *I've become a camel,* she'd said to her oncologist, *storing water as if I'm heading into the desert.* She was due back in hospital so they could drain it, but she was determined to attend the memorial. She picked out black jeans and an almost-new green shirt for Antonello. They both took jackets. There was a cover of dark cloud across the sky, and Paolina said she could smell rain.

'It's cold, Paolina. You should stay home.'

'Are you worried some old girlfriend might turn up and I'll cramp your style?' She smiled and winked and Antonello shrugged, pointing to his pot belly and pulling at the loose skin under his chin.

'Sure, they'll be lining up to get their hands on me,' he said, and then moved closer to her, kissing her lightly on the lips. 'Button up your coat, *bella mia.*'

By the time they arrived, there were several hundred people under the bridge. Mostly men, mostly unionists, wearing badges and t-shirts and windcheaters with slogans: *Putting workers first; We bridge the gap; Stronger together; Dare to struggle, dare to win.* Some of the workers were wearing safety jackets; in the crowd, they created rivers of yellow and green. There were union banners and TV cameras. Forty years was a long time, and young men were old, but some faces were so familiar, it seemed impossible all those years had passed. He recognised them, the weathered outdoor men who'd been his workmates. They recognised him. A smile. A nod. A slap on the back. Men moved across the crowd to stand by him, next to him. They called him Nello, and he was surprised they remembered, but then their names slipped off his tongue as if he'd seen them the day before. Dennis, Angelo, Steve … a tight pulley was winching him back to the young Antonello, a twenty-two-year-old rigger, a boy, agile, smooth-skinned, carefree; a man with mates who called him Nello, with workmates who called him *dago* and *wog*, and whom he called *bludgers* and *racist shits*. But no matter what they said, no matter what arguments and disagreements they had, when they were working up high, they looked out for one another. And all of them, all those men, stayed on the site for days after the collapse, digging in the mud, hammering at steel and concrete, using welders and jackhammers and cranes, all of them searching for the bodies of their mates. The grip of their handshake, his reflection in their eyes, time so elastic that Antonello wasn't sure he could keep himself upright.

He was looking for Sam when Paolina pointed to Alice, but Antonello would've recognised her anywhere. She was talking and laughing, and a circle had already formed around her.

'Alice comes every year to every memorial, to be with Sam. She lives up north with her second husband and her children,' Paolina said.

'How do you know?'

Paolina grinned. Of course: Paolina and Alice had kept in contact all those years. He didn't know. How many other things didn't he know about his wife? How many things that Paolina hadn't told him? He was thinking about this, and about the short time they had left together, when he was distracted by a reporter interviewing a man standing behind him. The man was in his sixties, tall and solid, flanked on either side by his sons. He was familiar, but Antonello could not remember his name. The likeness between the father and sons was unmistakable. Both of the younger men had his build, but it was the eyes that were distinctive: three sets of bulging brown eyes, set in hollow sockets, under thick dark eyebrows.

'Do you think about the collapse?' the reporter asked.

The son standing on his left answered, 'My father wakes up screaming some nights.'

The father put his arm around his son's shoulder. The son, in his early forties, would've been a toddler at the time of the collapse. Antonello remembered him. Des. He had been a boilermaker.

'A few bad nightmares,' the father said to the reporter, 'but I got off lightly. I saw my sons grow up.'

'Nello,' Sam called out to him, and they walked through the crowd to where he was standing talking to a woman also in her sixties. Her grey hair was set in a style that reminded Antonello of his mother and of the Queen Mother. 'Mick's wife,' Sam said, motioning to Antonello. 'Rosa was widowed at twenty.'

'I don't remember you, but then I didn't meet many of Mick's workmates before the accident. He loved this bridge. He used to say, "Wait until it's finished, and then we're going to drive over it, all of us, with the kids."' There was no bitterness in her voice. 'I wish,' she said, 'that he'd seen his children grow up. He loved his girls so much.' She pointed to three women standing behind her. One of them wearing a union logo, the same logo worn by Des's sons. *Bridge builders breed unionists*, Antonello thought.

The speeches were heartfelt and respectful, but for Antonello the references to the bridge as a monument to the workers who died was difficult to listen to. The bridge wasn't their legacy. For survivors like Sam, who took the tragedy and fought to improve safety, the legacy was a safer future for working men and women, tougher laws, and harsher punishments to stop employers taking shortcuts with workers' lives. That was a legacy he could stand behind. Not a bridge.

'Never again,' the crowd shouted after one of the speeches.

Sam hadn't let his nightmares define his life. Sam had joined together with other survivors and made a difference.

'Never trust the bosses again,' one of the other speakers said. 'That was the lesson. That's our motto.'

The last speaker read out the names of the thirty-five dead. Men took off their beanies. The crowd bowed their heads.

Sarah arrived at the bridge after the speeches were over, and the crowd was thinning. She stood in front of the memorial. The wreaths and bouquets laid out by the mourners created a tiny carpet of colour under the mammoth bridge.

She walked towards Williamstown on the path that ran alongside a row of grey and red stone pillars, a sculptural installation. Each pillar was slightly different. Each represented one of the men who'd lost their lives. Sarah ran her hand over the surface of one of the pillars. Overhead, drivers kept driving. There was no stopping on the bridge, except for emergencies. She supposed that for Ada life had been unbearable, death an urgent desire.

Sarah walked on, to a small clearing. Here a new plaque acknowledged the death of a thirty-sixth worker in 1972 on one side, and on the other it read: *Forty years after the tragedy of 1970, the workers of the WEST GATE BRIDGE strengthening project remember the sacrifices of an earlier generation. They left us a mighty legacy. The struggle continues and in the words of a great philosopher — 'Now and then the workers are victorious, but only for a time. The real fruit of their battle lies, not in the immediate result, but in the ever expanding union of the workers.'*

Sarah knew the quote was from Engels and Marx's *The Communist Manifesto*. Why didn't the unionists name the philosophers? It was government land, so she could easily imagine the careful negotiations between union and government officials that had led to this compromise.

From her position in the small clearing, the bridge looming over her was ominous. Her brother Paul had studied the West Gate in his engineering course, examining the reasons for the collapse and the lessons that could be learned about the structure and architecture of bridges. 'But their downfall was ego,' he told her. 'They thought they were so clever. These were the best bridge designers in the world, supposedly. A couple had been knighted for their bridge-building contributions.'

Sarah understood about ego: there were plenty of egos knocking into one another in the legal profession. But while some lawyers, some people — more men than women — were good at shouting out their own virtues, at making grand gestures, at pushing themselves forward, of thinking about how they might get ahead, that wasn't her problem. Her problem was the doubt and the self-loathing, and that had been Jo's problem too. A damaged ego could be as harmful. She had to find another way to live.

Sarah had gone to see Jo in the prison the week before the bridge memorial. She was in Castlemaine for a meeting of a working group of the Prison Reform Committee. She took Jo a stack of novels, some magazines, and chocolate. During the visit, Jo didn't ask for anything, and didn't complain. She was working, she told Sarah, on prison maintenance, painting the social areas. 'It's better having something to do,' she said. 'It's good to see you. It's good to talk to someone who isn't — who is outside. Good to remember there is a world outside.'

'You don't have many visitors?'

'Mum and Nan have been coming once a fortnight, but it's hard. Nan cries most of the time. The strange thing is that a little while ago, I started receiving photocopies of pages from Ash's journals. They're out of sequence, some more recent, some from years ago, but they are pages where she's talking about us, about me, about being good friends. It's weird. Some of it's surprising, not what I thought she was thinking and writing. How could I have been so wrong?'

'Someone wants you to know that Ashleigh loved you.'

Jo didn't know who was sending them, though she suspected it might be Ashleigh's grandfather.

'We'll apply for parole as soon as we can,' Sarah said.

'It's better for everyone,' Jo said, 'if I do all the time I was given.'

'You have to forgive yourself, Jo, and stop trying to make things harder than they already are.'

'I know, but I killed her … and I doubted her friendship, and it was all in my head, stuff I was making up. Lots of time to think in here and dissect things.'

'You could study,' Sarah said. 'There are some education programs; it'll help when you get out, and stop you going over and over things you can't change.'

'I know, I'm not ready for that yet. But I'll think about it.'

At the end of the visit, Jo gave Sarah a hug. 'Thank you. I realised I never said thank you for everything you've done for me and for my mother.'

On her way home from the bridge, Sarah went to visit Mandy, and, just as they did during those months before the trial, they gravitated to the backyard.

'Did you go down to the anniversary memorial?' Sarah asked.

'Just for a little while. I listened to some of the speeches. It was teeming with rain, but there was a big crowd. It's good to see that people remember.'

They talked about the bridge and about Jo. It would be the last time Sarah would visit — the house was sold, and in a few weeks Mandy was moving to a farm cottage outside Bendigo. She'd be closer to Jo, would be able to visit more regularly. Sarah would miss Mandy.

'Drop in if you are ever up that way,' Mandy said as they embraced at the door. It was a casual invitation, and Sarah knew she shouldn't make too much of it.

———

After the memorial, there was a party in a nearby hall. A local band was playing seventies covers, and Antonello recognised one of the guitarists — he'd been a young carpenter on the bridge, one of Slav's crew. The band played the 'Ballad of the Westgate Disaster', and by the last line most people were openly weeping. The band continued with Mark Seymour's 'Westgate'. When they stopped, young men standing close to the stage called out, 'Play Lennon,' and the band members nodded and the crowd clapped as they played the familiar chords of John Lennon's 'Working Class Hero'. There was nothing heroic about working long hours in dangerous jobs — Antonello knew that better than most — but he could not help being carried away by the song, and he sang along with his mates.

Alice and Paolina sat in a quiet corner together, reminding Antonello of the young women they once were, of the nights they had spent together at the San Remo Ballroom, of the dancing and the music. When someone patted Antonello on the shoulder, he turned, expecting it to be one of the men, but it was his son. Alex with Nicki, Rae, and Jane. Alex gave Antonello a hug. And they both got teary. It had been forty years since the bridge and more than twelve months since Ashleigh's death, but they were all still hurting.

'You refused to talk about the bridge all those years,' Nicki said, giving him a quick peck on the cheek.

'I'm sorry, Nicki.' He drew his daughter into an embrace; there was a moment's hesitation, before she also wrapped her arms around him.

'It was a tough thing to deal with,' Nicki said as they moved apart.

'Other blokes managed better than me.'

'We aren't all the same,' Alex said.

Back at the house, they sat around the kitchen table. Paolina carried in a dusty box, from which she pulled out two sketchbooks and a framed sketch wrapped in newspaper.

'The only ones I managed to save,' she said, handing them to Alex and Nicki.

In the books, there were sketches of Paolina, Emilia, and Franco, of the river and, of course, of the bridge, in all its stages, and of the many bridge builders, including Sam and Slav and Bob. Antonello watched his children flicking through the sketchbooks. He watched Jane unwrapping the framed watercolour sketch of the half-made bridge.

'You were talented,' Alex said. 'Mum said you were good at drawing, but we always thought she was deluded.'

The sketches seemed so naïve to Antonello — drawn by a young man blinded by love, and by ego. Sketches of the glorious bridge he was building.

'Your grandmother wanted him to be an artist,' Paolina said. 'That's why she named him Antonello. It was the name of her favourite painter from Vizzini: Antonello da Messina.'

'Mamma used to say we were his descendants and that art ran in our blood.'

'I remember that print of the Madonna with a blue veil you had in the old house, was that one of his?' Alex asked.

'Yes, the *Virgin Annunciata*. We had the same print in our room at primary school,' Antonello volunteered.

'I gave it to your father as a wedding gift,' Paolina said.

Antonello thought about all the stories he had not told his children, stories and memories he had locked away and kept to himself. Stories he would never have the chance to tell Ashleigh. But it wasn't too late to tell his children and his remaining grandchildren — Jane and Thomas.

It was sunset. Paolina, exhausted, had fallen asleep on the couch, and the house was quiet. Antonello unfolded the rug and covered her. He watched her sleeping. She was beautiful; she was his home.

He left the house and headed back to the bridge, long and lean in the distance. It was oblivious to its own history, to the blood and bones crushed and buried under the silt and mud, beneath the concrete.

A neighbour waved as she stepped out of her front gate with her Cocker Spaniel, and then she pointed to two teenage boys sitting in the gutter smoking, and frowned. Antonello kept going without responding, making his way past the Mobil Oil terminal, the tanks glistening under the setting sun. Across the road, Jo's house looked dark and tired, but a *Sold* sticker over the *For Sale* sign promised a chance at another life.

As he approached the bridge, Antonello could see that the West Gate memorial plaque was surrounded by dozens of floral bouquets and wreaths, left over from the anniversary ceremony. He made his way to the small white cross that marked the place where his granddaughter died; he bent down, touched the cross, and whispered, *I love you*. Ashleigh and Bob and Slav were no more. Paolina might not make it to the end of the year. Death was everywhere — but so was life. And for the moment, he was alive.

Acknowledgements

When the West Gate collapsed during construction in 1970, I was a schoolgirl, living with my brother and working-class migrant parents in Yarraville, less than ten minutes drive from the bridge. The thirty-five men who died were workers whose employers failed to ensure a safe workplace. It is Victoria's largest industrial accident, and it has haunted me for more than forty years. The real cost of progress is often borne by the working class, but while politicians, designers, and engineers might make it into the history books, the workers are forgotten. This novel is a work of fiction and none of the characters are based on real people. However, I have written it as a tribute to the men who built the West Gate Bridge — the victims and the survivors — and their families, to give voice to their stories.

This novel is also dedicated to my dear friend Teresa Corcoran, who passed away in 2005, and who believed we each have a responsibility to leave the world a little better than we found it. She was a humanitarian, storyteller, teacher, and gardener. I continue to miss our long and animated conversations, which always included lots of laughter and politics.

A substantial part of this novel was written while I was working as a full-time academic at Victoria University. My thanks go to the university, the College of Arts, and my colleagues for their support. I would also like to thank the City of Melbourne's Arts Grant Program and Victoria University for funding that provided some of the time and space for me to focus on the novel.

My gratitude to Patricia Hayes, who was my research assistant in 2011 and spent time digging up archival materials on the West Gate; to John Tully, for talking to me about rigging; to the staff of the University of Melbourne Student Union Advocacy and Legal Service, who gave me advice about sentencing lengths and conditions for culpable and dangerous driving; and especially Danny Gardiner, from the West Gate Bridge Memorial Committee, who provided some archival materials and stories early on in the project and later read and provided feedback on a draft of the West Gate sections of the novel. I would like to acknowledge the work of the West Gate Bridge Memorial Committee and their website (http://www.westgatebridge.org/), which documents the collapse of the West Gate and commemorates the lives lost; Bill Hitchings' book *West Gate*, published by Outback Press in 1979; and the many Melburnians I have met along the way who, when they heard I was writing about the West Gate Bridge disaster, shared their memories and recollections. I am grateful to everyone who was willing to offer their knowledge and experience. However, the facts are not always clear. While my aim has been to stay true to the historical circumstances of the collapse, not everything is known and sources differ.

To all my friends and family who have continued to show interest in my work, and faith in my ability to tell this story, my ongoing gratitude for your friendship and love. In particular I would like to thank:

Deb Warren and Robyn Williams, for their generous hospitality and for providing an inspiring space in which various sections of this novel were written.

My gifted readers for their thoughtful and insightful feedback: Helen Cerne, Barbara Brook, Bruno Annetta, and Megan Evans, who read a full draft of the manuscript, and Susan Holmes and Bronwen Hickman, who read various sections.

Vivienne Hadj, Helen Cerne, and Arty Owens for their enthusiasm and readiness to engage in long conversations about writing and literature, about life, about politics, and about the West Gate. These discussions have helped shape my thinking and my writing.

My gratitude to Alice Pung for making the time to read this novel and for her generosity and support.

I would like to thank everyone at Scribe Publications and especially my editor, Julia Carlomagno, for her perceptive and scrupulous editing, and for her commitment to and belief in the novel. *The Bridge* has been enhanced by her input. And thanks to David Golding for shepherding the novel in its final stages from manuscript to book.

Special thanks to my husband, Bruno Annetta, who has lived with this project as long as I have, for the thousands of conversations, for his love and partnership, and for his passion, generosity, and creative spirit; for believing in me even when I don't believe in myself and for making every day a joy.